UNDERCOVER MAGE

BOOK ONE OF THE MAGE AND THE BIRD CALLER

KAAREN SUTCLIFFE

Publisher: Inspiring Publishers,
P.O. Box 159, Calwell, ACT Australia 2905
Email: publishaspg@gmail.com
http://www.inspiringpublishers.com

 A catalogue record for this
book is available from the
National Library of Australia

National Library of Australia The Prepublication Data Service

Author: Kaaren Sutcliffe
Title: Undercover Mage
Genre: Fiction
ISBN: 978-1-922792-51-8

ACKNOWLEDGEMENTS

I'm excited to return to being a writer!

My heartfelt thanks extend to all those who so kindly and professionally helped me, Everand and Lamiya on the journey. A big thank you to my trusted readers who waded through early drafts, providing encouragement and constructive suggestions. Stand up and take a bow — Annette, Jody-Ann, Garry, Ed, Maxine, Martin and Donna. Thank you also to the volunteer judges of the Romance Writers Emerald Competition of 2021 for their most encouraging scores and helpful comments. Making it through to the top fifteen and round two of the competition made my year.

Next, my esteemed professional colleagues, members of the Institute of Professional Editors, who fine-tuned the story with precision. To AJ Collins, AE, and her gun assessor Liz, thank you for an insightful assessment that was instrumental in taking the story to another level. For the next steps, I am eternally grateful to Gail Tagarro, AE, for a meticulous edit and for her further encouragement and support, including some fabulous brainstorming about the ending to book one.

For the initiating inspiration my thanks go to Nature Coast Dragon Boat Club, who took me training on the scenic Moruya River and taught me to paddle. We had some fun and exhilarating moments, and I hope the book does the sport justice and inspires some readers to give paddling a go.

A special mention to those who work hard to support survivors of breast cancer. Thank you to Dragons Abreast Australia, who encourage survivors to take up paddling as part of their recovery. And to the Jane McGrath Foundation for funding the wonderful, compassionate breast care nurses. See the back of the book for more details.

I am indebted to the tireless and patient team at the Australian Self-Publishing Group. Many thanks for all your support, and for transforming my story into a great looking book.

To every reader, thank you. Enjoy the story, and I hope you have as much fun reading it as I had writing it.

Kaaren Sutcliffe, AE

Cast of Characters

Axis

Everand	Mage, spy, member of the Mages' Guild
Mantiss	Mage, Head of the Mages' Guild
Agamid	Senior Mage, assistant to Mantiss
Beetal	Deceased, Mage and former mentor to Everand
Tiliqua	Mage, daughter of Mantiss
Pelamis	Mage, member of the Inner Council

Riverfall

Dragon boat team (glide*, paddlers 1 to 10, drummer)

Tengar, Melanite, Mookaite, Selenite, Kunzite, Zeol, Persaj, Zink, Acim, Ybur, Beram, Micate

Atage	Town leader
Ejad	Reserve paddler — cloth maker
Lyber	Town second-in-charge
Thulite	Atage's wife
Vogel	Old man, historian
Mizuchi	River dragon
Mizukaze	River dragon

Riverplain

Dragon boat team (glide, paddlers 1 to 10, drummer)

Lamiya, Lazuli, Larimar, Laza, Lopa, Levog, Lattic, Lapsi, Lepid, Luvu, Ejad, Lulite

---

* In modern day paddling, the steersperson is usually called the 'sweep' or the' steer'. I found a reference to a 'glide' somewhere, and felt it suited the fantasy terminology. The two lead paddlers are often called 'strokes' as well as 'pacers'.

Riversea

Dragon boat team (glide, paddlers 1 to 10, drummer)

Cowrie, Conch, Chiton, Limpel, Clommus, Summel, Pippel, Spirula, Charonia, Clama, Nawpra, Chella

Riverwood

Dragon boat team (glide, paddlers 1 to 10, drummer)

Malach, Torrap, Magle, Mahog, Kwah, Tiek, Perid, Melan, Meralb, Kerish, Folnak, Yosper

THE ISLAND OF OSSILIS

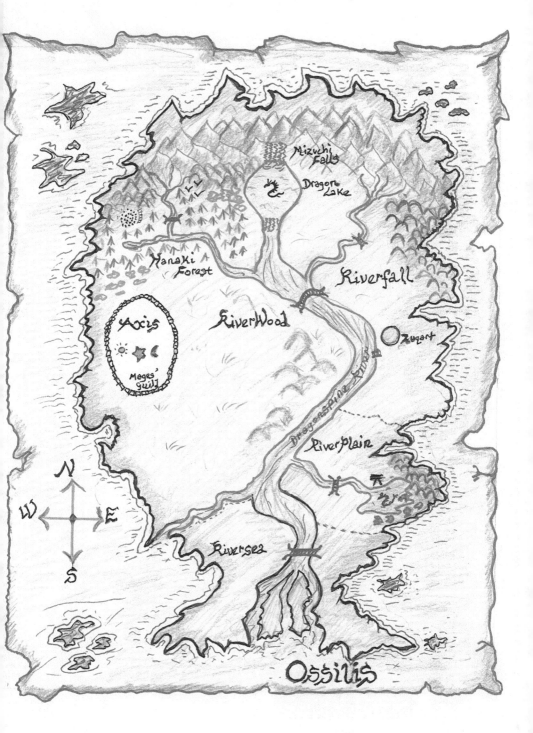

Ossilis

PROLOGUE

The shadow of an eagle darted across the lake, trailed by echoes of the bird's shrill cries.

The river dragon pushed off the lake bed, clouds of mud swirling around his legs and ripples eddying in his wake. A shoal of red and silver fish flashed past his nostrils.

Submerged, the dragon coasted with the current as the eagle's shadow skimmed to the western shore. He glided under the churning, cascading ribbons of the waterfall to observe the shore. The fading light stretched shadows from the line of trees behind the beach and silhouetted the man standing there, the eagle now perched upon his shoulder. What did this man want? He'd come several times to stand at the lake's edge and stare at the water. The man raised his arms, dislodging the eagle, and his feathered cloak slipped back over strong, muscled shoulders.

The dragon felt a beckoning nudge, a suggestion to approach, bump against his chest. Was that supposed to be a magical summons? His mother had warned him, over and over, not to trust people who held magical power. He ignored the nudge. After a pause, the man dropped his arms. Amused, the dragon blew bubbles through his nostrils.

The man produced a bag from behind his back and walked along the edge of the water, placing items at intervals. The eagle hopped behind, inspecting the fare. The dragon's ears pricked. An offering? For him? On this western shore? When he was a weanling dragon, people had come to the eastern shore to leave piles of fresh fish and sweet things for his mother. She had liked those people who came with laughter and children, telling him they were good people who needed rain to grow their crops. She told him stories of the early days, of when these people without any hint of magical power had first arrived. They had raced boats across the lake to play with her, beating glorious drums. Those people, she said, could be trusted.

Age finally claimed her, and his mother's bones now lay in glistening white arches in the centre of the lake. Irritation coursed through the dragon. Not once had people brought offerings for him, on either shore. Feeling discarded and grumpy, the dragon thrashed his tail.

The eagle screeched and the man stopped what he was doing and stared directly at where the dragon lay submerged. Again, the man raised his arms and the whispering nudge skimmed across the water. Why did this man call him, without ceremony and with meagre offerings? Where were the boats and drums his mother had spoken of? This man had power, weak though it was. The dragon reversed under the gurgling waterfall.

The man stood staring for a long time in the fading light. The dragon stared back. Once, many seasons before, an older man clad in brown robes and reeking of magic had tried to coax him. The strength in *that* summons had been difficult to resist, but the dragon had avoided the powerful call by diving deep under the waterfall. Was this man the lanky boy who'd come with the robed man? Was this weak nudge the best he could do? The dragon snorted clouds of bubbles.

Darkness fell, the tree shadows reached for the water's edge and the man walked away, soon swallowed by the trees.

When silver moonlight danced in dainty steps across the lake, the dragon slid out from the waterfall and swam to the beach. As he surfaced, silver wraiths of glistening mist rose around him. He waded out of the water and crunched across the pebbles. Reaching the items strewn along the stones, he lifted his head and, on detecting no lurking presence in the dark trees, clawed his way to the first item.

Lowering his head, he sniffed at a large, white-scaled fish, its glassy eye glinting back at the moon. He pushed it with his nose and a tingling sensation zinged into his whiskers and nostrils. He shook his head, but the tingles lingered. Riding the scents of the fish, an acrid taste crept along his tongue. Something was not right. The offering was a trick.

The dragon clawed over the pebbles to the next item, a decent sized bird, black eyes open and beak agape. A bitter aroma hovered over the bird's carcass. Not a spice — a potion. Poison? A stronger lure? His mother was right; these devious people with power were to be avoided. No matter what they wanted.

Disappointed, the dragon shifted his weight to his haunches. Having the little people with no magic come with laughter and offerings, respect and company would be welcome. He wanted to race a boat and hear the drum. Fury rising, he swished his tail, scattering pebbles with a clatter. Deep in his chest he growled at the cold disc of the moon. Mother had told him that after the little people raced their boats to ask for harvest rains, she'd melt the snow and conjure bulging clouds to drench the crops. As she had taught, he did this every season when the leaves budded. Without any company or races.

He roared. After this deceit the tricksy man and all the little people could wait and wait for their rain.

Forever.

CHAPTER ONE

Everand woke abruptly and lay blinking; his room was still shrouded in darkness except for the pale light fingering the windowsill. The communication horn on his desk chimed. Was that what woke him? The horn chimed again and he sat up. A summons in the dark? His warm blanket beckoned, but perhaps something had happened. Reluctantly, he rose and padded across the marble floor to his desk.

'Everand?' Mage Agamid's voice came through the horn. 'Come to the Great Hall. Mantiss and I are waiting. Hurry.'

Any questions died: something *must* have happened. 'On my way.' Hastily, he changed into his azure robe and laced on his favourite sandals. He took two steps towards the door and turned around. He should feed Mizu in case this impromptu meeting ran into the formal council one scheduled for just after breakfast. Weak primrose light from the arched window stole into the fish tank and his steps faltered. No bubbles, no flashes of white and red, no swish of a fan-shaped tail. His fish was floating on the surface on her side.

He leaned his hands on the sides of the tank, his breath forming patches of mist on the glass. *No, no, no.* Mizu was fine last dusk, gobbling her meal of ant eggs and warbling bubbles at him. Perhaps she was playing a new trick on him instead of hiding underneath the yellow lily pad. On tiptoe, he opened the lid of the tall tank.

4

Another chime reverberated, echoing off the marble walls. He frowned; Mage Mantiss was not usually so insistent. The echoes of a further chime mingled discordantly with the previous ones and his heart raced. What was going on? Shifting his grip on the lid, he spread his fingers above the immobile fish and murmured a spell of stasis. His heart skipped a beat when Mizu's fan-shaped tail twitched. The water in the tank turned to a clear gel, and Mizu's body straightened and stiffened. This would have to do for now.

Hurrying out the door, he created a small orb of light and jogged along the corridor of the circular building. His forehead twinged. What could have happened to make the Head of the Guild and the second most senior mage summon him in the dark? The corridors and stairwells were empty, and the slapping of his sandals on the tiles bounced eerie echoes off the walls. Had no-one else been summoned? Or was he late and they were already all there? He trotted down the final winding staircase to the lower level.

Halfway across the crushed pebble path that led to the administration building, he glanced up at the gold emblem displayed above the entrance. The sun and crescent moon with a star hung between them glinted in the pre-dawn light. The motif reflected the motto of the Mages' Guild to protect during the light and the dark, their power augmented from time to time by the magical star-shaped stone. He slowed to take more measured strides.

An urgent meeting hadn't been called for seven seasons, not since the full-scale battle to contain the ambitious Mage Beetal. The treacherous mage, his former mentor, had tried to wrest control from the Guild through an army of winged dragons that he had discovered on another world. Everand's pulse quickened. The battle was an epic moment in Guild history, and he'd played a large part in uncovering the mage's plans! Pride trickled through him. He squashed this warm feeling before it triggered memories of Elemar. That was then, this was now.

Shadow encasing him, he hurried up the broad, lacquered steps to the Great Hall and passed through the ornate wooden doors. His footsteps muted while he crossed the large silk rug. He glanced down at the woven images of the Last Great Battle of two generations earlier, admiring the bold mages who fought from astride their gigantic, armoured battle insects. Would Mage Mantiss commission a new rug to show the more recent battle with Mage Beetal?

Two generations of peace had passed between those two battles, and yet he was being summoned to an urgent meeting already, only a handful of seasons since the second one. Energy seeped into the soles of his feet as he mounted the steps to the wooden dais — and stopped dead.

Forcing his eyes away from the strangely clad figure sitting at the table, Everand bowed to Mage Mantiss, Head of the Mages' Guild, seated at the head of the table.

'Good of you to come so promptly.' Mage Mantiss stood with a rustle of his green silk robe and reached out to grasp Everand's hands.

Agamid, clad in his signature purple robe, stood and nodded a greeting.

Everand bowed again and then looked at the vacant seats around the large oval table. The dark mahogany gleamed softly, the matching wooden-backed chairs all tucked in neatly. So, this was an emergency meeting of three, and not one of the Inner Council of Ten. Agamid waved a hand and the enormous doors creaked closed, the locks sliding into place with ominous clicks. He swallowed: a clandestine meeting.

Everand sat in his customary chair, which placed him directly opposite the stranger. Was this man one of the non-mage humans who lived in Axis who'd committed a crime? Or — unease trickled into him — was the man from elsewhere and there'd been another breach in the wardspell? The last breach was when Elemar and her flying horse fell through it, alerting the Guild that a rift had been created. His previous mission had been to find out by whom and why. He looked to Mantiss for elaboration. Both senior mages appeared unsettled, their foreheads creased and shoulders tensed.

Agamid spoke, his hazel eyes troubled. 'Now you're here, we will question this man, who I found at the edge of the granite wall. We'd value your views, given you've had more interaction with outsiders.'

Everand assumed Agamid was referring to the time he'd spent with Elemar and her warrior friends. Reporting covertly to Mantiss, he had first unravelled how they got into Axis, and then pieced together a timeline of Mage Beetal's traitorous actions. It had taken much effort and considerable patience because Elemar's primitive lifestyle, values and concepts were so different, and she didn't speak Ossilian.

He eyed the man seated opposite him now: he sensed no power, so he was not mage-born, and the clothes were different to those worn by the humans who worked for the Guild. The man was covered in grime and dried sweat, suggesting he had travelled.

'Perhaps you could start at the beginning,' he said. 'How did you know he was there?'

Mantiss waved a robed arm at Agamid, who spoke steadily. 'The alarm to the wardspell sounded several times just as the moon was waning. Mantiss sent me to investigate the sounds, which came from a little way south of the Guild, on the eastern side of the granite wall.'

Everand looked across the table. The man was swallowing repeatedly and clenching his fingers, but listening as if he could follow their discussion. 'Can you understand us?'

The man gulped, briefly met his eyes, and nodded.

So, the man was from nearby and not from another world, like Elemar had been. 'Do you mind if I ask him a few questions?' Both senior mages waved assent, looking relieved. Trying to keep his face relaxed and not too stern, Everand asked the man, 'Where have you come from? Do you have a name?'

'Riverfall. Beram.' The man spoke with a lilting accent.

Everand frowned. Was one a place and the other a name? 'You came from Riverfall and your name is Beram?' When the man nodded sharply, he asked, 'Why?'

'We need help.' Beram fidgeted, struggling to find words.

Mage Mantiss leaned forward, his green eyes stern and wispy silver beard projecting sharply. 'While the Mages' Guild is aware of the riverland provinces to our east, we do not interact, having no need to trade or mingle.' Mantiss drew a breath. 'In this light, your request will need to be most compelling.'

Agamid leaned on the table with a rustle of his purple sleeves, and said, 'We must consider carefully. The Guild does not meddle in the affairs of others.'

'Agreed, this could …' Mantiss scouted for the right word, 'this could establish future expectations.'

Everand raised an eyebrow when Mantiss clamped his mouth shut and steepled his fingers, and Agamid leaned back in his chair. He considered Beram's clothing of a rough cotton tunic and comfortable-looking trousers. The man looked harmless enough, but why bring him to the Guild if they had no intention of helping him? Motes of dust hovered above the table in the early light, as if they, too, awaited direction.

His thoughts clustered like butterflies. Why summon just him and not convene the Inner Council of Ten, or the full Outer Council of Twenty? Last time an outsider arrived, it had heralded a plot that nearly unravelled them all. There was an odd undercurrent to this meeting. Last time, he'd reported only to Mage Mantiss, but now it seemed Mage Agamid was fully involved. What did this signify? And what did the senior mages expect him to do?

'Perhaps Beram could outline the problem?' he proposed, given that the oddly reticent senior mages seemed at least prepared to hear what the man had to say.

Mantiss waved a hand at Beram, inviting him to speak.

'I come from Riverfall, the province to the north-east. Our town sits on the banks of Dragonspine River.'

Everand cast a sideways glance at Mage Mantiss when his master suddenly sat straighter. Was that information important?

Beram rubbed a hand over his chin, which was covered in bristly stubble smeared with dust and grime. 'We're a farming and water people. We rely on the river.'

Concentrating to make sure he understood properly given the man's lilting accent, Everand nodded to show he was following so far. This all seemed tranquil, the nature of the issue difficult to predict.

'The river traverses four provinces and all of us use it.'

Everand held up a hand. 'Where does the river start, and finish?'

'The origins are in the mountain range above our province. In cold-season the mountains are ice-bound, and the growing-season melt helps renew the flow. Good rainfall helps.' Beram's jaw tightened.

'And the far end?' prompted Everand.

'The far end reaches the sea, in Riversea. In between, the river meanders, covering much land, and its tributaries mark the province boundaries.'

Everand flexed his fingers and glanced at Mantiss. No guidance there; Mantiss' face was unreadable. 'I don't understand the problem, though.'

Beram's face flushed and he twisted his hands together. 'The last five seasons have been dry, with not a single drop of rain. The river runs lower in its banks and the tributaries are becoming shallow. With no rain in sight, we try to use less water.'

Everand slid his glance to Mantiss, who remained impassive. He cast his mind back over the past few seasons. Perhaps there had been an unusual amount of blue sky and sunshine, but that hadn't affected the mages, who relied on an eternal underground spring for their water.

Beram's face grew a deeper red and he plucked at the hem of his tunic. 'If it doesn't rain before the harvest, tensions may develop. Just as we're trying to forge closer relations and begin trade among the four provinces.'

Agamid raised an eyebrow and murmured, 'There are now four provinces?' He exchanged a look with Mantiss.

Everand frowned. How did this involve the Mages' Guild? Did the province people want the Guild to make it rain or to magically increase the water in the river? He sat back. *Could* the mages even achieve this? No, because mages are not allowed outside the granite wall. Ah. *This* was why Mantiss hadn't summoned a full council! To help Beram and his people in any way would require a breach of Guild Laws. And if interaction *was* commenced, the notion of exercising power over the provinces would be too tempting for some.

Already, some of the younger mages were expressing frustration with the limitations of their duties. Over the last few meetings, Pelamis and Simoselaps in particular had pushed Mantiss, arguing for a broadening of their research and access to more power.

Everand drummed his fingers on the table, thinking hard. That kind of argument was precisely how Mage Beetal had shown his early ambitions — and the same pattern was recorded in the annals about Mage Thrip, the ambitious mage from two generations earlier. Twice, history had shown the Guild the danger of the allure of power. Twice, mages who had travelled outside the granite wall and breached the wardspell had wreaked havoc. Guild assistance to the river provinces could generate … yes, expectations was a good word. *Expectations. Responsibility. Change.*

Everand leaned back heavily, feeling the support of the wooden chair across his shoulderblades. That still didn't explain why they had collected Beram in the first place. What could *he* do? His specialty was sleuthing information. He frowned. He was also the only mage who had already breached Guild Rule Nine. In order to collect evidence against Mage Beetal he had, with Mantiss' sanction, travelled through the rift to Elemar's world with his treacherous mentor. Was this what Mantiss wanted? Information and an eye into what was happening beyond the granite wall?

Leaning forward, Everand asked Beram, 'How long did it take you to get here?' Out of the corner of his eye he saw Mage Mantiss' subtle smile.

Beram grimaced. 'On foot it took me two full suns, with no rest.'

'Why come to Axis? Who knows you are here?' asked Everand.

'Two others know of my journey, made at their request.'

Everand arched an eyebrow. For someone who supposedly needed help, the man was not very forthcoming. 'Because?'

'Because?' Beram tensed in his chair.

'Because,' repeated Everand, 'only two others know because?'

An interesting shade of mottled crimson spread up Beram's neck and seeped into his face. While waiting for an answer, Everand guessed that Beram was about his own age of twenty-six. He looked fit, muscled, strong, even for a farmer.

'We don't know who we can trust,' blurted Beram.

Everand glanced at Mantiss, who gave approval to continue the line of questions. Resting his hands lightly on the table, Everand asked, 'What do you fear will happen?'

'Someone is attacking us. We don't know what to do.' Beram's hands trembled and he clasped them together in front of him. 'We find irrigation trenches blocked. Crops crushed by rocks.' A sweat formed on his brow and his eyes turned a deeper shade of grey. 'The sun before my journey, large moths attacked the town and there was an explosion in the marketplace. A trading table was destroyed and three people were injured, including a child.' Beram stopped with a gulp.

Realising the background sound was coming from his fingers drumming on the table, Everand made them still. 'And you've no idea who is responsible?'

Beram looked directly into his eyes. 'In eight suns we'll hold the festival of the Full Harvest Sun. We've invited the other three provinces to join us. There'll be trade markets and boat races. Negotiators from each province will discuss the possibility of regular trade. We must find out who's doing this and stop them. In case ...' Beram's eyes pleaded. 'I was asked to come to the Guild. We had nowhere else to turn.'

Agamid held up a finger. 'You risked death by approaching the granite wall. Did you not know this?'

Beram squared his shoulders. 'Yes. But so much is at risk, I volunteered.'

Everand warmed to the man. He was brave, like Elemar and her people. 'How did you survive the wall?'

Beram shrugged. 'I threw rocks at it and saw the red crackles as they exploded. I figured someone would notice.' He frowned. 'I was more scared when the mage arrived with his enormous beetle.'

Impressed by the simple ingenuity, Everand repressed his smile, noting the annoyed thinning of both Mantiss' and Agamid's lips. Many thoughts rushed at him, but one stood out. 'You need to know why,' he said. When the others stared at him, he cleared his throat. 'You need to know why, otherwise you can't reason with them even if you do find out who it is.'

Mantiss placed his arms on the table, his green eyes intent. 'What do you propose?'

Everand closed his eyes. Mantiss was hoping he would spy for him again. With a deadline of seven suns and in an unfamiliar environment. Now they'd brought Beram to the Guild they could hardly just send the man away again, or kill him. A subtle warning wriggled in his gut; there had to be more to this. But Mantiss was relying on him! His heartrate lifted. The meetings of the Inner Council of Ten were not *that* interesting. The boat races sounded intriguing and he'd never seen a boat, not in inland Axis. A new mission held appeal.

Everand looked at Mantiss. 'I will go. If you wish it.'

A look of relief crossed Mantiss' face and he glanced at Agamid, who dipped his head almost imperceptibly.

They had wanted him to offer! The warning in his gut squirmed again. Did they know something else or want more than was being stated?

Beram's mouth dropped open and he addressed Mantiss. 'How will that help?'

Mantiss made a chopping motion with a hand. 'We need more information and Everand is a master at this.' When Beram opened his mouth again, Mantiss held up a firm hand. 'Out of instinct you kept your mission here secret. Let's keep it that way and aim for less violence, not more.'

Everand stood up when Mantiss rose and came around the corner of the table to grasp both of his hands.

'Everand, my son, your loyalty is beyond bounds.' Mantiss raised an eyebrow in query. 'You can disguise yourself? There must be *no* hint of the Guild's involvement, *none* whatsoever. Find out who and why, and prevent more attacks if you can.'

Agamid stood too. Then he reached down beside his chair and retrieved a rolled-up parchment, which he placed on the table and rolled out.

Everand held down the corner nearest him, immediately seeing it was a map of the large island of Ossilis. It depicted the Guild in Axis surrounded by the protective granite wall. The coast was close-by to the west, grasslands stretched east and south, and to the north were dense forests and then mountains. His neck prickled: how did Agamid know they'd need the map? Exactly *when* had Beram been found? Questions clustered in his throat, but before he could ask any the council summons chimes rang out loud and clear, reverberating across the Great Hall.

Agamid scowled and said briskly to Beram, 'Where is your town?'

Beram gaped at Agamid, confused by the rapid onset of action.

Mantiss leaned on the table for support, and looked sharply at Everand. 'I need your eyes on this. In accordance with Guild Law, no other mage has been outside the wall for three hundred cycles, except for Mage Thrip and Mage Beetal, and they are dead. You are the only mage alive who has been out, and sanctioned to do so. If the provinces around us are growing and now interacting we need to know more. Solve this issue and find out all you can about them in the seven suns.'

Everand hesitated, towering over his master. Mantiss looked disturbed and a tad subdued. Who had sounded the council summons? Mantiss called him 'son' and had covertly coached him in stealth and advanced magic since he was twelve, but what exactly was the *this* his master alluded to? Perhaps Mantiss intended to provide additional information in secret later. Swallowing, he pushed his concerns aside. 'Yes, master, of course I'll go, and I will be discreet.'

Agamid interrupted. 'We're taking far too long! We must send Everand right now, otherwise we'll have to consult with the council.'

Pulse racing, Everand stared at Agamid, who did not usually tell Mantiss what to do.

Mantiss turned to Beram. 'Mage Agamid will take you back to our border unseen and let you through the wardspell. From there you must make your way home on foot so others don't know of your contact with us.' Mantiss then regarded Everand, the green hues in his eyes reflecting myriad emotions. 'Everand will go by magic now. Who are the two people he can trust?'

Everand's mind churned. He felt like a small stone in the strategy board game they had played when he was younger. Did he really mean *now*? Wait, what about Mizu?

Agamid jerked his head at the unfurled map, holding it open with wide-spread hands. 'Quick man, point to a good location.'

Everand frowned, watching Beram lean forward, scan the map, trace a finger along a blue line that represented the river, which did indeed twist and turn, traversing the length of the map. It looked almost like a large lizard with tributaries for legs and arms.

Beram looked at Agamid, his brow furrowed. 'This is an old map? The provinces are not marked?'

'Hurry, man!' snapped Agamid. 'You must know where you live in relation to the river!'

Beram gulped, looked down and then stabbed his finger about halfway down the map on a grassy area next to a point where the river meandered in a curve to the right.

'Everand,' Mantiss swung his gaze to him. 'I regret the haste ...'

Wait! Mantiss and Agamid were preparing the spell of translocation! Were there no more instructions? How would he communicate what he found out? What about Mizu? How would he get back?

Footsteps echoed on the steps and the locked door handle rattled. Alarmed, Everand watched Mantiss stretch one hand towards the river on the map and direct his other hand, palm up, at him. Agamid directed both hands, palms up, at him. Their mouths moved in harmony as they intoned the spell and the Great Hall began to shimmer around him. 'The two names?' he gasped.

Through a tunnel of swirling grey and white, tinged with auras of green and purple of Mantiss' and Agamid's signature colours, Everand heard Beram gasp what sounded like, 'Grrr' or maybe 'Brrr'.

The Great Hall vanished in a shimmering grey light, dissipating into a perception that he was weightless and surrounded by pale-blue sky. Cold air ruffled past him. Abruptly, he hung suspended but on opening his eyes saw only pale sky. He was cold and his arm wouldn't move to reach out in front of him. His robe flapped and the air around the hem sparked and crackled with red warning energy; he'd reached the wardspell. He drew in a breath as lines of purple energy spread in front of him, tracing a doorway — Agamid, parting the wardspell. An invisible force butted his back, shoving him through.

Excitement trickled into him. Breaking Guild Rule Nine without the authority of the Head of the Guild was punishable by obliteration. And here he was with a new mission and the sanctioned opportunity to explore! Pale-blue air glimmered all around, and more cold air buffeted him. Everand flexed his fingers, gathering power and energy for whatever would happen next.

A ribbon of blue-green hue rushed towards him.

Chapter Two

Air rushing past his cheeks, Everand wished he was better prepared. A cloak would be useful, and without a communication orb how would he tell Mantiss when he was ready to be translocated back? Or would they just recall him in eight suns, assuming his mission was completed?

A cluster of orange and pink-toned structures zipped past below at a speed that predicted a far-from-comfortable landing. Ahead, the blue ribbon swirled and wrinkled, a mass of moving blue-green … oh no!

He plunged head-first into cold, choppy water. His chest and throat clenched with the press of the water that pushed and rolled all around him. His robe clung to his legs and ankles and he kicked, trying to free his feet. Small bubbles seeped from his mouth while he flailed his arms and legs to keep from sinking deeper. Dizziness crept in at the edges of his vision. Curse it! He couldn't drown straight off. A silver fish swam by, peering at him with glassy eyes. The water was pulling him along, its power disconcerting.

Everand muttered a spell of rising, the light grew stronger and his head breached the surface. Gasping in air, he moved his arms in circles and kicked his legs. Where was he? A wave slapped him in the mouth. Mantiss and Agamid would pay for this. He bobbed, trying to judge the distance to land amid the choppy water. He could see greenery and orange-pink buildings, but the river was carrying him away from these.

Should he translocate to the bank and risk being seen? No, as unpleasant as the notion was, he should swim.

Splash! Splash! Splash! Lowering his gaze, he found himself staring at the mouth of a blue and gold dragon bearing directly upon him. Large white fangs gleamed and a red tongue protruded. The dragon's beady black eyes were fixed straight ahead. Everand spluttered around another face-full of water. Dragons! Here? The beast was nearly upon him and he dived. Holding his breath, he floundered underwater as the shadow of the beast passed over him. The long, narrow, straight form glided above, multiple legs dipping rhythmically into the river to propel it. How odd; he thought dragons only had four legs. Perhaps this was a water species?

As soon as the shadow of the beast's raised tail had passed, Everand surged to the surface and gulped air. That was a close call. 'Yosh! Yosh!' He heard chanting in time to the splashes of the dragon's legs. Frowning, he eyed the receding beast. He saw heads and backs. Were people *riding* it? No, wait, this was a boat! It must be part of the boat races Beram had referred to. He hadn't realised the boats would be made to look like dragons. Odd. His history lessons hadn't included references to dragons. He thought they lived on other worlds, like Elemar's.

A woman was standing at the rear of the dragon-like boat, just before the stiffly raised tail. Sunlight sparkled off her flowing brunette hair, tinged with threads of caramel and blue. Falling down her back, the rich brown hair was wavy, like the water. Muscles rippled on her bare arms that wielded a long wooden oar. The muscles also stood out on her shapely legs as she balanced impeccably. Mesmerised, he watched her thigh and calf muscles bulge and relax as she moved for balance. The regular splashing was the oars hitting the water; the calling was to keep the time. He felt like giggling. Then the boat began to turn in a curve and the woman at the back called instructions to the others.

The dragon head faced back towards him. The woman called, 'Lift for twenty!' and the boat charged at him. What should he do? For an agonising moment he trod water, then he kicked hard, propelling himself out of the boat's path. Holding his breath, he sank under again to wait for it to pass. As the boat skimmed by, he admired the blue dragon scale-like artwork along its side.

After the tail had passed above, he bobbed back up and found the woman at the rear looking directly at him with piercing grey-blue eyes and a sharp intelligence. Some spy; his mission was already compromised. Snatching a breath, he sank again. Perhaps she would think she'd imagined seeing him. Stupid! He should have made himself invisible earlier. He hastily mouthed the spell and, too unnerved to translocate, swam towards the bank.

His legs quickly fatigued, feeling heavy and awkward. His breath came in gasps, his chest clenched with the cold. It took forever. The boat came back past, the woman frowning and searching the water. Once more, he sank underwater as she stared intently right where he was. Could she see him even when he was invisible? How could that be? Or was she guessing? Finally, the boat receded downriver.

Several times, he stretched his feet down only to find he was still in water deeper than his full height. When his toes at last touched a solid base, he put careful weight on his feet, finding the surface was smooth mud and the few stones he encountered weren't sharp. There was a short, narrow mud ledge, and he struggled onto that trying not to cause ripples that could be observed. Catching his breath, he regarded the bank with trepidation. Some roots protruded from a couple of bushes and he tugged on one. It felt strong enough, so he used it to lever himself up the bank. Grabbing handfuls of tough grass, he pulled himself up the rest of the way.

As soon as he found level ground, he plopped down, shivering, his arms and legs aching. His sodden robe clung to him and water was seeping from his hair and trickling down his back. Curse Mantiss and Agamid! They should have paid more attention — although landing with such speed on solid land may not have boded well for his mission either. An annoying chattering sound caught his attention and he realised it was his teeth. He'd never been so cold! Rounding up his scrambled thoughts, he cast a spell of warming. Soon, it felt as if he was sitting in warm sunshine and his robe began to feel less sodden.

Voices! Listening, he realised that people were travelling along a pebbly road behind him. Heading into the town? Looking down, he saw grey tendrils rising on the grass beside him. *What the ...?* The steam from his drying robe was casting shadows on the grass! He ceased the spell. *Be more careful*, he scolded. *Or you'll be discovered before you even get organised.*

Practical observations rushed at him: clothes, a new name and identity, a reason for being at the festival, food, drink, a roof, coin to purchase these ... the list seemed endless. He sighed. This would have been so much easier with the names of the two trusted persons. And a whole lot more information. No good feeling sorry for himself. He closed his eyes and the image of the woman on the back of the boat, hair flowing, muscles rippling, flashed into his mind. He shook his head: no time for sentimentality. He had a mission to perform.

His teeth stopped chattering and his robe no longer gripped his legs. Time to see where he was. Everand stood up and eased the tension in his neck. *All that cold water couldn't be good for you.* After a few tottering steps he stopped and shook the stiffness out of his legs. *Even invisible, it wouldn't do to go bumping into anyone.*

He stepped onto the road and, scuffing the surface with a foot, concluded it was made from crushed pink-white stones. These reflected in the sun, making him squint. To his right, the road stretched south, following the glistening blue river. The water looked quite appealing if you were not *in* it!

The green banks opened out into flatter, multi-coloured fields. Crops? He swung his gaze to his left, north. The road led towards a collection of buildings, mainly domed, elongated like cocoons. None was higher than one floor. Inefficient, compared to the ten-level marble domes of Axis. Low buildings consumed more land space. Keeping to the edge of the road, he strode briskly towards the town, hoping he was where he was supposed to be.

His long robe swished about his legs and protected his arms from the sun, but he started to sweat. One extreme to another. He slowed his pace as he reached the first buildings, constructed of melded pinkish-orange oblong shapes. Simple in design, there were spaces for a window and a door. Narrow paths of crushed pebbles led away from the road to the entrances. He moved on, observing how different things were to his Guild lifestyle.

After the cocoon-shaped buildings, he approached a high curved wall with a formal arched entrance to the town. Hesitating at a loud rattling sound, he flattened himself against the wall when two unfamiliar creatures erupted through the entrance, the pebbles crunching under their hooves. He barely had time to register that the creatures were attached by straps to a wooden, wheeled platform. As they receded apace, he saw a person seated on a bench in front of the flat platform. Behind the person were several oblongs of what appeared to be rolled-up cloth. He paused, listening, but it was quiet so he stepped around the edge of the wall.

He was in a large courtyard. The smooth orange wall curved around the space, which was open save for some bushes and small trees planted in square pots. Large, double wooden doors were pushed back flush on the inside of the walls. So, this town could be locked up after dark-fall. The courtyard seemed to serve as a gathering place, and on the far side was another archway.

Everand edged his way around the perimeter, keeping alert for any further unexpected activity. Pausing at one of the pots, he fingered the leaves of the bush. A glossy, dark green, they were smooth to the touch. Small, white buds exuded a faint perfume.

Moving on, he edged through the second archway. Another courtyard, but bigger and the curved walls were higher, stretching up to half his height again. There were squat wooden tables evenly spaced along the perimeter. Behind each of these was a wooden bench, and above was a wooden frame with a line of neatly rolled cloth. Used to provide shade, perhaps? Trees planted at intervals cast creative shadows onto more wooden benches. This must be the marketplace, sensibly placed near the main entrance.

He stood, absorbing the sense of the place. A chill wafted across the back of his neck: the lack of activity felt wrong. This was a space intended for bustle, shouting, trade and enjoyment.

Everand tracked his gaze around the perimeter. A chill gripped at his neck. Against the centre of the wall on the left side was a black, sooty smear that spread the height of the wall and covered the area of two tables. The two tables and benches looked new; the wood was a lighter brown and not at all worn or scratched. He crept closer, a charred smell drifting into his nostrils. Or was he imagining that? The wall was pock-marked, but intact. So, the clay bricks were robust and not readily consumed by fire. Standing between the new tables, he looked down.

The fine dust was marred by scattered splotches of dark stain. A faint metallic odour permeated, and a sense of violence assaulted him. Everand considered what Beram had said about the precipitating incident for his request. How had someone contrived an explosion so deep within the town walls? Small wonder the people weren't sure who to trust. He scuffed his toes around the area looking for clues. What was that? Squatting down, he prodded one of the tiny slivers of a darker grey with a finger. The slivers were from a different kind of stone. But that didn't explain the explosion.

And three suns had passed since the incident, diminishing any other traces of evidence.

CHAPTER THREE

Everand stood up, brushing the dust from his hands. Seven suns to establish who was doing these things and stop them. *A festival with people from all the river provinces*. Being dropped into the river felt entirely appropriate — he'd been plunged into this mission — and he was on his own here. Giving a shiver to dispel the mantle of foreboding, he continued.

Slinking along the wall, conscious that even invisible he'd cast a shadow, he edged his way through the next archway and stopped short. Numerous people were walking briskly between structures, coming in and out of doorways, some empty-handed and others carrying bundles of cloth or baskets of colourful produce.

He watched for a moment and concluded there was a pattern. The structures to the left were larger, and people bustled in and out of these with goods. *Traders*. In front of the trading buildings, all made of the pink-orange blocks, was a strip of verdant grass and a scattering of the same glossy, ornate shrubs. A wide, cleared path traversed the centre of the town.

To his right was another strip of grass, more shrubs and what looked like playthings for children. There was a plank resting across a log and some roughly built wooden climbing frames. On the far side of these were many more pink-orange domes, smaller and with colourful cloths hanging across doorways and windows. *Dwellings*. He counted at least eighty. So, maybe three to four hundred people lived here. Was there a building similar to the Guild's Great Hall, where meetings were held and where he might find one, or both, of the trusted contacts? 'Grrr' or 'Brrr' wasn't much to go on.

First things first, he should obtain some clothes and concoct a credible story of why he was there. His forehead twitched. In such a contained and ordered place this would not be easy.

He made his way towards the trading domes, keeping out of the direct paths as best he could. Peering into the entryway of the first dome, he waited while his eyes adjusted to the dim interior. A man, with his back turned, was rolling out a bolt of cloth. Along the walls were wooden shelves with neatly stacked bolts of cloth. The array of colours was impressive: from vibrant and vivid to soft hues in all the colours of the sky-arch that appeared after rain. Absorbed, Everand jumped when his elbow was jostled. He hadn't seen another man enter the dome, who looked his way with a puzzled frown, trying to work out what he'd bumped into.

'Ho, Acim. What can I do for you?' The man who'd been rolling out cloth greeted the newcomer.

Everand melted into the shadows inside the doorway and held his breath.

'May the sun shine on your fine wares, good Ejad. Tengar asked me to suggest new colours for our team. He wants to coax good fortune back our way. We must please the river dragon.'

Everand watched with interest as Ejad cracked his knuckles and smiled broadly. Both men looked to be in their early twenties and had well-muscled arms and shoulders. Both were a good head shorter than he was. Even by mage standards he was tall, so his height would be a disadvantage on this mission.

'I'm honoured.' Ejad tilted his head to one side. 'You wish to match Mizuchi's colours, yes? Blue and gold?'

'Yes, but something different to the current tunics. Tengar says we mustn't leave anything to chance this festival.' Acim looked worried, twisting his fingers together as he spoke.

24

'And your colours must differ from the teams of the other provinces?'

Acim inclined his head.

While the two men pored over various shades of blue cloth, Everand absorbed what he'd heard. So, Acim would participate in the boat races, and they competed in teams. Given the blue and gold colour, he'd probably nearly been run over by this province's boat. *Please the river dragon?* Did they believe there was an actual dragon? Or was it a boat racing expression? Who was this Mizu-something? Mizu? Like the name of his fish? That was weird.

Ejad and Acim had narrowed the choice to a bolt of striking blue, like the river in bright sunshine, and an equally vibrant gold.

'Well,' said Ejad, straightening up, 'this should attract the dragon's eye!' The two men laughed.

'And dazzle the other teams,' said Acim with a wide smile.

Everand liked this man with his ready smile, honest face and curly brown hair.

'If you set aside the bolts needed to clad the whole team, I'll race to Melanite's dome to ask her to sew the tunics.' Acim opened a cloth bag that was hanging from his belt and withdrew a number of tokens made of the pink-orange clay of the domes. 'How much? Tengar wants me to pay you.'

'For the team, a special price.' Ejad stood a moment, doing some calculations. 'How about six bushes for the blue cloth and two fishes for the gold?'

'Are you sure?' Acim responded. 'That's most generous.'

'Yes, yes.' Ejad flapped his hands.

Everand wondered how Acim was going to produce bushes and fishes, if he'd heard correctly with their accents. Acim sifted through the pile of tokens in his palm and selected two shaped like a fish and another six that were round but had an image traced on the flat surface. Everand deduced the fish tokens were

25

worth more than bushes, and the currency was these ceramic tokens.

Once Ejad's hands stopped flapping, Acim placed the tokens on his palms. 'You know,' he said with a kind expression, 'if you keep training you might be on the team too next time.'

Ejad's face lit up with hope. *Interesting.* So, being on the team was important?

The two men bowed to each other and Acim turned to leave. Everand flattened himself against the wall. *Stupid. They can't see you.* As soon as Acim had passed through the arch, he peeled away from the wall and slunk after the man, hoping the prospect of sewing new tunics for a whole team might distract the next trader long enough for him to steal — he frowned — *borrow* some clothes. He could always return them later. Or pay later. But then he'd have to steal — borrow — some tokens. His forehead ached: this mission was so poorly planned.

He almost ran up the back of Acim, who had paused outside the third dome. *Another close call.* An annoying bead of sweat trickled down his face.

'Melanite? Hello?' called Acim.

Everand slowed his breathing and stood still as a woman came to the entrance, a smile on her face.

'Welcome, Acim! Come on in. How can I help you?'

Acim followed the woman into the dome, saying, 'Greetings, may the sun shine upon your fine wares.'

Everand counted to three then slid inside the entrance. This dome contained clothes, hanging in neat rows from chest-height wooden racks. The racks near him were filled with tunics, scarves and long skirts in an array of bright colours. A bit further along, the clothes looked larger and were in more earthy colours — greys, browns, creams, greens and olives. Men's tunics. He stole that way and slipped behind a slightly higher rack.

'The whole team!' the woman exclaimed. 'Tell Tengar I'm honoured.'

Everand peered over the top of the rack. Acim was beaming, a little flushed, and the woman was toying excitedly with the beads of her necklace. She wore a simple pale-green tunic top that curved nicely down her ribs to flow into a long, elegant, light-brown skirt. She looked remarkably fit and muscled for a clothes-maker.

'When do you need the tunics by?' the woman asked Acim.

Everand eyed the clothes on the rack in front of him. There was nothing in his preferred colours of cobalt or blue, but a storm-grey tunic caught his eye. He scanned the next rack along and considered it might match the darker green trousers at the end. But what size? He could hardly start lifting clothes off the rack to hold against himself. He looked over to the others again.

'Stand over here.' The woman led Acim by his elbow to the other side of the dome. 'I'll measure you up while you're here. Tell the others to drop by as soon as they can …'

Blocking out their chatter, Everand eased the tunic and then the trousers from the racks, sliding them out backwards ever so slowly. The others didn't notice. Spying a head-height square wooden frame with cloth screens on all sides standing against the back wall, he extended the spell of invisibility to cover the clothes in his arms, sidled along the wall and stepped behind the screen. Would his robe become visible once he took it off? He was about to find out.

After making sure Acim and the woman were still busy, he peeled off his robe. It promptly appeared as a swathe of dark cobalt. He dropped it onto the floor, kicked it next to a wooden stool, and hurriedly pulled on the trousers. The material was soft yet crisp beneath his fingers and felt like it would breathe well. The hem of the trousers brushed just above his kneecaps, a little short, but they fitted well around his waist. It took him a worrying few heartbeats to work out how to put the tunic on. Eventually he established that he needed to lift it over his head

and put one arm, and then the other, through the holes at the top
of the short sleeves. The cloth then settled across his torso. He
swung his arms experimentally; he could move.

'Hello?' called a woman's voice. 'May I enter?'

'Lamiya! Welcome!' the clothes-maker trilled. 'How goes
your training?'

'Hah!' replied the new voice. 'You think I'd answer that
question from you, and with Acim standing there?'

'Can't blame us for trying,' quipped Acim, and all three
laughed. 'When does your boat arrive?'

'Another three suns,' said the new voice. 'Thanks for letting
me train in your boat. It's good to get the feel of the river. New
team outfit?'

Everand raised enough courage to stand on tiptoe to peer
over the top of the screen, and almost toppled back down. The
woman from the back of the boat! The one who might have
seen him in the river! His heart hammered against his ribs. She
must not see him until he'd sorted a new identity. He heard
Acim mumbling a reply.

'Of course,' responded the woman with a laugh. 'You need
to change your luck. But I'm being disrespectful,' she said slyly.
'Riverfall will be an excellent host. May the winds favour your
boat.'

That sounded like a goodbye and Everand dared another
peek, but it was Acim who was bowing in farewell. *Curses.* He
frowned at Acim's back as the man exited. Dry-mouthed, he
watched the woman from the boat hold up a tunic and examine
it critically. The clothes-maker made a tut-tut sound, drew a
turquoise tunic from a different rack and held it up. 'How about
this one? It'll offset your eyes and hair just so.'

The woman reached for the tunic and held it against her
chest. Everand tried not to look at the muscles moving in her
arms. The tunic did indeed offset her eyes and the blue tints in
her mahogany hair. He swallowed.

'May I try it on?' the woman asked.

'Naturally,' beamed the clothes-maker, handing her a skirt the colour of a pale moon. 'Take this too. I think they'll work well together.'

With a nod, the boatwoman took the skirt and marched directly towards the screen frame. Horror flooded into him. She intended to get changed behind the screen. He was a complete idiot! He was pinned, unable to escape without the women seeing. Sinking to a crouch, he shuffled as far as possible into what best constituted a corner. His heartbeat boomed in his ears.

The woman bounced behind the screen. 'What about your team?' She started to undo the buckle on her belt.

Everand didn't hear the reply, busy shrinking into himself as the boatwoman dropped her trousers. Distantly, he noticed these were still wet in patches. He scrunched his eyes shut when she lifted her tunic above her head. The smell of river water, mingled with the distant scent of a flower, wafted into his nostrils and he pinched his nose to contain a sneeze. Unbidden, he recalled the Bellflower perfume that Elemar loved to wear. His soul gave a sigh and stillness settled around him.

He felt a subtle probe, a vague sense of presence. The boatwoman stood before him, her grey-blue eyes piercing as she looked exactly at where he crouched. Everand couldn't swallow, his throat clenched, his heart yammering. *Could she see him? Could she sense him? How?* He was too distressed to worry that she stood only in her loincloth.

'Lamiya? Do they fit? How do they look?' The voice of the other woman broke the moment.

Everand wilted as the boatwoman averted her gaze with a frown tugging at her eyebrows, and pulled the turquoise tunic over her head.

'I'll show you,' she said in a voice that sounded strong, confident.

Closing his eyes, Everand listened to the rustle of material as the woman pulled on the skirt. He withdrew his mind as far inwards as possible, his instincts screaming that the boatwoman had sensed his presence. He felt the waft of air as … what was her name? Lamiya? pulled open the far screen and stepped out. He imagined her doing a twirl as she asked the clothes-maker how the outfit looked. He must move. *Now!*

With shaking legs, he stood up and looked over the screen. The two women were absorbed, the clothes-maker showing Lamiya a scarf the colour of dark-fall sky with silvery clouds. A detail he did not need. *Get a grip. Move now.* He pressed out through the narrow gap on the opposite side of the screen and sidled behind the nearest rack of clothes.

'Done,' Lamiya said.

'You could wear them to the welcome feast,' said the clothes-maker.

'Wonderful idea!'

Everand assumed the clap of hands was from Lamiya.

When Lamiya made her way back behind the screen to get changed again, Everand peered between the hanging clothes. The clothes-woman was placing scarves and tunics back on a rack. Confirming the spell of invisibility was still in place, he slithered along the wall.

And bolted out the doorway.

Chapter Four

Squinting against the bright sun, Everand stumbled onto the patch of green grass and sat in the meagre shade of an ornate shrub. He propped his back up against the pot and took several shaky breaths, his hands trembling. Most unpleasant. He sat flexing his fingers until his sense of order returned. *Think! Focus!* He had clothes: what next? What about his identity and a name? How about Everd? Close enough to his real name that he'd recognise when people were speaking to him.

Where was he from? In his previous subterfuge, sticking close to the truth had always worked best. Besides, he didn't know enough about any of the river provinces to claim he was from one and he was too tall for such a claim to be credible. Mantiss had decreed: *No hint. None whatsoever.* The muscles tugged across his forehead. Surely the best option was to say he was from Axis, but that he was one of the ordinary people who worked for the mages. If anyone asked questions about the mages, he could pretend his knowledge was from observations based on his duties. That could work.

His stomach rumbled and his innards writhed. Was he ill? From the river water? His stomach lurched. Of course! He hadn't eaten breakfast because he'd been summoned so early. He also hadn't drunk anything, except a few mouthfuls of river water. There was a lot to be said for having meals delivered to his rooms by the kitchen people, and on time. Leaning heavily against the pot, he groaned. He'd taken so many things for granted. Food and drink were next on the list.

Everand stood up, brushed the grass from his trousers and continued along the path. Somebody must sell food, and the sun was almost at its peak. Did these people eat at sun-high? *Focus, look and learn.* He passed another three domes that contained cloths and clothes. How did people decide where to purchase their goods? Quality? Friendship? Price?

His nostrils twitched: that smelled like bread cooking. His stomach rumbling, he quickened his stride. The next dome had a long wooden table outside the doorway and a man was carrying towards it trays of what smelled wonderfully like bread. He timed his arrival for when the man put down his tray and disappeared back inside the dome. Grabbing a couple of hand-sized round loaves from the middle of a tray so their absence would be less obvious, he scurried past. Ignoring the pangs in his stomach, he strode away, looking for something to drink.

Two domes along a woman was arranging ceramic jugs and mugs on another outside table. He paused, waiting for the woman to turn and go back inside, then he grabbed the nearest jug and hurried behind the dome. Once settled on the ground between the back of the dome and the wall of the town, where people were unlikely to walk, he inspected his fare.

The bread was still warm. He eyed the unfamiliar small brown seeds scattered throughout the mixture, and took a bite. It tasted delicious and his stomach growled in approval. He dispatched both loaves. Where were his manners? He didn't usually bolt his food.

He sniffed the contents of the jug, which smelled like a type of fruit. Giving the jug a jiggle, he watched the pale-green liquid slosh about. No matter, he must drink. Raising the jug to his lips, he took a tentative sip. The drink was light and refreshing. Not quite a tart taste, not overly sweet. He forced himself to drink it slowly. He should return the jug. If he put it

32

on the ground next to the table, the woman might think it had fallen off and spilled.

Leaning against the wall of the dome, he closed his eyes, enjoying the warmth seeping into his back from the bricks. Since when had he enjoyed such simple things?

His heart thudded against his ribs and his arms twitched. By the heaviness of his eyelids, he'd been asleep! Shouts erupted, followed by the sound of running feet and odd bangs and thuds. Leaping up, he hurried to the front of the dome. People were running and shrieking. On the far side of the path, women were snatching up children and fleeing into the dwelling domes. Nearer him, the traders were grabbing their wares and tossing them into their domes. He noticed a knot of men forming on the path and recognised Acim and Ejad among them.

'Quickly, man!' someone yelled at him as they ran past.

Everand twisted to look behind, but no-one was there. Startled, he looked down at his trousers and sandals. Curse it! He was visible! So much for a subtle introduction to the populace. The next man that came running by grabbed his arm and tugged him into a run. With a grunt, he fell into stride, eyeing the wooden stave the man carried. A fight? As he ran he carefully replicated the man's stave and tossed it into his right hand. Another few strides and they joined the knot of men and stood, legs braced, facing the archway and gates at the northern end of the town. Everand licked his lips. The bread sat heavy in his gut and his heart was thudding against his ribs.

'What comes?' he croaked.

'Tree-moths. A swarm,' the man replied, his eyes fixed on the archway.

Everand shifted from foot to foot, trying to limber up. Recalling the glimpse of the map, he remembered that to the north were mountains. Why would moths be a problem? A musky odour drifted across his head, cloying his nostrils. A ripple passed through the men around him and the sound of wings drew closer and louder, following the odour. Gripping his stave, he looked for Acim. There, the man was near the centre and front of the group. He nudged his way forward until he stood behind Acim.

As if a cloud had dimmed the sun, the sky went darker and a mass of large, beige moths hurtled through the archway. Everand gasped: the torsos were half the size of a man, with a wingspan the size of a person. The moths waved their antennae aggressively. Horrified, he watched the first few moths fly directly at the line of men.

'Staves!' yelled a solid, strong man, running to stand next to Acim. 'Timing, yosh!'

As one, the first row of men stabbed at the moths. Two moths fanned their wings furiously, trying to disengage from the staves, and let out high-pitched screeches that rattled Everand's teeth. The rest of the swarm closed in, beating at the men with their wings. A fine dust drifted down and the cloying odour grew thicker. Everand's forearms itched when some moth dust settled on them. Hastily, he brushed it off and then ducked as a pair of wings swept over him. Curses! He struggled with his stave and raised it just in time. The moth suddenly arched backwards and screeched. Everand leaped sideways as it toppled and watched Acim put a foot on the moth's back and yank his stave out of the body. Their eyes met and he nodded his thanks. Acim spun around to tackle another moth.

Everand barely had time to lick his lips before the next moth flew at him. This time, he jerked his stave up with all the force he could muster. There was a sickening crunch when the point connected with the moth's abdomen. Breathing hard, he lifted the stave higher while the moth thrashed its wings. He gritted his teeth; the weight on the stave was crushing his arms. His back foot slipped and the moth jerked closer until its antennae waved dangerously close to his face. Sending magical energy through the soles of his feet, he gave an almighty thrust upwards. His ears rang with the moth's screeching, then the moth toppled away from him and crunched to the path. Copying Acim, Everand put his foot on the body and tugged his stave free. Stinging sweat dripped into his eyes. He shook his head and, on instinct, thrust his stave upwards as another moth dived at him.

For an eternity he parried and thrust, dodged wings, dodged other men, and tried to keep his focus amid the screeching, shouting and chaos. His arms and legs burned and his chest heaved. He couldn't keep this up much longer! Should he ignore Mantiss' decree and use his powers to annihilate the swarm? He thrust once more, and an eerie stillness settled over the group.

Blinking the sweat from his eyes, he leaned on his stave, panting. Around him, between the humped bodies of moths, men were all doing the same thing. His ears rang and his arms itched and burned. Red blisters were forming where the dust had landed. Biting his tongue, he resisted the temptation to scratch, suspecting that would make matters worse.

'Gather around,' commanded the same solid man who had led the fight.

Everand raised his eyebrows when the men around him stood straight and moved towards the man. He hovered at the back uncertainly.

'Well done,' said the man, casting his eyes across each man. 'Is anyone hurt?'

'My arms, Tengar,' said one, stepping forward to show his skin seething with red blisters. 'The cursed dust.'

'I'm here!' called a female voice. 'Let me through.'

A woman clad in a moss green tunic and darker green skirt wound her way through the men to stand behind the leader. Over her arm was a woven basket containing sprays of green and purple plants that looked like herbs, and small jars that Everand guessed would contain ointments and salves.

35

'Sit,' said the man called Tengar. 'Mookaite will treat the burns and any other injuries.' He scratched at his head. 'I'll find some traders to help us remove the moth bodies.'

Again, almost as one, the group of men lined up and sat down. Everand hurried to join the end of the line. He drew slow breaths, trying to collect his thoughts as the woman crouched before the first man, who held out his arms for her to inspect. His arms and legs ached and sweat trickled down his neck, back and sides. He'd need to 'acquire' more clothes already. Resting his chin on his chest, he considered what to do next.

A rustling of material and light footsteps caught his attention. 'Me too, I can help,' said a voice that sounded all too familiar. Lamiya had arrived. This woman seemed to be everywhere! Impossible to avoid. Subtly glancing sideways, he saw that she carried a basket of herbs and had moved to the next man in line to treat him. Well, he could hardly stand and walk away now. Perhaps the other woman would tend to him. Taking the opportunity to think through his story for his reasons for being there, he waited patiently, half-listening to the men's conversation.

'Why did the moths come?' murmured one.

'No idea. They shouldn't leave the forest.'

'Just as well we stopped them before they got to the cloth.'

'Indeed. Some festival if we had no cloth to trade.'

'Do you think they were sent?'

Everand latched onto the last question and listened intently to the two men.

'On purpose? But how?'

'I don't know, but we're a long way from the forest.'

'Another intended attack, you think?'

The second man shrugged. 'Either that or we've truly angered Mizuchi and he's abandoned us.'

That name again. What or who were they referring to?

'Show me,' said a soft voice.

Everand's eyebrows pinched together: how could he find out what the men were speaking about without being too obvious? This Mizuchi seemed important.

'If you don't show me your arms I'll tip this water over your head,' said the voice sternly.

Appalled, Everand looked up. Lamiya was crouched in front of him, holding up a jug with a smile tugging at the corner of her lips.

'Sorry!' he gasped. 'I am tired.' That sounded lame. Suppressing a wince, he held out his stinging arms. When Lamiya shuffled closer he averted his eyes.

She took hold of his hand. Her hand pressure was firm, but her skin was soft and silky. 'Not so bad,' she murmured. 'I'll apply some salve.'

Everand closed his eyes while she gently rubbed a pungent cream along the blisters on his arms. Underneath the strong smell of the salve, he detected the faint scent of flowers. 'Are you a healer?' The words popped out before he could consider whether he should engage her in conversation.

'I am many things,' she replied, tossing her head to flick a curl of luscious brown hair back, 'but yes, I am a healer among them.' Her eyes locked onto his face. 'We haven't met, have we?'

Not trusting himself to speak, Everand shook his head.

'Where are you from? I haven't seen you here before.'

Everand swallowed. This was it. 'I am Everd. From Axis.'

Her eyebrows arched elegantly. 'Axis! Really? What brings you here?'

'Just travelling,' he said and stopped, hoping this would suffice. By the way her eyes narrowed, it would not.

'All done?' asked the other woman, coming over with a slap of sandals.

To his relief, Lamiya gathered up her basket and stood.

'Well, Everd,' she said his name slowly and distinctly, 'nice to meet you.'

Imagining that she had added 'properly', he replied, 'Thank you, Lamiya.' He hoped he'd pronounced her name correctly.

Her eyes widened with that keen alertness, the look that seemed to see right into him. With another smile tugging at her lips, she turned away and followed the healer woman.

When the other men stood up and started to drift away, Everand lumbered to his feet. Surveying the area, he saw some different men pulling the bodies of the moths into a pile near the archway. What would they do with the bodies? Burn them? Bury them? Eat them? A shudder rippled through him. The intent look Lamiya had given him played in his mind. What had he said to attract that level of alertness?

His breath caught in his throat. She *had* told him her name, hadn't she?

CHAPTER FIVE

Drawing his thoughts away from Lamiya, Everand pitched in to help so he could listen and observe. Wordlessly, he approached a man grappling with the tail of a dead moth, trying not to brush against the limp wings. Analysing the size and probable weight of the moth, Everand concluded that pushing the body from the head would be the most helpful. He stood with his legs shoulder-width apart and cautiously grasped the moth's head. Nothing dreadful happened, so he leaned into the body and pushed. The man at the tail end looked up with a grunt and gave a nod when the moth slid towards him.

While they worked, Everand eyed the moth. It was about the same size as the silk moths in Axis, but those were benign, graceful creatures that worked for the mages spinning the valuable silk threads. The tree-moth was chunkier. Silk moths didn't like bright light, and the enormous breeding domes at Mage Agamid's estate were dimly lit to provide a perpetual dusky twilight. The rows of silk trees provided further shade and cool for the silk moths. Did these tree-moths usually fly during the bright sun? Why had they attacked? Were they usually aggressive? The men had anticipated an attack when they saw the moths coming. Wait, Beram had mentioned large moths. He hadn't realised Beram meant *this* big, though.

Unease shivered across the sweat evaporating on the back of his neck. Were all the insects in the provinces this size? Did

Mantiss and Agamid know there were moths this big, like the insects of Axis? Was that the *this* he was supposed to see?

Once they had shoved the body to the edge of the pile, he let go. Seeing the man looking at him, curiosity forming, Everand edged closer. Unaware of the usual form of greeting, he said simply, 'Greetings, I'm Everd, a traveller.'

'Zeol.' The man dipped his head.

'Is this usual?' Everand waved a hand at the mound of moths.

'This is the second time.' Zeol frowned, as if weighing up how much to say.

'Where are they from?' Everand thought this a safe question.

'Riverwood. They live in Hanaki Forest. Usually.'

Everand thought of the map Agamid had spread out. He vaguely recollected a forested area to the northern end of the provinces. 'Where's that from here?'

'From Zuqart?' asked Zeol.

Was Zuqart the town? Everand nodded.

Zeol gestured towards the archway leading out of the town. 'That way, a full sun of walking towards the mountains, and then further across Little Claw bridge.'

Everand felt his eyebrow quirk at the naming conventions. This was an incredibly long way for the moths to have flown. What else should he ask? He didn't want to seem like he was interrogating Zeol. A rattling sound heralded the arrival of two of the wooden-platform carts like the one he had seen earlier. The drivers directed the pairs of beasts and reversed them until the backs of the carts faced the moth bodies. Everand eyed the raised platform. How did they propose to lift the bodies? The four-legged beasts fidgeted and swished long, thin tails.

'What are these creatures?' he asked Zeol just as the man went to step away.

'Hopeepa,' replied Zeol, putting his foot back down. 'From Riverplain.' When Everand looked at him, he added, 'We trade cloth for them.' He waved a hand at the colourful splotches on the creatures' bodies. 'They're bred for their colour and patterns but we use them to transport goods.' He shrugged. 'We should help load.'

Everand hovered, intrigued, as a couple of men carried long wooden planks to the back of the carts to form a ramp. Next came coils of ropes, which were carefully hooked under a moth's wings. *Clever.* They were going to drag the bodies up the ramps.

The man called Tengar beckoned to him. 'You. Hold the creatures.'

Everand's mouth went dry. Tengar looked as if he were about to bark a further order, so he hastened to the nearest hopeepa's head and grasped the straps under its jaw. He swallowed when the creature swung its head, the same height as his, and peered at him, fluttering long eyelashes. Stretching its long neck, it sniffed at the salve on his arm, its oval nostrils flaring to show a lilac lining. Large, mahogany-brown eyes regarded him steadily.

Remembering the affection between Elemar and her winged horse, Everand lifted his other hand and gently rubbed the hopeepa's neck. The fur was soft and warm, and the creature leaned into his hand and fluttered its eyelashes more. An eddy of calm washed through him.

'Don't pat her,' admonished a man as he jostled past with a coil of rope. 'She'll follow you everywhere.'

The hopeepa gave him a limpid look, and Everand almost smiled. Then he thought of Mizu, stuck in stasis back in Axis, and the eddy of calm dissipated. Sensing his change of mood, the creature shot out a purple tongue and licked the back of his hand. Something nudged his shoulder. The pair hopeepa pushed at him. This one was slightly smaller and the blotches on its body and neck were a paler purple. However, it looked just as friendly. He gave the smaller one a brief pat and then the straps went taut in his fingers.

'You can let go now,' called a voice.

Everand dropped the straps and took a few steps back out of the way. Should he offer to go with them? That would be an ideal way to see outside the town. 'I can help, if you like,' he called up to the driver.

'Climb up then,' came the ready reply.

He hurried to the front of the cart, climbed up a wooden step and settled on the seat next to the driver. The man shook the reins and clicked his tongue, and Everand swayed backwards as the cart lurched. His sore back muscles tensed and he tilted forward, copying the man's posture. The cart rumbled beneath the wide archway and he took in the scenery. The driver was silent, concentrating on directing the creatures. Dust drifted back, raised by the wheels of the cart in front, mingled with the musky odour of the tree-moth bodies. Everand blinked to dislodge the gritty feel in his eyes.

The path headed due north, following the banks of the river. The land was flat and open and to the right of the path stretched rows of neatly planted bushes with glossy green leaves and crowns of fluffy white buds. Running along the base of the rows he saw shallow trenches made of pebbles and stones. Was this how they watered the crops? There were no domes in sight.

Discreetly, he assessed his companion. This man had a coppery tone to his hair, like Beram, and was of a similar build. Muscles rippled in his arms and Everand noted the breadth of his shoulders. He decided to attempt conversation. 'I am Everd, a traveller.'

'Persaj,' said the man, flicking a glance at him.

'How far will we go?' asked Everand.

Persaj hunched his shoulders. 'To the base of the hills. To bury these in a gully.'

Everand scanned ahead. Sure enough, to the east, a line of hills was emerging. 'Can I ask some questions? I've never been here before.' He took Persaj's nod to be assent. 'So, this land here, you only use it for crops?'

Persaj inclined his head. 'Yes.'

'To grow the plants to make the cloth?' Everand took a guess, based on the number of trader domes related to cloth and clothes. Also, Zeol had said they traded cloth for the splotched creatures.

Persaj shook the reins to make the hopeepa speed up, a gap having formed between them and the other cart. 'And food crops.'

This was hard work. Perhaps a change of subject would draw Persaj out more. 'Do you race in the boat?'

Persaj straightened up. 'Yes, paddler six.'

'I'm looking forward to seeing the races.' He tried to look enthused. 'Can you tell me about them?' When Persaj smiled, he decided the man was younger than he first thought, perhaps only thirty or so.

'There are ten paddlers in a boat, plus a drummer, and a glide to steer the boat and direct the team.'

'The glide stands up at the back?' Everand thought of Lamiya, brown hair waving in the breeze, and her steady balance on the moving boat.

'The glide is the leader. They set the pace and keep an eye out for any dangers.'

'What are the boats made of? Do all the provinces have a boat?'

'Wood from the tallest, oldest trees. We and Riverplain, our closest neighbour, have boats and team colours. We've raced each other a few times. But this festival will be the best because there'll be four boats racing.' Persaj waved his hands animatedly, and the hopeepa wobbled on the path as the reins flapped. 'Last time Riverplain beat us. We're determined to take back our title.' Persaj frowned. 'We must.'

Everand let the silence ride for a few breaths; there was more than winning the race on Persaj's mind. Absently, he noted they now passed fields of a tall, yellowish, stalky crop with seed heads on it. Beyond the fields, the land was a brown-green, the grass short. A fork in the path loomed ahead, with the right-hand path leading towards the hills, the hues of darker green and brown at the base suggesting trees. His thoughts hovered like butterflies again; there must be a pertinent question, one that would unlock what was going on. *Something about the festival.*

The first cart swung onto the diverting path. The creature he'd patted tossed her head and bellowed until Persaj pulled the reins and their cart swung onto the new path too. The rumbling of the wheels grew louder and Everand noticed the stones were rougher, not as finely crushed. A breeze caressed his face. *Focus.* 'The festival is important?'

Persaj gave him an astonished look. 'If we don't please Mizuchi our crops will fail.'

Everand's heartbeat thudded against his breastbone. That name again. 'How will you please this Mizuchi?'

With a wild wave of his hands, Persaj said, 'Our boat must glide supreme, fast and furious. We must churn the waters of the river with our paddles to leave the others bouncing in our wake. We must honour Mizuchi.' Persaj faltered, his voice breaking.

What were the consequences of failing to win? While Persaj regained his composure, Everand looked ahead at the huddled hills with a large copse of trees at the base. 'Forgive my ignorance, but who is Mizuchi?'

Persaj nearly toppled off the seat. 'You don't know?' he squeaked. 'Mizuchi is the river dragon. Without his blessing the rain doesn't fall from the skies, the rivers will fall and our crops will fail.'

Everand sensed that if he weren't holding the straps, Persaj would be wringing his hands. 'Is that likely?'

Persaj compressed his lips. 'It hasn't rained for five seasons. The dragon must be angry.'

Everand leaned his elbows on his knees and rested his head in his hands. So, Mizuchi was a dragon. A belief or a reality? Maybe real — after all, Mage Beetal had found dragons on Elemar's world. Those were winged dragons that lived in a volcano and although he hadn't heard of dragons living in water that didn't mean it wasn't possible. He only knew what Mage Beetal had chosen to show or tell him about his army of the beasts.

His nape tingled. Dragons were enormous, aggressive and ruthless. He grimaced; no-one had ever said anything about there being dragons in Ossilis, of any type. Did the mages not know? The Guild was proving to be most ignorant about the provinces and people surrounding them. He was about to ask whether Persaj had ever seen this Mizuchi when calls rang out.

'Persaj! Over here!'

They'd reached the trees and the other cart waited in the shade of the outer branches.

The water dragon — real or not — would have to wait.

CHAPTER SIX

The basket of salves and herbs weighing heavily in the crook of her arm, Lamiya walked back to the dome allocated to her team. The opportunity to train with the team from Riverfall in the early golden light had been wonderful. Their boat was sleek and fast and it glided smoothly over the water. Her boat would be hard-pressed to best this team. The Riverfall team's timing was nothing short of miraculous. What drills did they use to achieve this? How did they train for stamina for the longer races?

Her pace quickened as she considered strategy, then slowed again when she thought about the boat narrowly missing what she was sure was a person. In the river. Yet when she'd turned the boat around to look properly, there'd been no sign of anyone. She frowned. Her instinct insisted there *had* been a person. If she'd been with her own team she could have asked if they'd seen anything. But they were still three suns away, bringing their boat, Flight, by carts.

Nudging aside the hanging curtain, she appreciated the cooler air in the dome. The sun was unusually strong for the season and her hair clung dankly to the back of her neck. She placed the woven basket on the table in the corner and sorted through the contents. The jars of chamomile and lavender salve were both low after treating so many men. She squinted at the line of herbs hanging along one wall. There were three bulky sprigs of lavender and two bunches of chamomile flowers; enough for one more jar of each.

She shuddered: if the tree-moths returned they'd need many more jars. How had the terrifying moths grown so large? They'd more likely eat her precious birds than the other way around. Hopefully, they'd never fly south to Riverplain. Pushing away the dark thought, she fetched a mug of cool water to drink, and filled a small bowl to splash her face with.

Seated on the low stool, dabbing her face with a cloth, her thoughts drifted. The traveller, *Everd*. Why did she feel this was not his true name? It didn't sit well with his aura, which suggested a longer, smoother name. Why would he give a false name? Was he really from the elusive province of Axis? Why was he here? The image of him sitting with his arms outstretched to receive the salve on his burns overlaid the fleeting image of a head bobbing in the river. The pale colour of his hair, like spun starlight, was unusual. She gasped. Was *he* the person in the river? Why?

Her gaze wandered and came to rest on the pile of dark-blue cloth on the floor just inside the door. Another mystery. This material had been lying crumpled on the floor in the changing area in Melanite's clothing dome. Hiding it inside the skirt and tunic she'd purchased, she'd snuck it out with her. Did it belong to the traveller? She crossed the floor to retrieve the cloth.

When she picked it up her fingers tingled. The material was smooth and slippery and glimmered with its own sheen. She shook the material out and held it up high, both of her arms spread to full stretch. Deciding she possibly had the thing upside down, she reversed the material. Not a design she'd seen before, it looked like a really long tunic that would stretch from neck to toes. Was he tall? She had to hold it above her head. The cobalt blue was an exotic, mesmerising colour. Her breath caught: it matched his eyes!

She closed her eyes, willed her heartbeat to slow and took a slow inhalation through her nostrils. Her nose and fingers tingled. A strong sense of him ebbed into her, just like when she'd rubbed the salve into the burns on his arms. Her mind would not call him Everd. He was bigger, better, than that name.

She opened her eyes and felt them narrow. Had *he* been in Melanite's dome? He must have been because that was where she'd found this strange tunic. Was he the unusual presence she'd felt while trying on the new skirt? Why hadn't she been able to see him? Perhaps he'd taken clothes and left, and what she'd sensed was his lingering essence. Was that even possible? Or had she perceived his aura in the clothing left behind? *Too many ifs and maybes.* Her lips twitched. She could have some fun when she returned his clothing. Surely he'd be embarrassed beyond belief. And she might find out more about him. She folded the cloth carefully and placed it back in the corner.

What to do now? She stood with her hands on her hips. The people of Riverfall were pleasant enough, but it was boring being out of routine. She missed her birds and their bright fluttering wings and incessant chattering. She should have brought a couple with her, but not in small cages. No, the birds were better staying at home, especially with the breeding season approaching. A smile teasing her lips, she thought of the two brightly plumed males she'd found. Her favourite, Whirr, was especially intelligent and engaging. He was affectionate, often perching on her shoulder and playing with her hair or peeping into her ear. This season's chicks would be spectacular!

Absently, she rubbed at her tight calf muscles. Some stretching would help. She began her routine, stretching tall and rotating her hands and wrists above her head. Sweeping forward to touch her toes, she placed her hands flat on the ground in front of her. Carefully, she eased her weight backwards, feeling a pleasant stretch in her lower back. Next, she eased her hands and weight forward, wincing at the stretch in her calves and behind her knees.

Her mind focused on her goals. The team had sent her to Riverfall early; as the glide it was up to her to plan the strategy and ascertain the depth of competition. Tengar had kindly said she could train with them until her boat arrived — an excellent opportunity to find out more about Riverfall's training strategies. She swung her hips one way and then the other, looking forward to seeing her team. Lulite had promised to bring a new charm for her, something special. Lepid would be driving the lead team of hopeepa, no doubt proud that creatures from his herd were participating in the festival.

She paused. Lazuli would also bring his strongest hopeepa. The handsome and witty paddler had been increasingly attentive of late. Lamiya resumed her ankle rotations and added her wrists. Lazuli was forever asking her to comment on his technique and engaging her in conversation about drills and training exercises. By the way Lepid rolled his eyes behind his brother's back, she was sure it was more than competitive zeal driving Lazuli. What to do? Lazuli was her right-hand pacer and like a playful brother to her. Was he aiming to change this? Her pulse raced. Did she want him to? Her stomach clenched.

Taking a breath, she determined to focus on the more pressing problem that her team was one paddler short. Curse Latog for breaking his leg! What had possessed him to climb a massive tree before these races? On the other hand, if he hadn't broken his leg she'd be paddler ten rather than the glide. The team wouldn't otherwise have allowed her to test her prowess as a glide at this important festival.

She lifted her hair from her neck with both hands to allow cool air to wash over her. If Luvu, their most experienced paddler, hadn't managed to find someone, she'd have to scrounge a paddler from another province or the boat would be unbalanced. She swallowed. Luvu would be looking for any reason to find fault in her leadership, given he would have preferred his friend Latog to be the glide.

Crossing one leg in front of the other, she leaned over to stretch the large band of muscle running down the outside of her leg. So, the rumours were that Riverwood was sending a boat. Usually, the fierce hunters kept to themselves, hiding behind the dense Hanaki Forest. Her eyebrows clenched in a scowl; their boat would be an unknown proposition. Why had they decided to compete? A shiver passed up her spine and sat tingling at the base of her neck. She straightened up, dropped her arms to her sides, closed her eyes and breathed in deeply. *A premonition.*

Forcing all thoughts from her mind, she allowed sensations to drift over her. Images of large black and grey birds of prey circling a dense forest floated before her closed eyes. One screeched, a harsh, mournful cry. Her neck tingled again and her mind's eye dropped from the skies to enter the gloom of the forest.

Muscled men clad in skins and feathers moved through the trees, carrying crossbows and knives. A shiver raced through her at the intent of violence. *Ah.* They also carried a dragon boat. It was long and chunky with brown, grey and white scales along the sides, the head of a fierce eagle with an open beak and impenetrable black eyes at the prow. The wooden stern rose proudly, carved like a fanned tail of storm-grey and brown feathers. *Raptor*, suggested her mind. She shuddered. Was she seeing the Riverwood team on the way, or something more? How many men; was it the number for a team? Why would they bring weapons?

She started to count the men as they slipped through the trees. At their head marched a tall man with broad shoulders and a face as fierce as the birds of prey. He had grey feathers woven into the braids of black hair that framed his angled face and hook-shaped nose. Abruptly, he looked up. For an instant, dark, glittering eyes glared at her. Then the wall of tree trunks shifted and merged, blocking her view.

The vision faded. She was standing in the dome at Riverfall, breathing hard.

Chapter Seven

Everand was impressed by the way the men from Riverfall worked silently and efficiently. Soon, all the moth corpses were rolled into a heap at the bottom of a deep, jagged ravine and numerous branches had been sawed down and thrown on top to cover the mess. The knot of men stood on the lip of the ravine and waited for instructions from Tengar. Everand used the sleeve of his tunic to wipe the sweat from his face. A dull ache was settling into his lower back and the backs of his legs. He'd never done this much physical exercise at once. Did they use bathtubs here? He could use a long, hot soak. Wryly, he supposed these men would be more likely to dunk themselves in the cold river water.

'Good work, everyone,' said Tengar, with a nod of approval.

'Should we burn the bodies?' asked a man Everand hadn't met yet.

Tengar put his head to one side. 'I reckon not, Lyber. It's been so dry we daren't risk a forest fire. We'll have to leave them to rot.' He straightened his shoulders. 'Let's get home before dark-fall.'

After clapping one another on the shoulder, the men divided into the previous two groups. Everand hastened to catch up with Persaj, who was striding towards the further cart. After scrambling stiffly up the step, he sat beside Persaj just as the man took up the leather straps. This time, he leaned forward ready for the initiating lurch. The taller hopeepa shook her ears

51

and let out a call. As before, they followed the other cart and Everand could see the four men on it murmuring to one another.

The scenery looked different from the reverse direction. The trees fell away and rolling plains of short, wiry grass stretched before them, with the town walls rising slowly larger ahead and casting purple-tinged shadows. Persaj drove in mute concentration, occasionally flicking the straps to make the hopeepa keep the pace. Everand considered what other questions he should ask, but the butterflies were hovering listlessly in his mind. What had they been talking about before? Ah, yes, the river dragon and the possible failing of the crops. Feeling a spark of energy, he straightened from his slouch and observed the countryside more keenly.

Away from the riverbanks the grass did look dry, mainly brown with occasional wispy tufts of green. The river water gleamed a dull blue-grey in the fading light. If he squinted, he could see the neat rows of bushes closer to the town. His head perched heavy on his neck and his eyes were gritty and sore. Sleep! Where would he sleep this dark-fall? The movement of the cart gently rocked him to and fro. If only he knew the name of the two people he could trust.

Before him, the rumps of the two hopeepa swayed, the lilac blotches moving in a sinuous pattern. The ears of the larger hopeepa flopped in time with her steps. The creatures seemed friendly and kind. Not dangerous. He turned to Persaj.

'Where are the hopeepa kept? Do you need help to settle them for the dark-time?'

Persaj gave him a weary look. 'I accept your offer.'

Everand nodded, wondering exactly what he'd just offered. His chin drooped and he dozed, lulled by the movement and the softening twilight.

A nudge to his ribs woke him. 'We're here,' said Persaj.

Opening his eyes wide, Everand found they were back inside the town walls and the cart had stopped in front of an elongated dome with wooden doors across the entry. He sniffed at the peaty, grassy odour wafting into his face.

Persaj slid down and tied the long straps to the front of the cart. 'Help me undo the harness?'

Everand slid down, the solid ground jarring his feet and his back giving a warning twinge. Wordlessly, he moved to the larger creature and, frowning in concentration, copied as Persaj unbuckled various straps in a set order. The hopeepa pushed him repeatedly with her head, and Everand tried to elbow its nose away while he fumbled with the buckle of the chest strap.

'Don't let her get too friendly,' cautioned Persaj, leaning across to tug the buckle from its keeper. 'They're meant to be working animals.' Persaj tugged the smaller hopeepa towards the stables using the strap running down its cheekbone.

Everand copied, and his hopeepa followed, but kept licking the side of his face. The rasping tongue tickled and the more he tried to squirm out of reach, the more persistent the creature became. Persaj gave him an exasperated look.

Inside the long, squat dome were several stalls divided by wooden railings. A couple already contained hopeepa, and these swished their tails and called soft greetings. He followed as Persaj led his hopeepa into the second furthest stall and jerked his head at the final one. Everand was dragged into it by the enthusiastic hopeepa. 'Whoa!' he exclaimed.

Persaj laughed. 'She's keen for her food. Remove the straps first and I'll show you what they eat.'

Everand fumbled with the straps while the hopeepa alternated between licking his hands and stepping on his feet. He could see Persaj trying not to laugh. Finally, he scurried out of the stall and Persaj showed him how to slide the entry rails into the box keepers. In the feed area, he mimicked Persaj by measuring handfuls of various grains into a square wooden tub.

'Not too much corn,' said Persaj, indicating the hard yellow kernels, 'or they get silly.'

Everand carried the tub of grains and placed it in the hopeepa's stall. The creature buried her nose in the tub, her tail swirling as she crunched on her food.

'Check she has enough water.' Persaj pointed to a large ceramic bowl at the rear of the stall. 'And check there's enough dry grass on the floor.' Persaj scuffed at the long dry stalks with the toes of his sandals. 'Should be enough.'

An awkward silence followed. 'Well,' said Everand brightly, 'thanks for showing me all that.' He walked to the exit as if he had somewhere to go.

At the doors, Persaj gave him a friendly clap on the shoulder before hurrying away into the near darkness.

Everand stood a moment, taking in the darkening sky, sensing the quiet falling over the town. Soft light glowed behind brightly coloured curtains. There was minimal movement on the pathways. These were good people: straightforward, hard-working, honest and kind. So far, he'd seen nothing to suggest any reasons for the violence Beram had described. He looked up at the pale stars twinkling amid wafting strands of high cloud. How long until Beram arrived? Perhaps things would move more quickly when he had help. His stomach reminded him he hadn't eaten since sun-high. No matter, sleep was the greater imperative.

Confirming that nobody was nearby, he melted back into the shadows of the stables. The hopeepa was delighted, flopping her ears and nudging him with her nose. He crept into the back corner of her stall, piled the dry stalks of grass higher and lay down. As his eyes closed, the hopeepa buckled at the knees and sat down next to him, her long legs folded beneath her. Her eyelashes tickled him where she rested her head on his arm. Calm washed through him and he smiled. His disguise seemed to be working, and surely Mantiss would be pleased that he had found out so much already.

He fell into a deep and dreamless sleep.

CHAPTER EIGHT

Mage Mantiss sipped the last of his apple wine. The sun had dipped below the horizon and a pale slip of moon was edging up into the purple-grey sky. Where was Everand now? Was he safe? Mantiss placed the glass back on the dining table, controlling the tremors in his hand by sheer force of will. Curse this failing body! There was so much more to be done.

Clasping his hands together and resting them on the table, he stared out the window. His arms felt weighted by fatigue. That was a close call this sun-up. Too close. Agamid had barely disappeared with Beram, translocating to his country estate, when Pelamis had started to pound on the doors to the Great Hall. The impudence! His lips twitched. He had translocated out into the gardens and young Pelamis had not looked so confident when he'd approached him from behind, coming along the pebble path and ascending the steps to apologise to the gaggle on the doorstep that the meeting was cancelled.

The others might not have believed his explanation that Mage Agamid was delayed dealing with some issue at the moth breeding domes, but he was the Head of the Guild and they had no choice but to accept the meeting was postponed for two suns. As he had pointed out, overriding their grumbling, they should have waited for *him* to sound the summons. By the depth of Pelamis' scowl, he deduced it was him who had taken the initiative. Mantiss reached for his glass, and found it was empty. Pelamis needed to be taught his place — soon — or he would have another Mage Beetal on his hands.

Using both hands to push himself up from the table, he wandered over to the alcove where his reading desk sat snugly between two pillars. Reaching behind the desk, he placed a palm flat on a smooth marble tile indistinguishable from the others in the wall and murmured the words, 'note-scrawl-Lapemis'. The tile dissolved, and a flat tray with an ancient, crinkled notebook on it slid out.

Gingerly, Mantiss picked up the notebook. By the time he had sat at his small desk, the tile had formed back in place. With a sigh, he caressed the notebook's dry cover and traced his fingers over the etched title.

He uttered the code words again, and the cover opened and flattened itself, offering him the first page to read. His throat tightened at the memory of the previous Head of the Guild, Eremius, lying on his death bed and passing the book to him with tremulous hands and clouded, rheumy eyes. Twelve season-cycles ago. Reading the notebook back then was enough. The weight of the knowledge contained inside had pressed on him every time he paused to think about it. Still, at sixty-eight cycles, he would have expected more time in the position of Head of the Guild. Eremius was eighty-five cycles when he passed, and the three incumbents before him were also in their eighties before they'd handed over the reins.

The quiet of the room and the calm of dark falling enveloped him. Trusting, loyal Everand had gone out beyond the wall to please him. The least he could do was refresh in his mind the details of the true history of the origins of the Guild. Although his savage injuries looked healed on the surface, his body was telling him the battle with Mage Beetal had irrecoverably cost him, physically and mentally. Before long, he would need to pass this notebook on to a new Head of the Guild. Agamid would be a logical choice, but did he have the fortitude?

What about ... Everand? Although young, he was powerful, incredibly intelligent, analytical and, most importantly, he could always be trusted to work for the greater good. A frown pinched his forehead. This impromptu mission would give Everand yet another chance to prove his mettle. But he was an odd one; difficult to read, he kept largely to himself, and being a spy had only enhanced these qualities. The other mages were unlikely to elect him.

Mantiss shook his head: wait and see what information Everand brought back. If the provinces around them were growing and uniting, perhaps some level of change would have to be wrought. After all this time. In the meantime, he must prepare by reading the notebook again. Slowly and carefully. He dropped his eyes to the opening paragraph.

From the scrawlings of Mage Lapemis

The arrival

We were exhausted. The turbulent seas had taken their toll; we were sick and parched, out of food and water. Paralysed with cold, we dreaded the great sea serpent would harry the boat again. We were about to abandon hope when a long, green and grey knob of land rose out of the sea mist. I cradled Dtella's limp hand until the boat surged into a craggy inlet. All hands to deck, the shredded sail moaned with one last gust of wind and drove the prow onto the rocks. The front of the boat shattered and water tumbled in. A mere twelve mages and six humans staggered onto a stony beach. The cries of the others pierced my soul as the waves swallowed them.

Next thing I remember, I woke face down with sharp stones sticking into my nose and cheek, sun warming my back. Old Pygopus hadn't survived. Now we were eleven, with only Dtella, Pogona and Aprasia to bear offspring to continue our line. How far we had fallen! Eleven left out of a guild of a

57

hundred proud and talented mages. For two hundred season-cycles we had protected that realm of humans. A bitter taste crawled into my mouth. Despite our efforts and advancements, we were no match for several thousand warriors from the north. Too few, our energy and power were depleted over a raging battle lasting eleven suns and moons.

I swallowed my bitterness. Thank the stars I'd had the foresight to conceal *Wavestrider* in a sheltered cove — or we'd be none. I cast my eyes over the huddled and weeping humans. We had failed them: broken our tryst to 'protect by sun and moon' in exchange for having menial duties taken care of so we could focus on our expanding our magic and teaching the next class of apprentices.

Rally and rebuild, we must. I gathered the survivors and allocated them tasks. The humans cast about for edible plants and wood for a fire, while Aclys and Hemiapsis scoured rock pools for small fish and crabs. When the moon rose, we crowded around the fire and replenished our bellies.

'What now?' Hemiapsis asked, everyone's eyes looking to me.

'We find a new home,' I replied, warmed by the subtle straightening of their backs. They needed hope. 'We explore until we find the right place. And we will, I feel it in my bones.'

At sunrise, we trudged inland following a stream. Hiking uphill, we found the water fresh and drinkable once away from the sea. From the crest of the craggy headland, I gazed down at the broken, listing boat. One more storm and the remnants would be taken by the sea, then neither the serpent nor the northern warriors would know where we were. I muttered a heartfelt farewell to *Wavestrider*.

Roaming my gaze in all directions, I understood we'd found a large island, big enough to hide on. I couldn't see the far reaches of it. Water was plentiful, with a wide and twisting river originating in a range of mountains to the north. The plains and other lands looked arable. Of any movement or population, I detected no sign. Was it possible we had this land to ourselves? Hope beat in my chest. Gathering our energy and power, we walked on, taking food and water as we went, warming ourselves at dark-fall and making plans.

'We should form a new Guild.' I broached the subject. 'It will take time, but there are enough of us.' *If we don't lose anyone else.* I kept that thought to myself. 'What do you say?' I looked into each face before me. 'We rebuild, with the same agreement in place as before?' I looked at Marek, the oldest of the humans. He nodded, without conferring with the other humans. So, they had already discussed this.

Everyone agreed we would start afresh and form a new Guild. The humans agreed they would once more provide for us, expecting that we would study hard to augment our powers and protect them. May their trust that we could do better not be misguided.

To my humble honour, I was named to lead this new Mages' Guild. Such responsibility!

Mage Mantiss rubbed his eyes and closed the notebook. Emotion coursed through him; he'd forgotten how powerful this tale was. The pressure of his office leaned heavily across his shoulders. Lapemis had shown extraordinary insight and courage; it was not easy to tread wisely in his footsteps. Especially not if another significant test was imminent.

CHAPTER NINE

Something tickled his nose and voices disturbed the darkness. Everand flicked his eyes open, confused by the grassy spikes that greeted him. A large shape loomed over him. He jerked awake: he was in the hopeepa stall, and men had arrived to feed the creatures. The hopeepa moved to stand at her gate rails, bobbing her head and swishing her tail. Shrinking into the dry hay, he whispered the spell of invisibility. Then he crept to the railings and slipped out through them. Recognising Persaj and Zeol, he snuck along the wall and out the doors. The sun was already up and he blinked in the bright light. Ceasing the spell of invisibility, he gave a few brisk stretches, and ambled back into the dome.

Persaj jumped. 'Come to help again? Perhaps you're as fond of Crystal as she is of you.'

Everand frowned. 'Crystal. Is that the creature's name?'

Persaj handed him a tub of mixed grains. 'Give her this, and a sheaf of hay.' He jerked his head to a wooden cubicle. 'From there.'

Laden with the tub and a wispy sheaf of hay he headed towards Crystal's stall, and Persaj called, 'Be quick! Atage has called a town meeting.'

Everand hurried. A meeting sounded promising; he might learn more. Running his tongue over dry and cracked lips, he wondered if it was too much to hope that the meeting included food and drink. He was beginning to feel light-headed with the intermittent sustenance. Soon, he was walking with Persaj and

Zeol, heading towards the large market area. People emerged from numerous domes; everyone headed the same way. His stomach growled when he noted a few women were carrying baskets of loaves.

They passed under the archway into the market area and Everand smiled at the sight of tables laden with baskets of breads and fruits. These were being handed out freely and he gratefully took three small loaves and a round pink fruit. Juggling these, he nudged his way through townspeople to rejoin Persaj and Zeol, who were making their way towards a group clustered at the front of the crowd. He hovered while the small group clapped Persaj and Zeol on the back in greeting. Then he recognised Tengar.

'Ah. You've brought the traveller with you. Everd?' At Everand's nod, Tengar continued, 'Thanks for your help with the moths. Please, join our group.'

At what appeared to be a formal welcome, the others crowded around to introduce themselves. He recognised Melanite as the clothes trader and Mookaite as the healer. Another woman was introduced as Kunzite. The way the muscles in her arms rippled was distracting. Were all the women built like warriors? The young man he'd followed when he first arrived introduced himself as Acim. The names became a blur after that, although he remembered that Ejad was to supply the cloth for the team's new uniform.

The loaves were starting to stick to his palms. Would it be rude to eat them now? The group began to banter among themselves and Everand gratefully bit off half a loaf. With no water to wash it down, he chewed carefully so as not to choke, and started on the second loaf.

Persaj nudged his elbow. 'And this is Selenite.' Another fit woman stood there, curiosity in her brown eyes.

Everand hurriedly swallowed his mouthful and gave a polite nod.

Selenite stepped aside and he found himself looking at Lamiya. The cursed woman smiled broadly at him and raised an elegant brown eyebrow. 'You must be hungry.'

Everand fumbled for a reply, his hands full of sticky food. The sides of his neck seemed to be growing warm. Before he could conjure a suitable response, Tengar intervened.

'Lamiya! Join us for training after this meeting?'

Lamiya's face lit up. 'I'd be honoured. Just give me time to fetch my paddle.'

'Good,' said Tengar. 'I have a new drill to try.'

Lamiya's face shone and she gave such a big smile that Everand wondered if they were speaking in some form of code. The group all looked strong and fit, with muscled, broad shoulders, and he now saw that Ejad was holding a collection of wooden sticks with a wide, flat base. Were these the paddles? He was standing with the Riverfall boat team! Tengar must be the captain by the way everyone respected him. Lamiya's attention was now focused on a discussion with the other women, and Everand chewed thoughtfully on his last loaf. The other women had darker brown hair and their skin was more olive. Perhaps Lamiya was not from Riverfall? Could she be from another province, sent early before the races? She clearly knew all the others, but the way Tengar had invited her to join them for training suggested she wasn't part of their team.

Lamiya looked over her shoulder, her eyes directly meeting his. A shudder rippled through him as he again felt that she saw more than she should. He swallowed, and the last mouthful of bread caught in his throat. Gamely, he fought to repress the instinct to cough. Trying hard to maintain a neutral face, he poked the crust loose with his tongue. It slid further down his throat. After three or four coughs that brought tears to his eyes, the offending piece shot into his mouth. He slid his hand up to remove it and looked up. Lamiya was laughing at him.

He was saved from having to react when a man climbed up to stand on a table that had been placed at the front of the crowd. The murmuring and movement ceased as the man began to speak. This must be Atage. Was he the head of the town? Everand winced again at the mages' limited knowledge of their neighbouring provinces. He should see if he could somehow remedy this. Assuming he survived this mission. He listened carefully.

'Dear people, the Festival of the Full Harvest Moon is close now and we've much to do to prepare.' Atage considered his next words.

The man looked to be about fifty, by the grey tinges in his dark hair and the lines in his face. He was slimmer than the other men, and Everand concluded he was not part of the boat team. He looked to be an administrator. Could he be one of the contacts Beram had mentioned? Although it was difficult to get 'Brr' or 'Grr' from 'Atage'.

'First, Tengar will speak about the arrangements for the boats.'

Tengar vaulted up onto the table and waved his hand towards the team. 'Our training goes well. Melanite is sewing us new uniforms to make sure Mizuchi smiles upon us.'

A great cheer went up from the crowd and Melanite flushed with pride, while the nearby team members patted her on the shoulder.

Tengar held up a hand for quiet, and Everand noticed the inked dragon coiled around the man's biceps. 'The boat from Riverplain will arrive in two suns. The glide Lamiya is already here.' He paused while Lamiya inclined her head. 'Their boat Flight will be housed with our Mizuchi until the other boats arrive. The boat from Riversea will arrive in four suns.'

'What about Riverwood?' someone called. 'Is it true they are coming?'

A wave of unease passed through the crowd and Everand sharpened his focus.

Tengar spoke slowly. 'Riverwood intends to compete. They didn't say when the boat and team would arrive. We'll set a dome aside ready.'

In the periphery of his vision, Everand caught movement in Lamiya's face. She looked as if she was trying to decide whether to speak. Did she know something? She compressed her lips and remained silent. Everand watched her carefully; there was definitely more to her than met the eye. Perhaps he should befriend her and keep track of what she was doing. When her head started to turn towards him, he returned his attention to Atage.

'What about the moths?' called someone else. 'What if we're attacked again?' A murmuring rippled through those gathered.

Tengar glanced at Atage and then replied, 'We'll have people ready in case they come again.'

'Thank you, Tengar.' Atage took the lead again.

Everand's attention wandered while Atage discussed several logistical matters, until a cheer from the crowd drew his attention back.

'I missed that,' he said to Acim. 'What is happening?'

'We're going to hold extra races and a small feast to welcome the Riverplain team when they arrive. This'll be fun!' Acim's eyes sparkled.

Everand smiled at the man's enthusiasm, and then wondered whether a gathering like this might provide a target for another attack. How could he prepare? He could offer to help with the races so he'd know what was happening, when and where. 'I'd like to help,' he said.

'Wonderful!' responded Acim, grabbing his elbow. 'Let's tell Tengar.'

Tengar gave Everand three sharp nods and an almost-smile. 'It'll be useful to have an impartial judge of the winners — someone who isn't in any team. We had been worried about that.'

Everand had an uncomfortable feeling he'd just agreed to far more responsibility, and prominence, than he'd anticipated.

Tengar gave him a calculating look. 'Are you staying for the festival? We could use your skills then.'

Adopting a neutral expression, Everand replied, 'Can you tell me more?'

He was certain Tengar's eyes twinkled before the man responded. 'I can explain the festival to you. Why don't you observe the team training and afterwards I'll add the extra details you need to know?'

Feeling a presence, Everand glanced sideways. Lamiya stood there, listening. 'Sounds good,' he said crisply.

'Can I listen too?' asked Lamiya brightly.

Tengar shook his head. 'See the depths of the rivalry between our provinces? This is why an impartial judge is a blessing!' he said to Everand before turning to Lamiya. 'You are lucky I will share this new drill with you!'

'Ah, but that's only because you need my expert opinion on it. Riverplain has its own secret drills, you know.'

Intrigued, Everand watched Lamiya stretch taller and give Tengar a challenging look. These teams were so enthusiastic about their boats and training. The image of the warrior woman Elemar running wild loops across the lawns at the Mages' Guild sprang into his mind. At first, he'd thought she was running away, astonished when she hitched up her dress and sprinted across the grass. He had panicked and prepared to bring her down with a stun spell.

Then she looped back towards him and he'd realised she was running for the sheer joy of it. Elemar had returned to him sweating and flushed but with happiness dancing in her eyes. Did racing the boats and training give these people the same depth of joy? The boats seemed to be a symbol of pride and identity for the town. Maybe there was something important to learn from all this.

Tengar raised an arm. 'Come, Mizuchi waits eagerly to tell us whether my new drill will work.'

'Yosh!' the group replied as one, before turning to Ejad and each grabbing what Everand supposed was their own paddle.

Wishing he had time to get a drink of water or juice, Everand trailed after the group as they formed into pairs and marched out the southern gate with their paddles held high like a small, moving copse of trees. Lamiya and Tengar walked at the rear.

Everand stifled a yawn; it sounded as if they were comparing drills.

CHAPTER TEN

Lamiya tried to focus on Tengar's discussion about strength drills, resisting the urge to turn to look at the traveller who walked alone behind them. Did he know anything about boats and paddling? Why *was* he here? There must be a way she could insinuate herself into his discussion with Tengar to find out more.

'… don't you think?' asked Tengar.

'Most likely,' she answered vaguely, with a wave of her hands. Her footsteps faltered and, dismayed, she gaped at her empty hands. 'Oh. I forgot to collect my paddle. Shall I go and fetch it?'

Tengar's eyebrows quirked in surprise. 'No, never mind. Ejad can lend you his. He won't be in the boat this session.'

'Thank you,' said Lamiya meekly. What was wrong with her? How could she possibly forget her paddle?

The group turned along the path that ran along the top of the riverbank. Lamiya knew the Riverfall boats were kept in large domes to the south of Zuqart, at the end of the cluster of domes that stored crops, grain and cloth. The sun beat down on the back of her neck and the top of her head; a bead of sweat trickled irritatingly past her ear. Where was the so-needed rain for these people to grow their crops and for the grass to grow to feed the Riverplain herds? Her birds needed the blossom and nectar from the flowers.

She knew the banter disguised an undercurrent of worry about the unusual heat and dry. Among the neat rows of cotton bushes they passed, women, swathed in tunics and scarves to avoid sunburn, were emptying jars of water at the base of each bush.

She looked at Tengar. 'You're hand watering?'

Tengar grimaced. 'It could get hotter yet. We conserve water in case.'

A shadow loomed behind Lamiya and the traveller said, 'May I ask a question?'

She moved aside so he could join their conversation. He stepped between them and asked Tengar, 'What are the cloth strips tied to poles above these bushes for? Are these the bushes that make the cloth you wear?'

Lamiya couldn't resist. 'That's two questions.'

The traveller gave her a sharp glance.

'To answer the last first,' said Tengar, 'yes, these bushes grow the balls of cotton we harvest to make cloth. The sun is unusually fierce for the season and we're seeing whether we can help the bushes by providing shade.'

While the traveller was absorbing this, Lamiya asked him, 'Do you have cotton bushes in Axis? What do you wear there?'

To her surprise, he took several steps to answer. It was not a difficult question!

'The mages wear long robes made of silk,' the traveller said slowly. 'Those who work for them wear tunics similar to here, but of a coarser silk and with bark belts and sandals.'

'Silk,' she said the word carefully. 'I'm not familiar with this cloth. Is it much different to cotton?' And would his description match the azure material she had found?

'It's softer, more flexible,' the traveller said, still speaking slowly. 'It's made from slender fibres produced by silk worms.'

'How interesting!' exclaimed Lamiya. 'Do the worms make it in different colours, or do you have to dye it?'

Everd looked distinctly uncomfortable, avoiding eye contact with her. 'The silk strands are pale silver, and the material is dyed from plant juice.'

She could sense him adding '*I think*'. Time to push him a bit more. 'Does the silver kind of show through the overlaid colour so the cloth shines?'

Everd put his head on one side, considering. She'd swear the colour drained from his face and his eyes narrowed for an instant. 'I suppose you could say that.' He shrugged and straightened his shoulders. 'It's not of interest to us workers, but perhaps the mages value it.' He quickly turned to Tengar and waved a hand at the domes they were passing. 'So, people don't live here? These are different domes?'

Tengar launched into an inordinately detailed description of the layout of the town. Lamiya let his babble wash over her and pondered the material. So, it seemed that the blue cloth was this silk, spun by worms. Wait! Hadn't he said it was worn by the mages? Her breath caught and she stubbed her toe on a stone. When she stumbled, his strong hand grasped her elbow to steady her.

'Thanks,' she mumbled. Her elbow tingled as she resumed walking. Could the traveller be a mage? Was *this* why she detected such a strong aura? If so, she'd better be more careful. Could he read other people's thoughts? She'd heard vague and ancient rumours about the mages from Axis, but no-one had ever met one.

Tengar's words drifted over her. Something wasn't right here. The people of Riverfall were tense, although her paddling friends had all been delighted to see her. Was it just the hot and dry season, or something more? Then this stranger turned up, from Axis of all places. Well, she enjoyed intrigue. This would be a good test of her emerging skills to see if she could work out what was going on. As a bonus, he was handsome. Tall, deep-blue eyes, and his hair colour was fascinating. She should try to befriend him before her team arrived and she was fully absorbed in race preparation.

Distracted, she almost ran into Persaj and Acim, just managing to stop before she had to put a hand on their backs.

The team had reached the side path leading to the boat storage dome.

Tengar brushed past her. 'Acim and Ejad, take the paddles down to the ramp. Lamiya, go with them and test Ejad's paddle for length. Everyone else, follow me to bring the boat.'

The group peeled away. She took three paddles from Ejad to share the load, then tiptoed down the grassy bank to the edge of the wooden slatted ramp that sloped gently into the water. Now that she was paying attention to how dry it was, her eyebrows rose at how far down the ramp the water level was. The wood that was usually covered was darker, less sun-faded than the planks that were usually exposed. The river had dropped almost half a person's height. Had anyone been north to see what was happening at the source of the river, near Mizuchi Falls? Or was this simply due to less rain?

'You need to borrow my paddle?' Ejad handed her a paddle with a small blue dragon etched into the blade.

'Thank you,' she said with a deferential bow. Ejad gave her a tight smile, clearly disappointed that he'd be left sitting on the bank. If Luvu hadn't found a tenth paddler, she could ask Ejad if he'd join her team. He seemed dead keen.

'Slow the boat!' Tengar's voice came from the top of the bank.

Lamiya stepped aside as the team carried the boat down the bank. Admiring the sleek lines and the bold blue and gold scales painted along the sides, she fancied that the dragon rolled his fierce black eyes at her. Tempted to caress the proud gold mane, she gripped her borrowed paddle. She looked up at the sun; it would be hot. Glad she'd put on her simpler tunic underneath, she slipped off her over-tunic.

Tengar looked at her. 'You can take Beram's place in the back row so we can discuss the drills while on the water.'

Tengar turned to the traveller. 'Can you help Ejad hold the boat while we load?'

Lamiya suppressed a smile when Everd paused at the edge of the water, realising he'd have to follow Ejad in to about knee-deep. The team pushed the boat backwards onto the water. She ducked her head to hide her smile when Everd had to jump out of the way; Ejad was forgetting to explain things. He then waded to hold the front, copying Ejad's moves. Tengar stepped over the rows of seats to take up his position at the rear, and when he had the steering oar ready in its slot, she hopped into the boat. She paused where the traveller was holding onto the rim, his face pinched in concentration.

Smiling, she said, 'We load the boat from the back first so the glide can position the long oar in the deeper water. We'll paddle backwards to get it out to the channel.'

Understanding spread across his face, and she skipped to the back row and sat. The traveller didn't know anything about boats or paddling — which gave her a good excuse to talk to him. She could insist on being helpful.

The boat glided away from the ramp and Tengar turned to run with the current. Busy watching Everd as he sat down on the riverbank, Lamiya was behind in readying her paddle.

'Paddles down,' said Tengar sharply. 'Lamiya, are you with us? Paddles up!'

Cheeks hot, she swung her paddle up ready. This was not the time to make mistakes in front of the opposition! At Tengar's command, the team smoothly plunged their paddles into the water. Lamiya sighed; she loved the start of a session when the muscles came to life in her arms and legs and the boat surged forward.

Soon, water was rushing past the sides of the boat and Lamiya fancied that the dragon head took a breath of delight. The banks slipped by, the storage domes giving way to fields of cotton bushes growing in impeccably straight lines. On the far side, Riverwood territory, the tall wild grasses were a green-brown hue, suffering from the lack of rain. She felt her back and shoulders relaxing into the rhythm and her heart lifted. Keen to see the new drill, she felt privileged to train with Tengar. Rumours said he'd not once fallen off the back of a boat.

After a while, they turned back upriver, working harder against the current, with Tengar exhorting increasing speed. Large bubbles of white water ploughed alongside. How did the team manage such smooth transitions?

Tengar called for the boat to stop. 'We'll try this drill five times. I want you to take five powerful strokes backwards, and then reverse and paddle forward. I'll count it for you.'

'How many forward?' called Mookaite from the front.

Good question, thought Lamiya.

'Fifteen. See if you can get Mizuchi's nose back up in that time. Paddlers, sit ready!'

Lamiya gave her shoulders a quick roll. The resistance when they changed to paddle forward would be tremendous, loading shoulders, backs and arms. She held her paddle back ready.

'Attention ... go!'

Lamiya thrust her paddle deep into the water behind her, so the water came up right over her hand, then clenched her core muscles, leaned against the resistance and drove her paddle forward through the water. She frowned; they were fast and she had to concentrate to keep up.

'Four ... five ... forward!' yelled Tengar.

Lamiya leaned forward and plunged her paddle in the water in front of her, straining for power against the water rushing in the other direction. It felt awful! It took eight strokes before the team regained their rhythm.

The team sat, breathing hard. 'What do you think?' asked Tengar.

Lamiya twisted around to answer. 'A tough drill. I can see how it'd improve race starts. Something's not quite right when we change direction; we're losing too much power.'

'Agreed,' said Tengar. 'This time, when we change to forward try paddling a little shorter and deeper for five strokes, then stretch out. Paddles back!'

Lamiya took shorter strokes when they reversed direction. It worked; she had more purchase on the water and in only four strokes the boat was moving forward smoothly. By ten strokes she felt the prow of the boat lift. Tengar was most clever. She couldn't wait to try this drill with her own team.

The rest of the session passed in a blur, and when they paddled back to the ramp sweat was running down her neck and back. No wonder the team was good. After practising the new drill ten times, as well as other speed and strength drills, her shoulders and arms ached.

Ejad and Everd stood up and brushed grass from their tunics when the boat glided towards the ramp. What would the traveller make of their training? Perhaps she should simply follow him and Tengar back to the town.

They'd be too polite to tell her to go away.

CHAPTER ELEVEN

Everand found it pleasant sitting in the sun on the bank watching the boat. Ejad didn't say much, so he was able to watch the training closely. He quickly ascertained that when the ten paddlers worked smoothly as a team and their timing was in perfect unison, the boat flew through the water. He admired Tengar's balance; standing on the back of a boat with the choppy water and the changing momentum took considerable skill and balance. The man seemed to be a natural leader and the paddlers followed his instructions without question. After each drill, Tengar leaned over to speak with Lamiya and he concluded that she was respected in her own right.

Casting his glance sideways, he saw the rueful expression on Ejad's face. The only time Ejad explained anything was when the paddlers changed which side of the boat they sat on, apparently to reduce the risk of injury from paddling too much on one side. Everand's eyebrows rose as each pair of paddlers took it in turn, one half-standing up in the middle while the other paddler scooted behind them to take the seat on the other side of the boat — while everyone else continued paddling and the boat skimmed along the water.

'We don't swap seats in races,' offered Ejad. 'The boat loses momentum.' Not by much, as far as Everand could see.

Soon enough, the boat headed in a direct line towards the ramp. When the gilded head drew close and the dragon's beady eyes glinted at them, Ejad jumped up and waded in by the ramp.

With a sigh, Everand followed. At thigh depth the water wasn't cold, but the mud squelched unpleasantly between his toes. How many pairs of sandals did the paddlers need? He'd need at least one more set of clothes. He wrinkled his nose; his tunic already smelled of a mixture of hopeepa, hay and river water. Imagining presenting himself before Mantiss and Agamid in this condition, his smile faded when he considered how little he would have to report. Around him, the team carried the boat out of the water and paused on the ramp.

'Good work, everyone,' said Tengar. 'Paddlers one to six, wash Mizuchi and put her away. Paddlers seven to nine, sweep the boat dome free of dust.' He looked at Everand. 'Our traveller has volunteered to help with the races, so I'm going to explain how the competition works and sort out where his skills can best be used. Come,' Tengar's hand clapped his shoulder. 'Let's find a good place to sit and talk.'

Tengar set off at a brisk walk and Everand jogged a few steps to catch up.

'So,' Lamiya's voice came from right behind him. 'What did you think of our training?'

Reluctantly, Everand allowed her to draw alongside. She smiled, not even appearing to be out of breath. She carried her over-tunic across one arm, her bare arms glistening with sweat and river water. 'It looks like hard work,' he answered honestly. 'The paddlers must be very strong.'

'Yes,' Lamiya agreed. 'What about in Axis? Do you have boats?'

He shook his head, trying to think of a way to deflect further questions.

From a few paces ahead, Tengar looked over his shoulder and stopped to wait for them. 'Lamiya, where are you off to now?'

'I thought I'd walk back to the town with you.' She gave Tengar a confident smile.

A glimmer of a scowl crossed Tengar's forehead. 'Of course.'

With interest, Everand observed that all the way back, Tengar sought Lamiya's opinion on various drills. A couple of times she opened her mouth to ask him something, but each time Tengar posed a new drill-related question. The man was deflecting her on purpose! Sweat prickled under Everand's armpits by the time they neared the town outer wall. The archway loomed invitingly, for the sun was burning down upon his head and arms.

Abruptly, he realised that 'Tengar' could sound like 'Grrr'. Was the boat captain one of his trusted contacts? From what he'd gathered so far, Beram was usually paddler ten, yet no-one was commenting on the paddler's absence, which meant it had to have been explained. Tengar, as team captain, would have to be aware. His spirits lifted; this confident and strong man would be a good contact to have.

They entered the outer courtyard. Still talking training techniques — the range of topics seemed boundless — Tengar led them into the traders' area. Everand's stomach growled at the wafting smells of fruits and breads and another familiar smell that he couldn't quite place.

'It seems our traveller is hungry,' quipped Lamiya. 'Can I get the meal for you both?' Tengar hesitated and she added, 'Let me repay your kindness in sharing your new drill.' She spread her hands wide and beamed at them both. 'It's the least I can do.'

Everand admired her bold approach. How could Tengar possibly refuse?

'Very well.' Tengar gave Lamiya a nod and shot a glance at him. 'We can talk afterwards.'

'Excellent!' Lamiya clapped her hands. 'Let's find somewhere shaded.' Then she asked, 'Do you like fish?'

Fish! Everand's nose identified the additional smell. 'Very much.' His stomach rumbled again.

Lamiya laughed and led them to a table under the shade of a large bush. Waving a hand at the bench, she said, 'Sit, and I'll fetch us a meal.' She bounced away towards the trader domes on the other side of the grass and path.

Everand sat opposite Tengar. Should he say something, or wait to see what Tengar said? Waiting usually served him better, so he quashed the temptation to comment on the heat.

'It's good you are here,' said Tengar, and Everand's pulse quickened. 'There'll be so many extra people at this festival.'

Everand held eye contact, willing him to continue. When Tengar didn't, he asked, 'Are you surprised everyone is coming?'

Tengar looked tense. 'We knew Riverplain would come. Riversea jumped at the invitation. Riverwood usually keeps to itself. They are ... a hunting people, a proud and fierce people.'

Tengar fought to keep his hands still upon the table and Everand remembered that the tree-moths had come from this province. 'You worry about more than the prowess of their boat,' he said softly, resisting the urge to look over his shoulder to check whether Lamiya was coming back. Tengar looked though, and gave a tight nod.

Everand steepled his fingers. Tengar *was* his trusted source. How to use this short time wisely?

'Here we are!' Lamiya stepped to the table, her arms laden with a long platter of delicious-smelling food.

Everand leaped up. 'Let me help you with that.'

She gave him a broad smile as he took one end of the platter and helped her lower it onto the middle of the table. 'I hope you like sliver-fish. It's one of my favourites.'

Everand looked down at the platter, which was filled with loaves, a mixture of pink, yellow and green fruits, neatly sliced, and a mound of tiny fish covered in a sprinkling of spices.

Tengar shuffled sideways out of the bench. 'I'll find us a jug of water.'

Lamiya slid onto the bench. 'The sliver-fish are the smallest that we eat, but they're full of flavour. These,' she said, pointing to each fruit in turn, 'are star-fruit, round-fruit and feeja fruit. They taste good after the fish.'

His mouth watering, Everand wished Tengar would hurry back. 'How do you cook the fish?' he asked to distract his stomach from the promise of food.

'At home we make a small log and grass fire and roast the fish on a stick above the flame.'

'Where is your home?'

'Riverplain; the next province to the south.'

'What do you do there?' He found the questions flowing out of him.

'Do?' She cocked her head at him.

'When you're not paddling in a boat, what do you do?'

She laughed and her grey eyes sparkled. 'I breed and train birds.'

His eyebrows quirked upwards. 'Birds?' The mages' world was filled with massive insects and reptiles, and fish in the ponds in the Guild gardens, but he'd seen pictures of birds.

Lamiya gave him a curious look. 'We value their soft and colourful plumage. We use the feathers for many things, such as clothes, decorations, bedding and toys for the children.'

'Tell me more,' he said simply.

Tilting her head, she regarded him thoughtfully. He tried not to look at the way her eyes moved with intelligence, or admire the contours of her cheeks and jaw. 'I breed a number of birds, from the very small ones we use to help harvest the grass seeds and fruit, to the brightly coloured ones whose feathers we use.'

Everand had difficulty visualising this. 'Do you keep them in a dome or structure? How do you know which are your birds?'

The look she gave him was intense. 'They come to me.'

Her grey-blue eyes held his and a subtle sensation crept along his forearms. Compelled to lean towards her, he suppressed a shiver. His body started to tilt across the table, his hands creeping towards her. *Block her! Raise a shield.* A bead of sweat eked down his forehead as he resisted her pull. A spell would give him away completely.

'Here we go.' Tengar plopped a jug and three mugs on the table. 'You waited? That was kind.' He shuffled onto the bench beside Lamiya, who looked down and moved along.

The sensation passed and Everand was once more conscious of the sun on the back of his neck, the leaves of the bush rustling in the breeze, the sounds of people moving along the path behind them and the smell of food wafting beneath his nostrils. He shivered: this woman could call more than mere birds.

As Lamiya had suggested, the tiny fish were delicious. The soft white flesh melted in his mouth, and the spices added a wonderful bite. Everand popped a slice of the green fruit into his mouth and closed his eyes as the tart juices fizzled on his tongue. Opening his eyes, he found Tengar and Lamiya regarding him with expectant looks. He sat taller; he must have missed a question. An annoying air of amusement drifted from Lamiya.

'How keen are your eyes?' Tengar repeated his question.

His eyes? Why did they need to know this?

Lamiya said, with a smile curving the edges of her lips, 'If you are to judge the winners, you need to have very good eyes. The races can be closely fought.'

'We thought,' added Tengar, 'it would be best to have a judge who is not aligned with any province. You can practise when we have the competition with just Riverplain in a few suns.'

Heaviness crept down Everand's arms as the muscles released a tension he hadn't realised he was holding. 'My eyes are good, if you're confident enough to grant me this responsibility. Where is the judge positioned? Do you have more than one?' A potential downside of being a judge was that he'd be in a highly visible place and unable to leave his post if he detected any untoward activity. Should he point this out to Tengar? Or wait and see how events unfolded in this first competition? His instinct nudged him to the latter course.

'Everd should have some training in a boat,' said Lamiya.

Everand glanced at her sharply.

'The more he understands the dynamics of the boat and paddlers, the more he'll understand what he is seeing and judging in the races.'

Warm air rushed into Everand's open mouth, and no words came to counteract it. Go in a boat? What if he fell in? Or made a complete mess of the paddling? To his horror, Tengar nodded.

'Excellent!' Lamiya clapped her hands in delight. 'We're down a paddler so he can train with us when our boat arrives. Until we select a paddler ten.' Her eyes were full of light and mischief. 'It'll be fun.'

Everand gave her a thin smile. Being in the boat was unlikely to be fun.

CHAPTER TWELVE

'I thought she'd never go,' admitted Tengar after Lamiya had finally stood up and bade them farewell.

Everand refrained from comment, feeling Lamiya had gained enough concessions in the time she'd stayed. His hands felt clammy at the thought of having to go in the boat.

'Anyway,' continued Tengar, 'now we can get you properly organised. Let me show you the dome you can stay in. I hope last dark-fall wasn't too uncomfortable?'

'It was fine,' Everand assured him. 'Some more clothes would be helpful.' He paused, something that felt horribly like shame rising. 'I'm not sure how to compensate you, though.' His jaw clenched. Everything was so *difficult* on this mission.

Tengar gave him a serious look. 'Finding out who's behind this, and a festival without incident, will be compensation enough.' He pushed up from the table. 'Come.'

Everand stared in relief. By these words, Tengar had confirmed he was one of the trusted contacts. He quickly stepped alongside as Tengar set off purposefully across the square, heading towards the dwelling domes near the southern gate. Tengar stopped at a small dome that was second from the end, just before the southern gate. The curtain had a pattern of blue and gold scales, the boat's colours.

'This is Beram's dome. I expect he'll return after dark falls. He lives alone, so this should suit.' Tengar held the curtain aside and swept his other hand out, inviting Everand to enter.

Everand went into the dome, which was a single room, with wooden shelves along one curved side, a ceramic oven and grill on the other and a short wooden rack where some clothes hung. Rolled up in the far curve was a thick mattress that he guessed would be the bed. He hoped there were two of these.

Turning, he cleared his throat. 'How do you wash?' An image of the pristine marble bathroom of his rooms at the Guild sprang into his mind. Running water, light, people to do all the cooking and cleaning — so many things he'd taken for granted. Shame edged into him; the mages cared so little about the neighbouring peoples. Guilty too, he'd regarded Elemar's people on her world of Terralis to be little better than savages. Yet, in the mages' own land of Ossilis were nearby people living lives that, based on his observations so far, weren't much more advanced. How had such a gap developed? Was it simply because the mages applied their magic? He closed his eyes, not at all liking this line of thought.

'Are you tired?' asked Tengar.

He hastily opened his eyes. 'I'm fine. Let's go over what you'd like me to do as a judge.'

Tengar arched an eyebrow. 'Your earlier question first. Follow.' Tengar went back outside and followed the curve of the dome to the back of it, to the space between the dome and the town wall. There, he opened a small door made of the same pink mud bricks but completely aligned into the wall, and inclined his head towards the space.

Everand leaned in, understanding from the faint odour that this was a covered in-ground toilet. Following Tengar back into the dome, he asked, 'How do you bathe here?' As anticipated, the answer was either swim in the river or heat up tubs of water.

'I must go,' said Tengar, taking a step back. 'I'll return after dark. Beram will be here and we can talk about everything. Rest up, our discussion will be long.'

After Tengar left, Everand explored the dome. Beram kept his space tidy. The rack of clothes showed Beram's preference for olive and brown tones. There were also three sets of team outfits hung together at the front. Underneath, six sets of sandals were lined up in a straight row.

Propped against the wall was an object that came to his mid-chest. Presuming this to be Beram's paddle, he carefully unwound the soft layers of pale-blue cloth. The smooth wooden handle and elegant blade brought a smile to his lips. Etched lightly into the blade in ornate lines was an image of a dragon head rising from a sea of small waves. The dragon looked proud, its eyes alert and the open mouth revealing sharp teeth and the tip of a tongue. The nostrils were flared, the whiskers and mane stuck out as if bristling. The small image was full of life. Had Beram carved this himself? Everand hefted the paddle in his hands, feeling the balance and weight. It felt light and strong. He carefully wrapped it again and propped it back against the wall.

On the other side of the room were three curved wooden shelves, arrayed in perfect alignment above each other in the centre of the wall. He liked this man and his preference for order and balance. Was this why Tengar had chosen Beram for his role? The shelves held an assortment of tools, cloths, ceramic plates and a tidy nest of wooden bowls. The tall jars on each side of the plates proved to contain herbs, grains and fruits.

Below the shelves was a small table, pushed against the wall. On this sat a small, pink, clay dome. Unable to determine its purpose by looking at it, he carefully hooked a middle finger into the small hole in the lid and lifted the upper half away from the base. Underneath he found a smaller dome nestled on top of a grille. Beneath this was a white mixture, with wooden wicks poking up. Leaning forward, he sniffed: candle wax. The wick tips were blackened, suggesting recent use. He knew what candles were for, but the purpose of this complex arrangement eluded him.

Spying some large square cushions tucked underneath the small table, he tugged these out from between the table legs, sat on the moss-green one and rested his back against the olive one and the wall. Closing his eyes, he took deep breaths to clear his mind and rest his body.

Sensing movement, Everand hurriedly opened his eyes. Beyond the dome entrance the light was the deep purple-grey of dusk. As his eyes adjusted, the curtain dropped back into place and a shadow moved. Too late, he realised his legs were stretched out before him and the person stumbled over his feet.

'Dragon's blood!' swore the shadow, righting itself.

'Sorry,' said Everand, tucking his legs up and hoping this was Beram.

'Mage Everand?' said a sharp voice.

'Beram?'

The shadow brushed past him and fiddled with something on the table. A soft glow cast a circle of light, highlighting Beram's dusty features, and a pleasant scent wafted past his nose. Intrigued, he saw Beram had lit the wicks inside the clay dome. 'What is that?' He frowned; surely he had more important things to ask!

'Actually, we haven't a name for it yet.' Beram rubbed his hands together, warming them. 'Mookaite designed it, and this is the first one she made. It creates light, scent and soft warmth. She is most clever.'

Beram looked underneath his table and Everand realised he had all the cushions. He hastily offered the darker green one to Beram, who took it and all but collapsed onto it.

Scrubbing his face in his hands Beram said, 'I hope Tengar brings food. I'm famished.' He grimaced. 'Your beetles fly so high! The ride tested my courage.' Beram scrubbed at his face again and his look became more alert. 'Have you discovered anything?'

Ruefully, Everand shook his head. He quickly explained about the attack by the tree-moths and said he had been learning about the town and the boats.

Beram sat quietly for several breaths. 'I wonder ... now that I've seen the enormous beetles of Axis ... these tree-moths are similar ... could there be a connection?'

Everand took a sharp breath in. This had been bothering him too. 'I assume the other insects here are all tiny?'

Beram nodded.

'Ho!' Tengar's voice came from the now-dark entrance.

'Welcome,' said Beram. When Tengar stepped in, he added, 'Doubly welcome. You bring food.'

Everand pulled the small table away from the wall so Tengar could put down the platter and jug. His hands freed, Tengar reached to the bundle pinned under his armpit and passed the wad of material to Everand. 'Clothes.'

Beram fetched another cushion and they sat around the table, Everand copying the others' cross-legged posture. In the centre of the table the small dome that Mookaite had designed gave off gentle warmth, a yellow light and a pleasing hint of lavender. Tengar passed around loaves of crispy bread and small leaf-wrapped parcels of grilled fish. They ate in silence, then Beram fetched mugs and Tengar filled these from the jug. Beram took a sip and closed his eyes. 'This is good.'

Tengar inclined his head. 'My best. We've been saving it for several moon cycles.' He looked at Beram fondly. 'You earned it. Good to have you back safe.'

Everand took a cautious sip, deeming the drink to be a wine or spirit. A sharp taste fizzed on his tongue and his throat felt warm after he swallowed. *Strong. Better not have too much.* He had a number of logistical questions, and when he sat taller the others looked at him.

Clearing his throat, he asked, 'Given the distance between the provinces, how did you invite the others? Is there regular contact with the other provinces?'

Putting down his mug, Tengar wiped the back of a hand across his mouth. 'As you'll soon see, the provinces and their people are quite different. Lamiya's people are best known to us. They're the closest, and for a couple of harvests we've been exchanging goods.' Tengar looked at Beram, who nodded thoughtfully. 'We traded some of our finest cloth for four hopeepa and the two carts they pulled. This gave us the means to travel to Riverplain. After this festival, Atage hopes to trade goods for more animals, and to breed some of our own.'

Everand nodded; this made sense. 'You don't travel up and down the river by boat?'

'We do,' Tengar replied. 'However, the Riverplain dwellings are mainly inland closer to a large lake, so if we want to trade cloth, it's easier to take the road and the carts.'

Everand thought perhaps there was still an element of novelty in having the creatures, given how proud Persaj and Zeol were of their animals. 'You've raced against Riverplain before?'

Tengar and Beram nodded so enthusiastically he winced, determining to limit the discussion about the boats.

Rubbing his hands together, Tengar said, 'Riverplain has a large, oval lake and they already had similar boats and held their own swimming and paddling races. The Riverplain captain and glide, Latog, is a wise old fisherman and boatman. Between us we agreed to have ten-paddler boats of a similar size and form to make the contests truly about paddling skill.'

'They're our main rival,' interrupted Beram, his eyes dancing.

'Latog?' asked Everand. 'I thought Lamiya was their glide?'

Putting his head on one side, Tengar replied, 'Latog is the true captain. But he broke his leg so Lamiya, the glide in training, must take on the role. A big task for a large competition.'

Beram nodded, 'She is skilled though, so we're not relaxed!'

Everand didn't want to talk about Lamiya. They were getting side-tracked. 'How about the other provinces?'

Tengar sat back. 'Riversea was invited by messengers from Riverplain. They sent their pacers, Lazuli and Larimar, with an invitation on our behalf. Lazuli breeds hopeepa, and he rode one all the way back to tell us Riversea accepted the challenge. The Riversea captain, Cowrie, is also the chief of their town. Lazuli said their boats are a bit different, but similar enough to make it fair.'

So far, this seemed straightforward. This left Riverwood, home to the large moths. 'And Riverwood?' Unease rippled off Tengar and Beram and they shuffled on their cushions and looked at each other. Surprisingly, it was Beram who spoke.

'This was strange. I travelled by cart with Persaj towards Riverwood. We know nothing about them because they keep to themselves. Easy to do since the bridge, several thousand paces to our north, is the only access to Riverwood. Beyond the bridge, we believe there's a tributary that runs into Hanaki Forest, and there may be another bridge. But you can't see any sign of dwellings or people from the river and the land looks wild and untamed.' Beram stopped and took a breath. Tengar flapped a hand, compelling him to continue. 'So we went to the bridge, prepared to explore until we found people.'

Everand's interest sharpened. 'What happened?'

'Well, we got to the bridge and three men were waiting in the centre of it.'

Everand's eyebrows pinched together. 'Waiting?'

'They knew we were coming.' Beram swallowed. 'We have no idea how.'

A cold shiver eased down Everand's spine. How could this be possible? 'Did they know why you were there?'

Beram gave a tight nod. 'Before we even spoke, their leader said Riverwood would attend the festival and they'd bring a boat team.'

Silence ensued. Tengar and Beram watched his face, waiting for his reaction. Realising his left leg had gone numb,

Everand uncrossed his legs and straightened them while he thought. How could they have known? A deep ripple of unease travelled through him. Did they have magic? Riverwood was closest to Axis and the great granite wall that separated the mages. Could there have been a breach? His throat felt tight. Dismayed, he stopped drumming his fingers on Beram's table and put his hands in his lap. The others were still watching him. 'Then what happened?'

'The leader, never said his name, bowed and said they would arrive just before the festival.' Beram shrugged. 'We didn't know what to do, so we nodded and turned the cart around.'

The weight of their expectation sat heavily, but Everand couldn't say anything reassuring: he had no explanation. Was there a spy in Riverfall who was providing information to someone in Riverwood? Was this odd incident why only two people knew about the request for assistance? 'Who else knows about this?'

Tengar replied, 'Only Atage, our town leader and the festival master.'

'And maybe Lyber,' added Beram. 'He's second in charge to Atage.'

While silence stretched again, Everand sensed the stillness outside the dome. A beam of wan moonlight shone through the door, insects buzzed and chirped, but all else was quiet and calm. It must be late, and they hadn't even started to talk about the boat competition. 'Let me think on it,' he said finally. 'Perhaps we can talk about the boat races after we've slept?'

Tengar smiled and leaned forward. 'Actually, I think Lamiya is right. You need to go in a boat to understand properly.'

Everand swallowed hard.

Tengar stood up, brushed his hands down his tunic and said to Beram, 'Bring our traveller to training tomorrow. Can you lend him a team outfit?'

Both laughed, and he had the distinct impression this was due to the look on his face.

CHAPTER THIRTEEN

Mantiss kissed Elytra and bade her sleep well. Then he tiptoed back out to the dining area. It didn't seem fair that whatever this ailment was, it had touched Elytra as well. Did he look as pale and frail as she did? Perhaps not yet because, Agamid aside, others hadn't commented — although he had caught the assessing look Everand gave him right after he volunteered to go on the mission. Hopefully, his spy would be too absorbed in the mission and learning about the provinces to think on his condition further.

His mind replayed the sharp glance Tiliqua had given him when he told the Inner Council the meeting had been cancelled. When the meeting did reconvene, Everand would be absent. How could he explain that? A shiver travelled across his nape and he paused, resting his hands on the back of his desk chair. Could he confide in Tiliqua? He might have to. His daughter would notice something was amiss soon, if she hadn't already. Perhaps she was biding her time, choosing when she might confront him.

Pulling out his chair, Mantiss settled onto it, then murmured the code words at the tile in the wall. It dissolved and presented the notebook to him. He created an orb of soft reading light to hover above his shoulder. The words wavered and blurred on the open page, and he struggled to pull his mind onto the task. No use fretting about where Everand was now. The young mage was resourceful and clever. Mantiss blinked to make his eyes focus. Everand was also exceptionally good at what he did. But what information would he bring back, and what would it mean? With a feeling of foreboding, he turned to the next page in Lapemis' notebook.

From the scrawlings of Mage Lapemis

The lake

On the third sun, we came down grassy, rounded hills to a valley with trees and vibrant foliage. The crater was filled with a lake of turquoise water that lapped at the toes of the hills. A tranquil place, we washed and refreshed ourselves. Dusk fell and we made a fire on the pebbly shore and sat around it telling ourselves that fate was kind to us, for this island was plentiful and seemingly uninhabited. Every minute detail of what happened next is seared into my mind.

The water rippled and the head of a great serpent emerged to stare at us, moonlight glinting off an armour of green scales, golden horns and barbed spikes. The air around us throbbed with its roar. The humans shrieked and hid behind the mages while we scrambled to form a shield. Sound and fire bounced off our shield. Unexpectedly, the beast turned away and dived under the water. We traced the current of ripples as the serpent made for a darker-than-dark spot at the base of the tallest hill.

'In legend these creatures hoard treasure,' whispered Notechis in my ear. 'We should take it.'

'Fight a serpent?' said I. 'We barely fended off the other one.'

'Yes, but Lapemis,' said he, 'we know how to defeat them. Shards of death-power shot into the eyes.'

True, I thought. Finding the body scales impenetrable, we had in a last act of desperation blinded the sea serpent attacking *Wavestrider*. The great beast had retreated. All looked to me for a decision.

We left Dtella, Pogona and Aprasia on the shore to conserve our females, with Carlias, the youngest mage, to protect them. The other seven of us gathered what power had returned, warded our bodies and created bubbles of air around our faces. We dived into the cold but clear lake and swam to the yawning mouth of a deep, dark cave. Myriad colours of light glinted far inside the cave, and the water eddied with the presence of the serpent. My heart raced! We formed a curve across the entrance and I sent a bolt of energy into the darkness.

The massive green-and-gold serpent emerged, spurting scalding steam from its fanged jaws and raking the talons of powerful forearms at our faces. Aclys and Canthopis raised an outer shield while Hemiapsis, Notechis, Nactus and I hurled pointed shards at its face. Golden irises the size of our heads glared down, the textures dancing and shifting. I felt my mind becoming transfixed.

'Beware the eyes!' I yelled, averting my gaze and throwing more shards.

The creature roared and railed at us, its talons screeching against the shield while we threw a stream of death-shards at its face.

Finally, one of my missiles embedded in its right eye. The creature bellowed and clawed at it, driving the shard deeper. Inky blood seeped into the water. Hemiapsis shot three shards into its left eye. More ink spilled and the water became murky and dense. Turning around, the creature drove its massive, barbed tail down on top of us. Canthopis was crushed and the shield wavered.

Without thought, I ran onto the tail and up its back, dodging the spikes. Reaching the beast's neck, I created a massive spike of death and drove this into the flat top of the serpent's head. It thrashed and wavered. I jumped clear as it fell, the lake bed shuddering beneath its mass. Ignoring the awful groans as it writhed and died, I swam past and entered the cave, drawn by the glittering colours. The others followed me.

In the darkness, I perceived pulses of mighty but restrained pure magic.

The cave

The cave twisted around a bend, luminous lights refracting off the walls. I reinforced my ward and edged around the final curve, emerging into a smooth, rounded cavern with a kaleidoscope of light and energy dancing off the walls and roof. My eyes went straight to the enormous, pearly eggs collected against the back wall. In their midst sat a star-shaped stone with all the colours known shifting inside it. About the size of my head, the stone oozed magic. Entranced, I stared. If we could access the magic inside that stone then we could magnify our power a hundred-fold and reclaim much of what we'd lost.

The shadows by the wall shifted and my breath lodged in my throat when a red-and-gold serpent nudged into the light of the star. Behind it, more shadows shifted. A blue-and-gold creature lifted its head and a second set of golden irises fixed upon me. Frozen, I gulped air and made a rapid assessment. These serpents were lither in build, and seemed wary. Perhaps they were younger and were the females of the species. I deduced we had killed the male. Still, this made them no less dangerous, and we had them cornered.

The red creature stepped forward, placing herself in front of the eggs and the stone of magic.

I signalled with my hands and instructed the others to spread out, so we could attack from multiple sides. Creating an orb of incandescent silver light, I floated this above us so its beams bounced off the rocks, casting shadows behind us and making the air glittery and uncertain.

The blue creature lumbered to its feet and I noticed its extended belly, bulging with eggs. A pang of pity shot through me. Although deadly, these creatures were majestic. I considered. The green serpent had not fully attacked us, but had fled back to its cave. Although similar to the sea serpent, these beasts were not the same. These had four powerful legs, a clear neck, body and tail and a longer face, shaped like that of a horse. The one before me felt sentient, graced with power and elegance. Thoughts flashed through my mind while the red creature loomed above me, looking down its nose.

'Try to stun or bind it,' I croaked. The others regarded me with astonishment.

The creature's nostrils flared and its eyes flickered. Did it perceive my intent?

'We want the stone,' I said in a commanding voice. 'Give us the stone and we'll leave you be, with your eggs.'

The red creature tilted its head as if it understood. The textures in its eyes writhed and danced. It flicked a long, forked, purple tongue from its fangs, trying to get a better sense of us. But it remained on guard in front of the eggs and the alluring stone. Twisting its massive neck so that the burnished red scales gleamed in my light, it rumbled at the blue creature. The blue one edged sideways along the cavern wall, aiming to pass us.

'You want us to let the other one go?' I asked the red beast directly.

It arched its neck like a bridge and dipped its head. Steam swirled from its oval nostrils.

'Step to me,' I commanded the others. 'Let the blue one go.'

'But Lapemis,' hissed Hemiapsis, 'what if they come after us later? Isn't it better to kill them all?'

'I concur,' said Notechis. 'Take no risks.'

I hesitated, ranging my eyes over the mighty creature before me. The others were right, we should take no risks, but if we could take the stone while showing mercy ... that would be a far more auspicious beginning for our new Guild. And this red beast had enough intelligence and honour to try to save her fellow female. Emotion surged through me and my heart constricted.

'Let's try mercy,' I decreed. 'But we can't afford to lose more of us, so if we can't get the stone, we forsake mercy and attack. Let the blue one pass.'

I held my breath while the blue serpent waddled around us and disappeared down the tunnel, an eddy washing back from the movement of its tail.

Then I faced the red creature.

Heart racing, Mantiss leaned back in the chair. For over three hundred season-cycles there had been no word of such a creature, or anything similar. Surely, after all this time, it had died. Mantiss closed his eyes, his heart pounding disconcertingly.

When Mage Beetal's winged dragons had encroached on the Guild Hall seven seasons ago, he was convinced the fearsome beasts had come to claim the Staropal. But the creatures were under Beetal's command, and transpired to have been brought here from another world altogether — Terralis, Elemar's world. Mage Beetal had used the beasts' might to force him and the councils to raise the Staropal from its secret nesting place and yield it to him. However, there had been no hint of recognition in any of the dragons' faces, and they'd made no move towards it, simply responding to Beetal's commands.

Once Mage Beetal was dead, killed by one of the farseers from Chrysalis, the dragons had hovered around the Guild Hall, directionless. Until Everand somehow spoke with the scarred black beast that seemed to be the lead dragon and persuaded all the dragons to return to Terralis. Once the dragons had left, the Outer Council of Twenty combined had sealed the illicit rift and reinforced the wardspell tight. No more dragons. No more excursions, no more intruders. Mantiss ran his tongue over parched lips. May it stay that way.

Perhaps he should read the rest of the notebook when it was light; it would be difficult to find sleep now.

Chapter Fourteen

Far too soon, the first rays of light peeked below the curtain of the dome. Everand lay listening to Beram's steady breathing. He jumped at a sudden movement near his ear, but it was just Beram twitching a foot. With only one mattress they had slept head to toe, Beram bowing profusely and promising to borrow a second mattress.

Seizing the moment of quiet, Everand reviewed what had happened so far. He agreed there was a risk to holding the festival — from Riverwood, or was that too obvious? If Riverwood kept to themselves, why would they hold a grudge against Riverfall? Although the water supply didn't seem critical, was it to do with the river, given the unusually hot and dry conditions? The river was lower but was still deep enough for boat races and well managed irrigation.

Was it to do with the festival itself? The first festival where all four provinces were invited? Did somebody not want the provinces to mingle? Why not? He couldn't shake his discomfort that Riverwood was adjacent to Axis. Surely this had nothing to do with the Mages' Guild? Needing movement to dispel the notion, he slithered from underneath the blanket.

Beram stirred and rubbed his eyes. 'Is it light already?' He yawned and rolled his shoulders. 'I'm stiff and sore. A paddle to loosen up will be good.'

Everand tensed, then told himself the thought of paddling might be worse than the reality.

Going to the entrance, Beram peered out. 'Good, we have time for some food first.' Looking over his shoulder, he added, 'I'm afraid my supplies are low, so let's stop by Kunzite's dome.' When Everand opened his mouth, he added, 'Don't worry about the cost. Tengar has given me tokens from Atage to cover it.'

Humbled, Everand mumbled a thank you. Soon kitted out in one of Beram's team outfits, he followed his host, who marched ahead with his paddle resting over a shoulder. He wished he shared Beram's enthusiasm, and that the tunic had more space beneath his arms. He didn't relish the idea of chafed armpits. Beram stopped at the fifth trader dome where the woman with darker brown hair and matching dark-brown eyes appeared, also clad in team uniform.

'Beram!' she said with a broad smile. 'Are you feeling better? Tengar said you were sick?' She paused when she saw Everand. 'Oh. You've brought the traveller. You met him already?'

'I'm well now,' Beram replied, adjusting his paddle on his shoulder. 'Tengar dropped by and asked me to bring Ever– the traveller … to training.'

Everand admired Beram's quick thinking and kicked himself for not providing his disguised name. 'Everd,' he said distinctly to Kunzite. 'I think we have met?'

The woman nodded and looked straight back to Beram. 'What do you need? Bread?' She bustled back into her dome and returned with a cloth containing loaves of different shapes and colours, some whiter, some browner, and two round green fruits.

Beram handed her some tokens and took a step backwards. 'See you at training.' He set off towards the southern gate, saying, 'Let's eat by the river.'

Everand lengthened his stride to match Beram's eager steps and they soon reached where the ramp led down to the water.

Beram chose a flat grassy spot overlooking the boat ramp and sat cross-legged. He put his paddle down and placed the cloth of food between them, indicating Everand should choose a loaf. Everand gratefully bit into the brown loaf and savoured the taste of the grains. The food here was basic, but tasty and nutritious. And devoured all too soon. He was losing weight, his tall frame requiring more than these people seemed to eat. Becoming light-headed would not help his spying prowess. The mission was not going well as it was.

Brushing the crumbs from his hands, he said, 'You'd better tell me about the boat and how it works. I watched the last training session but Ejad didn't explain much.'

Beram laughed. 'Ejad is shy. The most important thing is for the ten paddlers to be in time. The tip of the blades ...' he picked up his paddle to demonstrate, '... must enter the water at the same time.' He swung the paddle into a forward position, holding it at an angle where Everand saw how the tip would spear into the water. Beram held the paddle on his right side, showed him the two-hand position and mimed the movements.

When Beram stood up, he hastily stood too. He *could* do this, although he'd prefer not to make a complete fool of himself. Beram thrust the paddle at him and he went through the motions.

'Not bad. Don't forget to breathe!' Beram smiled encouragingly.

Relaxing his shoulders, Everand felt his breathing deepen. The rhythm could become hypnotic.

'Nice,' said Beram. 'Now try the other side. It'll be easier when you can feel the motion of the boat and see the movements of the rest of the team.'

Everand swapped sides and his arms began to ache; no wonder these people were so well-muscled if they paddled for several thousand strokes each time. The back of his neck prickled when a shadow fell across his feet.

'You started already?'

'Lamiya!' exclaimed Beram. 'Are you training with us?'

'Better,' said Lamiya with a mischievous smile. 'You are all training with me!' She flung her arms wide for emphasis. 'Tengar has been called to a meeting with Atage and asked me to take the boat out.'

When she spun to observe him, Everand felt foolish standing there on solid ground with the paddle poised, so he handed it back to Beram.

'Does he have a paddle?'

Everand looked from one to the other while they discussed him. Uncomfortable, he thought this must be how Elemar had felt when she landed in Axis and the mages discussed her while she sat meekly present. How rude they must have appeared.

'No, but I imagine Ejad will lend his.' Beram's eyes narrowed. 'Have you found a tenth paddler?'

Lamiya shrugged. 'I won't know until our boat and team arrive.' She tilted her head to one side. 'If we don't have a tenth, I was going to ask Tengar if we could borrow Ejad.' She glanced at Everand and her lips twitched. 'Unless our traveller proves to be a brilliant paddler and then I'd steal him.'

Everand's mouth fell open while Beram and Lamiya laughed.

Beram regarded him with amusement. 'You can relax! Tengar already has a role for you.' He looked at Lamiya. 'Ejad would be thrilled. He's desperate to compete. And ready, I feel.'

'Fair enough,' said Lamiya. 'Well then, let's see what mettle our visitor has. He can sit next to you at the back, where I can see what he's doing.'

Everand stifled a groan. Movement caught his eye as the rest of the team arrived and headed to the boat dome.

Lamiya looked over her shoulder, and then back at him. 'Let me run through some of the glide commands while they get the boat.' She focused her remarkable grey-blue eyes on him. 'They'll be keen to train, so you need to learn quickly.'

He wondered whether there was a subtle spell he could use to help him remember the commands. But if Lamiya were so close, would she be able to detect it? It was tempting to find out. He tried to pay attention while she quickly ran through a dozen commands.

'The glide is the captain,' concluded Lamiya primly. 'I'm in charge, so *always* listen for my calls.'

Everand hurriedly stepped back out of the way when the team brought the boat down the ramp.

'Follow me,' said Lamiya. 'The back loads first.'

'Wait,' said Everand as Lamiya and Beram headed towards the boat.

'What, Traveller?' asked Lamiya with an eyebrow arched. 'Are you nervous?'

Everyone looked at him. He fought to contain a smile and said seriously, 'I know my hands are large, but don't I need a paddle?' It was harder to control his smile when the whole team burst out laughing.

'Ha! Got you there, Lamiya!' said Zink.

Lamiya flushed pink up her neck and cheeks and compressed her lips.

Ejad held his paddle out to Everand. 'Here.'

Everand accepted the paddle with a nod of thanks. Lamiya turned and danced her way across the seats to take up her position. Beram followed her and flapped a hand at him to board. He waded into the water and stepped into the boat. From inside, the boat felt horribly narrow and tipsy. Tightening his grip on Ejad's paddle, he stepped carefully over the seats until he reached the last bench and wedged in beside Beram.

The bench was snug; their hips nestled against each other. Copying Beram, Everand wriggled as far to his side as possible, placed his feet under the seat in front of him and held the paddle flat on the surface of the water, which Beram said helped to stabilise the boat. The rest of the team boarded and Ejad pushed the boat away from the ramp.

'Paddles back!' sang Lamiya. 'Go.'

The team paddled backwards slowly and Everand kept up. Something brushed the back of his neck and he flinched. On turning his head, he found Lamiya had leaned forward and a wisp of her hair was tickling him. She said softly, 'If the boat tips over, swim back to it. We must count and make sure we know where everybody is.'

If the boat tips … Everand licked his dry lips.

'Paddles up!'

No time to think further, he held his paddle in the position Beram had shown him.

'Go!'

The boat moved down the river and he realised his height was an advantage as he could easily see Melanite and Mookaite in the front row as the two pacers. He tried to mimic the rise and plunge of their inside arms.

'Not bad,' said Lamiya after fifty strokes or so. 'Try to push your blade deeper into the water, so that your outer hand gets wet.'

Everand tried this and immediately felt his blade had more power.

'That's it,' said Lamiya encouragingly.

'Don't be fooled,' murmured Beram. 'This will get harder very soon.'

He was still pondering what Beram meant when Lamiya called, 'Lift the rate!' Mookaite and Melanite began to paddle faster. Everand snatched a breath and frowned in concentration while he kept up. He'd just got the hang of it, when Lamiya called for another lift. He snatched a breath and paddled faster again. The sun felt warm on his back and arms.

'Good,' muttered Beram. 'Don't worry about your power too much, just keep in time.'

In the periphery of his vision, the riverbanks flowed by on either side. Wasn't it Riverwood land on the far side of the river?

'Timing!' snapped Lamiya, and Beram grunted at him. He began to appreciate that paddling was discipline for the mind as well as the body.

'Longer!' called Lamiya.

Glancing at Zink seated in front of him, he observed that the young man was leaning further forward as he plunged his paddle into the water. It took two strokes before Everand could match this stretch and his shoulders and back felt the extra pull along the water. He felt the boat nose lifting in the water, the prow skimming along and bubbles of white water rushing down the sides of the boat. Tiny waves slapped against the wood and the team paddled in harmony, muscles rippling. Time blurred with the rise and fall of his arms and he stretched, pulled and breathed.

'Let it run!' Lamiya called.

Everand almost bashed his nose when Zink stopped paddling and sat up, whereas he'd leaned forward to take a stroke.

'Traveller,' called Lamiya, 'you alright?'

Everand sat taller. 'Yes, fine.'

'Don't look too keen or she'll flog you on the way back,' muttered Beram. 'Roll your shoulders or something.'

Obligingly, he rolled his shoulders and tilted his head to stretch his neck muscles.

'Change sides,' called Lamiya.

Impressed with their deft actions, Everand watched the front paddlers who were already swapping from one side of their bench to the other. He was glad Lamiya had stopped the boat.

'What is that?' said Lamiya just as Zink and Acim started to swap seats. 'Sit!' she screeched. 'Paddles flat!'

Everand looked up to see a large bubble of water moving swiftly towards the boat. Before the team could react, the bubble hit the front of the boat hard, and it bucked in the water.

'What the!' said Beram.

'Look out!' yelled Lamiya.

This time the bubble rammed into the far side of the boat and it tipped precariously. Everand held his paddle flat with all his might, trying to push back. The boat continued to lift and, frantic, he sent a surge of magical energy down every paddle on the left side. The boat thumped back down level with a loud swish and a wash spread away on the far side.

There was a splash behind him. He looked over his shoulder — at the vacant back of the boat, the oar dangling in its socket. Lamiya!

'Hold this!' He thrust his paddle at Beram and leaned over the side to scan the water. Was that Lamiya's brown hair below the water behind the boat? Yes, it wasn't a clump of weed, he could just discern the caramel and blue threads in the strands. Why wasn't she surfacing? The other paddlers waited with their paddles flat, casting anxious glances around. They hadn't realised Lamiya had fallen in.

'Must get Lamiya,' he gasped at Beram.

Beram had barely managed a white-faced nod when Everand slid over the side of the boat, trying not to tip it. His teeth chattered when the water clutched at his chest, as unpleasant as his original arrival had been. He must find Lamiya. Taking a deep breath, he dived towards where he'd seen her hair. Above, the tail of the boat glimmered in the sunshine, in a world that seemed far away. Below, the water grew darker and murkier. He took powerful strokes to pull him through the water and resisted the urge to close his eyes.

There, brown wavy hair fanning out in the current. Lamiya was drifting downwards with her hair floating around her. Blood seeped from a gash on her forehead and her arms draped limply sideways. She was unconscious — which meant he could use his magic undetected. He drew her to him and placed his hands under her armpits. Her hair wafted over his face and tried to sneak up his nose. He squashed rising panic and turned her around so her back was to him and he could rest his chin on top of her head. *Better.* Gently exerting a lifting spell, he drew them upwards until they emerged beside the tail of the boat. Startled faces peered down as he floundered in the water, struggling to keep afloat with Lamiya's weight.

Beram leaned his arms over the side. 'Pass her to me!'

Everand edged closer and sent a pulse of energy and strength down his arms so he could lift Lamiya high enough for Beram to grab her.

'You push, and I'll pull,' instructed Beram.

Kicking his feet strongly for leverage, he nudged Lamiya upwards. Her legs and feet swung out, catching him under the chin. He gave another shove, and her limp form crumpled over the rim of the boat. Then he clung to the side, still kicking, and his teeth resumed their chattering.

'Hang on,' said Beram. 'I'll prop her in my seat and take the glide position so there's room for you.'

Everand gritted his teeth, sure he was turning blue. Beram stood up cautiously at the back of the boat and Acim reached a hand down to help him clamber in. He made his body weightless and pulled on the rim until he toppled face first towards the bench. *Most undignified.* It took a few breaths to disentangle his arms and legs, particularly with Lamiya slumped across half the bench. Eventually he managed to perch on the bench.

'Can you hold her against you and we'll paddle back?' asked Beram.

Body aching, Everand adjusted his weight and put an arm around Lamiya so she sat with her head resting on his shoulder and her body leaning against his. She felt cold, so he discreetly warmed himself and let it seep into her.

'Paddles up! Go!' called Beram and the boat moved forward. Beram steered a wide curve to head them back upriver and towards the ramp.

The paddle home was silent, the eight paddlers in front of Everand retaining their rhythm and form, but with a tense set to their shoulders and arms. He took a few calming breaths. Beside him, Lamiya snuggled more into his shoulder. *Nice. But what will she think when she finds out?* He itched to ask Beram what the bubble in the water was, but that felt like a question to be asked once they were safely back on dry land. For now, he observed the landscape, appreciated the sun on his face and arms and enjoyed holding Lamiya beside him, her hair tickling his jaw.

When the boat ramp came into view, disappointment rippled through him.

CHAPTER FIFTEEN

The lurching sent a wave of nausea through her. Why was it dark? Lamiya tried to open her eyes, but stabs of light and pain advised against it. She squeezed them closed and concentrated on what she could feel. She was moving, but her feet were not on the ground. Her head hurt and there were tight bands around her arms. Her heart raced as panic set in.

'Breathe slowly, I have you.' She followed the advice and the panic receded. The voice was familiar. The lurching movement felt like walking. Clouds and stars! Was she being *carried*? She reached out with her senses. Yes, the bands around her were someone's strong arms. Her face was pressed against a chest. She could feel the fabric of the tunic and, beneath that, the drum of a heartbeat. How embarrassing! Why was she so weak? She tried to wriggle, to say she could manage, but no part of her body responded.

'Nearly there,' soothed the voice. 'The healer lady will tend to you.'

Healer lady? Did the voice mean Mookaite? A cold flush washed through her. The traveller! She was being carried by the traveller, for everyone else would know Mookaite's name! How awful! Was she hurt? What had happened?

'You're making this harder,' said the traveller. 'Just relax. I won't drop you.'

A pulse of warmth crept through her, making her limbs and mind heavy. She released the tension in her neck, allowing her cheek to sag against his chest. 'Better,' he murmured so gently she relaxed further.

Freeing her mind from worrying about what had happened, she used the opportunity to sense him. She could feel his ribs, he was lean. His arms felt strong, his chest broad and warm. His heart beating against her ear sounded strong, capable and steady. She breathed in through her nostrils. He smelled like river water. *Odd.* She breathed deeper, trying to gauge his unique smell. Images of piney trees and enormously tall, bright yellow flowers with black faces flitted behind her eyelids. *Even odder.*

When he took an abrupt turn, the images were banished by a surge of nausea and she gagged.

'Sorry. We're here. I must bend to go through the curtain.' His face came closer and his breath flowed warm over her cheeks. Instinctively, she clenched her arms around his neck when he tilted forward. 'Let go, the bed is beneath you.' She released her arms and gave a sigh of relief as soft mattress greeted her back, buttocks and legs.

'Thank you, Traveller. Step aside now.' Mookaite's voice.

A knot of disappointment formed: he was leaving. She should say something. Why was her body refusing to obey her? A great weight seemed to be pressing her into the mattress, and her eyelids were glued closed. Would he come back?

'Lamiya, Lamiya,' tutted Mookaite. 'Hold still. I must bathe the gash on your head. You are lucky, you know. It's bad but it could've been worse.'

The scent of aloe vera, lavender and calendula reached her nose just before something cold landed on her forehead.

'Keep still. The salve will ease the pain and clean it, but you know this.'

Lamiya tried to relax, to let Mookaite's murmuring wash over her. Then a pungent drop of liquid plopped into her mouth.

'Sleep. You must rest.' Her arms and legs grew heavier, her jaw unclenched and she wriggled her toes. Vaguely, she felt a warm blanket being drawn over her, and allowed her mind to fade into welcome darkness.

☼

'Is she awake?' The words bounced around in her head. The wall of darkness became lighter at the edges.

'Not yet, Traveller.'

Traveller! Yes, yes, she must be awake! With effort, she pushed the darkness aside. Flashes of light appeared.

'Wait. Maybe. I saw her eyelashes move.' Mookaite's voice, then a warm hand on her shoulder. 'Lamiya? Are you with us?'

Finally, she pushed her eyelids up and saw Mookaite's face, brows raised in concern. 'No, don't sit up yet.' The pressure of the hand on her shoulder pinned her to the mattress.

But the traveller? She wanted to ask.

'You must be thirsty.' Mookaite's face disappeared and she heard rustling and clinking.

'Can I talk to her?'

At the traveller's voice, she tried to push herself up.

'Can it wait?' Mookaite sounded cross.

Lamiya managed to flap her hand and heard the traveller rumble a reply.

'Help me to prop her up so she can sip this, then.' Mookaite sounded resigned.

The faces of Mookaite and the traveller appeared, side by side. She wanted to giggle; they looked so worried. A light pressure under each armpit, and the dome tilted as she was brought to a half-sitting position and a cushion was edged behind her head and shoulders.

'Just a few sips,' said Mookaite, holding a small cup to her lips.

A trickle of water entered her mouth. She let it dribble over her tongue, which felt fuzzy, then slide slowly down her throat.

After five sips she felt a bit better, more with it. It was still light, judging by the sun streaming beneath the dome curtain.

The traveller fetched a cushion and lowered his long frame onto it, sitting cross-legged by her side but positioned so she could see him. She should thank him, but she wasn't sure what for. Last thing she recalled was being on the boat. Her forehead pinched and her eyebrows drew together. The traveller lifted a hand, as if he would soothe her face, but hurriedly put it back down. She swallowed her disappointment. What was wrong with her?

'You want to know what happened?' he asked. Behind him, Mookaite hovered and bustled, tidying jars and clunking things. His expression looked earnest.

She managed the smallest of nods.

'We were on the boat. You were the glide.'

She stared at him. *He* was on the boat?

'We stopped and were swapping seats.'

He must have been there, so much detail.

'A bubble of water attacked the boat and almost tipped it.'

She closed her eyes. This was starting to feel familiar. A dream, or had it happened? Strong, warm fingers encased her hand and the essence of him pervaded her. His voice sounded in her ears and in her mind.

'This is important. You fell off the boat and hit your head. But did you see the bubble? What was it?'

His fingers traced small circles on the back of her hand. *Nice. Calming.*

'No, don't go to sleep again. The bubble? Think, Lamiya.'

Why was he so insistent? A pulse of energy sank into her hand and travelled up her arm. A sense of alarm followed it. She snapped her eyes open, her mind replaying a vivid image of the mound of fast-moving bubble heading purposefully towards the front of the boat. Her standing there, powerless to stop it, powerless to protect the paddlers all mutely seated before her. Her chest grew tight. He held her hand with both of his, his face closer to hers. His eyes were such a hypnotic dark blue, willing her to remember. She could smell the river, feel the sun and sky. Saw the bubble reaching the front of the boat, a dark movement beneath the mound of water.

'I couldn't stop it.' Her words caught in her throat.

'No. But you warned us.' He squeezed her hand tightly. 'Did you see it?'

She frowned, ignoring the tug on her tight forehead. She had a brief sense of a dark shape below the bubble, a fin, a tail thrashing to propel itself at such speed. 'A jumping fish,' she said, surprised.

Mookaite appeared behind the traveller. 'A jumping fish? Are you sure?'

Lamiya nodded. 'Fin, tail, size, speed.'

'But they're harmless. They usually play with the boats!' exclaimed Mookaite. She looked at the traveller. 'They often leap from the water and frolic around the boat's prow, chattering to us.'

The traveller relaxed his grip on her hands, looking thoughtful. 'So, like the tree-moths,' he murmured, 'aggressive when not usually so.' A deep frown etched onto his face. She curled her fingers around his, not wanting him to withdraw. His gaze came back into focus and he looked into her eyes. 'Well done.' He paused. 'You are brave.'

'Oh,' said Mookaite. 'I need more aloe vera. Traveller, will you mind her while I fetch some?'

'Of course,' he inclined his head and Mookaite gathered up some jars and her basket and hurried out of the dome.

Discomfort and embarrassment washed through Lamiya. Mookaite had left on purpose! Now what? Realisation flooded into her: someone, probably the traveller, must have pulled her from the water. She now remembered drifting, unable to swim, the river encompassing her in a cold, clammy embrace. 'You saved me,' she whispered.

The skin on his neck turned red and he looked down.

She squeezed his fingers. 'Thank you.'

He gave her such a gentle smile that her spine tingled. 'Your team needs you.' His smile became lopsided. 'Although when you said, "if the boat tips" I wasn't expecting you to test me that thoroughly on the first outing.'

Despite everything, she laughed. 'Well, Traveller … I can't keep calling you Traveller. What is your name?' When he opened his mouth she added, 'And don't say "Everd" because I know it isn't that.'

He closed his mouth and she sensed him debating whether to ask why she thought that. After a few breaths, he said, 'Everand. But call me Traveller in front of others.'

'Why?' He was placing his trust in her!

'A long story,' he said, withdrawing his hands. 'Mookaite returns.'

Lamiya stared at the curtain hanging over the dome door. A few breaths later, Mookaite pulled it aside. How had he known that?

The traveller pushed to his feet. 'I should go.' He glanced down at her. 'Beram and Tengar still need to explain what I am to do during the races.'

She licked her lips, ignoring the open curiosity on Mookaite's face, although the healer was doing her best to look busy fiddling with jars and sprigs of herbs. Dare she ask if he would come back later? In the end she merely nodded. With a last small smile, he turned and left.

'Well!' exclaimed Mookaite, hurrying over to sit by her side with a wicked grin. 'Perhaps next time I'll throw myself in the river if it means being carried and tended to by a tall handsome stranger!'

Lamiya felt the heat rising up her neck and cheeks. She could not deny she found him handsome, intriguing and now kind.

With a twinkle in her eyes, Mookaite patted her hand. 'Oh my. This will prove interesting.'

Lamiya winced. Deciding not to say anything about the traveller, she touched the bandage on her forehead. 'How bad is it? Will I be able to glide?'

Mookaite's expression became serious. 'The gash is quite deep. I'll apply salve frequently to hasten it along. If you don't suffer from dizziness or nausea you might be back on a boat by the sun-up after next.'

Lamiya groaned. 'But my team will arrive soon. What about the races between Riverfall and Riverplain?'

Mookaite looked thoughtful. 'Maybe we can ask Tengar to wait an extra sun. We still have time before the other provinces arrive.'

'Would you ask?' Lamiya latched onto the idea. 'I can't let them down like this.' Her chest grew tight and tears burned the back of her eyes. The team had awarded her such honour to be the glide at this all-important festival. How could she possibly let them down? Latog would be eternally disappointed in her. Luvu, always critical, might insist she couldn't be the glide. She *must* recover, and fast.

'For you, dear friend, I will ask.' Mookaite's expression grew playful. 'I'm sure the traveller will appreciate the extra time too. I doubt he's in a hurry to get on a boat again!'

Lamiya winced. Hopefully he hadn't been put off boats entirely. While Mookaite prepared another batch of salve, she lay quietly, thinking. Her hands tingled with the memory of the traveller's hands upon them. Did he like her? Or was he only seeking information? He'd looked so serious when he realised the bubble was a jumping fish behaving out of character. What did it mean? Why *was* he here? Why was *he* asking the questions? And Beram, who'd been curiously absent since her arrival, seemed to know him. How could that be? First the tree-moths, then this. Something wasn't right.

The people of Riverfall were edgy, which she'd put down to the responsibility and excitement of the first all-provinces festival, but maybe there was more. An undercurrent of tension, and was ... *Everand* ... here to help them in some way? Her plan to stick close to him and observe seemed sounder than ever. Perhaps even bigger, more exciting things were happening.

A wave of fatigue tumbling over her, she lay back and closed her eyes. The sounds of Mookaite tinkering and humming nearby were soothing. Soon her team would be here. It would be so good to see them. Lazuli's face with his dark-grey eyes and smudgy-blond hair curling at his shoulders sprang into her mind. She swallowed. Lazuli would be concerned at her injury and was likely to be more attentive than ever.

This could get complicated.

CHAPTER SIXTEEN

Everand took a moment to get his bearings. Which way was Beram's dome? Should he try to find the man? His stomach rumbled; he was constantly hungry on this mission. And thirsty, his dry tongue suggested. He needed to do better than this lurching from mishap to mishap. An ache building in his forehead, he decided to find Beram and ask about more food.

He set off along the path and the image of Lamiya lying on the bed in Mookaite's dome filled his mind. A lump clogged his throat, she'd looked so weak and disoriented. The salve on her head, the warmth of her hand and the way she had squeezed his fingers … *stop it! Focus on your task*. She said the boat had been attacked by a normally playful jumping fish. The villagers said they'd been attacked twice by the large tree-moths, yet the large insects in Axis were all benign. Why were the tree-moths so large when the rest of the insects in the province were tiny? Given the proximity of Hanaki Forest to the granite wall, was it possible the moths had come from Axis?

His pace faltered. Even if the moths had originated in Axis, why were they aggressive? And could the moths, and now this jumping fish, have been *made* to attack a designated target, such as the town or the boat?

His breath quickened, his heart thumped against his ribs and his feet stopped moving as he remembered Elemar running around the staghorn beetle's stable fighting for her life. At that time, he was apprenticed to Mage Beetal and his mentor had said he wanted to show him something. The mage had insisted he bring Elemar, his charge from the other world. His stomach roiled at the recollection of how he'd been made to forcibly lift her onto the peaty floor in the staghorn's stable. His mentor had clucked to call the beetle, dripping a dark-red potion onto a leaf which he'd then fed to the insect.

Instantly, the beetle had gone into battle-stance, waving its long horns aggressively at Elemar. Powerless, he'd watched Elemar fight for her life, kicking off her shoes, lifting her silk dress and running around the stable. He'd so admired her courage as she ripped a stretch of cloth from her dress and tried to throw this over the staghorn's head as it repeatedly charged. His throat aching with tension, he thought of how he'd surreptitiously replicated a stable fork and positioned it in the peat so she'd step on it. Warrior that she was, she'd used it to kill the staghorn.

His mentor had been outraged, spluttering, his dark beard bristling. Before his mentor could strike Elemar down, he'd used a stun spell and she'd dropped like a stone into the oozy peat. Thwarted, Mage Beetal had let her live.

Everand scowled; his mentor had been triumphant that his 'personality adjuster compound' had worked. Swallowing hard, he fought to slow his heart rate. *Could* someone be using this same compound? What had happened to all the items in Mage Beetal's study once the mage had been killed? Mantiss and Agamid had removed key items and sealed the rooms. Could they have erred, not recognising the compound as something sinister?

He'd assumed this mission to Riverfall would be about disentangling squabbling ordinary people. What if they were wrong and magic was involved? Why had Mantiss and Agamid decided they needed to know more about the provinces? The curiously intent look in Mantiss' eyes at the end of the impromptu meeting came back to him. *'I need your eyes on this'*, his master had said. What did —

'Are you lost?'

He blinked rapidly, relieved to see it was Beram standing there peering at him.

'Are you alright? You look like you've seen a wandering spirit! Why are you standing here?'

Everand brought a smile to his lips, struggling to squash the unease rippling through him. He couldn't reveal his idea about the compound just yet: he needed more evidence. 'Actually, I was trying to work out where you might be.' He adopted a pained look. 'I feel faint. Is there any possibility we could get some more food?'

Beram laughed and touched his elbow. 'Let's do that, and we must speak. This way.' Beram headed towards the trader domes. 'How is Lamiya, by the way?'

After they were seated at a table in some scant shade, with an array of food before them, Everand told Beram about Lamiya saying she thought a jumping fish had tipped the boat. Beram stared at him, a crust of bread halfway to his open mouth.

'This becomes stranger and stranger.' Beram put the crust in his mouth and chewed. 'Atage apologises he hasn't spoken with you yet. He's waiting for more visitors to arrive so you blend in more and it won't draw attention if you two speak.'

Everand nodded. That made sense, and surely Beram and Tengar could pass on any messages. 'Is there anything you and Atage want me to do?'

'Atage thinks the plan we have so far is a good one. He's worried about the races against the team from Riverplain, but these will be a good test.' Beram paused to drink from his mug. 'Speaking of which, let me explain how the races are held.'

Everand ate as much as he could while he listened to Beram outline the rituals and ceremony accompanying the races. On one level, it sounded wonderful and exciting. On another level, his anxiety multiplied ten-fold at how difficult it would be to detect any threats and to protect everyone. Especially if magic was involved. What if the attacker arranged for a swarm of tree-moths and a shoal of aggressive jumping fish at the same time? There would need to be more than one of him to counteract threats both magical and physical, and it would become impossible for him to continue to conceal his powers and hence his true identity. Did these peaceful people have no weapons at all? Could he suggest they make some? But what kind?

A cheer went up from near the southern gate and he raised his eyebrows at Beram in query. In a swirl of dust, a cart came clattering up, with Persaj and Zeol waving excitedly. Persaj hauled on the reins and the two hopeepa slithered to a halt.

Beram stood up. 'Are they coming?'

'Yes!' shouted Persaj above the fidgeting hopeepa. 'The team from Riverplain has almost reached our boat dome.'

'Great,' said Beram. 'I must fetch Atage to welcome them.' He ran over to the cart and clambered on the back. 'Give me a lift.'

With another cheer, Persaj slapped the reins on the creatures' backs and they took off at a loping trot.

Everand watched them go, noting how the nearby people all cheered and small children ran behind the cart, shrieking and waving. He sat down again and eyed the last loaf and pieces of fruit. Who knew when food might next be available? He drank the remainder of the jug of juice as well.

The boat team jogged past, clad in their team outfit and carrying their paddles. Men and women walked towards the gate, many accompanied by children who held small sticks with strands of brightly coloured cloth. Everand brushed the crumbs from his tunic, grateful he was wearing one of the new ones, and made his way to the gate. On arriving, he nudged his way through the throng until he had a good vantage point, where he could see easily over the heads of those in front of him.

'Yosh!' called Tengar and the team lined up, half on each side of the gate, holding their paddles up in a salute. People moved away from the path, and Atage and Lyber hurried to take up position a short way inside the arched entry. Both men wore smart dark-blue tunics and brown trousers. Atage looked nervous, his fingers twitching as he stood with his hands by his side. Lyber, the offsider, kept his face neutral.

Where was Lamiya? Everand looked at the team line of honour and realised Mookaite wasn't there. Even as he made this observation, the people on the other side of the gate from him parted and Mookaite shouldered her way through with Lamiya hanging onto her elbow. He watched Mookaite murmur to Lamiya and then take up her position at the front of the honour guard, opposite Melanite, the other Riverfall pacer. Lamiya came to stand next to Beram at the end of the line, looking pale but determined.

'Yosh!' shouted Tengar and the team held their paddles higher as the heads and necks of the first team of hopeepa passed under the archway.

Everand's eyebrows lifted as the boat and team from Riverplain rumbled into Zuqart. The boat was placed on three broad wooden-wheeled trolleys, one under the front, one under the centre and one towards the rear. Each trolley was pulled by a matching pair of hopeepa — attached to the sides, rather than the front. The lead creatures had purple splotches, like the ones Riverfall owned. Even to his untrained eye, these creatures were magnificent: strong, broad-chested, the array of blotches pleasing to the eye.

The man leading them wore a proud expression. He was tall, also broad and muscled with a strong and capable-looking square face and jaw framed by smudgy-blond hair that curled at his shoulders. On the other side walked a wiry, also tall man, with dark hair. Were these the Riverplain pacers? The man with the smudgy-blond hair glanced over and did a double-take when he saw Lamiya with her bandage. A kind of static passed between them and she shook her head. The man fixed his eyes forward again, looking at Atage.

The middle trolley was pulled by a pair of hopeepa with blue-green blotches. Not quite as impressive as the lead pair, but they were still handsome creatures. Observing the array of colourful feathers woven into the creatures' manes, tails and harnesses, Everand remembered that the people of Riverplain valued colour and breeding. The rear pair had purple splotches, but looked smaller. Perhaps they were younger creatures because the handlers were keeping a tighter rein on them.

The team stopped ten paces away from Atage and Lyber. Lamiya walked out to stand next to the Riverplain pacers and together they bowed. Behind them, the rest of the Riverplain team bowed.

'Welcome to Riverfall!' exclaimed Atage. Whatever else he was saying was lost in the cheer that went up and the excited shrieking of the children who were madly waving their sticks and cloth streamers.

Buffeted by the cacophony, Everand felt a surge of warmth; these were such good-hearted people. He must not allow anything, or anyone, to harm them. Before his mind could follow that negative path, he cast his eyes over the boat. Even sat solidly on trolleys out of the water, it was impressive. The shape was similar to the Riverfall boat, but the decorations made it clearly from Riverplain. The base colour was yellow, with a pattern of green and orange leaves made to look like dragon scales. The mane was a vibrant red, as were the horns, and the body and tail spikes were a mix of fiery red and vivid orange. Long, exotic feathers were attached to the mane and tail and he wondered what sort of bird they came from.

The dragon face looked as proud and fierce as that of Mizuchi, but its horns were shorter, its yellow-gold eyes slanted and the tongue was crimson instead of purple. The arch of the neck was elegant, and Everand had an uncanny sense the dragon depicted was female. The array conjured the image of colourful foliage and birds, very different to the cool colours of the

Riverfall boat reminiscent of water. He started to have an inkling of how massive this festival would be, with boats from all four provinces. The children shrieked and he winced; the noise was likely to be deafening.

Quiet rippled through the crowd when Atage raised his arms to speak. All faces turned expectantly towards the town leader.

'Welcome,' Atage lowered his arms, 'welcome to our good friends from Riverplain.' People started to clap and he held up a hand. 'Hear me out. Lyber needs at least twenty more people to help set up domes for our visitors. More people will arrive from Riverplain.' He turned to look at Lamiya, still standing at the front of her boat. 'The team will take a rest sun, and on the sun after we'll hold races to celebrate their arrival and warm the teams up. After all,' he paused for effect, 'we want Riverfall's victories to be fairly won.'

The Riverfall team raised their paddles and called, 'Yosh!' In response, the Riverplain team raised their hands and yelled, 'Yo!' The crowd applauded.

When the noise subsided, Atage called, 'This dusk we will feast in honour of their arrival.' Atage and Lyber bowed; Lamiya and her pacers bowed back. Then Atage and Lyber began to walk away up the central path.

Everand watched as people started to drift back to their domes. Some of the children looked as if they wanted to touch the boat, but were daunted by the hopeepa swishing their tails and turning their heads towards anyone who approached. The children quickly retreated and held a parent's hand. Not surprisingly, the two teams crowded around each other, shaking hands and exchanging greetings.

Forgotten for the time being, he stood quietly. The Riverplain team had three women other than Lamiya, and the men looked to be a mixture in age from mid-twenties to forty-plus. Their hair was predominantly blond or mid-brown, and their skin fairer than that of the people from Riverfall. Naturally, they were all muscled and fit.

Each team member approached Lamiya and exclaimed over her injury, and he thought she looked embarrassed and uncomfortable. When the oldest of her team, a stocky man, stood before her she bowed a number of times and appeared to be trying to reassure him that she was fit. The man regarded her impassively, unimpressed. Everand stored that piece of information. So, Lamiya was being tested here. When the stocky man went to turn away, Lamiya grabbed his elbow and called out to Ejad. Hurrying over, Ejad bowed to the man, clutching his paddle tightly. Lamiya spoke rapidly, waving her hands around. By the grin on Ejad's face and the profuse bow he gave, Everand guessed the young man had been invited to paddle for Riverplain.

The tall, strong pacer with the square jaw stepped closer to Lamiya, put his paddle down and touched the bandage on her head. His lips moved as he spoke to her. Clenching his teeth, Everand resisted the temptation to use the enhanced hearing spell. Not appropriate: of course she would be close to people from her province. Was this tall, handsome pacer her partner? She hadn't mentioned him, but why would she? A pocket of disappointment formed in his stomach. *Never mind. You have enough else to worry about.* But his disappointment lingered.

Lamiya looked past the pacer, directly at him, and he felt like a fool, idly standing there. She smiled and beckoned and when he didn't move, his feet oddly reluctant, she beckoned harder.

'Traveller!' she called. 'Come and meet my team.'

Persuading his feet to lift from the ground, he walked over, schooling his face into a neutral expression.

'Gather around,' she said when he stopped three paces away. 'Everyone, I want you to meet this traveller. He'll be helping Riverfall to judge the races.'

'Ah, always good to be friends with the judges!' boomed a stocky man, who stepped over and bowed. 'Levog, paddler five.' He straightened up and stepped aside.

The tall pacer turned. The man's dark-grey eyes showed intelligence and he eyed Everand intently. 'Lazuli, pacer and breeder of hopeepa.'

'Everd, from Axis,' Everand responded, wondering whether Lamiya had forgotten his supposed name.

Lazuli looked as if he were about to ask a question when two women pushed him aside. 'Lopa, paddler four,' said one as the other said, 'Lulite, the drummer.'

Lamiya laughed and Everand was rapidly introduced to Larimar, Lattic, Lapsi, Lepid and the stern older man, Luvu. His mind struggled to disentangle so many names beginning with the same letter, but this meant it would be easy to recognise paddlers from Lamiya's team. The team was a mixture of breeders of hopeepa, breeders of birds like Lamiya, fishermen or builders.

'You'll want to remember Larimar,' said Lamiya. 'His fish recipes are divine.' The young man blushed modestly.

'The boat, Lamiya,' interrupted Luvu gruffly. 'Where are we supposed to house it?'

Everand caught the fleeting dismay on her face as she looked at Luvu. Had she forgotten to ask Tengar, as implausible as this seemed? Before she could reply, he said, 'The boat dome is back that way, you passed it.' Avoiding looking at Lamiya, he said, 'There's plenty of space in this courtyard if you'd prefer to leave it here this dark-fall. Some of the town people may appreciate the opportunity to admire it.'

A stunned silence followed and both teams turned to look at him. Lamiya's mouth was slightly open. He sought Tengar's eyes and willed the man to understand that the boat might be safer inside the town.

Tengar gave him a curious look before he stepped forward. 'Our traveller has a good point. Others may want to see the boat. We shut these gates at dark-fall so your boat will be quite secure.'

Persaj stepped up, hands clasped neatly, and addressed Lazuli. 'The hopeepa stables are near the northern gate. It'll be less distance to take your animals from here. Zeol and I will show you the way.'

Lazuli looked at Lamiya and arched an eyebrow. 'Glide?'

Lamiya smiled brightly. 'Excellent. Let's get the hopeepa housed and find somewhere to eat, drink and catch up.'

Mookaite touched Lamiya's elbow. 'Let me apply more salve and change the dressing before you get too busy.' She smiled at Tengar. 'I'm sure the men can secure the boat?'

Lamiya ducked her head and turned to go with Mookaite, but not before glancing at Everand from beneath her long, brown eyelashes. Perceiving a 'thank you' in her look, he became aware that Lazuli was watching him. 'Can I help with the hopeepa?' he asked the man.

Persaj said with a grin, 'He's good with them. Just don't let him pat them!'

Lazuli raised an eyebrow and, gesturing to the rear of the boat, said, 'You can help Lepid.'

Everand approached the rear of the boat and watched Lepid fiddling with the chest harness of the nearest hopeepa. The man's build and square jaw reminded him of Lazuli despite the difference in their hair colour. 'Did you breed these?' he asked.

'Yes.' Lepid passed him the lead rein to the nearer creature. 'Lazuli and I borrow each other's stags to progressively strengthen the line.'

'They're brothers,' explained Persaj.

Everand tried to store all this information. A tongue rasped over his forearm, and he found the young hopeepa fluttering its eyelashes and licking his arm. He gently rubbed its neck. When he looked up, Persaj rolled his eyes and shrugged, as if it were a mystery why he had this effect on the animals. A warm sensation seeped through him.

If only he could also have this effect on some people.

Chapter Seventeen

Grateful that Mookaite set a modest pace, Lamiya followed the healer back to her dome. A wave of fatigue and anxiety displaced her joy at seeing her team and boat. The noise had made her head pound, the sun seemed way too bright and the back of her neck felt clammy. How could she possibly recover fast enough?

Mookaite turned and touched her elbow. 'Another sun will make a big difference, but you need to take it easy.'

Lamiya forced a smile, welcoming the cool of Mookaite's dome and the aroma of herbs. She lay down and closed her eyes so Mookaite could change the salve and bandage.

'It looks good,' murmured Mookaite, her fingers gentle. 'There's no infection. It'll heal fast and you might not even have a scar.'

'A testament to your skill,' said Lamiya. 'When my head hurts less, will you teach me the salve recipe?'

'Of course,' Mookaite patted her arm. 'Perhaps we can trade recipes?' The healer sat back. 'I'll make some brew and you can tell me more about your birds and what you do.'

A shadow fell across the curtain to the dome and her mouth went dry. The traveller? Or, more likely, Lazuli?

'Permission to enter?' called a female voice. 'It's Lulite.'

Relief surged; her bird mentor and friend. Mookaite rose and held the curtain open for Lulite.

'Ooh, it smells nice in here,' said Lulite with a broad smile. 'How are you, Mookaite?' She rummaged in a pocket of her tunic. 'I brought you a small something.' She handed Mookaite a bracelet of finely woven plain-grass strands with small seeds and a tiny red feather embedded in it.

'Beautiful!' exclaimed Mookaite. 'You shouldn't have. Lamiya and I are talking about exchanging salve recipes. Chamomile brew? I'm just making some.'

'Please,' nodded Lulite. The drummer came to sit on the mattress and took Lamiya's nearest hand. 'Before you explain what happened, I have something for you.'

Lamiya noticed the front of Lulite's tunic was bulging and moving. Was that a small peep? Her heart quickened when a dark beak nudged aside the tunic collar and a small colourful head and beady eyes peeked out. 'Whirr?'

Lulite shrugged and the small bird climbed out and hopped onto the blanket. 'He followed us. We didn't realise until he came to sit on my shoulder after we stopped and made a fire for our sun-fade meal. Sorry, Lamiya.'

The bird ran up the blanket and snuggled under Lamiya's chin. Overwhelmed by his soft feathers and familiar scent, she blinked back tears. She missed her birds, and having Whirr here was beyond belief. *A good omen.* The bird fluttered his wings, pecked at her chin a few times and settled down to sleep on her chest.

'Well,' said Mookaite, holding two mugs of steaming brew, 'that will make it difficult for you to drink this.'

Lamiya nudged the bird down onto her lap and sat up to take her mug. She sipped thoughtfully while Lulite and Mookaite exchanged news and discussed the pending races. Energy crept into her. Had Mookaite added something to her chamomile? Or was she just happy to see her friend and much-loved bird? Her fingers stroked Whirr's downy back while he peeped happily.

125

'I'd best go and see what the team is doing and let you rest. Besides, I'm sure you'll have other visitors.' Lulite winked and stood up. 'Thanks for the brew,' she said to Mookaite. 'See you at the feast.'

'I'll be sure to wear this.' Mookaite smiled, twisting her arm to reveal the bracelet.

Once Lulite had left, Mookaite bustled over and tucked the blanket higher under her chin. 'Try to rest a while. It'll be busy enough later. I'll be back soon.' Mookaite gently touched her forehead. 'Sleep, if you can.'

Lamiya closed her eyes, feeling relaxation ebbing down her arms and legs. Whirr nestled under her chin, his feathers tickling. She allowed the darkness to wash over her.

Higher she flew, feeling the warm current underneath her wings, gently lifting, the sun beating on her back. Beneath her, the river sparkled myriad blues and greens, flanked by waving grasses. Along a pebbled path, people walked with a long boat pulled by three pairs of hopeepa. Swooping low in a graceful curve, she recognised her team bringing Flight to the festival. She swooped lower, almost clipping the ears of one of the front hopeepa then flitting upwards as it shook its head and tossed its horns. She felt her face crease in a smile. A fly buzzed by and she snapped it up. She dived again, clipping the ear of the other hopeepa, darting away as Lazuli shook his paddle. This was fun! The smile reached her ears.

A warmer eddy of air pushed her upwards and she rode it, ranging ahead of the people below. The ribbon of river wound ahead, the grasses wilder and longer on the far side before feeding into a line of hills. Behind the trees she could see a rising grey mass: the wall of granite? A peep escaped her. The trees were cast in shadow, defeating the light and sun. Despite the warm air current, a chill settled on the back of her wings. She looked the other way. Much better: the Riverfall crops grew away from the river in neat lines. Far, far ahead a cluster of pink buildings glinted.

A shadow fell on her back. A cloud? Looking up, she saw nothing but blue sky. Gamely, she flew on, the warm eddy encouraging further heights. The sense of shadow grew, and when the feathers along her back ruffled in warning she folded her wings and dived. A large beak snapped shut right above her. Enormous grey-black wings disturbed the air and a large beak snapped closed again. She dived harder and curved back under her path, speeding towards the people and boat far below. The air whistled past her face as she held her wings tight in the dive, flapping her tail feathers and fighting panic.

She shrilled a warning; saw Lazuli look up. A thumping reverberated through her: her heart beating, urging speed. The cruel black beak snapped at the back of her neck. She scrunched her head in and dived, dived, dived. Saw Lazuli raise his paddle and stand ready to swing it. Saw the hopeepa twitching its ears and shaking its head.

I see you, the voice boomed in her head, accompanied by the image of the face of a mountain eagle. Fierce yellow eyes glared at her from behind a cruel curved beak. The yellow eyes grew brighter, more piercing. Inexorably, she was being pulled into the gaze.

Something sharp stung her cheek and she cried out and bolted upright, chest heaving. She blinked furiously and the inside of Mookaite's dome came back into focus. Whirr pecked her cheek, peeping wildly, his feathers ruffled. Her heartbeat resounded through her entire body. *What was that? Another vision?* Or was she seeing something that had happened to Whirr and he was telling her? Blinking more, she focused on the small bird. Gently grasping him in her cupped hands, she faced the bird towards her.

'Is this you? Did this happen?' She probed his back and neck, seeking any damage from raking talons. Although Whirr seemed fine and chattered excitedly, the sense of dread would not leave her. *I see you.* That felt aimed at her, not her bird.

Drained, she lay down, but her heart pounded so hard she sat back up. She needed a distraction. Perhaps she could make more salve for Mookaite. A much gentler activity than she'd prefer, but it would pass some time.

She pushed off the mattress, chose several sprigs of fresh chamomile and sat at Mookaite's small table. Concentrating, she separated the flowers, leaves and stems, and started to gently crush the flowers and leaves in a small bowl. Whirr flew over to perch on her left shoulder.

'So,' she addressed the bird. 'You decided not to be left behind? Who is looking after your hens for you?'

Whirr peeped. Allowing her gaze to soften, her eyes to see-but-not-see, Lamiya focused on Whirr. Her connection with this bird surpassed anything she'd tried before. This was a perfect moment to try to extend her ability. Images and words flitted into her mind. She frowned. 'Slow down, my excitable friend.'

The images became clearer, more ordered: Whirr tucked inside her tunic, peeking out while she stood as the glide, the backs of the paddlers stretching away from her, their arms rising and falling in perfect harmony. She felt her eyebrows rise. 'Oh, so you decided to be the boat mascot?'

The bird chattered and flapped his wings, and she laughed in delight. 'And so modest, too!' A thrill shot through her: this level of clarity was astounding. How far could she take her ability?

Whirr gave a loud chirrup and she heard footsteps approaching the dome. Mookaite? No, whoever it was had stopped outside the curtain.

'Lamiya?' Lazuli's soft query made her heart skip a few beats. 'May I enter?'

'Yes, I'm awake,' she replied.

Her heart skipped more beats when Lazuli nudged the curtain aside, his grey eyes fixing on her, his face creased with concern.

'How are you feeling?' Lazuli sat on the other side of the table and looked at Whirr on her shoulder. 'I see you are reunited with your trainer, you cheeky bird.'

Lamiya couldn't help but smile at the way Whirr fluffed his feathers indignantly. 'Was he trouble on the journey?' she asked. Lazuli's answer might reveal whether the incident with the eagle had happened in reality.

Lazuli pulled a mock stern face as he counted off on his fingers. 'Let me see, diving at the hopeepa's ears repeatedly, vanishing without telling us, pecking a hole in the sack of seeds and helping himself ...' Lazuli threw up his hands. 'Need I say more?' His eyes narrowed. 'I put it down to poor training.'

She laughed and Whirr hopped up and down on her shoulder with a high-pitched squawk. When she put the bowl down, Lazuli grasped her hands, his grey eyes serious.

'Tell me *properly* what happened. I don't believe you fell off the boat!'

She flushed at the compliment and his confidence in her ability.

'Zink said something about a bubble of water?' Lazuli said, prompting her. 'Tipping the boat?'

She swallowed. He deserved a proper explanation, but the traveller and the Riverfall team, Tengar and Beram in particular, weren't saying much. When his grip tightened on her fingers, she reluctantly met his eyes. Briefly, she described the sudden appearance of the bubble and how it had rammed the boat.

'It tipped us almost completely over.' Her fingers twitched; she would have spread her arms for emphasis but he was still clutching her hands. 'I remember losing my balance and falling towards the water.' She stopped. The next thing she remembered was being carried. By the traveller.

Lazuli looked astonished. 'A good thing you could get back on board.'

So, they hadn't told him that part. Taking a deep breath, she met his look. 'I didn't. The traveller pulled me from the water.' Panic surged through her as she bit back: *or I may have drowned.*

'What?' gasped Lazuli. 'Lamiya!' His eyes went to the bandage on her forehead. 'How bad is it?' He tipped forward, clearly wanting to snatch her up into an embrace. Lucky the table was in the way.

'I'll be fine. I just need a bit more time,' she murmured. Did she want him to hold her? Lazuli was clearly considering his next move. She peered at him from underneath her eyelashes, admiring the way his hair curled around his nape, the intensity in his deep grey eyes. The traveller's lean face, hair the colour of spun starlight and deep, deep blue eyes appeared. Confused, she shook her head. Perhaps she'd hit her head harder than she acknowledged.

'You look sad,' said Lazuli wistfully. He brought her hands to his mouth and brushed the back of them lightly with his lips. 'I know this is a setback on your first festival, and such an important one.' He placed her hands back on the table. 'You are our glide. We are confident.' He sat back, readying to leave.

She swallowed at his kindness. On her shoulder, Whirr gave a soft peep. When Lazuli stood up, she wished her feelings were clearer. Why was she so muddled? She stood too.

'Sorry, I am a bit tired.' She managed a smile. 'Thanks for coming to see me.'

Lazuli gave her an odd look. 'Let me know if I can help.' He paused. 'You know I would do anything for you.' He gave her a brusque, short bow, as if alarmed by such an open declaration. Then he backed out of the dome and the curtain swung gently into place.

Still standing, she clenched her hands. Curses! She'd forgotten to ask Lazuli if there had been an eagle. Perhaps she could ask him at the feast. She could wear the new tunic and skirt she'd bought from Melanite … her lips twitched. Then she remembered the faint sense of the traveller when she was trying on the outfit. The large blue robe! Hidden safely under her head-cushion in the team dome, it was possibly made from the material that might be the silk only worn by the mages of Axis ... How could she conjure an opportunity to give it to Everand? Yes, Everand felt like his true name. She'd better keep calling him Traveller, otherwise she might let slip his name. A long sigh escaped.

She had known the festival would be a challenge: but not on so many levels.

Chapter Eighteen

Everand followed the others, listening to the conversations. Each time the young hopeepa that he led stepped on his feet, he elbowed its shoulder to nudge it away from him. A distant ache set up in his chest at the lively exchanges and evident bond between the paddlers, the camaraderie and sense of belonging. The mages were a community, he reflected, but they were bound by tradition and hierarchy — an aloof and self-contained collection of people with power.

The young hopeepa bellowed and barged into him. Two running children skidded to a stop nearby. The rope he was holding yanked at his arm as the animal stood on its hind legs, waving its forelegs ready to strike out. He tugged sharply on the rope, but the hopeepa bellowed and shook its head, loosening his grip.

Quickly, he stepped in closer, put his other hand on the long, flat shoulder blade and sent a calming spell coursing down his arm and into the creature's fur. The hopeepa blinked, gave a bleat and came back to all fours. Then it put its forehead against his chest. Relieved, he scratched at the wiry mane nestled between its stubby horns. A ripple passed through the animal and he felt its muscles relax.

'You alright?' Lepid gasped, taking the rope from his hand.

Everand nodded. 'The children startled it.'

'He's young,' said Lepid. 'You did well. They can be skittish in strange surroundings.'

By the look on Lepid's face, he guessed the man was wondering how he'd calmed it so quickly. To deflect any questions, he said, 'You must train them well. How old is this one?'

The group moved forward again, and Lepid retained his hold on the rope to walk beside him. 'This one is only two full season-turnings. After the harvest I'll give him a couple of does to breed with.'

Everand let out a breath. 'How many animals do you have?'

Lepid talked easily now, relaxing into his topic. 'My herd has a hundred animals, with another twenty expected this growing season. I have two stags. One is getting old, so I hope this young one will prove his worth.'

'Does he have a name?' asked Everand, wanting to keep the conversation going until they reached the stables.

'Bounder, for his long stride.' Lepid sounded proud. 'My other one is Skimmer.'

'Good names.' After a pause, Everand asked, 'What about Lazuli's herd? Are his animals related to yours?'

Lepid glanced at him. 'Lazuli began his herd with an unrelated stag and doe from my herd. We don't breed animals closely related because it produces weakness. He also bought some does from Levog.'

'I see,' said Everand, unsure whether he did.

'I'll keep hold of Bounder while we settle them in,' said Lepid. 'The presence of unfamiliar hopeepa will set them all off.'

Sure enough, when the group paused at the entrance to the stable, the creatures inside called out and Everand heard stamping hooves.

'Come,' Persaj tapped his elbow before hurrying into the dome.

Everand strode after him. Inside, the hopeepa were loping around their stalls, necks swaying and long legs sending up stalks of hay and dust.

133

Persaj thrust a head harness at him. 'Crystal and Topaz need to be moved into the far stall together.' He jerked his head at Crystal. 'You move Crystal and I'll get Topaz.'

Everand opened the gate to Crystal's stall carefully. She loped up to him and licked his hands. He fumbled with the harness, surprised that she kept her head lowered until he got it on. He opened the gate and led her out, turning towards the far stall. The rope snapped taut as Crystal made a break the other way. He groaned. Of course, she wanted to go to the stags! He tugged harder. She planted all four hooves and he found himself rebounding to slam into her chest, whereupon she licked his face. Swallowing a curse, he saw Persaj struggling with Topaz. Placing a hand on Crystal's chest, he sent the calming spell until she lowered her head and meekly followed him into the stall.

Then he went to help Persaj. Discreetly putting his hand on Topaz's far shoulder, he calmed her also and soon the two does were licking at each other, secure in the end stall.

Persaj used a sleeve to wipe the sweat from his face. 'You really do have a way with them.'

Everand shrugged modestly. 'Maybe being tall helps.' Persaj gave him an odd look and opened his mouth but then the Riverplain paddlers and the stags clattered into the dome.

Once the six stags from Riverplain were secured, three to a stall, in the two stalls furthest from the does, Persaj tapped his elbow and headed towards the sacks of grain and the hay. Before he went to help, Everand glanced at the others. Lepid, Levog and Lazuli stood in a tight bunch near the entrance, talking. Lazuli took a slow step backwards, Lepid speaking to him urgently. Levog just shrugged.

Lazuli waved his hands as if to make a point, said, 'Lamiya,' then took long strides out of the dome.

Everand deduced the man was going to see Lamiya. The pocket of disappointment reappeared in his stomach. *Not your business*, he chided. *You'll see her at the feast.* He turned to help Persaj mix tubs of grain.

☼

Dusk turned the sky into a layered blanket of pale to dark mauves as the sun slowly dropped behind the distant hills to the west. Everand paused just outside the northern gate to watch for a while. West: where Axis lay. Were Mantiss and Agamid thinking of him and his mission? How was he supposed to tell them when he needed the wardspell parted so he could be brought home? He imagined himself standing forlornly at the base of the wall, throwing rocks like Beram had to attract attention. He sighed. *No use dwelling on that now.*

He needed to complete a circuit of the town before people started to gather. Would there be an incident at the feast? He walked towards the river, considering. On balance, probably not, due to the risk of discovery. The enemy seemed determined to remain undetected. The boat races were a more likely target — the races were the highlight and disrupting these would wreak the most havoc. He glanced both ways up and down the riverbank and, seeing nothing untoward, turned to head back. It was getting too dark to see much anyway.

Taking several long paces to the other side of the town entry, he paused again, listening and watching. The grasses rustled sibilantly in the breeze and insects chirped. The flat terrain stretched away from him, melding into darker shadows where it reached the hills. He mouthed the enhanced hearing spell and the insect chirps and buzzes became a chaotic chorus rising from the grass. The grass heads scratched together. *There.* Another sound. Above. Peering skyward, he perceived a shadow pass high above him. *Ker-chuck, ker-chuck, ker-chuck.*

Probing, he reached out: a large, dark-feathered bird was circling above the town. His forehead pinched in a frown. So far, Riverfall hadn't mentioned large birds. The wing beats faltered and a tingle coursed down his spine. The bird was turning and would pass above him. Hurriedly, he dampened his reaching spell. *Coincidence?* Throwing a cloaking spell over where he stood, he listened while the flapping travelled slowly past, and the bird swung away and flew towards the river. Slowly, he exhaled. Given that the other incidents had involved creatures, this was not a coincidence. The town was being watched.

He heard the voices of men approaching to close the gates. Good, Beram had heeded his advice about securing the town gates at dusk. Leaving the cloaking spell in place, he slipped through the gate and crept along the wall until he'd passed the men. Ahead, yellow and orange light flared up. The large bonfire in the centre of the market courtyard had been lit and the feast had begun. He dissipated the cloaking spell, tugged his tunic straighter and secured the thong that bound his hair back. At least he was clean. Beram had brought pitchers of water to their dome so they could wash. The water from the well was fresh and clear, but he'd not liked the temperature when he stuck a hand in. Beram was delighted when he used the warming spell so they could have a hot wash.

Mingling with the townsfolk, he headed towards the market courtyard, his mouth watering at the aromas. He vowed to relax for a while before he told Beram and Tengar the town was being watched. Everyone deserved to enjoy this feast.

The archway flitted above him and he stopped to take in the scene. The pile of wood was an impressive yellow-orange mound, so high that it would burn until the moon waned. Even from where he stood, warmth caressed his arms and cheeks. Small wonder people left a decent gap around the fire. Numerous tables of food and jugs of drinks were set closer to the walls. The celebration was skewed to the left side, given the boat from Riverplain was nestled on the right. He smiled to see numerous people and children crowding around the boat, Lepid and the stocky man, Luvu, showing them the boat's features.

He should eat and drink first so he could then mingle and listen unfettered. Approaching the tables, he recognised the paddler with dark-brown hair and brown eyes. He waited while she piled up plates of breads for a family and then stepped to the table.

'Traveller!' Firelight danced over Kunzite's happy face. 'What would you like?'

He opened empty hands and looked at Kunzite. He didn't have any tokens!

'Don't be shy. Atage is hosting the feast, so take as much as you can eat.'

Relieved, he said, 'Thank you. What do you recommend?'

Delighted, Kunzite chose a small, dark-brown loaf sprinkled with black seeds, a white one with brown chunks in it, and a flat brown loaf that had slices of a green vegetable over the top of it. She handed him the plate and pointed to each in turn. 'This one is sour and the cottonseeds are crunchy. This is sweeter, with dried fruits, and this one is my favourite. It's heavier bread with grilled olive.' She smiled. 'Let me know which you like best.'

Unsure what he should say, he settled for, 'Paddle well in the races.'

Still smiling, Kunzite waved a hand towards a table two along. 'Make sure you try some fish from Zink and Acim.'

He stepped aside to let the next person approach and followed her advice.

'Hey, Traveller!' called Acim as soon as he saw him. 'Try my fish!'

From behind the next table, Zink took a sideways step and elbowed Acim. 'His are bony and flavourless. Try *my* fish!'

'I clearly need to try both so I can compare.' He laughed as they both rushed to select fillets of steaming fish and elbowed each other to pile up his plate. Clutching his plate tightly, he bowed. 'Paddle well.'

'Yosh!' they responded, clapping their right hands together.

He laughed again, marvelling at their good humour. Extricating himself from the queue, he carried his plate towards the cluster of tables, many bulging with bodies packed in tightly along the benches. He saw the Riverplain team seated together at a table near the fire. Tengar was with them, deep in discussion with Lazuli. Selecting a vacant table in shadow at the edge, he sat down and eyed the haphazard pile of fillets: so much for comparing the fish! Every fillet tasted wonderful and he didn't find a single bone. Finishing his last mouthful of bread, he agreed with Kunzite's choice: the square bread with the vegetable was very pleasing to the tongue, and the salty taste lingered.

He roamed his gaze over the groups of people. Where were Beram and Lamiya? The older townspeople were gathered closest to the fire and he observed the cheer in the men as they quaffed from their mugs, and the happy faces of the women. Many had weathered faces and grey sprinkled through their hair. Atage, Beram and Lyber sat with a group of older men at a table not far from the Riverplain team. Mookaite appeared, juggling a plate, and made her way to the Riverplain table where she squeezed between two women paddlers. Perhaps now was a good time to become invisible and listen to some discussions.

'Why do you sit in the shadows?' Lamiya's question came out of the air behind him. Her clothes swishing, she came around and edged onto the bench on the other side of the table.

Staring, he took in the way she had braided the front part of her long hair into a crest over the top of her head. The remainder cascaded in luxurious mahogany waves over her shoulders and down her back. She wore the clothes she'd tried on in Melanite's dome when he was hiding there. The turquoise tunic did indeed accentuate the blue flecks in her grey eyes and bring out the blue strands in her hair. The caramel threads glinted in the firelight. The skirt the colour of a pale moon clung to the curves of her hips and folded elegantly about her legs. A flowery scent wafted across the table.

'Well?' She arched an eyebrow. 'You're sitting by yourself in the shadows because?'

With difficulty, he swallowed around the lump in his throat. 'You look nice,' he blurted, hurriedly adding, 'I was trying to decide who to sit with.' That sounded stupid, but Lamiya looked flustered. Perhaps telling her she looked nice had distracted her. She opened her mouth to speak, but his eyes darted to the front of her tunic, which seemed to be *wriggling*. He was preparing a stun spell to protect her when the head of a small bird poked out of her tunic neckline. It cocked its head, snapped its black beak and let out a series of rapid peeps.

Astonished, he watched the bird climb out and hop onto the table. Even in the flickering firelight the bird's plumage was stunning. Its chest was a vivid gold and its back and wings a deep jade. *Elemar's favourite colour,* his mind prompted unhelpfully. Its face was a golden yellow, with a black bar across the top of its beak and curving around the eyes.

'Whirr!' exclaimed Lamiya. 'Be nice.' She met his eyes. 'He says you should close your mouth.' She giggled.

Firmly closing his mouth, he eyed the bird hopping around on the table. Where had it come from? Had she just spoken with it? Watching her face, he said, 'This is one of your birds? That you breed?' As soon as she nodded, he said, 'And you can talk with it? You said you could call birds, but I didn't realise you meant you could understand them.'

She tilted her head to one side, reminiscent of how her bird cocked its head, and fluttered her eyelashes prettily. 'I can call many birds, but with some, like Whirr, I can also grasp what they're saying. If I concentrate, they send me images.' Her mouth twisted wryly. 'A skill I wish to hone more fully. My mother was renowned for her ability with birds.' She held up a hand. 'Before you ask, she is dead. So is my father.' Her eyes glinted.

Drumming his fingers lightly on the table, Everand took a few breaths. 'I am sorry,' he said, hoping she wouldn't ask after his parents. That unhappy tale was best forgotten. 'Are you alone now or do you have other family?'

Her face brightened and she held out a finger for Whirr to hop on to. 'No brothers or sisters. Lulite is like an older sister to me. She and Lapsi live by the lake, near me. Lapsi often brings me fresh fish from his catch.' She gently stroked Whirr's back with a finger. 'Lulite breeds birds, so we exchange birds and skills. She's teaching me how to make feather ornaments.'

Everand's spirits lifted. No mention of a partner. But he dare not ask. He ran his tongue around his teeth; she was looking at him with a serious expression. No doubt difficult questions were coming.

'Can I ask ...' She paused and his heart beat more rapidly. Her throat bobbed with a large swallow and his wariness increased. 'I need to ask about the creatures attacking us.'

Making his drumming fingers still, he clasped his hands together. Good, she was not going to ask a personal question. But she was likely to ask questions uncomfortably related to his mission. Stiffly, he nodded.

Lamiya let out a breath. 'Is it possible for someone to make creatures attack others?'

Everand hesitated. His instincts said he could trust her, confide in her, but was this only because he liked her? *Too much.* He closed his eyes to shut out how attractive she was, and sensed her. *Intelligence, integrity, caring ... and a wanting* came through to him. He quickly opened his eyes. That could get complicated! His heart beat harder against his ribs.

140

'A good question,' he began slowly. 'I'm wondering the same thing. The tree-moths, then the jumping fish.' He eyed her. 'Is there more?'

She cupped Whirr in her hands. 'On the way with the boat, Whirr said he was hunted by an eagle.' He waited while she chewed the corner of her lip. 'Eagles do hunt small birds, but when Whirr was relaying the images of what happened,' she swallowed, 'the eagle looked right at me and thought *I see you.* That was for me, not my bird.' Her last words came out in a whisper.

Alarm coursed through him. This confirmed his fears: there *had* to be magic involved. His fingers drummed a rapid tempo on the table until a sharp pain went through the back of his hand. He looked down just as Whirr delivered another peck.

Lamiya grasped his hand. 'I see from your face the answer is yes. What does it mean?' Her anxiety leached through her fingers, making them feel cold upon his.

Reluctantly, he met her eyes. 'I'm not sure.' *Trust her. Tell her. She might be able to help you.* 'That's why I am here. To find out.'

She sat back, surprised. A smile of delight spread across her face, making her cheeks dimple. 'I knew it! I knew something was amiss. Can I help?'

Wriggling on the bench, he stifled a groan, his thoughts tumbling. He'd done it now. Dare he hope she possessed common sense as well as her apparent enthusiasm? And that he wouldn't get her killed. He'd need to tell Beram.

'And,' she drew his attention back, a coy smile adorning her lips, 'I have something of yours.'

He felt his eyebrows rise.

'It's hidden in my dome.' She was teasing him, stretching it out, her smile brimming with mischief.

He frantically tried to work out what he'd lost. The answer arrived just as she spoke.

'I have a long tunic made of a wondrous blue material that could be this silk you spoke of.' She paused for dramatic effect and looked right into his eyes.

'The silk you said the mages of Axis wear.'

CHAPTER NINETEEN

The look on Everand's face! Lamiya burst out laughing. It had been well worth waiting for just the right opportunity. Whirr flapped his wings, picking up on her energy. When Everand leaned across the table towards her, she stopped laughing.

'You mustn't tell anyone,' he said earnestly. 'Don't speak of this to anyone. Except Beram,' he amended, 'Beram knows.'

Lamiya stilled, eyeing him carefully. So that was why he was staying in Beram's dome. The yellow-orange reflection from the flames played over his face, and she liked the way his angular cheekbones became prominent, the deep hue of his eyes. With his hair bound back, the overall impression was austere. What would he look like with his starlight hair loose? And wearing his robe? The way he was looking at her sent a shudder down her spine.

'You must be careful,' he said softly. 'I know you have much to prove at this festival, but for some reason you are of interest to this elusive enemy.'

The next shudder that travelled down her spine was cold. She wanted to follow this traveller, yearned for adventure — but she might be a target herself. Why? Was it to do with her vision of the Riverwood men with their weapons and the way the leader had sensed her scrying? Or was it her ability to work with birds? Should she ask Everand? He was looking over her shoulder and frowning.

He swung his eyes back to her face. 'You should join your team. They're looking this way and Lazuli is getting ready to come over.'

Panic swirled within her. 'What shall I do? Say?'

After a small smile, Everand said, 'Be yourself. Focus on preparing for your races. I'll find you if I need you, or if anything happens.'

Lost for words, she stood up. Whirr ran up her arm and nuzzled at her cheek. With a farewell smile, she headed towards her team. After a few paces she glanced over her shoulder but there was no sign of Everand. How had he done that? When she reached the table, Lazuli slid sideways to make room for her.

'There's space here.' Lazuli patted the bench.

Summoning a smile, she squeezed in beside him and was bombarded with questions.

'How are you?'

'Can you glide?'

'Does your head hurt?'

'What drills will we do?'

'What will the races be, do you know?'

Laughing, she held up her hands. *Be yourself*, Everand had said. 'Thanks to Mookaite's skills, I will glide for our races.'

The paddlers clapped hands with the person seated opposite them, and then with the person next to them. Warmth spread through her. Lazuli somehow managed to put an arm around her and nudge her so that she leaned against his shoulder. It felt nice with his strength seeping through the light contact. She sighed; it would be so good to be on the water in the early sunlight, with Flight skimming across the sparkling surface. The bubble speeding towards the boat flashed into her mind's eye. She shook her head and resolved to be far more alert on the water. Elation rippled through her: Everand had confided in her!

'Try this.' Lazuli handed her a mug. 'They call it feeja wine. Take it easy, it's strong stuff!' he added when she took a gulp.

144

She spluttered at the bite to the liquid, but enjoyed the warmth coursing down her throat and pooling in her stomach. This might help her sleep.

✿

Mage Mantiss sighed and settled himself at the small desk. Dark again, but there had been no time to read more of the notebook earlier. He retrieved the notebook and nestled it on the desk in front of him. Leaning back in his chair, he closed his eyes, fatigue washing down his arms and legs.

The council meeting had been difficult. The other eight members present were grumpy that the meeting had been delayed without adequate explanation, and Tiliqua had asked why Everand was not present. She had snapped her lips closed tight and given him a snippy glance at his lame explanation that Everand had requested time to research a topic in the library and prepare a new research proposal for the council.

He frowned. His daughter showed subtle signs of attraction to Everand, who remained polite but distant. He should encourage Everand, the ideal match for his astute and powerful daughter. Then he could truly call him 'son' and acknowledge the fondness he held for him in his heart. Perhaps he could broach the topic when Everand returned from this mission.

The furrows in Mantiss' brow deepened. Was Everand merely hiding his feelings, which, by the stars, he was astoundingly good at, or did he not return Tiliqua's attraction? Thinking of the minute cracks in Everand's façade when he intervened to save the life of that primitive warrior woman, he concluded reluctantly that it was the latter. But Everand showed no interest in anyone else, so the possibility of a match might be worth pursuing.

Just as well the warrior woman had returned to Terralis with her friends! How could he ever have sanctioned her remaining with Everand when Guild Rule Eight was unequivocal: *Mages must only breed with other mages to keep the lines of magic pure. Accordingly, the humans of Axis must only breed with other humans.*

Opening his eyes, he sat straighter and prised open the notebook. Fate had sided with him and he hadn't had to resort to devising a tragic accident for the warrior woman. He had rewarded Everand for all his efforts, with graduation from apprentice to full mage status and promotion to a place on the Inner Council of Ten. Sometimes, though, he wished he could read his spy better, as loyal as he seemed to be.

He drummed his fingers on the desk beside the book. He had erred gravely by sending Everand on this mission without a communication orb. Not only had he left Everand without any means of calling for assistance — in the unlikely event he should need it — he had no way of knowing whether Everand was safe and what was happening until the festival had been held. Another five suns hence.

He dropped his gaze to the open pages. It might take him that long to read the rest of this cursed notebook.

From the scrawlings of Mage Lapemis

The red serpent

My heart pounded in my throat while the beast and I each waited for the other to make a move. The creature lowered its massive, red-scaled head and I hastily fed more strength into my ward and conjured a death-shard in my right hand. The forked tongue rasped over the top of my ward but I held my ground. Notechis came to stand beside me, and I glanced at the bundle of shards he held ready.

'Wait!' I gasped. Notechis gave me a dark look.

Aclys slithered to my other side and raised an eyebrow in query.

'Prepare a massive stun spell,' I said softly, relieved by his nod.

The red beast closed its jaws and took a shambling step backwards. The other mages stepped up behind me. Water ebbed around us, the stone glinted alluringly behind the beast, the pearly eggs glowed under my incandescent light. I wanted our new beginning to be auspicious, but the patience of my fellow mages was waning. Flexing my fingers, I drew a stun spell to me.

'Great red serpent, yield,' I said loudly. 'Give us the stone.'

The beast's eyes flashed with rage and fire and it towered higher.

'Now!' I yelled at Aclys, raising my arms and making a throwing motion.

Aclys mimicked me and we cast the stun spell over the creature like a net. She wobbled and wove her head from side to side. Notechis' death-shard zoomed into the water where her head had been, arched down and pierced an egg. The shell shattered and a tiny foetus spilled onto the rock floor.

The red beast roared, and staggered half-stunned towards the broken egg.

'Again!' I yelled at Aclys, sorrow coursing through me.

We cast the stun spell once more, with Hemiapsis and Nactus joining in. The red beast's enormous hindquarters buckled, and she toppled onto her side, breaking more eggs beneath her mass. Before I could react, Notechis leaped forward and smashed the closest eggs.

'Desist!' I commanded. 'The beast is down.'

When Notechis lifted his hand to cast a bolt into the last remaining egg, Aclys raced forward and yanked him away.

'Lapemis leads!' hissed Aclys. 'Follow his orders.'

I nodded my gratitude to Aclys and eyed Notechis with disfavour. The others stepped close to me in a gesture of solidarity. Notechis shrugged and moved away from the egg.

The lights in the cave dimmed. The red beast lay stretched out on her side, the huge arch of her rib cage rising and falling, her eyes closed to slits with golden light seeping out.

My heart sank.

She had fallen on top of the stone of magic.

The stone of power

'How do we take the stone now?' Notechis said, his face twisted in a sneer.

I held up my hand, thinking. 'We have to lever the body up and transport the stone out.' Keeping my face calm, I quelled my rising fears. What if the stone was sentient and refused to come? What if it was protected, and death came to anyone who touched it?

Aclys drew closer. 'We will lift the body and you, our new Head of the Guild, can clasp the stone and convince it our intent is pure.'

My nod was of gratitude as well as agreement. Whatever this stone was, wherever it had come from, it should be treated with respect and awe. The others positioned themselves and gathered their magic ready to raise the back of the red beast. I took deep breaths and wrapped my mind around the concept of a new Guild, one with honest intentions to dwell on this land and replenish the line of mages and magic, while protecting a population of humans. I thought of the arable and tranquil lands, and vowed we would do nothing to destroy these.

'Lapemis?' Aclys queried. 'Ready?'

I fixed my intent and will on the area where the stone was. Magic hummed down the arms of my colleagues and gently, with invisible force, the back of the creature tilted upwards and sky-arch beams of light cascaded out. Stepping closer, I held out my arms, palms upwards, and coaxed the stone to me. The colours within the star whirled and roiled, shining bright then dim then bright again. I took another step, maybe two, and leaned towards it.

'Magnificent stone, come to me. Help us rebuild,' I pleaded.

The colours whizzed in all directions, faster and faster, and the water around the stone began to hum and quiver. The colours adopted a red hue, like streaks of churning blood. I frowned. This was not a good omen. I took another step and projected images to the stone of a Guild built of beautiful white stone with glints of minerals, then I envisaged an emblem of a sun and a moon with the star-stone hung between them, of classes of mage apprentices learning magic, of large moths and worms spinning glorious silk to create fine robes, of a colony of content humans working the land and raising their children in a time of peace.

The whirring reds slowed and mingled with shades of blue — azure, cobalt, sapphire, sky, turquoise, aquamarine — and the star-stone slowly lifted away from the last remaining pearly egg. I spread my hands, and to my never-ending wonder the stone floated to me and perched upon my palms. Its star points were not sharp as they settled onto my skin, the opalescent surface felt smooth and hinted at warmth. 'Thank you,' I breathed to it. 'We will honour you.'

I stepped back, giving the others space to lower the beast.

'Gently,' I called, despite the beads of exertion adorning their brows. 'Don't break the last egg.'

With grunts and muttered curses, the others lowered the red creature to the floor of the cavern.

Tearing my eyes away from the wonder of the stone, I said, 'Let us leave, quickly.' I clutched the star-stone tightly against my chest, feeling the magic thrumming within it, and swam for the cavern entrance.

Guilt throbbed through me when we swam over the carcass of the green creature, its once golden eyes unseeing and clouded with grey film.

Mantiss scrubbed at his face. For three generations, the mages had been taught that the Staropal had been found buried in the eternal spring in the centre of Axis, and that Lapemis and the others had interpreted this to be the sign they should build the new Guild here. Apprentices were taught that the stone contained a finite amount of power that needed to be conserved, and hence the stone was accessed only rarely to draw minimal extra magic from it.

New spells and abilities were to be discovered through research and practice, a key role for the Guild. The texts in the library were filled with volumes of research and experiments, and academic ability was regarded highly. As was innate strength of power.

An oppressive weight draped around his heart. Was it this burden of forbidden knowledge that caused his body to wane before its time? Neelaps had examined him using his healing abilities and had found nothing wrong. Were his problems founded in the shock of having to deal with Mage Beetal's treachery and the almost-failure of the Guild? Without Everand's help, he'd have been branded the Head of the Guild who had failed abysmally and lost everything Lapemis and the others had worked so hard to rebuild. Mantiss closed the notebook.

May his spy's current mission prove to be as simple as he hoped.

CHAPTER TWENTY

Lamiya felt that she had barely closed her eyes when her body started to shake. She tried to burrow into the mattress.

'Lamiya! Wake up!'

She opened her eyes.

Mookaite was shaking her shoulder and Whirr hopped excitedly on her pillow. 'Not too fast,' said Mookaite when she tried to lurch upright.

Lamiya sat up and blinked. Her tongue felt fuzzy and her mouth dry. Memories of the feast came flooding in and she licked her lips. 'That feeja wine outdoes any sleeping potion.'

Mookaite gave a tinkling laugh. 'Lazuli is naughty. Sorry, I didn't realise until he'd given you a third mug. How is your head?'

Lamiya tilted her head from side to side, stretching her neck. 'I'll manage.'

Mookaite patted the blanket. 'Good. I have juice and bread ready. You need to hurry.'

Lamiya forced herself not to bolt her bread and hurriedly got into her team tunic. Mookaite left before her, suggesting she meet them at the boat ramp as the teams had already gone to fetch the boats.

Beneath an already bright sun, she walked briskly towards the southern gate with Whirr peeping happily from her shoulder. 'You should have woken me,' she scolded, worried that Luvu would comment on her lateness. Her injury felt much better,

151

but her head ached dully. What had Lazuli been thinking? She had a vague memory of leaning against him as he took her back to Mookaite's dome. Frowning, she reflected *that* had been his plan. Firmly, she pushed all thoughts of Lazuli and the traveller aside. This training was important: she needed to prove her mettle and not be distracted by intrigue and men. She considered her favourite drills, deciding it would be best to work on speed and timing and not overdo it. Her feet felt lighter as her plan formed and she broke into an easy jog once she had cleared the gate.

On reaching the ramp, she saw her team settle Flight into the water, and then Larimar sat on the prow, behind the dragon head, to steady the boat. Maintaining momentum, she swept down the ramp, past her paddlers, and stepped onto the prow. The startled look on Lazuli's face made her grin. She bounced over the benches to take up her position, quickly putting the steering oar into its socket.

'You may board,' she called. Running footsteps made her look up to see Ejad jogging down the ramp. 'Wait for Ejad, our new paddler ten. 'Welcome, Ejad.' She flashed him a smile. *Be yourself.* Whirr squawked as if to say *but don't overdo it.* Ejad flushed and stepped over the benches to sit beside Luvu, who grunted at him.

While her paddlers settled themselves, Lamiya looked around. The Riverfall team was poised at the top of the ramp waiting to bring their boat down, Mizuchi's blue and gold head glaring at her in challenge. Her heart pounded: these would be hard-fought races between two proud boats and two skilled teams. A bundle of nerves settled into her stomach and she stood taller. She *could* do this. She *would* do this. She swept her eyes over the Riverfall team. No sign of Everand.

'Glide?' Luvu grunted. The team was waiting with their paddles poised.

Calm washed into her as the boat slid smoothly away from the ramp. Once Flight was mid-river, she faced the boat north.

Drawing a deep breath, she imagined the orange and green dragon waiting, its spirit strong in the boat. Her team sat ready, listening.

'This session will be a loosener,' she began. 'You've journeyed hard to get here and next sun-up we pitch our skills against Riverfall.' She waited while the team predictably yelled, 'Yo!' This was followed by laughter as the Riverfall team paused while boarding their boat and responded, 'Yosh!'

Lamiya tossed her head, loving the way the breeze rippled through her hair, nudging it away from her face. The sun already sprayed warmth over her cheeks, arms and legs. The dragon beneath her felt coiled, ready to spring out over the water. Drawing another deep breath, she repressed a strong urge to call the dragon. Birds came to her, why not a dragon? She exhaled. What *was* she thinking? Were delusions an after-effect of this feeja wine? She focused on the ten backs sitting before her.

'Five hundred strokes easy, then merge into intervals of twenty fast, fifty long and powerful, twenty fast. Five sets.' Luvu grunted, whether in approval or not she couldn't tell. 'Paddles up! Go!'

The team paddled strongly. Lamiya watched Ejad find his rhythm and soon his timing and reach were seamless from the others. The set to Luvu's shoulders eased, and she concluded he approved of Ejad. That bode well. At the front of the boat Lazuli and Larimar's muscles bulged and relaxed as they drove the boat through the water, setting a solid rate. Flight skimmed along the river and the banks sped by on either side. The dragon felt happy. Whirr crept into the front of her tunic, with his beak peeking out. A glance over her shoulder confirmed that Tengar had taken Mizuchi the other way, south, so the teams couldn't be tempted to race each other.

Soon they were ploughing past the northern wall of Zurqat. 'Well done! Middle power and speed,' she called, and the boat settled into the water as the paddlers lowered their rate. Once past the gate, she called for a series of lifts until they approached the large waterwheel perched next to the bank. From there, they should be able to see the bridge in the distance. 'Stop the boat!' The paddlers dug their paddles in, creating a wash. 'See the bridge up ahead? That's the finish of the long race.'

Her paddlers took the opportunity to roll their shoulders and stretch their backs. 'The first, shorter race will start at the boat ramp and go to the southern gate. The second one goes from the ramp to the northern gate. Crowds will gather along the bank to watch.' Heads nodded.

Lazuli twisted around. 'How many strokes do you estimate for the long race?'

Good question. She'd intended to pace it out but too much had happened. 'Tengar said at training pace it's close to six thousand strokes. So, at race pace about three hundred less.'

'Long way to paddle home after,' muttered Luvu. 'Why don't they do a turn race?'

Lamiya straightened Flight when the prow drifted in the current. 'Tengar said there used to be a race to the bridge in the past, and Atage wants to revive this tradition.' Even as she said this, she realised paddling to the bridge would take them closer to Riverwood and Hanaki Forest. Her eyes flicked that way.

From where they were she discerned the dense, dark blanket of treetops to the north and left of the bridge. A breeze picked up, and she fancied it carried threats and shadows. Whirr vanished and his feathers tickled as he nestled deep between her breasts. Along the riverbank, tall grasses swayed and whispered. A prickle passed between her shoulderblades. *Don't look up. Turn the boat*, her instincts shouted, perceiving a shadow, eyes, high above. Whirr gave a muffled peep.

'Let's head back. Turn the boat.' Too slowly for comfort, her sense of vulnerability increasing with each breath, the boat turned to face south. 'Paddles up! A hundred long and strong,' she called. The sooner they got back to the town, the better.

The boat ramp came reassuringly into view, and she released a sigh. What was Everand doing? Should she tell him what she'd sensed? Looking down at the backs of her team paddling so strongly and smoothly, her chest grew tight. The very next sun her team would be on the water racing Riverfall. Should she tell them there might be danger? How could she not?

You mustn't tell anyone. Don't speak of this to anyone. Everand's face had been so stern. There seemed to be two of her.

One part of her was guiding the boat neatly into the ramp, the other part debating: *did she trust the traveller?*

CHAPTER TWENTY-ONE

Lying flat on his back in the darkness, Everand stretched his legs and toes until he felt the floor at the end of the mattress. Glad Beram had found another mattress, he listened to the steady breathing on the other side of the dome. From sun-high until dusk, he'd roamed the riverbanks as far south and north as he had time for and discovered nothing untoward. Disappointingly, he didn't see Lamiya at all, other than in the distance on the river training her team. When he returned from his surveillance, Atage had invited him, Tengar and Beram to the sun-fade meal, giving him no opportunity to find an excuse to talk to her.

On arriving at Atage's dome, the town leader had grasped both of his hands warmly and expressed his thanks, and Everand worried he'd done nothing to warrant such approval. Their trust that he could protect them was disturbing.

Over a delicious meal of grilled meats and baked vegetables, they had discussed the details of the races. He'd found it easy to praise Atage's wife Thulite, a skilled cook. They had talked about the festival and races until long after moon-rise, sitting around flickering candles and sipping herbal brew. Everand flexed his fingers. He now knew more than he would ever need to know about dragon boats, paddling technique and the races. Judging the races between Tengar's and Lamiya's boats would be much needed practice.

Pausing mid-stretch, he thought of Tengar's comment that they wouldn't practise the long race. On asking, he'd discovered the final race would be all the way to the bridge that spanned from Riverfall to Riverwood. *Curses!* He hadn't explored that far. Could this bridge be at risk? In the festival, the four racing boats would pass beneath it, people would be standing on it and it connected the provinces on this side of the river to Riverwood on the other. It was the only bridge across Dragonspine River. His forehead hurt. If he wanted to disrupt the festival, what would *he* do? He'd damage the bridge or destroy it. What would be gained? Isolation for Riverwood? Loss of goodwill between the provinces?

He must see the bridge. There wasn't much time left and he still had no idea what was going on. The people from Riverfall and Riverplain seemed honest and straightforward. Riversea was unknown, but there was no sense of threat. Riverwood felt tricky and ominous and, so far, the indicators pointed that way. Or was this too obvious? Had he missed something? Atage would hold discussions with the province leaders the sun after the races. The man had spoken animatedly about his idea for regular trading between the four provinces.

Everand drummed his fingers on the mattress, the squishy feeling on his fingertips less helpful than a solid table. Could trade be the problem? Not the festival itself but the idea of regular trade? Surely everyone stood to benefit? He was getting nowhere. Pale light nudged under the dome curtain and Beram woke up with a snort and a gurgle.

✿

After a hurried rinse with warmed water and hastily swallowed breads and juice, he followed Beram, who was clad in his team outfit and clutching his paddle. Everand wore the new clothes he'd been given — the slate-grey tunic had hues of his favourite deep blue, and he liked the soft grey trousers. Melanite had thoughtfully provided a matching slate-grey thong for his hair. On balance, he preferred the feel of his silk robe flapping around his legs and ankles, but he had to admit the trousers were more practical.

'Follow me to the boat shed,' said Beram. 'Atage will come with the cart to take you to your judging position.' He grinned over his shoulder. 'You can wish us luck!'

'Ha!' responded Everand. 'I'm the impartial judge, remember!'

Beram laughed and narrowly avoided colliding with two children who ran right in front of him waving streamers. Everand took longer strides because Beram was almost jogging. He dodged numerous townspeople hurrying to take goods to their trading domes, chasing after children, or heading to the riverbank to make sure they had a good view. He scanned each courtyard as they passed through: so far, nothing looked out of place.

The outer courtyard was empty where the Riverplain boat had been. Was Lamiya feeling confident? Had she recovered enough? From his trial pacing, he knew it was six hundred of his long strides from the start at the boat ramp to the finish at the southern gate. Would he be too far away if mishap occurred early in the race? At the dusk meal he'd suggested to Atage that the men make more wooden staves to repel any tree-moths and have strong men positioned at intervals with these. With a look of dismay, Atage had agreed, but the staves wouldn't be ready in time for these races.

As they hurried along the path, he saw women in the adjacent planted areas pulling trolleys and tipping jugs of water at the base of the bushes. They worked methodically in pairs, one pushing the trolley and handing a jug to the other, who watered the bush and placed the empty jug back on the already moving trolley.

Beram paused for a stride and said, 'Blue sky for as far as we can see. If it doesn't rain soon we'll struggle to produce enough cotton. We need a happy and strong festival to appease the river dragon.' He strode off, more quickly than before.

Everand hesitated. He'd almost forgotten they believed there was a dragon in the river, although no-one had actually seen it. He stopped dead: what if there *was* a fierce river dragon? What if this elusive enemy was practising on tree-moths and fish but the real target was the dragon? Hence the stealthy approach. The dragon wasn't visible — yet. What if it did appear and the enemy worked out how to control it? The boats and paddlers wouldn't stand a chance! Images crowded him of boats tipping over, a dragon's strong tail shattering them, powerful jaws picking off paddlers as they floundered in churning water.

Walking slowly, he thought hard. How could he find out if there was a dragon? His mentor had shown him that dragons could be trained. But it took time, and dragons were hard to conceal. Mage Beetal had kept his dragons hidden in a volcano on Elemar's world, where he had discovered them. If Elemar hadn't fallen through the sky rift Mage Beetal had created and landed in Axis, he'd never have uncovered his mentor's plot until it was far too late. He forced his mind back to his current task: where would the river dragon be? At the river source? He *must* find out. He *must* go look for it.

Looking down the ramp, he eyed the waiting boats, all decked out for the event. The Riverplain boat had enormous bright red and green feathers attached to the carved dragon's mane and tail, and the paddlers had feathers in their hair. Standing at the back, casually working the oar, Lamiya was clad in a vivid orange tunic and short green trousers. Her mahogany hair tumbled over her shoulders, the front part adorned with slim braids patterned with brightly coloured beads and sweeping long green feathers. She looked stunning.

As he stared, entranced, she looked up and uncurled her fingers from the top of the oar in a subtle greeting. On the other boat, Tengar caught his eye and gave a short wave. The Riverfall team had necklaces of coloured tokens around their necks and the women had blue tokens and beads woven into their hair.

A rumbling noise behind alerted him that the cart had arrived and he turned around. A man he hadn't met was steering the hopeepa because Persaj and Zeol were in the boat. Everand walked up to the cart to speak with Atage and Lyber, and the nearest hopeepa promptly licked his face and fluttered her eyelashes. *Crystal.* He pushed her away with a friendly nudge and found Atage and Lyber regarding him with astonished expressions.

'Climb up,' said Atage, indicating the platform at the back of the cart.

He complied and, selecting one of the cushions on the flat platform, sat with his back against the side railing so he could still speak to the others at the front.

Atage stood up and faced the boats. 'May the sun shine upon your paddles! Paddle fast and strong! May the best boat win!'

Everand grimaced at the chorus of 'Yosh!' and 'Yo!' He felt his head tuck in towards his shoulders as the traditional calls were drowned out by the beating of drums. Sitting taller, he peered at the boats. Both boats had an extra person at the front, facing the paddlers. Drummers. Before their knees sat round wooden tubs with an animal hide stretched over them. The drummers hammered the hide with a wooden stick. What else would be produced for the festival, and how much noise would four boats make? Enough to wake the dragon?

The cart lurched forward and he put his hands flat on the floor for balance. The hopeepa broke into a long lope and the sideways lurching made him feel queasy. The noise of rumbling wheels and thudding hooves precluded conversation. Soon enough, the entry to Zuqart loomed and the hopeepa were pulled back to a walk. The driver turned the cart onto the grassy stretch at the top of the bank and faced it towards the river.

Atage said, 'Come up here with us. The driver will hold the hopeepa.'

Everand climbed over the back of the seat and sat next to Atage, on the downriver side. Lyber retrieved a cloth bag from underneath the seat and Everand watched with interest while the man undid the strings at the top and eased the cloth down over a small wooden frame. Across the frame were five strings, stretching from side to side. Each string was threaded through a cluster of clay tokens, a different colour for each of the top four strings. The bottom string had four different coloured pieces of string tied to it. Before he could ask, Atage explained.

'Lyber will keep score. There's one row for each team: blue for us, green for Riverplain, white for Riversea and brown for Riverwood. After each race we move the tokens across. This sun, with only two boats, the score is two tokens if the boat wins, one token if it is second. The bottom row is the overall score and we retie the coloured strings in the overall position. The team with the highest score is the winner.'

Lyber added, 'Of course, on festival day with four boats the score will be four for the win, down to one token for fourth.'

Simple and clever. Everand sat back and looked around. He had a clear view down the river where the water glittered in the sunshine, a mesmerising shifting pattern of blues, greens and flashes of silver. The breeze was light, but the water seemed to be flowing south so the boats would be working against the current. If he squinted, he could see the two boats poised in the distance.

On the far bank, tall grasses waved in the breeze and the scents of grasses and hints of flowers teased the tip of his nose. Ripples reached the bank with a soft slapping sound.

161

He extended his senses: insects and small creatures foraging, nothing untoward. *Not yet, anyway.* On his right, townspeople were gathering along the bank in front of the town wall, many carrying blue and gold cloth streamers.

Two men emerged through the gate carrying a long wooden stave with a bright yellow cloth flag attached. They approached the cart.

Atage pointed to a spot in the grass about five paces in front of the hopeepa. 'Around there.' He remained standing as the two men carried the stave to the spot, put the sharp point on the ground and held it vertical. Atage looked at Everand. 'The finish line. Is that straight in front of you? You will call the winner as the boat's nose passes the flag.'

Everand looked at the stave through half-closed eyes. 'About half a pace downriver,' he said. The men moved and held the stave straight. Now the stave was directly before him, making a clean line across the river. 'Yes, there's good.'

One of the men produced a stone block from a pocket and they hammered the stave into the grass. Then they left and merged into the crowd.

'How much longer?' Everand turned to Atage.

'Soon. The starter must make sure the boats are lined up straight for a fair start.'

His heartrate quickening, he looked down the river. The surface glinted bright silver, the sun warmed his face and arms, the crowd murmured eagerly. Unease drifted into him; he couldn't see the boats properly. Use the enhancing spell? Atage and Lyber wouldn't detect it. Would the enemy, though? Was it worth finding out? He squinted against the shimmering light, trying to see the start. Three breaths later he gave in and silently mouthed the enhancement spell.

The glittering water was almost blinding, but he could discern the boats: blue and gold on this side; orange and green on the far side. The silhouette of a person stepped down the ramp and the paddlers leaned forward and placed their paddles in the water.

A horn sounded, and with a flurry of movement and water the boats shot forward. He narrowed his focus, blocking out the sounds of the crowd. After five short, fast strokes Tengar's team changed to longer strokes while Lamiya's team maintained a higher rate. The orange and green boat edged ahead. Lamiya's boat swapped to longer, stronger strokes and the drummers beat a rapid rhythm in time with the paddles. The boats skimmed towards him, straight as arrows. With incredible skill, the paddlers' arms lifted and fell, the two teams in time with each other. *Astonishing.*

At halfway, the orange and green boat held a marginal lead, and he relaxed the spell. Sounds rushed in: people cheering, the beating of the drums now not quite matched, the calls of 'Yosh' and 'Yo', the splash of paddles and swishing of prows pushing through water. Another few breaths and he heard Tengar and Lamiya exhorting their teams. Tengar was gaining on Lamiya. The boats loomed larger and he focused on the stave. From front on, the boats looked to be head and head.

'Lift!' Lamiya shouted and her team became a blur of arms rising and falling, feathers waving behind them. The front of the boat lifted in the water. For a breath, the boat shimmered into the form of an orange and green dragon, tongue flicking, tail held proud, scales glistening along its sides. Everand blinked. *Concentrate!*

He flicked his eyes to the stave just as the orange and green nose passed the yellow flag, with the blue and gold nose a mere head-width behind. The crowd cheered and stamped their feet and he sat up, heart pounding. Before him, the paddlers slumped over on their benches, sides heaving. Tengar gave Lamiya a sharp nod of acknowledgment. Good, they too knew who'd won.

'Riverplain, by a nose,' he said to Atage.

'I thought so,' responded Atage.

Lyber shuffled the tokens across on the strings and they made a pleasant clacking sound against the wooden frame. Lyber was grinning, which Everand thought strange given that the Riverfall team was second.

'Your son paddled well,' Atage said to Lyber.

Lyber's grin grew wider. 'He's thrilled to have the opportunity. I'm so happy he excelled.'

It dawned on Everand. 'Ejad is your son?' Lyber's sustained happy grin answered him. Abruptly, he realised Atage was speaking.

'… so good Lamiya was recovered enough. I'm glad we waited an extra sun-up.'

Everand dipped his head in agreement.

Atage looked at him. 'You must stand up and announce the winner.'

'Me?' They hadn't mentioned this part.

'Yes. You're the judge! Go on.'

Quickly running his tongue over his lips, he stood up on the cart. To his relief, the crowd quieted down. With over two hundred faces and pairs of eyes all watching him, his knees felt far away, numb. He took a breath. Down the bank, the paddlers sat erect, waiting. *Think of something to say!* He raised his arms.

'Congratulations all paddlers! A swift and hard-fought race.' The paddlers smiled and Atage murmured in approval. *So far so good.* 'This first race goes to Riverplain. Flight's nose crossed the line just ahead.'

Before he could consider what else he should say, the Riverplain drummer beat the drum in a frenetic tempo and the team waved their paddles, shouting, 'Yo! Yo!' The crowd erupted with more cheers while Tengar and his team bowed to Lamiya and her team. Then Lamiya looked up at him with shining eyes and tossed her head so that her hair rippled and the long green feathers moved. His heart soared and he smiled at her.

Atage nudged him. 'Tell them to head back to the start for the next race.'

'That was race one,' called Everand. 'We eagerly wait to see race two. Glides, please take your boats back to the start.' After a formal nod of dismissal at Tengar and then Lamiya, he sat down. *Quite enough prominence!* How could he possibly intervene in any untoward actions while displayed like this in front of hundreds of people?

The driver climbed back up and Lyber obligingly moved to the back of the cart. The cart rumbled slowly towards the northern gate, waiting for people to clear the path.

'No need to hurry,' murmured Atage. 'It'll take the boats a while to line up ready. Thulite will bring us something to eat and drink.'

Everand liked the idea of sampling more of Thulite's cooking. Prompted by the realisation that Ejad was son to Lyber, he asked Atage, 'Do you have children?'

'Sadly, no.' Atage shrugged. 'We weren't blessed enough. Still,' he opened his hands in a resigned manner, 'it means I have time to be the town leader. In a way, all the townspeople are my children.'

Everand regarded Atage. Instinctively, he liked this man, and his sincere wish to improve the town and the lives of his people. This moment of quiet seemed a good time to propose a visit to the bridge. 'You said there's a longer race for the festival, all the way to a bridge in the north.'

'Yes,' agreed Atage. 'The long race is the climax.'

'I'd like to see the bridge,' Everand said, conscious that Lyber and the driver were listening. Atage opened and shut his mouth. 'It would be good for me as the judge, and the two glides Tengar and Lamiya, to orient ourselves with the finish line.' When Atage still didn't speak, he added, 'Perhaps Beram could drive us in a hopeepa cart?' The inclusion of Beram would surely alert Atage that this was to do with his mission.

After a worrying hesitation, Atage asked, 'When would you like to go?'

'Next sun-up,' said Everand.

Lyber's curiosity was evident in the man's open-mouthed stare.

'Very well.' Atage frowned. 'Are you sure you wish to take Lamiya?'

'To be fair, both glides should go.' Everand sat up straighter. To deflect further questions, he added, 'She has a perspective that might be useful.' He willed the man to agree.

'True,' said Atage, residual concern lacing his words. 'I'll speak to them after the second race.' The cart slowed and the driver turned the hopeepa to face the river again. 'We're here.' Atage smiled broadly. 'And here's Thulite with our food!'

Thulite handed out small, sweet cakes that were soon washed down with a juice from the tart pink fruit. They climbed back onto the cart to wait and Everand flicked sweat from his forehead with his fingers. The sun was fizzling on his arms, the river gleaming a deep, hypnotic blue. The earlier breeze had dropped and he had an eerie sensation that everything stood still around him. Even the tall grasses on the far bank were silently erect. The town's concern for their crops was well placed. His tunic was stuck to his back, and he was just sitting on a cart. It would be hard work for the paddlers. Now to his left, townspeople were hovering in the shade of the town wall, talking in subdued tones, and the children were sitting down rather than running around.

'Honk!' The horn sounded. Everand applied the enhanced senses spell once more. As expected, the boats were racing side by side in another close race. As before, they travelled impressively straight. He felt a smile forming: Lamiya was proving her worth and her team would be so proud. The drums grew steadily louder. The boats drew level with the southern edge of the town, and still raced side by side. Focusing, he

166

made out the movement of the paddlers, saw Tengar and Lamiya adjusting their oars and calling to their teams.

A sudden chill settled on the back of his neck. He sat up, suppressing a gasp. Cold brushed over the back of his neck, like a caress from an icy hand. Far above, a black speck circled against the blue sky. He ceased his enhancement spell.

Atage gave him a sharp look. 'Is something wrong?'

Everand shook his head and focused on the boats, wishing his heart was not beating so rapidly. *Focus! You're being watched! Forget that, focus!* He blinked a few times. The boats were fifty paces away, battling it out neck and neck. Admiration threatened to overwhelm him. *Get a grip. Focus.* The drums beat faster and faster, the paddles rose and plunged in a blur. Tengar and Lamiya screamed orders and the fronts of both boats lifted.

'Lift!' Lamiya yelled.

'Yosh! Bring it home!' shouted Tengar.

Townspeople swelled to the riverbank stamping, hooting, shouting and waving their flags. Atage barked at someone who crossed before the finish flag. Everand leaned forward. He must get this right; he stared hard at the stave and the limp yellow flag.

Mizuchi's blue nose flew past, with Flight's green and orange nose half a head behind. Sitting up, he felt glad; one race each was a good result and would make the competition at the festival more exciting. Drained, he wiped his forehead with the back of his hand. 'Riverfall wins.'

Atage and Lyber clapped each other on the shoulder and the noise along the riverbank was deafening. Lamiya bowed to Tengar, whose grin stretched from ear to ear. Unexpectedly, Everand's chest seethed with emotions: pride and joy. He blinked. This would not do: he must remain detached. Complete his mission.

He closed his eyes, blocking out the sights that were affecting him so much. *The bridge.* He must see the bridge and ascertain the danger. *How can you do that when you don't know what's going on? And why did you ask to take Lamiya?* Eyes still closed, his forehead pinched as he recalled the way Lamiya's boat had shimmered into a dragon-like form. *Because you will need her. Do you? Or do you just like her? You will need her, just as you needed Elemar's help.*

Not liking this connection of Lamiya to Elemar, he took a slow breath. It felt inexplicably right to take her too, though. He had such little control over anything on this mission he might as well run with this wild idea.

Atage's cough made him open his eyes. 'Can you announce the winner?'

Everand pushed away his inner debate and stood up to declare Riverfall the winner.

CHAPTER TWENTY-TWO

Lamiya stepped off the boat, trying to ignore the shake in her legs. Her head was pounding, not that she was going to mention this to anyone. Except Mookaite. Before she had properly attained her land balance, she was enveloped in hot, sweaty hugs. Multiple hands thumped her back; not helpful for her head. She held up her hands to deflect the attention and inside her tunic, Whirr peeped in alarm.

'Well done,' said Larimar, patting her shoulder. 'The extra fast strokes at the start worked!'

She smiled tiredly, appreciating the praise.

Lazuli nudged Larimar aside and said, 'We could've taken them in the second race.'

She put a finger to her lips, conscious the Riverfall team was also milling around the ramp, using tubs to wash down Mizuchi. His eyes glittered in understanding.

'Clever,' he said quietly. Holding his paddle loosely in one hand, he reached out to stroke her cheek. 'How is your head?'

'Fine, but I might see Mookaite and rest for a while.'

'Good idea.' Lazuli hesitated, his eyes fixed on her too discerningly. 'Will you sleep in Mookaite's dome or return to the team dome?'

She watched Lazuli's face. As wonderful as it would be to rejoin her team, a quiet sleep and care from Mookaite would be better. She must recover enough for more races. Besides, she needed to think about what had happened near the end of the first race. A thrill passed through her stomach. Never before had she *felt* the dragon move beneath her. A niggling sense that this was important tugged at her, and Whirr fidgeted, his feathers tickling her breastbone.

'Lamiya?' Lazuli prompted.

'I'll celebrate with the team for the meal and spend one more dark-fall under Mookaite's care.'

Disappointment crossed Lazuli's face. 'Fair enough.' Standing taller, he said, 'Should we put Flight back in the courtyard or in the dome with the Riverfall boat?'

Lamiya glanced to where the rest of the team was washing Flight. Noticing Atage speaking with Tengar off to one side, she held a finger up, indicating Lazuli should wait, and approached them.

'Ah. Lamiya,' said Atage, and when she stopped a polite distance away, he beckoned. Surprised, she stepped closer. 'Next sun-up, the traveller wants to go with you and Tengar to see the bridge and the finish of the long race.' The man looked uncomfortable.

'He does?' She bit down her 'why'. Everand must have good reason to suggest this. *He wanted her to go!* Elation surged through her. Suppressing a smile, she adopted a serious expression. 'It will be useful to have a feel for the finish area.'

Tengar and Atage both gave her a startled look, as if they'd been expecting her to argue.

'How will we get there?' She deployed Everand's tactic of asking questions when he thought someone might ask him something he didn't wish to answer.

'Beram will take you in a cart. You'll leave at first light.'

Lamiya inclined her head. 'I'll be ready. I'll stay with Mookaite this dark-fall.' As the silence stretched, she remembered why she had approached them. 'I came to ask whether we should put Flight in the boat dome or take her back to the courtyard?'

Tengar replied, 'The dome. Let's keep the racing boats together, and it's faster to the ramp.'

Lamiya went to tell her team. Predictably, Lazuli was hovering near the front of the boat. Just as well she'd decided to stay with Mookaite — Everand would have carefully chosen who he wanted to go to the bridge. *Tell no-one.* Trying to stop Lazuli from going too would be nigh impossible. This way, she'd have left before he realised.

✿

The top of the town outer wall glimmered dusty pink with the hint of light and Lamiya walked quickly. The town was quiet, curtains hanging limp across dome entrances. The leaves of the bushes were unfurling, the small white flowers starting to open, and the musky scent buoyed her spirits. The entry to the hopeepa stable yawned darkly, the door already open. Hearing the thudding of hooves, she stopped and Beram emerged leading the hopeepa. The creatures looked grumpy, ears flattened against their heads and twirling their tails.

Tengar and Everand followed the cart, gave her brief smiles and then slipped past her to open the northern gates. She tiptoed after the cart as it rumbled through, hearing the gates creak when Tengar and Everand pulled them closed.

Outside the wall, she revelled in the view. Mist coiled up from the river, giving the banks a mysterious air, and ahead the hills loomed as dark shadows with fingers of silver light eking down the sides and sneaking into the folds and crevices. Her skin prickled in excitement. Beram climbed up onto the driver's seat, Everand quickly following. That left her and Tengar to sit in the back, and she chose the side behind Everand.

Beram shook the reins and the cart moved off. One of the hopeepa bellowed and Beram slapped her back with the reins. The creature gave an indignant huff, but fell quiet. Lamiya

171

chewed at her lower lip. Despite her best efforts at stealth, Mookaite had stirred and asked where she was going. 'The glides are going to check the course for the long race. Back soon,' she'd replied vaguely, slipping out before Mookaite could ask anything more. Should she tell Everand? Surely the paddlers would realise they were missing anyway?

'So, the long race starts at the northern gate?' Everand asked Beram. 'Can we take the cart closer to the river's edge?'

Lamiya felt the cart veer left and the noise from the wheels lessened as they rolled over grassy verge instead of crushed pebble path. Tucking her legs underneath her, she grasped the back of the driver's seat and pulled herself to standing. Keeping a firm hold as the cart lurched along, she looked down at the river. Everand's shoulders tensed at her proximity. 'I haven't seen this part of the river,' she explained.

He twisted to look at her. 'You can sit up here if you like. We can make room.'

To her delight, he moved closer to Beram. With a broad smile she climbed over the seat. Warmth spread through her elbow and arm as he helped her to balance and then sit.

For a while, they watched the river glide by in silence. Ahead, the land became a muted yellow as the sun cleared the hills to the east. The river was changing from grey to blue, and the tendrils of mist were dissipating. Water birds hooted and warbled, splashing among the reeds. Whirr stirred and gave a series of chirps. Everand looked at her with his eyebrows lifting comically and she laughed. Focusing on the river, she thought the far banks seemed to be drawing closer.

Leaning forward, she asked Beram, 'Does the river narrow here?'

Beram flapped the reins to encourage the hopeepa to step out more before responding. 'Yes. The river meanders and the bank curves outwards making the river narrower, then it curves wider again before it feeds under the bridge. After that it follows gullies and valleys until it reaches Flat Mountain.'

'The river source is there?' asked Everand.

Beram nodded. 'Mizuchi Falls pour down from Flat Mountain and tumble into Dragon Lake. The lake then drops down a steep lip and feeds into Dragonspine River.'

'Waterfalls!' said Lamiya softly. 'I'd like to see those.'

'Does this mean the river is widest in Riverfall?' asked Everand.

Lamiya turned so she could see his face. His brow was furrowed.

'Crystal!' said Beram sharply. 'No eating!' He slapped the reins. Crystal flapped her ears in annoyance and the corners of Everand's mouth twitched.

'Sorry,' said Beram. 'We think the river is widest and deepest as it passes Zuqart.' He shrugged. 'This is probably why the ancestors chose to build the town there.'

Tengar spoke up from the back of the cart. 'The river is deep enough for four boats to race all the way to the bridge.'

She swallowed when Everand suddenly faced her. 'What about in Riverplain? What does the river look like there?'

Wishing she could understand his line of thought, Lamiya considered. Eyeing the river beside them, she said, 'It's about the same width as we pass now. I think it's a similar width all the way through our plains and fields.'

'It's your main supply of water?' Everand's serious look sent a trickle of alarm through her.

'There are two tributaries, Dragonscale River and Dragonleg River.' His blue eyes invited more. 'I live near the southern tributary, which feeds into Dragonfoot Lake. The lake is also filled by run-off from the hills. So, we have plenty of fresh water.' Curiosity overwhelmed her. 'Why do you ask?'

Everand took his time, and she noticed he was flexing his fingers. Her alarm grew stronger.

'Why do you ask?' she repeated, and the others also looked at the traveller. The cart rumbled onwards and still he didn't answer. Lamiya wanted to shriek at him: why was he asking questions about the river? The river had always been there, it sustained them. Then it hit her: what if it *wasn't* there? What if it stopped flowing? Her chest tightened and her whole body felt chilled. Was it her imagination or had the cart slowed? She drew in a gulp of air.

Beram shouted when both hopeepa slowed and turned their heads to look over their shoulders. Crystal bellowed, and Topaz twirled her tail in agitated loops. Lamiya grabbed Everand's arm, disconcerted by the inward look on his face.

His look became sharp. 'We're being followed. A cart approaches, coming fast.'

Why was he staring at her? A flush rushed up her neck and face. 'Lazuli?' At his nod, guilt flooded her. 'I'm sorry. Mookaite woke up just as I was sneaking out. She must have told him.'

Everand's expression softened. 'It seems the pacers refuse to be left out. Larimar and Mookaite are with him.' He looked as if he wanted to run his fingers through his hair in frustration. 'This complicates things, but we need to see the bridge.' He sighed. 'We might as well wait for them.'

Lamiya sat with her head bowed. He'd confided in her and she'd let him down. Tengar passed around water and pieces of fruit and she shook her head, her stomach churning. How could she regain his trust? Curse Lazuli! He meant well, she knew that. The sun grew warmer on her cheeks and the top of her head. *Pull yourself together.* Lazuli and Larimar mustn't realise this was anything other than a visit to see the race finish. Whirr crawled up to sit on her shoulder. Blinking, she pushed down the feeling that the three men with her emanated disapproval.

She sighed and turned to Everand. 'I'll travel in their cart and explain what we're doing.'

'Good. Then we can keep going.' He gave her a small smile. 'They might prove useful.'

Feeling forgiven, even though she hadn't earned it, she climbed down from the cart to stand on the grass. The plume of dust on the road formed into Lazuli's stags travelling at a fast canter. She fiddled with her fingers while she waited.

Lazuli pulled the hopeepa to a stop. The creatures were lathered, dark sweat along their necks and flanks, white froth at the edges of their mouths. Lamiya's lips compressed: Lazuli wouldn't usually treat his prized animals so.

Tengar stood up in the back of his cart. 'You want to see the race finish too?'

Lamiya took this as her cue and called up to Lazuli, 'Can I travel with you?'

'Do,' he said tersely.

She'd upset Lazuli as well. Mutely, she climbed up onto the seat next to him.

From the back, Mookaite mouthed 'sorry' at her, and said, 'We asked Melanite, but she's too busy finishing the team tunics. I said I'd fill her in later.'

The two carts moved off, and to deflect questions about why they hadn't been invited, Lamiya prattled on about how Tengar had asked her to come as the other glide. She explained that they were checking the river course and depth and familiarising themselves with the bridge and the finish line.

'We're lucky,' she finished, seeing Lazuli's shoulders relax as he accepted her explanation. 'The other two glides won't have this opportunity.' She waved her hands, as if enthused. 'By the time we reach here the boats might be quite separated. It'll be good to know where the channels and currents are.' The truth of this filled her. 'We didn't think to ask you pacers given it's the glide's role to chart the course.'

Lazuli looked thoughtful. 'Why is the traveller here? He won't be in a boat.'

Lamiya shrugged. 'I guess as the judge it's good for him to get a sense of the light and what he'll be able to see. The best position for him to stand in.' Lazuli looked sceptical. 'Come on,' she said with a teasing smile. 'It might be a close race.'

'You think?' said Mookaite. 'All you need do is follow in our wake!'

Larimar laughed and Lazuli grunted.

For a while, Lamiya watched the river continue to narrow until it was barely wide enough for four boats to race side by side. She hoped the glides from Riversea and Riverwood were skilled enough to keep a straight course. On the Riverwood side a variety of grasses swayed and rustled. What did those people do, other than hunt? The bank had a wild air to it, not grazed or cultivated in any way. She searched her memory for snippets she might have heard. The people of Riverwood were gathered in the north, where she'd heard there was a forest of massive trees. The vision she'd seen of the fierce hunters slipping between densely packed trunks seemed to confirm this. Quickly, she pushed this aside, not wanting to encourage any more ideas of being watched by the man with the face like an eagle.

Squinting against the rising light, she saw a darker structure rising from the blue of the river.

'The bridge,' she murmured.

Lazuli stirred. 'It is indeed a long race. May your endurance drills prove their worth.' He smiled wryly. 'I doubt Latog would've pushed us the way you have.'

Surprised, she looked at him.

His grey eyes bored into her as he murmured, 'Don't doubt yourself, Lamiya. You will glide us to victory.'

Words failing her, she leaned against him, allowing his warmth and strength to seep into her. It would be easy to be with this man. *To love this man.* So why did she hesitate? Was there something wrong with her? For so long she'd nursed her ailing parents, watching the life-light fading from their eyes, the skin shrinking on their bones. For an eternity she'd wandered the lake shore lamenting their passing, placing flowers and seeds at their grave stones, wanting their spirits to return from the lake mists to guide her. Grief rushed at her. Was she afraid to lose anyone else? Was that it?

Mookaite tapped her shoulder. 'We're here.'

Peering against the too-bright light, Lamiya looked around. Lazuli stopped the cart next to the other one, on a patch of longer grass so the hopeepa could graze. Several paces away an arched bridge of wood and stone reached away from the bank. Excitement bubbled within her. The bridge was massive! Larimar stared at the bridge with his mouth open while Lazuli tied ropes from a front foot of each hopeepa to a hind foot so the creatures couldn't wander. Mookaite linked an arm though hers and they walked together to where Beram, Tengar and Everand waited.

'We need to check three things,' said Tengar. 'The depth of the river, the flow of the currents, and the best place for our judge to stand.' He looked at Everand. 'Which do you want to do first?'

Everand was staring at the bridge with an unreadable expression. 'Let's go see the bridge first.'

Lamiya had a strong sense he wanted to check several other things not mentioned. Hovering close to him, she added, 'We need to check there's enough room to turn the boats after we've passed under the bridge.'

Everand glanced at her and then took such loping strides towards the bridge she was obliged to run to keep up. She nearly ran into him when he stopped suddenly at the base of the bridge. When he flinched at finding her so close, she gasped, 'Sorry!'

He raised an eyebrow and walked, not up onto the bridge as she'd expected, but towards the river, following the wall of the bridge as it rose steadily from the bank and reached out above the water.

'What's he doing?' hissed Lazuli, arriving beside her.

She shrugged, watching Everand fumble down the bank, stepping sideways so he didn't slip on the tufty grass.

'Let's follow.' Lazuli insisted on holding her hand as they slipped down the bank, until they reached the flat bed of stones at the base of the bridge.

Everand craned his head back to observe the underneath of the bridge. 'How is it made?' he asked.

'I don't know,' replied Lazuli. 'We need to ask Tengar.'

Intrigued, Lamiya watched Everand glance up at Tengar, still at the top of the bank, and then move to stand completely below the bridge, in its shadow. Reaching up, he put his hands flat against the underneath of the bridge. Beside her, Lazuli fidgeted impatiently.

Everand called out, 'Is this high enough for the boats to pass underneath? With a glide standing up?'

'Stupid question,' muttered Lazuli. 'Riverfall wouldn't suggest the race if it weren't. And we'll be in the middle of the river, where the bridge is higher.'

Lamiya felt she should defend Everand's question, but on balance she agreed with Lazuli. Looking at the traveller as he stood with his hands against the bridge, she concluded he was deflecting them and using his mage senses to check something else altogether. She said nothing.

Everand dropped his hands and stepped back to them. Looking at Lazuli, he said, 'How can we check the depth of the river here?'

That, Lamiya thought, was a good question. The watermark on the bridge was lower than usual, judging by the darker exposed struts, which would help the boats pass more comfortably underneath but could be a problem if there were rocks or other obstacles in the river channel.

'Could we walk in to test it?' asked Everand.

Lamiya stared. *They might prove useful*, he'd said. Was he manipulating Lazuli to wade into the river?

Lazuli squared his shoulders. 'Larimar and I will test it. Let me find a branch to probe with.'

Did she imagine the flicker of amusement that crossed Everand's very blue eyes?

'Can you do this while we check the top of the bridge?' He gave Lazuli a curt nod and started to climb back up to the road.

Lamiya touched Lazuli's elbow. 'Thanks. Look for mud banks and the way the current flows. Any advantage you can give us ...' Feeling guilty at the resigned look on Lazuli's face, she scrambled up the bank, passing Larimar on his way down with a long branch.

She followed Everand and Tengar onto the bridge. Both stamped on it, testing how robust the wooden slats were. The bridge was wide enough for a cart, and long given that the river was some seven hundred paces wide. There were no steps, just a gradual climbing arch, a flatter section in the middle, then a decline. The banks on both sides were high enough to keep the bridge well above any flooding, and gave ample space for boats to pass under.

What was Everand investigating? How could she help? She absorbed as much detail as she could. The pillars supporting the start of the arch of wooden slats were a mixture of stone and wood, held together by packed earth and the neat way they were jammed in. On the bridge itself, the slats were hewn trees cut in half lengthways, the flat sides forming the surface. These would have been heavy. How had they been put in place? Squatting, she ran her hand over a seam. The logs were held together with thick wooden pins, fixed into holes in the logs. Everand seemed to also be inspecting the structure closely.

Next, she drifted to the retaining side rails. A single wooden rail ran at waist height, supported by uprights three long paces apart. These were regular, giving a neat effect. She ran her hand along the railing. Made from a lighter, thinner wood, it would stop a person from inadvertently falling off the bridge but would break if hit with force. Like a bolting hopeepa.

Everand reached the middle of the bridge and stood looking down into the river. She leaned on the railing next to him. Below her feet was a circle of wood, like a sawn-off tree. Leaning over and looking under the bridge, she saw there were four massive tree trunks planted squarely in the river base to support the centre of the bridge. Below them, Lazuli was wading into the river holding the branch, with Larimar hanging on to the back of his tunic to steady him. By the way they had their feet planted and arms out she guessed the current was quite strong. She noticed that Mookaite was sitting on the grass at the base of the bridge, and Tengar and Beram had stopped halfway up the bridge and were looking at something upriver. She touched Everand's elbow.

'I need to ask you something,' he said, and the intensity of his look made her shiver. 'I have a plan forming.'

Her lips parted, but she couldn't decide what to ask. *You are way out of your depth.*

He looked towards the mountains, and then swung his eyes back. For a moment she saw regret. 'We need to go to the river source. You and me.'

Astonished, she stared. *Why? How? You and me? Will it be dangerous?*

'Yes, just you and me and it may be dangerous. I'll tell you more when I work it out.'

Had he just read her mind? She gulped, then a splash drew her attention to the river. Peering over the side of the bridge, she saw Lazuli floundering in the centre, his branch floating away and Larimar laughing. Alarmed, she called, 'Are you alright? Can you stand?' Beram and Tengar rushed to join her and they both laughed. 'It's not funny,' she snapped.

Tengar patted her shoulder and wiped tears from his eyes. 'It *is* funny. We'll go fish him out.' He and Beram trotted off down the bridge.

She leaned on the railing again while the others got soaked pulling Lazuli back to the bank. The least she could do was go down and check he wasn't hurt. Leaving Everand standing on the bridge, she strode down and waited at the top of the bank.

Mookaite stood up, brushing grass from her tunic. The four men toiled up the bank and came to a dripping stop. She couldn't see any blood or bruises on Lazuli, but he was remarkably wet. She arched an eyebrow and was rewarded with a lopsided grin.

'Right-hand pacer reports the river is deep enough.'

Each time they ceased laughing, Lazuli extended his report.

'I recommend we be in the lead. The current has a left-hand pull.'

'The fish are too slippery so we should focus on the race.'

'The water is cold. Avoid tipping at all costs.'

After a time, her sides ached. She hadn't laughed like this for a long time. Lazuli's teeth started to chatter and she said, 'We should get you into the sunshine.' Looking at Tengar, she asked, 'Is there more to see?'

At his shrug, she looked up. Silhouetted against the sky, Everand stood high up on the bridge. He faced north, towards the mountains and the river source. Her humour faded and she swallowed. Laughter, belonging, easy camaraderie and a known life. Or intrigue, adventure and perhaps love and a different life. *Which do you want?* Everand looked so alone she yearned to go to him. Her feet did not move.

Perhaps he prefers to be alone. Perhaps you don't have a choice.

181

CHAPTER TWENTY-THREE

On the way back, Everand eyed the rumps of the hopeepa. Crystal and Topaz were setting a steady pace, glad to be heading towards their stable and a reward of grains and hay. The slope of the creatures' backs was steep, stretching down from the bumpy point at the base of the long neck to the top of the tail. The back of the young dragon that Mage Beetal had once made him ride was also sloped, but he'd been able to tuck his legs in front of the wings for stability. It would be difficult to ride the hopeepa, but a cart would be noisy, slow and much harder to sneak out. It would be challenge enough to get to the river source, try to find the river dragon and return before the sun rose. What if he put a strap around the hopeepa's neck and hung onto that?

'What do you think?' asked Tengar.

Everand pushed aside his planning. 'About the bridge?' He needed to give honest advice to Atage. 'The bridge is at risk for two reasons. Disrupting the end of the long race would bring disrepute to Riverfall and could result in injury, perhaps death, to the paddlers.' He winced at the open horror on Tengar's and Beram's faces.

'And the second reason?' whispered Tengar.

Drawing a deep breath, Everand laid out his best guess. 'From what I see of the land and the way the river flows, if someone caused the bridge to collapse into the river it would reduce the supply of water south of that point.'

'But …' stammered Beram, his hands shaking on the reins, 'why would anyone do that?'

'That,' confessed Everand, 'is what I can't work out. The river would still flow, just less vigorously. Being above the bridge, Riverwood would be unaffected, and it would remove access to their side.' He rolled his shoulders to ease the tension. 'When was the bridge built? No-one has spoken about going across it.' He looked at Beram. 'Other than when you went to deliver the invitation to Riverwood and they stopped you from crossing. What was the original purpose of the bridge?'

Tengar ran his hands through his hair and scrubbed at his face. 'Good question. The early arrivals must have built it generations ago, but no-one has used it for as long as I can recall. Destroying the bridge would certainly disrupt the races, and would make it more difficult for Riverwood to trade with us. How can we protect the long race?'

Beram chimed in. 'I think maybe it is more about the long race and damage to our reputation. Although, a reduced flow of water … especially if it doesn't rain soon … would be a problem.'

Slowly, Everand said, 'I think Lyber and I should be the only ones to stand on the bridge. I need to be there to judge the position of the boats, and Lyber needs to keep score. Everyone else should be kept a safe distance away.' He waited while they absorbed this. 'Watch out for Atage. Keep strong and agile people near him. It was his idea for an all-province festival followed by discussions about trade. His vision, he leads.'

Tengar frowned. Beram looked too shaken for words.

'The only thing I can think of is that the concept of shared markets and a mingling of the provinces is what set this off. But who wants to prevent this and why …' He spread his hands. 'My best guess is that destroying the bridge would achieve the goals of disrupting the races and ruining the trade discussions. The reduced flow could damage Riverfall and Riverplain's future crops, especially if it continues to be dry. Riversea might be affected as well, but I don't know enough about that province.' On reflection, he didn't yet know enough about *any* of the provinces. How could he find out more, and faster? Mantiss was expecting a comprehensive report.

Rubbing at his jaw, Tengar said, 'If we had to, with much effort and time, we could rebuild the bridge. But better that it remains intact and the races pass without incident.'

'Agreed.' Everand said, knowing they wouldn't like his next suggestion. 'On race day, you need men with weapons near the bridge, as well as placed at intervals along the bank.' Seeing the deep frowns on their faces, he added more gently, 'You can conceal the weapons underneath cloth so as not to worry the crowds. But you need them close by, in case.'

'I'll tell Atage,' said Tengar stiffly.

'How can we train people in time?' Beram looked upset.

'It's not ideal,' Everand admitted. 'But your people are fit and strong. You've already shown you can protect yourselves against the moths. You just need to be more prepared.' He thought of the jumping fish, and the possibility of eagles as spies. 'Can you make spears as well as staves? Something you can throw. And arrows or something to hurl stones at birds?'

'Like a slingshot?' asked Tengar.

Beram nodded. 'That could work. We can model them off the ones the children use for play, but make them bigger, stronger. I'll organise pouches of good-sized rocks.'

Everand had no idea what a slingshot was, but they had at least grasped the idea. Their discomfort was evident in their tense jaws and shoulders, and he felt sad. This should be a time of joy for the town, not anxiety and fear of possible violence. But he couldn't be everywhere at once, so they needed to be ready to help. 'I'll keep trying to find out more,' he said. 'I have some ideas to pursue.'

He had to move faster. If magic was involved, even his powers might not be sufficient to protect them. Time was running out. If the river dragon was possibly the end target, he and Lamiya should go to the river source *this* dark-fall.

Squashing the wriggle of anxiety in his stomach, he said to Tengar, 'I'll go to the river source this moon-rise. I need to go fast, and in secret.' He focused on Beram's face. 'Do you have a harness so I can ride Crystal?'

'I'll ask Persaj.' Beram looked troubled. 'Or Lazuli may have a harness.'

Everand frowned. 'Don't ask either of them. Leave me to work it out. Tell Atage, but no-one else.'

All the way back to the town, his niggling feeling of risk refused to subside.

✿

Mantiss let himself in to his dome. Delma, the woman in charge of his kitchen, hurried out into the hallway to ask if he needed anything.

'Bring me a glass of wine and a light snack, if you would,' Mantiss requested. 'I have some reading to do.' He sat at the dining table to wait for the wine and food. The setting sun was spectacular, hurling splashes of reds and golds across the sky. Anticipation coursed through him. He recalled enjoying the next part of the notebook, which was about the foundation of the new Guild. Mage Lapemis had been an insightful and skilled leader.

'Here you are, sir.' Delma placed a glass of white wine in front of him, followed by a small plate of oven-crisped strips of bread with fish paste smeared on top.

'Very kind, one of my favourites.' The cook beamed at him before striding away. He waited until he heard the kitchen door swing closed, then headed to his reading alcove, where

185

he ate the snacks and drank the wine before retrieving the notebook.

After carefully wiping his fingers on the small cloth provided, he opened the notebook.

From the scrawlings of Mage Lapemis

Trekking west

The others cheered when we rose up out of the water and staggered to the shore. The sun was low in the sky, for much time had elapsed. Everyone crowded around me, admiring the magical stone and its beauty.

'We must move,' I said. 'The red creature is merely stunned, and we know not where the blue one is.'

Disappointment on their faces, the others gathered up their cloaks and our meagre supply of food and water. Carefully, I wrapped the stone in a spare cloak and Aclys gave me his cloak to make a sling to carry it in.

Walking into the setting sun, its crimson-gold hues in our faces, we followed the beautiful turquoise lake and then a shallow tributary until we came to the broad river. We encountered no sign of the blue beast. I dipped my hands into the river and sensed traces of the blue beast passing, heading north, against the flow. Lifting my eyes, I regarded the hazy grey-purple mountains in the distance. Was there another lake at the source, where the creature might settle and lay its eggs? If so, we should continue due west and put as much distance between us and the rivers and lakes as possible.

I conveyed this to the others, and we agreed we should cross the river. The beasts were adept swimmers, but would be slow and cumbersome on land. Perhaps they could not survive for long out of water.

We divided ourselves into groups and translocated across the wide river to untamed grassland on the western bank.

Scanning south and north, I could find no sign of a bridge or any natural crossing point. The river remained wide, at least seven hundred paces across, with twists and meanders. When the light faded and the moon's face was rising into the darkening sky, we stopped, hoping we had made sufficient distance between us and the river. We ate and slept, resolving to continue west when it grew light. In the deep, still darkness I woke and lay listening to the chirps of insects and the hoots of a night bird.

Hearing the distant roar of the red beast echoing across the lake, I pulled the cloak-wrapped stone to my chest, feeling the disturbance within it. Was the stone responding to the beast's rage? Did they have an unbreakable connection and the red beast would know where we took it, despite our efforts and distance? It occurred to me that we should wipe the memory of the theft of the stone from the humans' minds, and not pass this knowledge down to the next generation of mages. My mind roamed, seeking an alternative, credible explanation for how we had come by it.

Sleep eluded me and I watched the first rays of light eke into the sky above the hills.

A new location

I roused the others and we continued. For a full sun we walked west across wild grassy plains, and hiked over small ranges of hills. Observing that there were no tributaries feeding into the river on the trajectory we took, I held our course.

We camped again at dark-fall. When their bellies were full and the humans had lain down to sleep, Aclys and I gently probed their minds and removed the memories of the green river serpent and of us diving into the lake and returning with the stone. I regretted the deceit, but Aclys agreed we should take the opportunity to conceal our transgression. Rearranging my small bundle of clothes and books, I hid the stone in with them.

No longer able to hear the beast, I slept better. When I stirred at the first hint of sunlight, I felt in my bones that we were close to our destination. We moved on and when the sun reached its zenith, we ambled down a gentle slope of hills into a wide plateau. The soil looked rich and arable. To the northern end were crags of enormous granite boulders, which gave way to tall, dense conifers. The land curved uphill, the forest growing denser and darker. We were a long way from the river and any tributaries.

In the centre of the plateau was a flat, marshy area, fed by an underground spring. Kneeling, I scooped up a handful of water. It smelled fresh and I risked a mouthful. The taste was clean and hinted at sweet.

'Here,' I said. 'Let's build our new Guild here.'

We walked the flat area, deciding where the boundaries of our new Guild would be. Assuming that over time we would return to our former status, we planned for a population of a hundred mages and twice that of humans. To the west lay steep headlands and a fierce drop to the sea and lethal rocks. To the south lay open, grassy plains and the soil looked less arable. The east was similar, and we now had two full suns of hiking between us and the river. Before the granite and woods to the north was a rocky, redder soil and sparse vegetation. Beyond the forest the land continued to rise, stretching towards the hazy mountains.

Making the spring the feature piece for gardens and wells for ready access to water, we planned outwards from there for tall domes of stone. We envisaged a library with classrooms, an administration building, a meeting hall and domes for residences. Immediately to the north of these, we needed houses for the humans with space designated for crops around them.

We used our magic to fell trees from the forest, expanding our line of visibility to the north, and translocated the trunks to where the humans could then build their houses. For our own domes, we found veins of white marble stretching down into the headland overlooking the sea. We extracted slabs of this and translocated them ready to build our domes. Fortunately, Nactus and two of the male humans were familiar with construction design and knew how to build in plumbing, light and ventilation.

The women found bunya and other small animals in the forest for food. There was also a variety of lizards and insects, particularly bees, beetles and moths. Aclys tried to teach Carlias how to replicate a shiny orange beetle and instead, Carlias made it the size of a cart-horse. When we stopped laughing, Carlias approached the massive beetle and jumped onto its back. He found it amenable to instruction, and lo, we had a new means of transportation that would help conserve our power. We put Carlias in charge of breeding and training transport beetles.

Construction progressed well, and the heat of the harvest season faded into red-leaf season. We decreed that the start of harvest season was the beginning of the New Guild season-cycle one.

A new Guild forms

By default, as Head of the Guild, I was in charge of the star-stone. I kept it concealed for twenty suns, and then claimed that I had found it hidden in a pocket of air within the bank of the eternal spring. The humans readily accepted this event. Hemiapsis, whom we put in charge of scribing the history of the Guild for future generations, collaborated with me and we composed a delightful tale of its discovery.

When I drew it out of its protective cloak, the stone responded to me, the blues becoming more prominent. It reminded me of the precious stone we called opal. After a time, it allowed me to reach my intent inside it and take small amounts of power to augment my own. This extra power I then passed on to the others. It enabled us to keep the pace of our construction work.

Becoming bolder, I asked the stone about its origin. I received images of an enormous cradle-shaped shell in the depths of the cave in the turquoise lake. I was shown tears of the red serpent dropping into the base of the shell, glinting with colour and crystallising into a small, translucent orb. Over time, the tiny orb grew and the serpent licked at it with her forked tongue, teasing out the points and helping it to transform into this magnificent star. The stone conveyed the term 'dragon' to me. Sadness whirled inside me when I realised the stone was born from the tears and innate power of the red dragon. Small wonder the creature had protected it.

Fear edged into my mind. Why had the dragon creature created it? Was it to do with the eggs, and was that why it was nestled among them? Surely, the dragon could not let us keep it. The magnitude of what we had done weighed heavily upon me. I consoled myself that the stone had accepted me, and was prepared to yield power to help our cause.

Carefully, carefully I went, a little light contact at a time, perceiving that I must retain the stone's trust. If Notechis or Nactus approached it, the red hues swirled and a sulky vibe emanated from it. I developed code words, murmuring 'lake-cave-star-opal' when I placed my palms upon it. The stone liked this, warming under my hands and responding ever more quickly.

One dark-fall, I jerked out of a deep sleep, an image of the stone flashing red behind my eyelids. With a gasp, I perceived a shadowy figure hunched over where I had placed the stone in a nook in the rocks next to me. I scrambled up, and a shrouded figure turned to face me: Nactus, with the stone gripped between his hands.

'Why should you be the only one to wield it?' he hissed, spittle forming on his lips.

Alarmed, I eyed the red streaks building inside the stone. Without the code words, Nactus could not access its power.

'Tell me how to use it! We should take more power.' Nactus' twisted face was lit with an eerie red glow.

In that instant, I perceived the danger attached to the stone. Its power could be used for good — or evil. Forcing calm, I stretched out my hands. 'Give it to me. See the lurid red it has become? It will not respond to you.'

Nactus clutched the stone to his chest, the lust for power glowing in his eyes.

Fear trickled into me. We needed a proper hierarchy and a set of rules immediately; clear order and protocol must be established. And once we had taken what power we needed to establish ourselves, the stone should be removed from sight and temptation. I kept my hands held out, waiting.

The stone pulsed with red light and heat, and suddenly Nactus handed it to me. The lust fading from his eyes, he turned on his heel and strode into the gloom. Shaken, I caressed the stone and murmured to it until it resumed its tranquil blue colours, like the lake glinting in sunlight.

I resolved to build a secure place to hide it under our new Great Hall. I further resolved that the code words would be known only to the incumbent Head of the Guild, who was to be elected by the mages. We would form councils, like those we had before, and a new law would be that the stone could only be raised by agreement of the entire Inner Council, and under the authority of the Head of the Guild.

So far, we had not seen or heard anything of the red or blue creatures. But I worried.

The more established we became, the easier we would be to find.

Mantiss snapped the notebook closed, wishing he hadn't finished his glass of wine. He concealed the notebook. The sky outside had grown shades of maroon and deep grey, and the orbs in the wall sconces had flickered into life, casting soft, warm light.

He breathed out: three hundred season-cycles later, the Guild had not been approached by any river dragons. Lapemis had wisely created Guild Rules Nine and Ten, which precluded mages from travelling beyond the granite wall, and forbade others from breaching the wall. No mage had come across or been seen by any river dragon, and no outsiders knew anything about the Guild.

By the stars and moon, let the creatures have died and no eggs hatched! What were the odds? Only one egg had been left with the red dragon, but the blue dragon Lapemis had let pass had at least one egg in her belly. If the Staropal was linked to the nurturing of the eggs, which Lapemis had alluded to, then if fate favoured them these dragons were now extinct.

But then why had Beram's people named the river Dragonspine River?

A shiver crawled across his nape.

CHAPTER TWENTY-FOUR

The time until dusk passed slowly. Everand walked around the courtyards observing the preparations for the festival. A group of women sat in a large circle on the grass making cloth tents and he admired their capable stitching. Nearby, another group was spinning the long strands of thread ready. Accepting the offer of loaves and juice, he watched a while longer and realised the women were sewing together panels of blue and gold cloth, the Riverfall team colours. Eyeing the piles of waiting cloth, he saw these were divided into orange, green and red, another of white, beige and pale blue, and another of grey and brown bolts. On asking, he was told the tents would be placed along the riverbank.

An array of mouth-watering aromas wafted from the trader domes. Each trader he asked explained about the special foods for the festival. Kunzite, delighted to see him and with much smiling and waving of hands, said she was making the sweetbreads to be offered to the river dragon. Zink and Acim were preparing leaf-wrapped fish fillets, seasoned with special grains to symbolise a strong growing season and harvest.

He found the Riverplain team gathered outside their dome, resting. After a brief greeting to all, he whispered to Lamiya to stay awake and wait for his call. Walking away, he felt Lazuli's glare burning into his back.

Next, he went to the hopeepa dome and ascertained that Persaj had made a rudimentary harness. He persuaded Persaj to show him how the harness fitted and hoped he'd remember how to attach the straps. It didn't look very secure. Crystal revelled in the attention, licking his hands repeatedly. Persaj fed her titbits as a reward, and he made a note to bring more to make sure she would be happy to go out alone.

Before he headed to Beram's dome, he scrounged food so he could avoid the sun-fade meal and rest until dark. Beram lit the small heat and light dome that Mookaite had made, and Everand lay on his back on his mattress. Ignoring the blanket of fatigue that settled over his limbs, he went over his plan. What could go wrong? What if he and Lamiya were detected? What if his theory was wrong? It was a wild theory disconcertingly proposed by his heart. Beram returned and collapsed onto his mattress and, judging by his deep breathing, fell asleep straightaway.

Everand waited until the crack at the base of the curtain took on a pale silver hue, indicating the moon was rising. He slid from his mattress, swallowed a mug of water and slipped out, murmuring the spell of invisibility. Taking long strides, he soon reached Mookaite's dome and hesitated outside. A spark of energy alerted him just before Lamiya pushed out through the curtain. How did she know he was there?

'Everand?' she called softly, looking right at him even though he was invisible. His skin tingled: her ability to sense others was exceptional. His wild theory might just work.

'Here,' he mumbled, reaching out to take her hand. 'Come, we'll both be unseen.' She flashed a grin at him, her warm hand slipping into his as he made her invisible too.

They crept to the hopeepa dome, her excitement and nervous energy tingling through her hand. At the entry, he used his will to ease the wooden bars from the gate and swing the gate ajar. He let go of her hand and made them visible so as not to spook Crystal. When Lamiya reached for the candle lantern hung on a rafter he shook his head and created a floating ball of silver light about the size of his hand.

Lamiya's eyes glinted silver. 'Pretty,' she breathed. 'Can you turn it orange?'

He did, and was rewarded with a gasp of delight. So far so good, she didn't seem to be afraid of his powers. Her amusement would fade if he had to defend the two of them. *Perhaps that would be a good thing. She needs to see who you really are. Then see if she still likes you.* A bubble of melancholy threatened, so he focused on the immediate task and reached into the feed area to extract the riding harness.

She raised an eyebrow. 'We ride?' At his nod, she added, 'Together? One hopeepa?'

He spread his hands. 'Only one harness.'

Wordlessly, she took the harness and slid the bar across the stall. Crystal and Topaz blinked sleepily against the light from the hovering ball that he had restored to silver. He fed Crystal a slice of fruit and she lowered her head so they could slip the head harness and reins on. Lamiya deftly attached all the straps. She must have seen this done before. *With Lazuli?* She led Crystal from the stall and, again invisible, they walked soundlessly to the gate, where he swung it inward enough for them to slink through. Outside, he nudged the gate closed and eased the bolts back into place.

'How will we get on?' He detected the smile in Lamiya's question.

Curses! They should have got on inside the stable where they could have used the stall railings. Looking around did not produce any convenient rocks or logs. Remembering how he had cupped his hands so Elemar could mount his travel beetle, he stepped beside Crystal and cupped his hands ready. 'You first.'

Unerringly, she put a hand on his invisible shoulder, stepped on his palms and swung up onto Crystal's back. *Impressive.* But how would he get on?

Lamiya gripped his arm in a strong hold and said, 'On three, jump. One, two, three.' She gave a mighty tug and he found himself tipping over Crystal's back. Shaken by her strength, he swung his leg over and sat behind her. Crystal took a few dancing steps and he sent a calming nudge at her.

Lamiya prodded Crystal with her heels and the hopeepa set off at a brisk walk. Everand concentrated on balancing. The fur was slippery; he'd have to put his arms around Lamiya. *Just as he had done with Elemar so many moons ago.* Stealing his arms around Lamiya, he hung onto the thick strap looped around the base of the hopeepa's neck, since she had a firm grasp on the reins. Warmth spread down the front of him when she snuggled back into his chest.

'Hold tighter.' She kicked Crystal into a trot. He bounced inexorably to the left until Lamiya's sharp elbow in his ribs pushed him back upright. She kicked Crystal and the hopeepa changed gait into the long lope. 'Better?'

'Yes,' he said, wishing he could bury his face in her hair and the back of her neck. 'You've ridden before?' Some conversation might help keep his mind focused.

'Once. Lepid wanted his stag to outrun Lazuli's and thought a lighter rider might help.'

'Did it?' he asked, intrigued at the idea of racing the hopeepa.

'Lazuli was furious,' she said around a smile.

She was brave; he had to give her that. Getting on a hopeepa and racing it at full tilt wasn't something that appealed. But then he wasn't the one who stood up at the back of a racing boat, either. Had she really almost changed the boat into a dragon?

'What did you want to talk about?' she asked.

Forcing himself to relax and sway in time to the hopeepa's strides, Everand asked, 'At the end of the first race, did something unusual happen?'

Lamiya wriggled. 'Let me ask you, what did you see?'

He'd wanted to hear her say it. Slowly, he said, 'For a breath, I saw a real dragon emerging from your boat.'

Her ribs expanded as she drew in a deep breath. 'I worried I imagined it, but I felt the dragon move beneath me.' She gave a small laugh. 'I didn't tell the team because they would've said it was to do with hitting my head.' When he didn't speak for several strides, she asked, 'Everand? What does it mean?'

Should he wait until they dismounted before he told her? Shadows lurked, gleaming black and silver under the moon steadily climbing its way to full height. Ahead, the arch of the bridge rose on their left. According to Beram, that meant they were halfway to the southern edge of Dragon Lake.

'Everand?' Lamiya prompted.

'I think it means you can call more than birds.' He frowned. 'Speaking of which, where is your bird?'

'I left him with Mookaite. Birds sleep after dark-fall,' said Lamiya. After a beat she added, 'And in case there is danger.'

'Wise. When we get to the lake, I'll explain.'

She nodded, her hair moving against his chin.

The bridge rose high on their left, the moonlight reflecting off the pebble paths, one leading to its base and the other feeding away to the right. 'Beram said we must follow the other road,' he murmured. 'The crops will stop and there'll be open land until we come to a smaller bridge over the northern tributary, but still in Riverfall.'

Lamiya pulled the rein to direct Crystal. At a brisk lope, they traversed open land with tufty grass and clumps of bushes. The scents changed to dry grasses and distant woody aromas. Insects chirruped and clicked and he felt the space around him, the air moving across his arms, legs and the back of his neck. The ground began to rise and Crystal slowed to a walk. Everand relaxed the spell of invisibility. They were a long way from any people and he wanted to see Lamiya's reactions. Each time Crystal hesitated, Lamiya nudged her onwards.

The path veered to follow a narrower arm of the river. Silvery tendrils of mist rose from the river nestled below the banks. To his right, the landscape grew dark with the shapes of hills. Crystal stopped.

'The smaller bridge,' said Lamiya. 'We should get off and check it's safe.'

Everand stiffly hefted his leg over Crystal's rump and slid down. The ground jarred his legs and feet. Lamiya jumped lightly down and pulled the reins over Crystal's head. Together, they stood at the start of the narrow, flat, wooden bridge. It was far less imposing than the other one and lacked the reassuring railings.

'Let's lead Crystal over,' suggested Lamiya. Without waiting for him, she tugged the reins and, after a bellow, Crystal followed her onto the bridge.

Everand followed her steps, keeping to the centre of the bridge. Mist wreathed around him, the chill suggesting the water was cold. A shiver crossed the back of his neck and he hurriedly finished crossing the bridge and stood quietly. 'Do you sense anything?'

Lamiya gave him a sharp look, but closed her eyes. After a couple of breaths she said, 'I feel uneasy, but nothing specific.'

'Let's walk from here,' Everand said, not wanting to have to focus on staying mounted.

'Good idea,' said Lamiya, setting off again. 'It'll get steeper and rockier. Not good for Crystal's hooves.'

Everand caught up to her and slipped the hopeepa a slice of fruit. The moon was at full height, beaming silver rays down on them. They must hurry. He marched rapidly through scrubby grasses and bushes. Ahead, the ground rose steeply and fed into the base of a mountain. Higher up, the rocky walls glinted with a silver hue, as if lit up from below. Was that a reflection from the lake? The rushing noise was probably not wind in leaves but the waterfall. The footing became difficult, the ground less even and strewn with larger pebbles and rocks, and the path narrowed.

'When we get to the lake,' he said, 'we need to find the dragon.'

'Mizuchi?' exclaimed Lamiya. 'The river dragon?' She tripped on a rock and stumbled.

He grabbed her elbow. 'I'm hoping you can call it.' He kept hold of her elbow since she seemed intent on looking at his face rather than where she should put her feet.

'Call the dragon?' she repeated. 'Why?'

Everand hesitated. How could he explain his wild theory? 'Because we want the dragon on *our* side.'

Lamiya stopped dead. 'What?' She turned pale, a ghostly sheen by moonlight, and her eyes opened wide. 'Oh. I see.'

Admiring her quick intelligence, Everand said gently, 'We must call the dragon before this unseen enemy does. You have great skill.' He smiled.

'If you alone can summon your boat's dragon, let's see if together we can reach Mizuchi.'

CHAPTER TWENTY-FIVE

The path twisted around larger rocks, ever climbing, and Lamiya dropped back to walk behind Everand when the path narrowed further. Crystal stopped frequently, planting her hooves and shaking her head. Lamiya scanned the terrain stretching away from the trail but there was nowhere suitable to leave the hopeepa.

'Perhaps there'll be some grass near the lake,' Everand said after the tenth time she'd tugged Crystal onwards.

Lamiya nodded. Her head was starting to throb, but she ignored it. The reflected light was growing brighter and the constant churning and rushing of water was loud in her ears. Ahead, the path rose to meet a steep lip of rock, which blocked the view of the sky. Dark water slid down the rocky face, flowing into the river below. Everand shivered and suddenly looked up.

'I felt it too,' whispered Lamiya, a tremor chasing across her nape at the sense of being watched. She hurriedly pushed away the image forming of the dark-haired man with the face like an eagle.

When Everand reached for her hand, she grasped his. Crystal tugged back on the rope and Lamiya clucked her tongue reassuringly. Soon, the path climbed sharply and disappointment flashed through her when Everand let go of her hand and leaned forward to manage the slope. Behind her, Crystal scattered stones, scrabbling for purchase.

The large muscles of her legs ached and her feet felt bruised, but she pushed on. Sweat trickled down her cheeks and back, despite the chill air. Spray sprinkled them from the water running over the rocky lip to feed into the river proper below. Gamely, she kept up, taking short breaths. At the crest of the rocky lip, she stopped when Everand bent over and resorted to all fours to crawl over the ledge.

Scrambling over after him, she nearly pitched onto her face when the ground abruptly levelled. She stood beside Everand, drawing deep breaths. Ahead, in a wide crater, a large circular lake gleamed blackly, silver ripples glinting across the surface. In the centre was a dappled reflection of the moon high above. Against the deep black backdrop of mountain, a curtain of silver water fell, twisting, tumbling and splashing until it plummeted into the lake. It looked like a hoard of falling stars with rainbow glints.

'Holy water spirits!' she gasped. 'It's magnificent!' The noise was like a dragon roaring, and even Everand looked awed as he stood staring and breathing hard.

With a great clattering, Crystal jumped over the lip. Lamiya fumbled for Everand's hand and clasped her fingers tightly around his. 'I've always wanted to see Mizuchi Falls.' She squeezed his fingers. 'So, this is the place of the spirit of the Riverfall boat we seek to beat.'

He gave her a wry look. 'Back to boats already?'

The warmth of his hand around hers felt good as he scanned the lake shore. The scrabbly ground tipped downwards until it met the water's edge. The shore stretching towards Riverwood was too dark to see properly. Instinct guided her to look to the east, and she roamed her eyes along the shore. There, a narrow band of pebbles, almost a path, followed the rim of the water. It looked as if it went all the way to the cascading waterfall. 'I think that way,' she said.

'Are you sure?' his whisper came in the dark.

She nodded. 'Feels right.'

'You lead,' he murmured.

She gripped his fingers and then let go and set off at a steady stride along the shore with her heart thudding against her breastbone. The pebbles glowed at her feet, magnifying the moonbeams. A shudder travelled through her, but this didn't feel like a place of evil. More of … expectation. Was there a dragon? Would it come? She half-closed her eyes, trusting her instinct to guide her. Near the waterfall the water would be too choppy to see into properly, but her heart led her that way.

The thunder of the waterfall dominated her thoughts. She imagined an open-mouthed dragon roaring, and shook her head. *Focus!* It seemed an eternity that she followed the glowing pebbles, misty spray from the waterfall tickling her face and arms. Without thought, her feet stopped and she faced across the lake. The enormous curtain of water fell from on high. She could stare for a lifetime into the tumbling, dancing columns of water. When Everand gently tapped her shoulder, she released a sigh and brought her mind back to their task.

In front of her, small waves lapped darkly at the shore. The water felt unerringly deeper, like a pond within the lake. She took a step, feeling Everand follow. *He senses it too.* Unspeaking, she stepped towards the water. Crouching down, she dipped the tips of her fingers in. Cold seeped up her fingers and she flexed them.

Moving to stand behind her, Everand put his hands on her shoulders. 'Sense the dragon, Lamiya. Imagine Mizuchi in his true form.'

Warmth flowed through his hands into her shoulders. The moon gazed down like a cool silver disc. Lamiya felt tranquillity steal over her; the ripples in the water flattened and the sounds of the waterfall retreated. Vapours of mist writhed, and from the depths she perceived an energy. When she exhaled, mist rose in front of her.

202

The air grew chill and the stillness became unbearable, as if time had ceased. She shivered, and Everand leaned more heavily on her shoulders. *Be brave. You can do this.* She reached within for her calling ability and pushed her fingers deeper into the water, allowing it to lap at her wrists.

'Mizuchi! I seek audience.' Her call reverberated through the water. *'Great Mizuchi, we would honour you. We would race against your might and glory.'* Images of the boats flitted into her mind, the paddlers striving for speed, the wash rushing along the sides of the boats, the drums beating.

'Show him Flight,' Everand prompted.

She adjusted her image and the orange, green and red boat flickered between the shape of a boat to glimpses of a scaled dragon ploughing through the water. The lake water held its breath.

Underneath the reflection of the moon, out deep, the surface bubbled. Ripples spread out in a circle. A tremor passed through her, then the image of the two racing boats reappeared, both shimmering as if two dragons raced and played. The orange, green and red dragon drew ahead and sashayed her tail at the blue and gold one. There was a splash in the centre and more ripples sped away from the spot. She wriggled her fingers in the water. *'Mizuchi, come to meet us.'*

The lake became a flat black mirror and the reflections of the faraway stars winked a pale white-silver. Lamiya stared at the dark water, willing the dragon to come; wanting it to come. She could do this. She *must* do this. Everand's mind subtly mingled with hers, bent on appealing to the dragon. The pride and joy of the Riverfall team etched into the idea and distant echoes of 'Yosh!' echoed in her head. The deeper water was moving like an unseen current, although the surface gave nothing away.

A strong sense of presence arrived. In the water below her fingers, two enormous red-gold eyes opened. She gasped, unable to look away. The eyes came closer to the surface, and behind them was a long, blue-scaled head, flaring dark-red nostrils, gold whiskers fanning out. The nose broadened to a wide brow above the eyes, a golden mane and sharp gold horns rising. The dragon was massive!

Lamiya hurriedly ordered her scrambled thoughts. '*Mighty Mizuchi! Our boats pale in your magnificence.*'

The dragon's whiskers flicked forward. The hypnotic eyes were pulling her into the tall dark abyss of black pupils, surrounded by fiery red-gold embers of eye. A tendril of doubt grew in her chest: how could they master such a powerful beast?

A large object hurtled past her vision and splashed into the water where the dragon's head was, shattering the image. Lamiya flinched at the frigid water showering over her. The air filled with an enraged roar, throbbing around her. Disoriented, she blinked as another head-sized object hurtled into the water. The area bubbled and roiled and the presence of dragon evaporated. An ice-cold chill passed across the top of her head.

The muscles in her shoulder twinged when Everand hauled her to her feet, spun her around and crushed her against his chest. His lips moved rapidly and she gasped as a protective shield, glinting with myriad colours, took form around them. Large rocks smashed into the shield and tumbled down around it, cracking when they reached the ground. She burrowed into Everand's chest, leaving his arms free to protect them. The dragon! Had it gone? Disappointment flooded her. More rocks crashed down. The shield trembled, and she felt Everand's body tingle as he fed more strength into it.

More rocks the size of her head boomed against his shield. She swallowed, averting her mind's eye from the gory idea of what would happen to *her* head if one connected. Was Crystal safe? The hopeepa had probably bolted. After a pause, more rocks thudded into the shield. Where were they coming from? She turned around and nudged her back against Everand's chest so she could look out.

'What can you see?' Everand's words buzzed against her back.

She looked up and saw the large raptors circling. 'Eagles!' she exclaimed. 'I see three eagles.'

'Eagles? Carrying the rocks?' said Everand. 'That explains the lull, when they swoop to get more rocks.'

'Is this a good thing?' she asked.

'Yes.' He sounded relieved. 'We're dealing with this enemy who can influence creatures. I can deflect eagles.'

Lamiya chewed her lip. How did he plan to deflect the birds? Would he kill them?

'Tell me when they approach,' he muttered into her hair. 'I'll have to drop the shield momentarily and this might be loud.'

Her heart raced. Just how much power did he have? 'There!' She pointed up and ahead, above the lake. 'One ahead, two flanking.'

Three dark forms flew swiftly in, moonbeams glimmering off the tips of large, outstretched wings. She felt Everand raise his right hand and a bolt of crackling red energy shot into the air. The lead bird banked with a shrill screech and the two behind faltered. Two more crackling bolts of energy surged out and the rocks crashed short as the birds wheeled away with sharp cries.

Lamiya waited tensely. Could the birds communicate with their master? What would they do next? What would Everand do next? The eagles circling above had stocky bodies and an impressive wingspan. The moonlight showed dark plumage around the head and back and a paler colour along the neck and chest. The yellow talons were sharp and cruel. The lead bird screeched. 'They're angry,' she said. 'Be ready.'

She swallowed, feeling him flexing his fingers and breathing in energy. The three birds spaced out in a circle above to create multiple targets. 'They come!' she called the instant the birds wheeled inwards and dived at them.

Everand pushed down on her shoulders, forcing her to her knees, and swung both arms upwards and outwards in a hurling motion. There was a loud crackle and three thuds and the birds plummeted like the rocks they had dropped. He'd killed them! She gave a cry of distress when their bodies crashed to the ground.

Yanking her back to her feet, he said, 'They're only stunned. We must flee.'

She wiped a hand across her eyes, relieved, although perhaps she shouldn't be. The eagles could have killed them. Everand grabbed her hand and tugged her after him, heading back towards the rocky lip. What about the dragon? They weren't going to try again? Where was Crystal? Her legs felt far away and she broke into a staggering jog to keep up.

The back of her neck and shoulderblades prickled with foreboding. The eagles had been stopped, but what of whoever was commanding them? They were so vulnerable out here alone, no wonder Everand hurried. As she jogged, she looked at his tense shoulders and realised he'd also revealed his powers to this enemy.

Just as they reached the rocky lip and prepared to scramble down, Crystal loped out of the darkness. 'Whoa!' Lamiya put up a hand to stop the hopeepa before she knocked them down the ledge. Crystal slid to a stop and licked Everand's fingers. He gave her a treat and patted her nose. He was an enigma, so gentle with the hopeepa but so powerful. *Powerful enough to kill with a wave of a hand.* She shuddered and her legs started to shake with fatigue.

Sitting down on the rocky lip, she dangled her legs over the edge. Just a brief rest before what promised to be a rushed and anxious journey back. Her hair clung dankly to her neck. She must look a sight. Everand gave her a startled look and then eased down beside her.

'Are you alright?' he asked, his voice tender.

She nodded. Her instincts were shrieking about wasting time but she needed a moment to absorb what had happened. 'We saw the dragon.' The image of the massive beast hovered in her mind. They had called it! She *had* helped him.

With a sigh, he put an arm around her shoulders. 'You did well. Really well.'

Twisting sideways, she threw her arms around his neck. 'I can't believe we saw it.' Excitement chased away her fatigue and she beamed up at him. He turned to face her and put both arms around her waist so they could sit balanced. His eyes looked wide and dark, and her heart beat more quickly. Would he kiss her? He looked as if he might. She gulped, her heart racing. He lifted a finger and gently caressed her cheek. She felt her lips part, and with a moan he tipped his head down and put his mouth over hers. Yes! She melted against him, her lips searching. His lips melded with hers, and she savoured his soft touch. The tip of her tongue brushed the tip of his tongue and he groaned.

Disappointment filled her when he pulled away and rested his forehead against hers. 'Lamiya, Lamiya.' His voice sounded croaky. 'We must leave this place.'

When she sat back with a sigh, he took both of her hands in his and brushed the back of them with his lips. 'We must hurry. We must be safe.' He conjured a smile and his words sent a thrill through her.

'I must protect our dragon-caller.'

CHAPTER TWENTY-SIX

The treacherous path gave Lamiya no time to think. Busy worrying about where to place her next step, she followed Everand as he slipped and slid down from the rocky ledge. A whirlpool of emotions lurked, but she forced her mind to focus. Everand suddenly stopped, standing sideways on the slope to keep his balance, and she nearly fell into his arms again when Crystal nudged her in the back.

'This is taking too long. The moon already wanes.' A deep frown pulled at his forehead. 'Not ideal, but I've already revealed my power so I might as well use some more.' He held out a hand. 'Bring Crystal closer. I'll take us to the bridge.'

The bridge? Unsure what he meant, Lamiya gripped his hand firmly. He smiled down at her, but he looked tired. As soon as she'd tugged Crystal's rope to bring the hopeepa nearer, Everand's mouth moved with silent words. Her whole body began to tingle and she gasped. *Hold tight. Keep calm*, sounded in her head and the air shimmered around her. She felt herself lifted, flying, and dark air rushed past. With a cry, she grabbed at Everand's arms. Something thumped her calf and she realised Crystal was kicking out in fear. She tugged the rope and murmured, 'Steady.' Cold air whistled around her and tears blurred her vision.

Hard ground slapped the soles of her feet and her legs buckled. Firm pressure on her elbows held her upright. Opening her eyes, she swayed. They were standing at the base of the *first* bridge. They were halfway back in the blink of an eye! Crystal gave an enormous shake, like she would to rid her body of dust or insects. Everand patted Crystal's neck and leaned against her large shoulder. Alarm rose within Lamiya. He looked as if he was leaning against the hopeepa because his legs wouldn't support him. He was drained and trying to hide it from her.

'Are you alright?' Her legs refused to take the steps towards him. *Was she afraid? Such power!* She chewed at her lip. This man, the traveller from Axis, was entirely desirable. The idea of a mage was intriguing and alluring. But the reality? What could someone so powerful possibly see in her? *Take the steps. Help him!* Her feet didn't move.

Everand pushed away from Crystal and shrugged. 'The spells take a lot of energy.' Discerning her inner turmoil, he gave her a sad look and picked up Crystal's reins. 'I'll take us one more stretch. We must reach the town before it gets light.' He ran the back of a hand across his face. 'I need a specific image to project us to. The gates are a bit too far. I need somewhere about halfway again from here.'

When he stopped speaking, she realised he was waiting for her to suggest a place. With a frown, she visualised the route they'd taken. There was a fallen tree just off the path. It had stuck in her mind because there were few trees, and because she'd admired the smooth, white trunk and the elegance of the twisted branches. 'There's a fallen tree.'

Everand stood taller and reached out his hands. 'Hold my hands and think the image to me.'

Her feet seemed prepared to move now, so she crossed the gap and gripped his hands. Closing her eyes, she thought about the white tree lying on its side, its smooth branches splayed out, the leaves withering and dropping to adorn the wispy grass underneath. The air whistled around her again but this time she knew what to expect.

She grinned when she opened her eyes and they were standing right next to the tree trunk. 'Impressive,' she murmured.

When Everand swayed she grabbed him and held him upright. Drops of sweat ran down his brow and his hair looked limp. He leaned on her with a worrying tremble in his arms. How far would he push himself to try to protect them? Why was he here to help Riverfall? What did the mages have to gain? So many questions! Really, she knew nothing about the mages of Axis. Nobody did. All her people knew was that there were mages with power hidden away behind some massive granite wall. Could she ask him about Axis and the mages?

She thought of the first time she saw him, floundering in the river when she was on the boat. 'I have a question. Why were you in the river the first time I saw you? Do you like swimming?' She paused. 'Or was that a mistake?'

His trembling ceased and he bristled. 'I was transported by others.' When she arched an eyebrow, he added, 'We only had an old map to work off. And we were in a hurry.'

'I see,' she said slowly. 'So, there are limits to this awesome power and ability?' Inside, she felt relief.

He gave her an odd look. 'We'd better finish our journey.' He gathered up Crystal's reins. 'Perhaps I'll tell you more as we walk.'

She moved into his path and, putting her palms against his chest, reached up to kiss him on the mouth. 'Thank you. For taking me. For protecting me.' Delight spread through her as he responded by putting his arms around her lower back and kissing her soundly.

When they broke apart his eyes were wide, dark and serious. 'This is not wise. I must remain focused until after the festival.'

Disappointment coursed through her, but he was right. With a sigh, she said, 'And I must glide us to victory.' Her smile slipped. 'And call the dragon if needs be.'

His lips brushed her forehead, leaving a tingling trail across her skin. 'You are brave and strong. I am glad of your help.'

He gently pushed stray tendrils of hair away from her cheeks. 'After the festival ... I would like to know you better.' His shoulders tensed and she wondered how difficult it had been for him to say those words.

'Agreed.' After a pause, she added, 'But we can be friends and I can ask you questions, right?'

His mouth twisted in a crooked smile. 'I doubt I could stop you, or your questions.' He gave her a push. 'Walk. The sun is rising.'

The northern gates to Zuqart loomed greyly ahead. Crystal scuffed her hooves, her head drooping. The hopeepa would be foot-sore for several suns, and Lamiya decided to ask Mookaite for a salve she could apply to help Crystal recover. While they walked, Everand suggested she sleep in her team dome from this dark-fall. He pointed out that she would be safer with more people, and Lazuli would defend her if anything untoward happened. Feeling like scuffing her feet like the hopeepa, she kicked at a stray pebble. How would she be able to exhort her team to full effort with so much to think about?

Everand made them invisible when they approached the gates, and they snuck inside and slipped Crystal back into her stall. He gave the hopeepa hay and handfuls of black seeds as a reward. Lamiya watched him with a smile; he was kind and seemed to value animals.

The primrose rays of sun-up bounced off the rooves of the domes as he walked with her to Mookaite's dome and made them visible again. After a brief caress of her cheek with the back of a finger, he walked away, heading back to Beram's dome. She stood watching him, trying to imagine what he would look like in his mage robes. *Taller. Stronger. Imposing.* With a sigh, she turned, lifted the curtain and stepped quietly through. Whirr peeped and hopped around on her empty bed in excitement.

Mookaite immediately sat up on her mattress. 'Where have you been?'

Lamiya's cheeks and neck grew warm and clammy. Before she could think up a credible response, Mookaite clapped her hands in delight.

'Lazuli? You must tell me all about it.' Mookaite winked and threw aside her blanket. 'I'll make us a brew. You look tired.'

Lamiya remained silent while Mookaite bustled about sprinkling herbs into mugs, lighting her small fire and producing breads from a basket on a shelf. Should she reveal she had been with Everand, not Lazuli? No, that would distract and divide her team. She swallowed. Lazuli would be devastated.

Fatigue pressed down from the top of her head all the way to her toes.

Chapter Twenty-seven

Everand nudged aside the dome curtain and entered, relieved to find Beram was still there. A mug of brew sat on the low table, steam coiling up from it.

'There you are,' said Beram around a mouthful of loaf. He waved a hand at his mug. 'Drink?'

'Please.' Everand pulled up the other cushion and plonked onto it. His elbow thumped the table and he winced; he was more tired than he wanted to acknowledge.

Beram put a loaded plate down, gave him a piercing look and went to rummage in the jars on his middle shelf. He added a small pink cake to the plate. 'You look like you've been working hard. The cake will give you energy. We often eat these between the races.' He sat down and took a sip from his mug. 'Eat first. Tell me after. I'll tell you what's to happen here.'

Grateful, Everand reached for a loaf. Truth be known, his legs felt hollow and distant. This level of fatigue was alarming. Was it due to the intermittent food and the activity, along with the need to use numerous spells so close together? This was something to think about. As well as learning and practising an increasing range and complexity of spells, perhaps the mages also needed to build stamina in using them. He must discuss this with Mantiss and Agamid. His mind was drifting ... he focused back on Beram.

'... after we put the boats away, we're to help with the festival preparations. We expect the team from Riversea to arrive before dusk.' Beram drained his mug, tipping it high. He plonked the mug onto the table. 'This means another welcome feast. Melanite and Kunzite, plus Tengar's wife, have been working hard.'

Everand started on the fruit and waved a hand for Beram to continue.

'We'll pitch the tents in the southern courtyard for the visitors from the provinces. The tents for watching the races won't be put up until the sun before.' Beram paused. 'I guess we needn't worry about rain ruining anything.'

'The boats?' said Everand.

'We've moved our reserve boat, so there's space for the four racing boats in the dome closest to the ramp.'

Everand considered. Having the four race boats together was wise and made it harder for a single boat to be damaged. But it also meant all four teams had reason to access the dome and boat area.

'What?' asked Beram. 'I can see you thinking something.'

'Will the boats be secure?'

Beram frowned. 'Ah. You think we should put a watch on them?' Before Everand could respond he added, 'Good idea. I'll find a few people to sleep in the storage dome each night. Just in case.'

Everand held his mug out. 'Is there any more?' It wouldn't do for him to become dehydrated; he knew this made the mind sluggish.

After Beram had refilled his mug, he said, 'Several things have happened. I need to tell you, Tengar and Atage what we know so far. I need more information about your river dragon.' Ignoring Beram's look of astonishment, he added, 'And Atage's vision for shared trading. I have a theory forming, but not enough context to be sure of it.'

Beram looked stunned but pleased as he rubbed his hands together. 'Your cake.' He pointed at the pink round cake still on the plate.

Everand picked up the cake: it was a pale pink and glistened with a dusting of fine white crystals. He popped it in his mouth. His tongue exploded in a burst of zinging and fizzling and he coughed. Tears sprang to his eyes and Beram laughed.

'The taste is strong, but there's nothing to beat these cakes for a burst of energy.' Grinning, he added, 'They've got extract from a red herb called fire-burst in them.'

Wiping his eyes, Everand croaked, 'Thanks.' He'd reserve judgement on the supply of energy. If it worked, he'd ask for a bag full. 'Can you arrange a meeting with Atage?'

'Straight after training,' said Beram confidently. 'I imagine you need to rest? I'll come back to collect you.' With that, Beram stood, dusted down his palms and fetched his paddle. He gave a brief wave as he pushed out through the curtain.

Everand sat sipping the rest of his mug, ordering his thoughts into a coherent report for Atage. Should he tell them about calling the dragon? What if it didn't come? But it might, and it could attack them. What did he suggest they do? Proceed regardless? He hated this nagging sense of pending failure for his mission. Was it because he was here by himself? This made him feel solely responsible for the outcome. Why, by all the stars, had Mantiss sent him without a communication orb or some other covert form of connection?

Did he have time to go and fetch help? Maybe, but he'd have to translocate through Riverwood to get to Axis. Going to the Guild, explaining and returning would take a full sun — and it would be exhausting. What if something happened while he was gone? He ran his hands through his hair and rubbed at his scalp, trying to tease out some answers.

If the Riversea team was to arrive at dusk, then the Riverwood team couldn't be too far away. His instincts advised he should be here when the Riverwood team arrived. Was that his source of angst? On his previous mission they had known who the enemy was: his own mentor, one of the Guild. On *this* mission the opponent remained unknown and thus nothing was falling into place.

An ache in his jaw alerted him he was grinding his teeth. His head said go get help; his heart said stay. *Don't forget Lamiya*, his heart pushed. *She is at grave risk. Yes*, his head concurred, *largely your fault.* He now understood why Mage Mantiss hadn't sent a group of mages. Being responsible for what happened to others was not a mantle to be worn lightly. Making the Guild responsible for the wellbeing of the other provinces was not a path to be trodden.

So, he would continue alone on this not-so-simple mission. Fatigue coursing through his limbs and weighing down his eyelids, he crawled to his mattress. His mind filled with the image of Lamiya stretching up to kiss him. *Another issue. But she might be the one to replace Elemar.* A deep ache settled across his chest. By the stars, he'd missed Elemar's exuberance and the challenge of trying to understand her. Was this why he couldn't respond to the subtle overtures from Tiliqua? No, he'd only just met brave, strong Lamiya and yet he yearned to be with her, tried to find excuses to take her with him. His head throbbed. Tiliqua, a fellow mage, was not what his heart sought, even though Mantiss would welcome him into the family.

He replayed the initial memory of looking up from the water and seeing Lamiya standing on the back of the boat, her hair flowing in the wind, muscles moving as she worked. The sharp intelligence in her grey eyes that saw right into him. Surrendering, he fell into a deep sleep.

✿

He jerked awake.

Beram stopped shaking him and sat back on his heels. 'Atage and Tengar are waiting.'

Everand stifled a yawn, and Beram added, 'Come along. Thulite will feed us.'

Pushing up off the mattress Everand stretched, easing the kinks pinching at his spine. Bright sunlight shone through the curtain. He splashed cool water over his face and neck, dragged his fingers through his hair until it seemed tangle-free and tied it back again. 'Ready.'

The short walk to Atage's dome refreshed his mind and loosened his aching limbs, although his feet reminded him with each step that they were bruised. The courtyard was a hive of activity and everywhere he looked townspeople were scurrying around carrying tables and chairs, platters, cloth cushions or woven baskets piled high with an array of goods.

They passed a group of children making streamers and flags under the guidance of a grey-haired woman. A small blonde girl, concentrating on threading her stick through the cloth pennants with her tongue poking out of her mouth, looked up and smiled at him. He gave her a small wave and her smile widened. How could he fail these people? He took longer strides, and Beram sped up beside him.

'Welcome,' said Atage, motioning to a dark-blue cushion.

Everand sat down with a brief nod at Tengar, who was already seated. 'How was your training?' The question popped out and he sighed. He was being pulled into the excitement of the competition.

'Good,' said Tengar, crunching a hand to pop the knuckle joints. 'We feel ready.'

Beram and Atage sat down and Thulite piled platters of steaming fish on the table.

'Beram said you have a theory?' asked Atage, indicating with his hands that they should take food.

Everand contemplated. Perhaps begin with the big picture then work his way down to the details. 'I need to know more about the provinces and what they produce to trade. My theory is that disrupting the trade discussions may be the intent behind the attacks. Someone doesn't want the provinces to mingle and trade. But I don't know who, or why.'

'So, the races will be safe?' asked Tengar, looking relieved.

He shook his head. 'The opposite. Ruining the races will jeopardise the trade discussions and damage Riverfall's reputation.'

Predictably, Tengar's face fell. Beram wrung his hands.

'We can't cancel the races,' said Atage slowly. 'What do you suggest?'

Everand wriggled on his cushion. 'Proceed, but keep a watch on the boats and the paddlers. As discussed, have people trained in weapons and place these groups strategically.' He looked at Atage. 'The finish of the long race carries the most risk. Only Lyber and I should stand on the bridge. Keep the crowds away and have strong men nearby.'

Atage gave him a direct look. 'You think Riverwood?'

Everand shrugged, uncomfortable. 'It looks that way. I hope I'm not missing anything.' He paused. Mantiss would not be pleased with him for revealing this, but they should know. They *must* know because lives could be at risk. 'I think our unseen opponent has some ability with magic.'

Atage dropped his mug and hot brew sloshed all over the remaining fish fillets. Tengar and Beram sat mutely staring.

'Tsk, tsk,' Thulite bustled over and dabbed with a cloth to mop up the liquid, now dripping off a table corner. She removed the plate of fish.

'How is this possible? What should we do?' croaked Atage. The man was disconcertingly pale.

Everand said slowly, 'Tell me about Mizuchi.' The change of topic earned him three frowns. 'You hold the races in honour of Mizuchi the river dragon. You say pleasing the dragon brings rain for your crops. Has anyone ever seen the dragon? How and when did this tradition begin? Do you have a recorded history anywhere?'

Silence stretched until Thulite came to stand by the table. Hands on hips, she said, 'You need Vogel. He's the only one old enough to recall the story. His ancestors have passed down the tale.'

'I'll fetch him.' Beram rushed out of the dome.

Thulite put a hand on Atage's shoulder. 'Why don't you move into the formal meeting room? The tapestry might help.'

Atage clapped a hand to his forehead. 'Why didn't I think of that! Come.' He pushed up from the table and gestured at an internal pair of curtains.

Following Atage through more soft curtains, Everand found himself in a large round room. A low polished table with six or seven plump cushions placed around it occupied the centre. His gaze was drawn to a faded oblong cloth that hung on the far wall.

'May I?' he asked, before going to inspect the wall hanging closely. Gingerly, he touched a bottom corner between his thumb and forefinger. The soft material felt ancient and was threadbare. He sniffed at the faint, musty odour. The faded images of the waterfall and the lake showed, beyond any doubt, precisely where he and Lamiya had gone.

The illustration showed a massive blue and gold dragon humping its way through the water beside a rough-hewn boat similar to the current one. The details were impressive, down to the multi-coloured pebbles on the shore, the light and shadow in the water and the shadowy copse of trees on the distant shore. The artist had captured the energy of the dragon and boats well. He concluded the symbolism of this hanging was akin to that of the enormous silk rug on the floor of the Guild's Great Hall depicting the Last Great Battle.

'Vogel will explain,' said Atage, coming to stand beside him. 'This tapestry was woven by the first ancestors who found the lake. It's passed down from town leader to town leader, along with the right to live in this dome.'

Thulite pushed through the curtain with a tray of mugs and plates. While she set these out, Atage touched Everand's elbow and invited him to sit. He chose a cushion from where he could see the tapestry. Thulite placed mugs and a plate of green and white cakes on the table.

Everand said, 'Can someone make me a list of the provinces and details such as how many people live there, where the main town is, what they grow and produce, what they're likely to trade?'

Atage nodded. 'I already have a list. I'll write a copy for you.'

Everand thought harder. 'I need a detailed map. One that shows the river, the bridges, the towns and the province boundaries.'

'Beram is our best drawer of maps. We have a few small maps but I'll ask him to produce a larger one, and to talk to people from the other provinces to gain more details.' Atage took a sip from his mug and put it down carefully. 'We can say we're preparing for the trade discussions.'

Everand inclined his head. 'Tread carefully with the people from Riverwood, but include them. We need to see if they resist the idea of sharing.'

Scuffling footsteps sounded at the curtain just before Beram eased through, with a hunched, wrinkled old man clinging to his elbow. Thulite gathered up two plump cushions and put them at the side of the table nearest the entry. Beram guided the old man to the table, took his stick and lowered the man carefully onto the cushions.

Atage bowed low. 'Welcome, Vogel. May the sun light your eyes for countless more seasons.'

'Unlikely,' rasped Vogel, 'but I appreciate the thought.' With a shaking hand he snaffled a green cake. 'You want to know about Mizuchi? You can always bribe a story from me with good cake.' The old man smacked his lips around the edges of the cake, and Everand realised he had few teeth left.

Wanting to hear the story, he said, 'Please tell us about the river dragon.'

Vogel squinted, assessing him or perhaps trying to recall where to start. He gummed the last morsel of cake and then spoke in a surprisingly clear voice.

'This is the story as told by my father's father's father. Spinel and Aura were among those on the first boats that came from across the sea.'

Everand held up a hand to ask the old man to pause. The least he could do was to capture the tale in a memory ball — then they could replay it whenever they wished, or scribe it. He put his hands in his lap below the table, quietly formed a clear memory ball and opened it to receive the words. He blinked, then created a second memory ball for the Inner Council, remembering that Mantiss had tasked him with finding out where all these people had come from. 'Sorry, can you say that again?'

Vogel gave him a withering look. 'This is the story as told by my father's father's father. Spinel and Aura were among those on the first boats that came from across the sea. Spinel told of fleeing violence and killing on their island. Invaders arrived from a larger island further east, intent on taking their island, perhaps for the fine cotton crops.

'Only forty people survived the massacre. They bundled food and blankets and nothing else into two boats, leaving under moonlight. For eight moon-rises and moon-fades they paddled the seas seeking land. Three people died from their wounds. The rest were almost dead from hunger and thirst when Spinel told it was Aura with her keen eyes who spied land.

'They paddled to the shore and the boats were dashed to bits on the rocks. Another person died. The survivors huddled on the rocks until the sun rose, then they caught crabs and fish in the rock pools, ate some berries and set out to climb the cliffs.

'It took two suns, but eventually they clambered over the clifftops and wound their way through the hills. There they found birds and small creatures and berries and nuts to replenish them. After another sun of walking, they came across a deep and wide lake, with cascading tumbling water.'

Everand stirred on his cushion. This tale was reminiscent of the history taught about the arrival of the first mages, but these people had landed later, and much further north. So, they found and named Dragon Lake and Mizuchi Falls. The others sat mesmerised, even though they had surely heard the story before. Vogel took a slurp from his mug and chose a white cake. Everand was relieved when the man took only a few nibbles and then resumed.

'So it was that thirty-six men and women stayed by the shore of this lake. They caught fish, found edible lake weed and foraged for nuts and berries in the nearby forest. On the third moon, a great serpent rose from the waters, roaring and breathing fire at them. Terrified, the people fled. Aura, ever wise, pointed out that no-one was harmed and suggested they make peace offerings to the great serpent. The next sun-up, they collected berries, nuts and pretty stones, and caught large fish. These they placed on the lake shore, on a small pebbly beach near the falling curtain of water.'

Everand thought this place sounded familiar.

'At the height of the moon, Spinel said the water of the lake churned and bubbled and the great serpent came to the shore and ate their offerings. The people bowed to it and named it the Great River Dragon, Mizuchi in the old tongue.'

Vogel's rheumy eyes shone for a moment. 'The beast had a head like a horse, golden horns, a long body of blue scales and a mighty powerful tail with barbs like knives. For a time, the people stayed there. They built two new boats and shaped them in the likeness of Mizuchi, with ornate carved wooden heads and tails. They painted them dark blue and pale blue and gave them names. Traditionally, the darker blue boat is always named Mizuchi, in honour of the great serpent. They made the boats long enough for ten people to sit on benches and wield paddles so they would be fast.'

'And they raced them!' exclaimed Beram, his face flushed with excitement.

Vogel looked at Beram. 'They raced the boats across the lake. As Spinel told it, Mizuchi would race with the boats, easily outpacing them. Then the great serpent would rear out of the water and roar at them before vanishing into the depths. And it rained. Many times they raced the boats, the dragon would come and it would rain.

'After two cycles of the seasons, Spinel realised the land by the lake wouldn't sustain them. Children would be born, the number of people would rise and they needed to move to a more arable place. They dismantled their shelters, built a small rock shrine to Mizuchi at the base of the waterfall, left a pile of offerings and called into the lake water that they had to go but would return to honour him each growing season. They named the lake Dragon Lake and the falls Mizuchi Falls.'

Everand rolled his shoulders. This made sense, so far. They waited while Vogel munched through his second cake, showering crumbs over his tunic front.

'The people carried their boats with all their goods inside, and descended the rocky plateau until they came across a tributary to the river. The land on the far side looked more arable, so they built a wooden bridge across the river.'

Everand assumed this was the second, smaller bridge.

'Where the river widened, the men got back in the boats and followed its course. They named it Dragonspine River, for it fed and sustained the surrounding lands. The women walked across the bridge and followed the riverbank. After two more suns of walking, they came across a flatter valley next to the river, with rich loamy soil. The land was full of pink stone and they found this was workable into clay.'

'And they built the first domes of Zuqart,' said Beram proudly. Tengar gave him a warning glance.

Vogel waved a gnarled hand at Beram. 'Indeed. They also found kapok — wild cotton — and realised its potential so they settled here.' Dribble oozed from a corner of his mouth and he licked it back. 'So, the seasons passed and the people grew, and the town of Zuqart grew.'

'And the races?' prompted Beram, earning a scowl from Tengar.

'Yes, my boy, each growing season the people kept their promise and paddled their dragon boats back upriver, carried them up the rocky lip and raced the great Mizuchi. They'd take bags of offerings and leave them by the waterfall. Afterwards it would rain.'

Everand was astounded at the effort that carrying the boats up the lip must have taken. The ancient people must have been truly convinced it wouldn't rain if they didn't race the dragon. He stirred as Vogel continued.

'Time passed; the town swelled to more than a hundred people. The crops of cotton, wheat, nuts and fruit were extensive. Aspen replaced Spinel, and then Aspen's son Zulic inherited as town leader and head glide. He suggested the boats race on the river next to the town. The people liked this because everyone could watch, and it took less time away from the crops. For a time, people were sent to Dragon Lake with the bags of offerings.'

Vogel paused and drained his mug with an odd gurgling noise. Everand curbed his impatience. So, what happened to alienate the dragon? They were getting to the crux of it. And how were the other provinces formed? Were they related? Finally, Vogel thumped his mug onto the table. It toppled and Tengar shot out a hand and righted it.

'In Zulic's time the town prospered, but things changed. Zulic had a falling-out with Lode. It is told they argued over the crops and the handling of birds and animals. Lode was a gentle man who adored all creatures. He wanted to build up herds of animals, but Zulic argued this wasn't a good use of the land.' Vogel raised a trembling hand and dragged it across his mouth.

Everand thought he could guess where this story was going.

'So, Lode gathered up his wife and children and twenty followers and their children, and they made their way south.'

Everand wanted to confirm. 'And they formed Riverplain? And became breeders of hopeepa and birds?'

'Yes, impatient young man. That is so.' Vogel twisted his leathery neck to stare at Atage. 'I welcome the renewed friendship with these, our people. Our ancestors would be pleased.'

Yes, thought Everand, but what about Mizuchi? Something must have angered the dragon. When Vogel said nothing for several breaths, he worried the old man might doze off. 'May I respectfully ask, what happened to the boat races and the great Mizuchi?'

Atage gave him a subtle nod.

'Ah, the great Mizuchi.' Vogel's eyes watered. 'Somehow, we've displeased the river dragon. Until the past five seasons, it's rained at the right time for our crops, but the dragon hasn't been seen since my father's time. In his time, people still left offerings at the waterfall and some claimed they heard the dragon roaring behind it, but the great serpent wasn't seen. Eventually, even this practice was forgotten.'

An awkward silence settled over the table and the air became tinged with regret. Everand wanted to drum his fingers, but kept them curled around the memory balls in his lap. Was the story over?

Tengar shuffled on his cushion. 'The offerings were forgotten, but not our love of racing the boats.' He gave a wry smile. 'As you might've noticed, it's deeply ingrained.'

Everand refrained from making a comment about this being an understatement.

Atage took up the thread, spreading his hands open. 'So, we still race the boats in hope. Until this growing season, we haven't been afraid of the dragon withholding the rain. We pray that four boats racing will please the dragon.'

Everand stopped the memory recording spell and sealed the memory balls. He slipped them into his trouser pocket. Was this why Lamiya was important? As well as her ability to call animals, did she represent a reuniting of the two peoples? This mission was becoming complex beyond belief.

Refocusing, he found everyone looking at him. A niggling thought surfaced. Vogel had referred to racing a dragon three generations ago, so how long did dragons live for? If he hadn't seen the dragon last dark-fall he'd have assumed it had died. Was the dragon old and grumpy and no longer able to make it rain? He frowned. No, the brief glimpse he'd had suggested a strong, vigorous dragon. The story at least answered his questions about how they knew of the dragon and how they knew its name: they'd named it themselves in their old tongue.

Beram gave a discreet cough to remind him everyone was waiting.

'I think it will work,' was all Everand said. The dragon *was* in the lake, but would it come? It hadn't seemed friendly. They thought the dragon was angry, and it certainly had looked angry. He didn't want to offer more hope than was warranted.

Atage sat back. 'Vogel, thank you for repeating the story. Beram will help you back to your dome.'

Beram stood up, retrieved Vogel's stick from where it was propped against the wall and helped the old man to his feet.

Everand stood also and bowed to Vogel. 'Your memory serves us well.'

Vogel's mouth stretched in what Everand supposed was a grin. Then Beram escorted the old man out of the dome.

Atage and Tengar remained standing but were looking at him again, as if he were the leader now. Everand shifted his weight from one foot to the other to ease the threat of pins and needles.

Then he fished one of the memory balls from his pocket and held it out. 'Atage, this is for you.' The man's face creased in curiosity. 'The ball contains the story that Vogel just told so it can't ever be lost. Please accept it into your hands.' Everand pushed the ball towards him and when Atage's hands closed over it, he muttered a brief incantation. 'There. Now all you have to do is clasp it with both hands and ask it to tell Vogel's story of the first ancestors.'

Atage and Tengar looked at him in awe and he realised this was the first demonstration of his power they'd seen. Suppressing a sigh, he thought hard about his next comment and sought Tengar's eyes. 'I can't explain fully, but you're likely to be closest to Lamiya during the races. It seems she has a role to play and she must be protected at all costs.'

Tengar gave him a thoughtful look. 'I see,' he said, although it was clear he didn't.

Everand drummed his fingers against his thigh. Perhaps they needed a little more. 'The opponent is using birds as spies, and Lamiya is a breeder of birds with an uncanny ability to communicate with them. She is at risk.' He took a deep swallow. 'I also think the dragon will probably come. And I think you are right, it is angry. We will need to convince it you want to be friends.'

To his surprise, Atage carefully passed the memory ball to Tengar, who handled it as if it were a live flame. Then Atage stepped around the table to grasp both of Everand's hands. 'We're so grateful you're here.'

Uncomfortable that their gratitude could be entirely misplaced, Everand extracted his hands, clasped them together and gave Atage a short bow. 'I wish I knew more. The outcome is not at all guaranteed.' He bowed again.

'But I can promise to try my best.'

CHAPTER TWENTY-EIGHT

Lamiya gasped when cold water showered over her head. Flattening her hands into paddles, she spun around, scooping water, and hurled it into Lazuli's face. He spluttered and laughed, splashing her back. She dived into the river, revelling in the fresh water, the tangy air, the blue sky above. Around her, the entire team was swimming or hurling water at one another. The training session had gone well and they all deserved to relax and have a swim. The team was as ready as they would ever be for the festival races.

A school of small white and red fish darted before her face, fleeing the commotion. She surfaced and stretched out into a long stroke, enjoying the way her arms sliced through the water and the pull of the muscles in her shoulders and arms. Small choppy waves broke over her, sending spray up her nose. Lazuli was encroaching on her heels so she kicked harder and was rewarded by a snort from behind. Taking a deep breath, she dived, tumble-turned and swam back underneath him. When she bobbed up behind and saw him scanning the water, she couldn't help laughing. He flipped around with a wide grin and lunged at her.

She dived again and saw the outline of his arms grabbing the water where she'd just been. Afraid she'd laugh and swallow water, she surfaced and took a gasp of air. Lazuli pounced, grabbing her shoulders. Giggling, she tried to splash water into his face. He became serious and his grey eyes seared into hers with an imploring look. Curse the water sprites! He was going to kiss her! She tried to break free, but he held tighter.

An alarm sounded in her head and she tipped sideways to look downriver, past Lazuli's shoulder. Two large bubbles of water were speeding towards them. She shrieked and Lazuli looked startled. 'Behind you!' she gasped.

'Nice try,' said Lazuli, pulling her closer.

'Not joking!' She gave another shriek.

The bubbles erupted right behind Lazuli and two jumping fish arched into the air above them, glossy skin shining darkly and blocking the light. Lamiya dived, heart hammering. The water churned around her flailing arms and legs. Her foot connected with something hard, stubbing her toes. The ache in her chest built and built, until white stars floated before her eyes. She had to surface. Hands grabbed her, and next thing she was treading water, crushed against Lazuli's neck.

'Are you alright? You're shaking!' Lazuli squeezed her in a hug and then swam towards the bank, pulling her along.

Scrunching her eyelids against tears of shock, she tried to breathe steadily, to dispel the tremors travelling down her arms and legs. Lazuli waded out of the water, tugging her with him. As soon as she felt the boat ramp firm beneath her feet, her legs buckled and she plonked down, facing the river.

Lazuli sat beside her and rubbed her back, his face creased in concern. He flapped a hand at Larimar and Lapsi, who were looking at them enquiringly.

'Sorry,' she muttered. 'I thought they were attacking us.'

Lazuli gave her an intent look. 'Just jumping fish, Lamiya.' He looked upriver and waved his free hand that way. 'There they are, heading upriver.'

She refused to look, focusing instead on the sun warming her and Lazuli's strong hand massaging between her shoulder blades. *Pull yourself together*. She had to be stronger than this for her team. *For Everand.* Was that a scare cleverly disguised? Or merely two fish on their way upriver? Shaking her head to scatter the buzzing thoughts, she turned to Lazuli. 'Thanks. I feel better now.'

'You can do this,' he murmured. The concern mingled with desire in his eyes made her feel guilty.

Giving him a shaky smile, she rallied. 'Only because I have *excellent* pacers.'

Lazuli's face relaxed into a smile. 'Better.' He stood up and pulled her to her feet. 'Come along, mighty glide, you should retrieve your team before they're completely water-logged.'

Her legs now supporting her, she gave him a grateful smile. 'Yes, and we need a team strategy talk. Will you call them?'

'Yo!' Lazuli's shout almost deafened her and she ducked as he waved an arm in a large beckoning circle. 'Yo! Team strategy!'

Pride coursed through her when the team ceased their play and waded out of the water. They toiled up the ramp, collecting their paddles on the way, and clapped a hand with Lazuli as they reached her. Taking two deep breaths, she imagined her worries and fears being neatly stacked under a small stone outside her hut back in Riverplain, and brought to the fore her planning for the races.

Addressing the team, she said, 'Let's use the time before Riversea arrives to go over our strategy. We can also do a stretch session.'

'Excellent idea,' said Lulite. The men nodded and grunted, and Ejad gave her a broad grin. The young man had slotted into the team remarkably well, although she wondered whether he would pass any of their strategy on to the Riverfall team. Perhaps she'd give Lazuli and Larimar more precise directions separately.

The sun scorched her head and the back of her neck while they walked back to the town, and steam wafted from everyone's sodden tunics. An eddy of worry wormed into her.

What would happen to the Riverfall crops, and to the grasses, seeds and fodder for the Riverplain hopeepa and birds if it didn't rain soon?

An image of the river dragon's head under the dark moonlit water appeared in her mind. They must win back this mighty beast's pleasure. In the middle of the session, as they were practising race pace, she had again visualised the dragon beneath her. And she'd felt the essence of the dragon infuse the boat. After ten strokes, she'd let her vision go in case the team noticed. A frown tugged at her eyebrows. Everything in her said that the dragon was female. Was it, or she, also called Flight, like their boat?

Surreptitiously, she eyed Lazuli, who was humming while he strode beside her. She took in his strong masculine jaw, the power in his upper body, the muscles bulging in his legs. Excitement flooded through her. Was it possible the great Mizuchi was male and was lonely? Did dragons mate? How long did they live?

'What?' asked Lazuli, breaking her line of thought. When she looked at him, he added, 'You laughed. For no apparent reason.'

Excitement still flowing through her, she said, 'I've just thought of a wicked new drill!'

Lazuli gave her a sceptical look. 'This close to a race?'

They walked a bit further and she noticed Lazuli was limping. 'Are you hurt?'

'You kicked me in the shin,' he admitted with a grimace.

'Oh.' She was going to apologise but thought better of it and sniffed. 'You have hard bones. Lucky I didn't break my toes, as *that* would make it hard to glide well.'

Lazuli leaned closer, a twinkle in his eyes, and murmured, 'I could kiss them better.'

'Hmm, I like the idea of you grovelling at my feet. Pacers can be so arrogant!'

He threw her such a startled look she feared she'd overstepped. Perhaps she should avoid men altogether. Negotiating these possibly-more-than-a-friend relationships was so delicate and complex. Nudging this concern aside, she turned her mind to the arrival of the team from Riversea, remembering that Lazuli had been to that province.

'Well, wise pacer,' she offered as an apology, 'you went to Riversea to invite their team. What do you think? Will they be strong?'

'They're different from us,' Lazuli said with a shrug. 'In build we're similar to the Riverfall team. From what I saw, the Riversea team will be shorter and more solid. They are compact, which will give them much power for the shorter races.' He shrugged again. 'I tend to think our lighter frame will give us an edge in the long race.'

'Interesting,' she said, thinking his assessment was probably correct, especially if the weather remained so hot. 'Let's hold our strategy discussion after we've seen them. We'll do a team stretch and muscle-ease for each other now.'

'I like that idea,' said Lazuli playfully.

She thumped his shoulder, words failing her.

✿

Time flew by as Lamiya led her team in an extended stretch session on the patch of grass close to the team dome. So far, everyone looked good, although Lazuli's left shin was turning an interesting shade of green and purple. She resolved to offer him some calendula salve, sighing as she anticipated his request for her to rub it in. Ejad's enthusiasm was infectious, and she noticed he'd become friends with Larimar, who was closest to him in age. Leading them in the stretch of arching their arms high above their heads, she gave Ejad a nod of approval. He beamed.

'Well done, team,' she said and dropped her hands by her sides. 'You all look strong and powerful. It's hot, so let's rest in the shade and take our meal.' The circle dispersed and she added, 'Keep your paddles handy for the traditional greeting.'

Inside the cool dome, Whirr greeted her with joy, hopping in circles and cheeping incessantly before he perched on the back of her wrist. After planting a kiss on the back of the bird's head, she saw Lazuli watching her. Embarrassed, she chose some food and sat on a cushion. To her relief, Lulite grabbed the cushion beside her.

'I'm looking forward to seeing what clothes and ornaments they wear,' said Lulite. 'Be quiet, Whirr,' she scolded, and Whirr fluffed his feathers in a huff.

'Me too,' replied Lamiya, glad to be having a straightforward conversation. 'I heard they use shells from the sea.'

'One of the women paddlers is a real artist, Larimar told Lapsi. He said the baskets she weaves are impressive. I'd like to meet her.' Lulite paused to finish her star-fruit.

'Lazuli told me there's a woman who tends to seabirds. I'd like to meet her,' Lamiya said, relaxing as she chatted with her friend. *This*, she told herself, was what the festival was all about: testing their skills, making new friends and trading ideas and products. Part of her wished she didn't know about the undercurrents. *Keep it simple,* she advised herself. Yet a tiny kernel deep within suggested the intrigue was far more exciting.

A loud, deep horn sounded and she exchanged an excited look with Lulite. 'They've arrived!'

The team rose as one, dusted off sticky palms and reached for their paddles.

'Wait,' said Lulite, snagging her elbow. 'Your hair!'

She stood impatiently while Lulite produced a comb from a pocket and dragged it through the knots in her hair.

'We can't have our glide looking dishevelled,' Lulite murmured. 'That would not make them tremble at the knees.'

'Pair up, in order,' Lamiya said to the men who were waiting with exasperated expressions. By the time they'd shuffled into order behind Lazuli and Larimar, her hair was combed and adorned with a red feather. She swept out of the dome. 'Let's go.'

She set a pace that made her team look fit and strong. The constant call of the horn stirred her spirit. For a heartbeat she wished the races were the very next sun-up. Her heart soared as she visualised Flight streaming ahead of the other boats.

'Steady,' called Lazuli, and she realised she was almost skipping.

Moderating her stride, she was delighted that so many eyes turned to watch when the team strode into the outer courtyard, paddles held high on shoulders. They took their place next to the Riverfall team who were already lined up on each side of the gate.

When she stepped into position behind Beram, he said, 'They came by water. They'll leave their boat at the ramp and bring the team in for the formal welcome before they put the boat away.'

Lamiya decided she would go and see the boat after this greeting.

Doo-doooo! The horn sounded extra loud. *Doo-doooo!* The two lines of paddlers turned to face one another, forming a guard of honour. Atage and Lyber hurried into position, both wearing formal tunics and their clay tokens of office. She skimmed her eyes over the crowd. Where was Everand? *Behind you,* popped into her head. *Don't turn around.* Inside her tunic, Whirr peeped a greeting to the mage. Across the gap, Lazuli cast her an excited smile and she twitched her lips in response and stood taller.

Doo-dooo! Doo-dooo! The echoes of the horn faded to be replaced by the sound of marching feet. Behind the teams, the gathered crowd murmured and fidgeted.

'Paddlers!' snapped Tengar, and in a smooth motion the Riverfall team swung their paddles up to form an archway.

'Paddlers,' sang Lamiya, her heart swelling with pride as her team fluidly followed suit.

The glide from Riversea stepped through the archway and she gasped. The man was so muscled his torso was almost square! His brown skin was decorated with elaborate ink swirls and patterns that shifted sinuously as he moved, and a head-dress of pure, gleaming white feathers sat high on his head. His eyes were a fierce pale blue, striking against the brown skin. This team would be a serious competitor. The two pacers behind him were also impressively solid, with slabs of muscle moving along their necks, shoulders and arms, also rippling beneath inked images of fish and waves. Lamiya swallowed. Their hair, an unusual grey-green hue, was pulled in a tight bun on top of their heads, with small white feathers protruding.

The team clinked as they stepped, and her eyes were drawn to the ornate shell necklaces around their necks and the intricate shell thongs around their ankles. The first six paddlers were all solid men and she felt her courage quail. Where were the women? Then she saw the last four paddlers were all women. They placed the women at the rear of the boat? Enchanted by the women's clothing, she swallowed with emotion. Although short and solid, the women were stunning with their long, wavy, pale-green hair, intricate dark-green ink swirls adorning their cheeks and arms, and entirely feminine in their rustling grass skirts, revealing hints of muscled thighs as they walked. She wished she could see Lulite's face.

The team came to a smooth halt before Atage and Lyber.

'Yee-ah!' The team saluted with their paddles, the blades adorned with images of fish and turtles. The other teams replied with 'Yosh!' and 'Yo!'

'Welcome, mighty team from Riversea!' Atage spoke loud and clear, and he and Lyber bowed low.

Intrigued, she watched the Riversea glide step forward and hold out a large gleaming white shell with elegant brown swirls traversing the surface and a wide valley of crinkled lip. Atage held out both hands to receive it. The Riversea glide motioned for him to hold the shell to an ear.

With a puzzled frown, Atage did so. A look of astonishment crossed his face. 'I can hear the sea!' he exclaimed.

The glide took a respectful step back. 'Cowrie, glide for Riversea.' His voice was guttural and hard to follow.

Behind him, each paddler gave a short bow and stated their name: Conch, Chiton, Limpel, Clommus, Summel, Pippel, Spirula, Charonia, Clama, Nawpra, and a female drummer, Chella. Lamiya mentally tried to sound out the names, observing that the women's names all ended with an 'a' sound. Paddlers eight and nine had a wispy aura to them, and she wondered if these were the two artists. They were both looking around in wonder, and she found herself looking forward to speaking with them at the feast.

The townspeople cheered and clapped. Thulite emerged from the tangle of people and came forward, and Lamiya guessed she would show the team to their dome and settle them in.

Atage raised a hand for quiet. 'Please make the Riversea team welcome. Gather back in this courtyard at dusk for the welcome feast!' He and Lyber then began to converse with Cowrie.

Lamiya watched Tengar approach the Riversea pacers. Were they going back to the boat ramp? Before she could move to follow, Everand's hand rested on her shoulder.

'Do you sense anything untoward?' he asked softly.

Her head to one side, she considered. 'No.' She turned around; it would look odd if anyone noticed him standing with a hand on her. Her heart skipped at his tall form, the deep blue eyes and starlight hair.

'Good,' he said, all seriousness. 'Neither do I.'

His inward expression made her want to jump up and down and yell, 'Hey! Look at *me*!' But she did no such thing, instead waiting to see if he would say more.

He gazed at her. 'What will you do now?'

She glanced over her shoulder. Her team stood waiting for direction, and Tengar and the men from Riversea were heading towards the southern gate. 'I'd like to see their boat. I was intending to go to the ramp.'

Everand gave a sharp nod. He felt like a distant stranger. 'Good idea. I'll come too.'

He behaved as if the events of dark-fall at the lake had never happened. Her emotions churned. Whirr clawed up out of her tunic and peeped.

Everand's expression softened and his eyes became a very dark blue. 'Your little friend is with you.' He looked up. 'And your larger friend approaches. I'll look for you at the feast.'

Lazuli arrived at her shoulder with a curt nod at Everand, who gave a curt nod back. Fixing a smile, she tapped Lazuli's elbow. 'Let's go and see the Riversea boat? You, me and Larimar and anyone else who wants to come?'

'Good idea,' said Lazuli, unknowingly echoing Everand's words.

All of her team wanted to see the boat, so they mingled with the Riverfall team and headed out the gate. Somewhere along the way, Everand merged with the paddlers and was chatting to Persaj. She nudged her way through the paddlers until she was right behind Tengar and the men from Riversea so she could listen and learn. Predictably, Lazuli appeared beside her. She glanced at him and put a finger to her lips: watch and listen. A smile lit his eyes.

'… from the wood of a tall ghost tree …' Cowrie was explaining to Tengar. 'They grow on the coastal bluff overlooking the sea. The white wood is hardy and the grain is good to work with.'

237

She couldn't quite catch Tengar's question, but heard Cowrie's response. 'Originally, we had benches for twelve paddlers. After your pacers explained the design of your boat, we took out a bench and extended the front part for a drummer. It should be suitable.'

Tengar rumbled more questions, then Cowrie added, 'Mainly we paddle to fish and trawl seaweed and shells from the sea. We have a lake too.' The man's massive shoulders moved in a shrug.

Lamiya listened and watched, fascinated. As the muscles flexed, it looked as if the inked fish on his upper arm was leaping over a wave.

'Of course, we race each other too.' Both men laughed. 'Our most skilled paddlers enjoy racing the waves when the seas are high, riding the crests and white water.'

Lamiya swallowed: that would take courage and awesome strength and balance. She looked at Lazuli who raised an eyebrow, probably thinking the same thing. Doubt nibbled at her: who was she to take on a team such as this? Annoyed at her lack of confidence, she brushed at a loose hair that tickled her cheek. Catching Lazuli watching her, she straightened her shoulders.

The men in front of her spread out when they reached the boat ramp. She veered to stand at the end of the curve of paddlers so she could see the river. Her heart thudded and a lump formed in her throat. The curved boat resting on the grassy bank was magnificent. The white wood glistened brightly in the sunlight and the carved head and tail were intricate beyond compare.

The head of the boat was a sea serpent, the nose longer and more tapering than a river dragon, the nostrils painted an inky blue, the bulbous eyes also an inky blue with silver slits for pupils. The horns were sharp spiral shells, and the mane was a cascading mass of dark-green seaweed scattered with ribbed shells.

Lamiya's eyes prickled with tears of wonder. All along the body of the boat were beautiful images of seasprites chasing fish and turtles amid the impression of waves and bubbles. A collage of seashells was artfully placed to give a lifelike effect. Warm fingers brushed hers as Lazuli took hold of her hand.

Lamiya swallowed. 'Beautiful. I bet she skims the water.'

'Flight is beautiful too, Lamiya.' He gave her a crooked smile. 'And our glide is significantly more elegant than theirs!' He squeezed her hand. 'Let's go closer.'

More emotions swirled within her at his kindness. What was wrong with her? Why couldn't she focus properly? She followed Lazuli, who was headed towards Tengar and Cowrie; she should introduce herself glide to glide. They reached the trio of men at the boat's head and Lazuli let her pass him. She dipped her head in thanks.

Tengar held a hand out and said to Cowrie, 'And this is Lamiya, the glide for Riverplain.' Looking over her shoulder, he added, 'Behind her are the pacers, Lazuli and Larimar, who you've already met.'

Cowrie gave a brief nod to her pacers and fixed his eerie light-blue eyes on her. To her surprise, he gave a low bow. 'May the winds guide your boat, Lamiya of Riverplain.'

Feeling inadequate, she bowed deeply and hastily replied, 'And yours, Cowrie of Riversea. May the sunshine light your path.'

Cowrie's brown face creased into a toothy grin. 'I be looking forward to testing our boats.'

Lamiya smiled. 'The design of your boat is beautiful beyond belief. May I ask who the artist is?'

The creases in Cowrie's face furrowed deeper and his eyes glinted. 'We be most proud of Seasprite. Clama did the ink drawings, and Charonia placed the shells.'

Lamiya recognised the names. 'They're here too?'

Cowrie rubbed his hands together. 'Paddlers eight and nine. I'll introduce you at the feast.'

'I'd be honoured.' Pleased, Lamiya shifted her weight from foot to foot, wondering how to extricate herself politely. Beram and Zeol marched up to tell Tengar the boat dome was ready, and she stepped aside as a collection of paddlers went to lift the Riversea boat. Hovering at the side of the ramp, she admired the clean lines of the boat and the carving of the sea serpent's tail as it was carried past.

She felt Everand's presence before he spoke. 'I didn't fully appreciate the intricacy and importance of this boat festival.' He looked down at her. 'You have much responsibility.'

Squinting at him in the bright light, she admitted, 'I am nervous. There's so much to think about, and the other teams are so strong.'

'And we haven't yet seen Riverwood,' Everand murmured, peering at her. 'You are strong too. And your dragon will be running with you.'

But what does that actually mean? Goose bumps ran down her arms, despite the heat. Would the boat disappear if it took the form of the dragon and leave them all floundering in the water? How would they win a race then? Aware she had opened and shut her mouth a couple of times, she saw Everand's expression change to concern. Was it fair to ask him what would happen when he might not know the answers? He, too, had much responsibility. His intent look sent a shiver tingling down her spine. She clenched her hands, wanting to throw herself against his chest, for him to hold her tight.

His fingers twitched a few times and he said quietly, 'I wish it too, Lamiya. Be brave. Focus on your races.' His lips quirked with the hint of a smile, then he turned and walked towards the town.

She watched him go, his erect stance reminding her that she still had his mage robe hidden beneath her pillow.

Perhaps she'd return it to him after dark-fall.

CHAPTER TWENTY-NINE

Mage Mantiss looked around the mahogany table. The members of the Inner Council were focused on him with expectant expressions and Agamid sat tensely on his left. He had barely got past the greetings before the challenge came.

'I ask again,' said Pelamis, leaning forward and shaking out the sleeves of his burnt-orange robe. 'What is Everand working on that is so important he is unable to attend council meetings?'

Seated next to Pelamis, Simoselaps also tipped forward. 'If it is so important, shouldn't the work have been approved by the council?'

Mantiss stifled a curse. He had hoped to stall any meetings until Everand returned, but Menetia had requested a meeting to discuss allocation of the young mages who were ready to begin their apprenticeship. She had never been keen to teach an apprentice, so it was a mystery why she had asked. Unless someone else had put her up to it. He looked at Pelamis thoughtfully, then glanced at Tiliqua, who sat with her deep blue eyes fixed on his face and her fine, blonde brows creased ever so slightly. She arched an eyebrow at him and he swallowed.

'I thought,' said Tiliqua smoothly, breaking the silence, 'that as well as preparing his new research proposal, Everand was interviewing the apprentices to ascertain their strengths and preferences. Didn't he want to be able to propose suitable mentors to you and save time at the next meeting?'

'Indeed,' said Mantiss slowly, feeling a rush of gratitude. He gave Pelamis a stern look. 'I was intending to explain this and schedule a meeting *after* Everand's feedback for the actual decisions of assignation. However, now we are here, I might as well ask whether any of you have particular preferences, and to confirm how many of you are willing to accept an apprentice?'

Pelamis scowled and Menetia flushed a pale pink and toyed with her numerous bracelets.

Mantiss turned to Saiphos. 'Can you scribe while I ask formally for preferences?'

Saiphos, former apprentice to Agamid, hastily straightened his writing pad and picked up the pen.

'So,' said Mantiss, 'there are four potential apprentices, three of whom are sixteen and one is seventeen. Do we have four mentors here, or do we need to convene the Outer Council of Twenty?' He sat back. It was unlikely there would be four volunteers from eight mages.

'I will mentor one,' said Agamid. 'No preference, whoever you deem most suitable.'

'Thank you, Agamid.' Mantiss listened to the pen scratching as Saiphos recorded Agamid's name. Tiliqua was regarding him pensively. Was she considering volunteering? He gave her a slight nod.

'This would be my first apprentice, but I am willing to try,' said Tiliqua.

'Thank you, Tiliqua. Either Agamid or I can answer any questions you may have, or talk through any challenges you come across.'

'I will mentor one,' said Pelamis loudly. 'I would prefer a bold apprentice with potential. Shall I speak with Everand?'

Mantiss took a breath. 'Thank you, Pelamis. No, that won't be necessary. Let's consider Everand's assessment as a group.'

'When will this be?' persisted Pelamis.

242

'Soon.' Mantiss swept his gaze around the table. 'Anyone else?' As he had thought, no-one else volunteered. Saiphos and Simoselaps lacked the confidence, Menetia was too self-absorbed, Neelaps was only interested in agriculture and Caimanops already had an apprentice. Tiliqua's boldness was pleasing, if unexpected.

'Thank you, all. Is there any other business? No? I will convene the full Outer Council in a few suns to finalise this.' He stood up to indicate the meeting was closed.

The mages hovered as if they would argue, but then gradually drifted towards the door. Tiliqua mouthed that she would see him at the dusk meal.

Agamid picked up the notepad and pen, and hovered by the table. 'They grow restless ... and bolder. Pelamis with an apprentice? Is this wise?'

Mantiss leaned against the back of his chair. 'No, but I could hardly refuse. We'd better hope Everand returns promptly so we can task him with interviewing the apprentices!'

Agamid's frown deepened. 'Things are moving too quickly. You might be forced to reveal his mission before you hoped.'

Mantiss sighed. 'I will ask Tiliqua to interview the apprentices so at least we can fulfill that promise.' When Agamid continued to hover, hazel eyes troubled, he said, 'What, my friend?'

'Do you think you should tell Tiliqua what Everand is really doing? She is astute, and understands you too well.'

'Plots within plots and secrets within secrets ... this is far from ideal, but you may be right.'

Agamid smiled. 'Plots and secrets are your forte. I must go. Let me know if you need anything.'

Mantiss walked to the door and down the broad steps with Agamid, then took the path to his dome while Agamid peeled away towards the library. *Secrets within secrets.* He and Lapemis had that much in common.

It was quiet in his quarters, so he headed directly to his desk.

From the scrawlings of Mage Lapemis

The wall of granite

Cold season arrived, with an icy wind howling down from the mountains. When Notechis and Aclys returned from hunting small animals in the forest, Aclys approached me.

'You know, Lapemis,' he said, 'there is a huge amount of granite in those outcrops. We could build a wall that would help break up this cursed wind and mark the boundary of the land we claim.'

A wall of granite — the concept had merit. A high wall would also keep out the red dragon if she ever made it this far across land. 'A sound idea,' I replied. 'Let's start work on it. We can replicate more boulders to build it faster.'

So, we mages used our power to transport massive, craggy boulders into a curve along our northern edge. The work kept us warm. It occurred to me that more people might find the island and decide to settle here, and the wall would serve us well then, too. Two of the humans worked with us, making mud to seal the cracks and gaps between the rocks where the smooth edges we created did not quite align. The other humans tilled a large area of land ready for crops and created wells into the eternal spring.

During the dark we gathered inside the marble dome we had finished, sitting around a fire pit and telling ourselves the future looked bright. I proposed that we create a new charter of laws for our Guild. Carlias offered to scribe. We created parchment from shavings of tree trunk, and each dark-fall discussed what our principles and rules should be.

All concurred that we should continue to keep the lines of magic pure, and mages must hence only breed with mages. This would be a key and immutable rule. Dtella agreed to be my wife, Pogona paired with Notechis, and Aprasia with

Aclys. The humans also paired up. Dtella and I frequently crept into a nook with blankets, aiming to commence the continuation of our line. Knowing that mages often only deliver one offspring, we reasoned we should start as soon as possible. I wished fervently for a daughter, for these were also rare.

Everyone agreed we should extend the wall of granite around our entire land. I could see the humans thought this proposal a tad extreme, having no memory of the red dragon. I explained that we would be better able to protect them, should the unthinkable happen and others settle nearby and invade us in the future. We congratulated ourselves again on our discovery of this bountiful island, but acknowledged that, over time, others might come.

Thinking of the Staropal, I proposed that we remain within the granite wall and not attempt contact with any others, should they arrive. Given that we could provide for ourselves, and especially until our numbers were replenished, this was readily approved. Relief filled me. If others outside the wall did not know of us, they could not relay information to the red dragon.

Cold-season drew to a close. The skies grew blue again, and the grasses and crops began to flourish. All of the women — mage and human — were with child. Over the growing and harvest seasons our work went well. The houses and a meeting place for the humans were completed, as was our mage residence building, which we optimistically made ten levels high. Carlias suggested we build an eleventh floor of stables and a training area for the transport beetles. He and Aclys added the idea of a flat rooftop with a ramp for the beetles to take off from and land on.

As Head of the Guild, I chose quarters on the tenth floor for myself and Dtella. Our quarters faced east; the others chose rooms that captured the western sun.

We extended the wall of granite so that it was two persons in height. By the time the first offspring were born, as well as curving across our northern border it stretched in a gentle curve all the way around the land we had claimed. We did not build a gate.

Of the red and blue dragons there remained no sign.

Mantiss stared at the threads of colour in the marble wall and thrummed his fingertips on the desk. In the three hundred season-cycles since Lapemis' vision, there had been two major breaches of the wall. The new Guild had fulfilled the early mages' expectations: there were now a hundred and thirty mages and almost three hundred humans. The lands within Axis were arable and well cultivated, yielding an impressive array of crops and produce. The eternal spring continued to provide ample fresh water. The stables were full of trained transport beetles and the silk moth program had expanded to six breeding domes. Axis was indeed comfortable — and entirely self-sufficient.

The research and testing of new spells had also developed well. The library, managed by Mage Hydrelaps, was brimming with interesting and well-written texts. The upstairs classrooms caught the sunshine, and had hosted classes for several waves of apprentices.

Mantiss frowned. Without drawing more power from the Staropal, they could be reaching the limits of new and useful spells. The younger mages were growing restless, Pelamis being the boldest so far. On reflection, it was amazing there had only been two breaches, by two driven, ambitious mages, over all this time.

Mage Thrip had snatched the Staropal two hundred cycles ago and had travelled to other worlds. History told that those remaining waited with bated breath. Their worst fears were realised when Thrip was overcome by a powerful race of half-humans and half-moths from a world called Chrysalis. Their world was dying, and they seized the opportunity to invade Ossilis. A bead of sweat trickled annoyingly down his brow and Mantiss brushed it away. The annals stated the battle had been fierce. The Guild had lost thirty mages, but managed to lure, trap and annihilate the small force from Chrysalis.

Afterwards, Mage Thrip was punished by obliteration. A shudder passed through Mantiss. The severest of sentences, in accordance with Guild Rule Eleven.

Mantiss sealed the notebook away and went to stand by the window, resting his eyes on the tranquil gardens. The second breach had happened under *his* leadership. The idiot Mage Beetal had also gone to Chrysalis, which was his undoing. Ironically, it was the traitor mage's army of winged dragons that killed the farseers and their insectoid soldiers. The idea had been suggested by the warrior woman, and Everand had somehow redirected the creatures' wrath. Too late to save Mage Beetal, though.

Which had saved him, as the incumbent Head of the Guild, from an unpleasant decision: a decree of obliteration for the mage's treachery. His left eye twinged. He'd nearly lost it in the battle, and the vision remained perpetually clouded.

Worry gnawed at his soul: was a third breach imminent? He had sanctioned Everand's travel outside the wall, reasoning that Everand had already gone out over the wall when he was spying on Mage Beetal. Everand's mission was for the greater good: it would give them the knowledge to *prevent* further incursions. Would the information he brought back be enough to prevent any unsanctioned *excursions*, though?

The strength drained from his legs and he leaned his arms on the glass.

Could his trusted spy save him again?

CHAPTER THIRTY

By the time Everand had warmed water to wash, devoured food and changed into the latest tunic and trousers that Beram had provided, the dome was filled with the purple-grey hues of dusk. Candles flickered softly on the shelves. Beram spent even longer arranging his hair and brushing down his clothes. Whose eye was he hoping to attract?

Finally, Beram patted his stomach and grumbled, 'Too many more of these welcome feasts and the boat will be too heavy to paddle! I wish Riverwood had arrived at the same time.'

Everand ducked under the curtain and walked with Beram to the courtyard. The babble of voices reached his ears and judging by the flickering orange light, the bonfire was already ablaze. Similar to the previous feast, on entering the courtyard he found tables with food and drinks piled high on the left side, and the massive fire burning brightly in the centre surrounded by tables and benches. The ones closest to him looked new, and he guessed the carpenters had been busy. Most of the townspeople were there, seated at tables eating or collected in small groups talking. Children ran weaving between the groups, or sat in circles near the fire playing games with clay tokens or pieces of wood. The courtyard was nearly full.

He surveyed the area, ascertaining where the various teams were. Tengar was seated with Atage, Lyber and Cowrie, the glide from Riversea. Also with them were the stocky older pacer Chiton and the oldest paddler in Lamiya's team, Luvu.

Were these older and more experienced men the negotiators for the trade discussions?

Two tables away, the rest of the men from the Riversea team sat with a mix of paddlers from Riverfall and Riverplain. None of the women were there. Feeling his eyebrow rise, he scanned further afield. A trill of laughter drew his attention and on the far side of the flickering bonfire he saw the women paddlers were seated together.

Momentarily, he watched Lamiya waving her hands around animatedly, deep in conversation with a young woman from Riversea. So far, she had astounded him with her courage and adaptability. Earlier, when they were watching the Riversea boat being brought in, he'd glimpsed her inner turmoil and held a brief uneasy fear that events might overwhelm her. That must not happen. Reluctantly, he'd walked away from the longing in her eyes, remembering all too well the same expression in Elemar's eyes when Mage Beetal had threatened her life.

A dusting of melancholy settled across his shoulders. With a deep sigh, he shrugged it off. He *had* saved Elemar. Now he must make sure Lamiya stayed safe. And he should take the opportunity to find out more about Riversea.

Amid much bantering with Kunzite, Acim and Zink, he piled his plate high and headed to the table of mixed paddlers, nodding at people who greeted him and stepping around knots of children. Persaj and Zeol shuffled along to make space for him and cheerfully introduced him as the traveller from Axis.

'He's going to judge the finish of the races,' said Persaj to the Riversea men.

'Conch, a pacer,' said the man seated opposite him, who Everand judged to be in his late thirties.

'Pippel,' said the younger man beside him. 'And my father, Summel.'

'Everd,' said Everand, just remembering his devised name in time, and leaping into questions before they could ask him about Axis. 'What are your skills?'

249

'Carpenter,' said Conch, 'and these two are fishermen.'

'Conch made our paddles,' explained Pippel. 'The oars we use are broader and longer. Sometimes we use a long oar with a blade on both ends.'

Conch nodded. 'The pacers from Riverplain explained how the boats needed to match to make it a fair competition.'

'Who made your boat?' asked Everand, genuinely interested.

Waving a hand towards Atage's table, Conch said, 'Chiton and Cowrie carved Seasprite. I only helped make the changes for the festival.' He then waved a hand at the women's table. 'Charonia and Clama did the decorations.'

Everand chewed his mouthful of fish, appreciating the flavours. 'Can you tell me more of the history of Riversea? As a traveller I'm trying to understand the history and lifestyle of the provinces.'

Summel spoke in a deep voice and he had to concentrate, for the man's accent was strong. 'We need Clommus for that. He be the master teller. Clommus!' Everand winced. 'Stop stuffing your mouth and come here! Traveller wants a history lesson!'

Pippel leaned towards him, grinning. 'Be warned, his stories take forever in the telling.'

'Eh?' shouted Clommus from the end of the table. 'An audience? On the way!'

Everand laughed as the solid old paddler elbowed his team mates off the bench and ploughed his way down the table until he sat opposite. Pippel and Conch sat back down beside Clommus whereas the older paddlers took the opportunity to shuffle away to converse with the Riverfall paddlers. Putting his hands in his lap, Everand created a memory ball ready to capture Clommus' tale for Mantiss.

Clommus took a long drink, wiped his mouth with the back of a hand and thumped the mug down. 'You be interested in history?'

Everand asked, 'How did Riversea begin?'

'Try the shorter version,' grunted Conch.

Clommus gave a snort and fixed his pale blue eyes on Everand. 'The pictures in the caves along the coastal bluff reveal this. Our ancestors came from lands far to the south, according to the rough map carved into the rock then coloured in charcoal and dyes from plants. They fled fighting and five boats set out, packed high with men, women and children. For a half-cycle of the moon, they rode the waves.'

Pippel rubbed his hands together. 'I like the next part. The adventure.'

After giving Pippel a dry look, Clommus continued. 'One dark and stormy dark-fall, when the moon was obscured by shadows and clouds … eh, I like how that sounds … One dark and stormy dark-fall, when the moon was obscured by shadows and clouds ... must remember them words … the boats were tossed like dry leaves upon a lakeshore.' He paused, and Everand could see him mulling over how that sounded.

'Get on with it!' snarled Conch.

'… tossed like dry leaves upon a lakeshore. Two boats be lost, with all souls aboard. Don't know why you like this part, Pippel. The other three boats were blown here and there, bobbing and lurching, until the people lay on the timbers quaking and exhausted. When the sun cast her pink fingers over the boats and seas …'

'*This* is the part I like,' interrupted Pippel.

'When the sun cast her pink fingers over the boats and seas,' repeated Clommus stubbornly, 'and the winds dropped and the swell eased, they stirred and sat up. Behold! A gleaming wall of white rock stood before them, with trees and vegetation waving greenly from the top. The oars were all broken, so they used their hands and paddled the boats closer, following the base of the rock until it parted into a broad river estuary.'

Pippel's eyes gleamed. 'Dragontail Estuary!'

'Who be telling the tale?' said Clommus gruffly. 'Aye, they paddled the boats up the estuary and found a sandy beach. According to the first drawings, fifty people landed. They found the rivers and tributaries full of fish, shells and other edible creatures. Above the sandy dunes they found palm trees, flax, broad grasses, herbs and berries. Look no further, they decided.'

'And over time, Caneo was built as the huts grew and the people multiplied,' squeaked Pippel, dodging the cuff that earned him.

Everand laughed, enjoying the byplay between the two paddlers and appreciating Clommus' way with words. So, he reflected, the people from Riversea were not from the same island as the people of Riverfall and Riverplain. The reason for their arrival was similar, but they were not related, as evidenced by the different build and appearance. What did they bring to the trade discussions?

'Who is your leader? Who will speak with Atage about the possibility of trade?'

Conch and Clommus looked taken aback at the abrupt change of topic.

Conch spoke slowly. 'Chiton is Master of Caneo and speaks for Riversea. Why do you ask, Traveller?'

Adopting an enthusiastic expression and waving his hands around like he'd seen Lamiya do, Everand said, 'From what I've heard, this festival with all four provinces is unprecedented. As is Atage's idea of trading across the provinces.' Forcing a grin that felt entirely unnatural, he added, 'We are living a historical event! As well as judging the races, I'm hoping to make a record of the events for the annals.'

Where had that come from? Now he'd have to do just that, although a complete and accurate record of what was agreed would be a sound plan and he was well placed to provide this service. Atage might already have something in mind, but he could at least make sure the record was robust enough to deflect disputes in the future. *Good idea, my boy, as long as you don't interfere with the decisions themselves,* he imagined Mage Mantiss saying sternly. He sealed the memory ball, assuming there was no more information coming, and slipped it into his trouser pocket.

Conch and Clommus regarded him with guarded expressions while Pippel shifted on the bench, glancing between them. Everand spread his hands modestly. 'Part of my duties in Axis is to record meetings and decisions so those doing the deciding are free to focus on the ideas and outcomes.' They didn't look convinced. 'I have the neatest writing.'

'Ah,' said Clommus, picking up his mug. 'Maybe you can record my stories then.'

Pippel laughed. 'But if he did that, we wouldn't need you to keep telling them!'

'That be an excellent point, young Pippel,' said Clommus, sloshing feeja wine as he waved his mug.

Everand joined in their laughter, then picked up his empty plate. 'I look forward to hearing more from such a master weaver of tales.' Clommus grinned widely. 'For now, more of the fine food.' He nodded a farewell and sauntered towards the food tables.

Plate refilled, he chose a quiet and shadowed spot near a glossy green bush, sat on the ground and nibbled at a cake. Unease wallowed in the base of his stomach. Instinct told him the people from Riversea came with good intent. But they were different, and those from Riverwood would be different again.

Atage had no small task before him to get four different peoples to trade with one another. Each province would seek the best advantage for their people — the boat races were a clear manifestation of their pride and competitiveness. Perhaps Atage would have been wiser to start with regular trade between Riverfall and Riverplain? Make the outcome desirable to entice the others to join in. Too late now, Atage had made his bold bid.

Absently, he picked up a piece of star-fruit. Think! You can't change this now. You must predict the problems. An image of Mage Mantiss' wise face appeared in his mind's eye, sadness tingeing the green eyes and a slim hand stroking the silvery beard. *This, my boy, is precisely why we do not meddle in the affairs of others. Men are unpredictable. It is difficult enough to keep a guild of mages focused.*

Focused for what? He choked as the sliver of star-fruit went down the wrong way. Suppressing the urge to cough brought tears to his eyes, but the offending piece of fruit slid down and he took a shaky breath. Focused for what? Why *do* the mages hone and expand their skills, living in their marble domes? *'To Protect by Sun and Moon'* said the gold emblem on the administration building. Protect who from what? The mages from the outside world? Why was it so important no-one go outside the granite wall and wardspell?

The muscles across his chest contracted painfully. Never before had he questioned the purpose and rules of the Mages' Guild.

His mentor had, though. The swarthy dark-haired mage had ranted about what he perceived to be the stagnation of the Guild and the enforced limitations on their powers. He would stride about his study, beard spiking in indignation and yelling his ideas at Everand. Mage Beetal's frustrations had led to violence, and the mages had indeed moved to protect themselves.

The taste of regret filled Everand's mouth at his mentor's death. His long-term mentor had been ambitious rather than evil and he'd thought, fleetingly, that he could turn him away from disaster. But the moment had passed, and his mentor had attacked the Guild with his winged dragons from Terralis in a bid to take the Staropal. Taking the stone shaped like a star, swirling with all the colours of a glittering opal, would have given Mage Beetal supreme power. And control of the Guild.

When the mages defeated Beetal's army, only with help from Elemar and her warrior friends, the Guild had once again buried the Staropal deep beneath the Great Hall. As Head of the Guild, Mage Mantiss had decreed that the lure of power was to be removed and sealed up tight. Everand tapped his fingers on his thigh. History taught that two generations before, Mage Thrip had also tried to take the Staropal and control of the Guild — for similar reasons to Mage Beetal. Perhaps Mantiss was right to remove the powerful stone from sight and all temptation.

But not everyone was tempted. He frowned. After the battle, the Staropal had bobbed towards *him*, its colours swirling hypnotically. He had touched its smooth surface, marvelling at its beauty, and Elemar had shrieked at him to take it, saying it wanted him to. However, he had readily passed it to Mantiss to conceal again, having no desire for such responsibility. Unease shifted in his stomach. Why had Elemar thought *he* should take the stone? He was a mere apprentice at the time.

His thoughts drifted to his ordered life. No longer an apprentice, he filled his time studying and researching, practising spells and attending meetings of the Inner Council of Ten. He'd been so proud to be invited onto the Inner Council when old Hydrophis died. All his basic needs were catered to by the humans who worked with them. Delma, the cook, had befriended Elemar when she arrived and helped him to understand the needs of the warrior woman from Terralis.

His throat constricted excruciatingly: the humans were just like those who lived in Riverfall or Riverplain. But the mages looked down upon them. The humans were protected and lived comfortably, but they did not have a voice in Axis. The food roiled in his stomach and he hurriedly stood up.

His feet carried him towards the northern gate, solitude by the river calling to him. As he walked through the courtyards, he saw that most of the domes were empty. Soft light emanated from a few, and the sounds of women putting children to bed. Perhaps he should check the northern gate; it would be easy for mischief with no-one there. He walked more briskly. On reaching the hopeepa dome, he thought of Crystal's cracked hooves and decided to check on her.

Easing back the door, he slipped inside and created a small ball of silvery light. The two largest stags from Riverplain looked down their noses haughtily, annoyed at being disturbed. In the furthest stall, Crystal ambled to the slats to see if he had any treats and rasped her tongue up the side of his face. He squirmed and patted her nose.

'Sorry, no treats.' Using the light of his globe, he squatted and inspected Crystal's cracked hooves. Someone had applied salve. The hopeepa licked the top of his head, his hair sticking to her tongue. Then she swung her head up, and he became aware of a shadow slinking into the dome behind him. The wood creaked as the door was pushed closed. His heart beat faster, although he didn't feel danger. His knees cracked when he stood up.

Holding the light out in front of him, he found Lamiya standing there with a bundle of material in her arms. This, she pushed at him.

'Your robe,' she murmured with a smile.

Everand rested the globe on top of a railing so he could take the robe. A knot of emotion rose as his fingers clasped the smooth silk. The robe was neatly folded, the material soft and smelling faintly of a kind of flower.

'I washed it,' said Lamiya. 'It was stiff with river water.'

'Thank you,' he said, moved by her thoughtfulness. An awkward silence ensued. Lamiya clearly had no intention of leaving, and that wistful expression was creeping into her face. 'Crystal's hooves are healing,' he said inanely.

Lamiya took a step closer. 'Good.' She put her head on one side most attractively, for it made the caramel and blue threads in her wavy hair sparkle in the reflected globe light, and accentuated her cheekbones. 'I like how you care about the animals. Do you have animals in Axis?'

Confused about the way the conversation was developing, he shrugged. 'I have a fish.' His guilt surged. He'd hardly spared a thought for poor Mizu in stasis, waiting for his return!

'What's wrong?' asked Lamiya, her eyebrows creasing together.

'My fish is sick. I left her, thinking I was going to a brief meeting.' If he hadn't been holding the robe, he would have run a hand across his jaw.

Lamiya took another step closer and touched his arm gently. 'Tell me about your fish.'

'She's silver-white, with large red patches and an elegant tail and fins. I named her Mizu.' He paused. 'Or maybe she came with that name.'

Lamiya smiled. 'She sounds like a Koi fish. I've heard there are many in Dragon Lake.' She waved her hands about. 'We have a smaller version in our lakes. Larimar was thinking about trying to breed some, for colour and form.'

Abruptly it came to him: he'd found the fish in a small bowl in Mage Beetal's study after Mantiss and Agamid had taken the important artefacts and any evidence they needed to record his mentor's treachery. Alarm jolted through him. Mage Beetal had disobeyed the Guild orders regarding travel, which he knew all too well because his mentor had taken him through the illicit rift that breached the wardspell and then through a second illicit sky rift into Elemar's world.

Had his mentor also travelled closer to Axis? The fish couldn't have been there all along or he would've noticed it during his regular lessons. He frowned. Beetal must have acquired the fish not long before his demise. The image of a torn scrap of paper on the desk next to the bowl came to his mind. It had the word 'Mizu' scrawled in Beetal's hand, but the paper was ripped next to it. Was part of the word missing? Had his mentor been to Dragon Lake? Did the piece of paper originally say Mizuchi Falls? Or, more worryingly, Mizuchi?

Lamiya was now standing almost on his toes, regarding him with a worried expression. 'What is it? You look as if you've eaten a handful of sour-berries!' She grasped both of his elbows.

'I ...' his voice cracked. Clearing his throat, he tried again. 'I remembered something.' He looked into her face properly. 'It's a long story. Too long for now.'

Disappointed, she gave a rueful smile. Everand floundered like a fish out of water trying to think what to say. A shove to his lower back sent him stumbling and, blinking, he found he was standing with his arms around Lamiya's lower back, still clasping the robe. She had somehow reached up to put her arms around his neck. Her face was tilted up at him, eyes glinting in the silvery light, her pupils wide and dark.

'Thanks, Crystal,' she muttered with an impish grin.

Words failing him, he rested his chin on top of Lamiya's head, allowing her warmth to seep into him, a welcome distraction from the painful thoughts emerging. Breathing deeply, he took in her subtle mix of scents, conjuring open plains filled with grasses and colourful flowers. He would like to see Riverplain; see where she lived.

He kissed her hair and she wriggled closer. She tilted her head further and he found his lips following the curve of her neck, softly brushing her smooth skin. An ache settled into his chest and spread towards his loins. His breath came in short gasps; he was losing himself to her.

'Lamiya,' his voice wavered. 'What of Lazuli?' He couldn't have his heart broken again. He had tenuously opened his heart to Elemar, and then the handsome warrior with chestnut hair had miraculously found a way through Beetal's rift and come to claim her. Elemar told him that her choice hadn't been easy. But she had left, nonetheless.

Lamiya leaned back to look him the eye. Chewing her lower lip, she said, 'I've known Lazuli all my life. He's like a brother and I care deeply for him. I don't want to hurt him.' She shuddered and looked troubled. 'But ... I can't explain ... *this.*'

Everand closed his eyes against the tide of hope crashing over him.

Lamiya narrowed her eyes. 'You haven't cast a mage spell over me, have you?'

Heart thumping, he stared. Was she joking or asking in earnest? Unable to tell, hurt rose. 'No, Lamiya. And you haven't used your calling ability on me, have you?'

A flush crept up her neck and into her cheeks. 'Not intentionally,' she whispered. The front of her tunic bulged and he sighed when Whirr climbed out, hopped onto his arm and clawed all the way up to his shoulder. The tiny talons were surprisingly sharp. Whirr then rubbed the top of his tiny, downy head against his chin.

Delight infused Lamiya's face. 'Whirr likes you!' She nudged Whirr aside and tipped her face up expectantly. Everand closed his lips over hers and revelled in the feel of her. When the ache inside became too painful, he broke away and rested his chin on top of her head again.

'I know,' she mumbled against his chest. '*After* the festival.' She lifted her head away from his chest and took a step back. With a waggle of fingers, she was gone.

He was left to sift through a morass of thoughts.

CHAPTER THIRTY-ONE

Lamiya woke to find the team already throwing off their blankets, sitting up and stretching or yawning. Her blanket vanished from her legs when Lazuli snatched it up with a grin. She grabbed the fast-receding corner and tugged it back. He threw the rest of it over her head. With a sigh, she pushed the blanket off and stood up. Whirr clung to her tangled hair with scolding squawks, and Lazuli laughed.

Around her, everyone was efficiently folding their blankets and rolling up their mattresses, stowing them neatly along the back wall. Lapsi and Lepid carried the low tables to the centre, and Lulite was already warming water for their brew. Lopa was humming to herself and breaking open loaves, with Laza beside her adding fruit to the plates. Lamiya hurriedly packed up her bedding and helped Larimar place the cushions around the tables. The team was soon seated and helping themselves to food. She put some grains on the table for Whirr and the bird fell quiet as he pecked at them.

While she ate, Lamiya thought about the training. This would be the second-last effort before the races, so something not too strenuous, but a sharpener to build confidence and refine their technique. A few more race starts holding the opening faster strokes for longer? She tapped her fingers on the table, considering the longer race. It was too late to build any additional strength, but a drill holding the anticipated rate of stroke over, say, six hundred strokes would boost confidence

260

and allow the team to ease out any stress. She tipped her mug up and realised it was empty.

'More?' It seemed Lulite had noticed.

'Please.' Lamiya passed over her mug. When Lulite placed a full mug before her and sat back down, she asked her drummer's opinion.

Lulite blew steam from her mug and looked at Lamiya over the rim. 'I agree. I think we need to work out the best sustained rate of stroke. We've never raced that far.' After a few cautious sips, Lulite added softly, 'This is the race you want to win?'

'Think of the glory in reaching that far bridge first,' said Lamiya.

'Do you intend to sacrifice the other two races, though?' murmured Lulite.

'Not if we can help it.' Lamiya shrugged. 'We'll need to paddle our best at all times. The other teams look strong.'

Lulite patted the back of her hand and gave a smile of encouragement. For a moment, Lamiya wished she could confer with Lulite about Everand and Lazuli. She would so value her friend's wisdom in these unpredictable waters! She must have looked downcast because Lulite patted the back of her hand again.

Lamiya clapped her hands to get everyone's attention and outlined her plans for the session. 'Any questions?' By his serious expression, Larimar was thinking about something. She waited for the shy paddler to form his idea.

'Perhaps we should practise speeding up for the finish at the end of the long race.' He clasped his hands together and leaned on the table. 'When we've been paddling at a steady rate for a long haul it can be difficult to persuade the arms to pick up the rate.'

Lamiya gave him a pleased nod. 'Good point. We'll add fifty fast strokes at the end of the sustained effort. Anyone else?' The team mumbled approval. 'Let's go then.' She looked at Lazuli. 'Can you collect Ejad on the way? You know where his dome is?'

In a short time, the team was clad in training tunics, paddles over shoulders, and marching out of the dome. Lamiya squared her shoulders and led her team through the town, acknowledging the cheers from the townspeople as they marched by, strides neatly aligned. *Excellent,* she thought. *We are a team to be reckoned with!*

They passed through the arch of the southern gate and she squinted against the silver light shimmering off the river. Already, she felt warmth in the sun's rays. It would be hot and hard work by the time they started the long race; she must make sure they brought adequate water with them. The cotton workers were already out amid the neat rows of bushes, hand watering.

Shading her eyes with a hand, she saw the Riversea team carrying Seasprite to the ramp. Her heart quickened and a ball of nerves formed in her stomach. *Stay calm. They'll be watching us as much as we're watching them.* Detecting running steps behind her, she glanced over her shoulder.

Lazuli dropped into place beside Larimar. 'Ejad is already at the boat dome. The Riverfall team is going out too.'

'Thanks.' She slowed down as she rounded the edge of the boat dome, then held up her hand and stopped because the Riverfall boat nose was coming out of the door. With smiles of welcome, the Riverfall team carried Mizuchi past.

'Train well,' said Tengar, looking at her. 'You'll need to!' he added with a sly grin.

Lazuli fidgeted, but thankfully didn't say anything. Piqued that her team was last to fetch their boat, Lamiya took a breath. *Save it for the races.* She entered the dome. Flight was alone in the centre of the large, airy space, and Ejad was waiting by the boat.

'Can I fetch your oar for you?' Ejad asked, hovering by Flight's tail.

'Thanks.' She watched him reach into the back of the boat to lift out the oar.

'Ouch!' Ejad exclaimed, snapping back up straight. He reached in again and leaped back with a yell, batting at his arm.

Horrified, Lamiya gaped at the narrow, dark snake dangling from his forearm, writhing so crazily the black body and green diamond pattern blurred. Ejad screamed and groaned. Whirr flew up from her shoulder, screeching. Lamiya froze; her mouth hung open and her legs seemed to have turned to rock.

Luvu roughly pushed her out of the way and swung his paddle down hard on the snake's head. Ejad screamed again, and the snake fell to the dirt floor, where it writhed in a large S-shape and raised its head to strike. Luvu planted his legs apart, grabbed his paddle in both hands, and drove it down on the snake's head with all force. With a sickening crunch, the blade severed the head from the twitching body. The snake tail thrashed then went still. Ejad looked at her, his face turning blue, and toppled to the floor.

Lamiya cried out and the team gathered around Ejad. Suddenly, Mookaite strode back into the dome, pushed her out of the way, looked at the snake's body then rushed to kneel down by Ejad. Finally persuading her legs to move, Lamiya hurried to crouch beside Mookaite.

'Cloth,' said the healer tersely. 'We must stop the poison from spreading.' Mookaite laid a hand on the moaning Ejad's forehead. 'Already he burns. Hurry, Lamiya!'

Lamiya ripped two strips off the bottom of her tunic and passed them to Mookaite.

'Hold his arm while I tie it.' Mookaite looked over her shoulder. 'Larimar, hold Ejad down. He must move less.'

With great difficulty, Lamiya managed to get a grip on Ejad's upper arm and hold it out straight while Mookaite slipped the strip of cloth above his elbow, held one end in her teeth, pulled it tight and tied a knot. Ejad screamed and tried to get up. Larimar was almost sitting on his shoulders to keep him down. Lamiya let go and eyed the puncture wounds just above Ejad's wrist, bile rising in her throat and making it hard for her to breathe. The fang holes were turning an angry red-purple shade, and Ejad was sweating profusely. She swallowed and looked at Mookaite. The healer shrugged, her face pinched.

'Even with my salves I doubt I can save him,' Mookaite whispered hoarsely. 'These vipers are deadly.'

Beside Lamiya's knee, Whirr jumped up and down, squawking. She snatched the bird up and spun him so his beak was not far from her face. Staring into the tiny bright eyes, she commanded, 'Get Everand! Now!' She threw the bird into the air, watching Whirr hover to give a peep and fly out of the dome, his tiny wings dipping at top speed.

Mookaite gave her a surprised look. 'The traveller?'

Lamiya said evenly, 'He has skills you don't know about.' Over her shoulder she observed her paddlers milling about helplessly. 'Can you stay?' she asked Mookaite. 'I'll get the team to take the boat out ready.' She pushed up from the floor and addressed the team.

'Lazuli, you're the fastest, run to Mookaite's dome and fetch her salves. The others, there's nothing more you can do here so take Flight down to the ramp and wait. I hope we'll still train.'

Lazuli spun on his heel and sprinted out of the dome. Luvu was watching her with a disgruntled look. She inclined her head. 'Good thinking to kill the snake. A healer is coming. Can you take the team through the ground warm-up?'

Luvu regarded her through narrowed eyes. 'As you say, glide.'

'Wait!' called Lamiya, mouth dry, when the team stepped towards the boat. 'Check thoroughly first. Look under all the benches, check *everything*.'

With bated breath, she watched while the paddlers searched the boat and found nothing else untoward. Luvu grunted and grabbed the boat near the tail. As one, the team lifted Flight and eased her out of the doorway. She was still looking at the door when a figure shimmered and emerged, shadowed against the light.

'What happened?' Everand strode past her and she blinked. He must have used his magic!

'A snake bit Ejad,' she said. Mookaite stared up at Everand in astonishment. Lamiya took a deep breath, walked briskly to the wooden door and pulled it to, then hurried to where Mookaite and Everand were crouched beside Ejad.

When she knelt beside him, Everand reached into his tunic and then passed Whirr to her. 'What actually happened?'

Lamiya licked her lips. 'Ejad offered to get the oar for me and the snake must have been coiled inside the boat.' Everand's forehead grew deep furrows and she faltered to a stop. He looked to Mookaite, who was starting to shake and look faint.

'How does the poison work?' he asked.

'It will stop his heart if it gets there,' said Mookaite.

Gingerly, Everand placed a hand on Ejad's forehead, snatching it back with a gasp. Lamiya wrung her hands while she watched Everand steeling himself, and then became intrigued when he closed his eyes and placed his palm across Ejad's forehead, his lips moving silently. Ejad squirmed once, and lay still.

'Is he dead?' squeaked Mookaite.

Everand shook his head. 'I've calmed him and slowed his heart down. This'll slow the movement of the poison and give us some time.' He sat back on his heels, considering. His eyes looked sad. 'I must extract the poison completely. The cloth on his arm was good thinking.' His shoulders lifted in a small shrug. 'If the venom hasn't spread past the cloth I might be able to save him.'

Lamiya sniffed, and noticed a tear trickling down Mookaite's cheek. Everand's command sounded in her head: *Tell her about me and swear her to secrecy.* She sniffed again and mumbled to Mookaite, 'Our traveller has powers we can't see. He's here to help us with a threat to the festival.' When Mookaite raised both eyebrows she added, 'You mustn't tell anyone.'

Everand shuffled to sit by Ejad's right arm. He cradled the limp arm in his lap, sitting cross-legged. Lamiya noticed that he kept the wounded hand lower, resting it on the floor. A small, clear bubble about the size of a clenched fist appeared around the puncture wound, sealing it from the air. Her stomach roiled, and beside her Mookaite took rapid, shallow breaths, as evil-looking purple-black pus seeped out of the fang holes and oozed into the base of the bubble. Whirr gave a strangled peep and crawled back inside her tunic.

'Magic?' Mookaite gazed at Everand in wonder.

'It's really important you keep this secret,' Lamiya said, observing Everand's face as he worked, fine blond eyebrows pinched together, eyes closed and face relaxed. Every now and then his lips twitched, and more pus dribbled out.

The dome was silent and still; she became aware of her heart thudding in her chest. Motes of dust hung suspended in the cool, shadowy air. Looking down at Ejad's slack face, she thought the blue tinge might have eased. When she glanced at Mookaite, she found the healer regarding her thoughtfully.

'There,' Everand opened his eyes. 'I think I have it all.' He mouthed some strange words, and the clear surface at the base of the bubble extended across the top of the fang holes and met in the centre. Then, he lifted the fully sealed bubble up and frowned. 'More than I expected.' He placed it on the ground away from him, making sure it did not roll. 'I'll scan the rest of him to be sure.' He knelt facing Ejad's face, and placed both palms flat on the young paddler's chest.

Lamiya held her breath, staring at Everand's strong hands, willing him to succeed. Without thinking, she moved closer, put her hands over his nearest hand and bent her senses into his touch.

266

'Close your eyes,' he murmured.

She perceived a faint buzzing sensation of energy travelling down his arms and through his hands into Ejad. A curious sensation of travelling through Ejad's body came to her, as if she were a small dot, systematically moving along the young man's life force.

'Don't analyse, just accept,' murmured Everand.

Time passed breath by breath, until she felt the warmth of Everand's skin beneath her palms, and the sensation of being inside Ejad receded. When Everand sat up, she dropped her hands to her sides. Mookaite stared wide-eyed at both of them. At her knees, Ejad stirred and sat up shakily, only to fall back again when Mookaite threw herself around him.

'You did it!' exclaimed the healer.

Ejad looked dazed, as if he couldn't work out why he was on the floor. Mookaite clung to the young man's left arm, tears rolling down her face.

'How do you feel?' asked Everand.

Ejad peered at him, his eyes not quite focused. 'Weird. Like I'm still asleep.'

'I forgot your heart rate,' said Everand. 'Wait.' He got up and stood behind the sitting Ejad, placing both hands on his shoulders.

Lamiya again sensed a buzzing of energies moving. Colour flowed into Ejad's cheeks, his chest moved as he took deeper breaths and the humour crept back into his eyes. When his lips broke into a wide smile, Mookaite burst into tears again. Ejad looked at her in such astonishment that Lamiya grinned. Relief raced through her, and she realised how responsible she felt for this borrowed paddler's wellbeing.

'Where's my paddle?' asked Ejad, trying to stand.

Lamiya liked the way Everand took Ejad's elbow and helped him up, not letting go until he was sure the young paddler was steady.

The sound of skidding came from the doorway, and Lazuli burst in with Mookaite's basket of jars and herbs clasped to his chest. He strode across the dome, his footfalls echoing against the walls, and stopped in disbelief when he saw Ejad standing up. Panting hard, he held the basket out to Mookaite.

'Thanks,' said Mookaite, taking the basket and rummaging in it until she found a jar with a pink salve. Looking at Everand, she said, 'I assume calendula and lavender will help? The punctures mustn't get infected.'

Lamiya stepped forward. 'Here, let me hold the basket for you.'

Ejad watched with over-bright eyes while Mookaite gently spread salve across the back of his wrist. 'Can we train now?'

Lamiya raised an eyebrow at Everand. He didn't answer immediately, and she thought he looked unsettled.

'If I'm honest, I don't know. You should be fine, unless I missed anything …' He looked at Mookaite. 'Can he go to your dome afterwards? Find me if he falls ill?'

'Of course!' Mookaite's response came out as a strangled squeak, and Lamiya wondered if the healer was overwhelmed by Everand's powers.

Everand said to Lazuli, 'Can you fetch a sack for the body of the snake? Is there a safe place we can bury it?'

Lazuli nodded tersely, sweat running down his neck. 'The next dome has some. I'll be back.'

Lamiya shifted her weight. Everand had taken charge of the event. Should she take back over and start their training? She tried to catch his eye, but he was speaking to Mookaite.

'I can take your basket back to your dome if you like, so you can train. Your team is still waiting by the ramp.' He glanced briefly Lamiya's way. 'I have a meeting with Atage.'

Lamiya groaned. Of course! Riverfall would be waiting for their pacer! She should have realised *both* boats would be waiting. What would the team from Riversea be thinking as they paddled up and down the river by themselves? Lazuli returned with a hemp sack, which he passed to Everand.

'Good, this will do. Thank you for your speed.'

Lazuli frowned, uncertain why the traveller was there. With a sinking feeling, Lamiya realised she'd have to explain. But how much?

Finally, Everand sought her attention. 'I think you can train now.' After a pause, he added, 'I'll dispose of the snake.' After another pause, 'Don't push Ejad hard.' She waited, feeling he wanted to say more, until he said distinctly, 'Take care. The snake wasn't meant for Ejad.'

Beside her, Lazuli stiffened. With a painful swallow, she passed Mookaite's basket to Everand. 'Thanks for your help,' she said formally. She looked at Ejad fondly. 'Paddler ten, are you ready?'

Ejad lifted his paddle and gave her a crooked smile.

Feeling as if her legs belonged to someone else, Lamiya led the others outside, leaving Everand to dispose of the snake. Lazuli was bursting with questions and his strides were choppy with annoyance. Ejad appeared to be oblivious to his near-death, and Mookaite kept giving her sly sideways glances. On reaching the top of the ramp, she quailed when everyone looked up in sheer amazement at Ejad walking with her.

'Yosh! Ejad!' The Riverfall paddlers almost dropped their paddles in their enthusiasm.

'Start to board. Now!' snapped Tengar, clambering into Mizuchi.

'Come by later.' Mookaite gave Lamiya a quick pat on the shoulder and hurried to take her place at the front of the boat. The other pacer, Melanite, greeted her as they pushed their boat out and climbed in.

Lamiya's courage almost left her at the way her paddlers were staring at her with dubious expressions. Flexing her fingers, she acknowledged she had some explaining to do.

Lazuli's annoyed grimace did not help. Grabbing Ejad's hand, she brought a bright smile to her lips.

'Ejad is a true warrior!' she exclaimed, ignoring the blush that rushed to the young paddler's cheeks. 'Despite injury, he insists on training.' She gave him a kiss on his near cheek. 'Give a cheer for Ejad!'

'Yo!' the paddlers rattled their paddles. Poor Ejad looked as if he might faint.

'With paddlers of this calibre, how can we lose?' cried Lamiya, hoping the other two boats were out of earshot. The paddlers rattled their paddles against the side of the boat, although Lazuli was regarding her intently. 'We're lucky the traveller and Mookaite knew what to do. We'll drink to them later. For now, let's train.'

Lifting her chin, she walked down the ramp and stepped on board and to her position. She eyed the oar before she threaded it through its anchor slot. Ejad and Luvu settled just in front of her. While the others were boarding, she leaned forward and said to Ejad, 'You are brave beyond belief, but this session is just training. If your wrist hurts or you feel weak, pull your paddle.' His shoulders stiffened. 'Pull your paddle,' she insisted. 'It's in the race we need you at full strength.'

'Yes, glide,' mumbled Ejad.

Lamiya straightened up and saw Lulite behind the drum ready and watching her.

'Paddles back … Go!' Flight glided away from the ramp. Lamiya balanced lightly while she scanned the river to see which way the other teams had gone. Both boats had gone south. Wondering why Riversea hadn't paddled north to become familiar with the stretch of river that would be used for the races, Lamiya turned Flight's nose to the north.

'Paddles up ... Go.' Joy sank into her as the boat powered through the water. So far, Ejad was paddling as he usually did. While the team warmed up, she reviewed her calculations.

'Keep paddling as I explain,' she called. 'I reason four hundred strokes for the first race. Then double that for the middle race, making it eight hundred strokes.' She paused to let the paddlers absorb this, or contradict her if they thought differently. Lazuli's head dipped in agreement.

'From the northern gate to the bridge is around six thousand strokes. So, we'll practise a running race start, a sustained long race effort with lifts, then I'll call bring it home. Let's see how it feels.'

Luvu grunted, and Ejad rolled his shoulders.

Flight ploughed steadily through the water in the slight current. Along the riverbank, teams of townspeople worked erecting cloth tents and setting up tables and benches. Some waved as the boat went by. Glad they weren't going to practise until they got to the second gate and there would be fewer observers, Lamiya gave small waves back.

The boat head drew level with the northern wall of the town. 'Paddlers ... Running start ... Go!' Flight leaped forward, a white-crested wash forming around her prow. After fifteen deep strokes, the team stretched seamlessly into a long, powerful stroke and Lulite began to drum. Lamiya's spirits lifted at the way the water rushed by, sparkling blues and greens, pockets of white bubbles forming from the effort on the blades. Each pull through the water was like a breath of the boat.

'Two hundred!' called Lamiya. 'Give me a lift!'

The muscles on Larimar and Lazuli's shoulders bulged as they reached further forward and pushed their paddles down and back, smoothly arching to reach again. Wriggling her toes to stabilise her balance, Lamiya felt Flight lift beneath her. Her hair blew away from her face and neck, and energy tingled through her. The team was good; the team was ready. Another two hundred strokes flew by and she called for another lift.

Now Flight was singing beneath her, the waves a slapping chorus as they bounced away from the chest of the boat. The dragon breathed, and Lamiya felt the head and neck stretch into the breeze, sensed the tail pluming behind her. The bubbles from the paddles were a constant river of silver-white mingled with the hues of the river streaming down both sides of the boat. Fighting the temptation to enter a trance, Lamiya counted again. Could it possibly be five hundred and fifty strokes already and the team still pulling so strong?

'Final effort, now!' She braced for the change in tempo. After a brief hitch in stroke, Ejad was still with everyone and Flight flew the river. The sensation of the dragon mingling with the boat was overpowering.

'Let it run!' called Lamiya, breathless and exhilarated. The sense of flying dissipated, the boat lowered in the water and the team slumped over their knees, rib cages heaving. If only they could repeat this in the long race!

She scanned the team: Ejad sat head and shoulders bowed, but he was still smiling. Luvu was gasping for air, and Lepid and Lapsi were breathing hard. Lattic rinsed his hand in the water and Levog was flexing his fingers. Laza and Lopa were lifting their hair away from their necks, trying to cool down. Larimar was rolling his shoulders and Lazuli was sitting bolt upright, looking ahead with a hand over his eyes. What was he looking at?

Her heart thudded against her breastbone. Was that a boat? Something came down the river towards them, the bridge a blur behind it. Unease displaced her elation. A boat coming from the north ... when the other teams had headed south ...

'Paddles up!' Her call came out as a croak. 'Turn the boat.' The boat felt clunky, with the paddlers' arms full of the after-burn of strenuous exercise. Lamiya kept them as close to the Riverfall bank as possible.

Lazuli twisted on his bench. 'A dragon boat comes!'

'I see it,' she replied. 'Make for the town. Paddles up ... Go!' Flight slid forward, nose to the south. To Lulite, she said, 'Tell me if it gets closer.' The drummer's responding frown was not encouraging.

The team paddled in silence, the river water lapping by fast. The back of Lamiya's neck prickled with tension and she resisted the temptation to keep asking the team for more effort. Ejad was starting to flag, but stubbornly refused to pull his paddle. The tension between her shoulders eased when they passed the northern gate, the town walls now sliding by on her left. 'Can you see the boat?' she called. Lulite nodded. 'What does it look like?'

Lulite squinted. 'A dark coloured boat. But the head has a beak, I think.'

A tremor passed through Lamiya's arms and she gripped the oar tightly. The previous vision of the fierce hunters from Riverwood and the boat with the head of an eagle floated behind her eyes. *Riverwood. Arriving unannounced!* She must warn Everand.

'Whirr, come!' Feathers tickled until Whirr emerged with bright eyes, cocking his tiny head. Her lips twitched. What would Everand think when her bird flew into his face for the second time? She told Whirr to stand on the top of the oar. *Find Everand ... I know, stop peeping and listen ... try Atage's dome. Tell him Riverwood is here. By boat. Tell him to go to the boat ramp. Go, and hurry!* Whirr gave his chest a quick preen and raised his wings. 'Fly low. Beware of eagles.' Whirr chirruped then swooped low over the water, heading for the town wall.

'They're closing,' said Lulite from the front of the boat.

Lamiya squared her shoulders. 'Hold the rate! Make for the ramp.' Lazuli set a steady rate to get them home. She refused to look over her shoulder; refused to give the Riverwood glide that satisfaction.

If they wanted the ramp first, they'd have to go around her.

CHAPTER THIRTY-TWO

Everand stood with the hemp sack loose in his hands while he studied the body of the viper. The snake in Lamiya's boat was unlikely to be a coincidence. He crouched by the body and reluctantly extended a finger to touch the scales along the snake's back. Still warm, the scales were dry and rasped sibilantly as he pressed. Ignoring a tremor of repulsion, he extended his senses. Travelling along the snake's veins, close to the severed neck he found the aftertaste of a strange liquid in the blood.

Releasing the contact, he sat back on his heels. This confirmed the snake had been influenced. How? He scrutinised the body, scale by scale. There, at the mid-point, were marks of depression in the scales, like fingerprints but sharper. Talons? It was a stretch of his imagination, but could the snake have come from Riverwood, been adjusted there and then carried by an eagle to the boat dome? Could it have slithered under the door in the dark and climbed into the boat to lie coiled and waiting?

Deep fury rose within him. *Such a coward to inflict death from afar.* No doubt the snake was intended for Lamiya, and neither she nor Ejad deserved such a painful death. Before he realised what he was doing, he blasted the body, leaving a desiccated and shrivelled pile of black ash on the floor. He scuffed the ash over the dirt floor with a foot, folded the sack and left it by the doorway and strode out the door. His fury grew with each long stride along the path. At the southern archway he took a deep breath, flexed his fingers and slowed to a brisk walk so he wouldn't attract undue attention.

Once outside Atage's dome, he straightened his hair and wiped the sweat from his forehead. He bit down a groan. Lyber would be present and he'd have to explain what had happened. Better Ejad's father hear it directly from him. After another deep breath, he called through the curtain.

'Welcome and enter,' said Thulite, holding the curtain aside with a smile.

As he expected, Atage and Lyber were already seated and poring over maps and lists. He fluffed a cushion and sat cross-legged at the table. 'Sorry I'm late.' He held up a hand when Atage went to speak. 'Something happened.' Their attention sharpened. Facing Lyber, he tried to speak matter-of-factly. 'Ejad was bitten by a snake, but Mookaite and I drew the poison out.' Lyber paled. 'Ejad is fine,' Everand said more gently, 'and has gone training.'

Lyber stared unblinking. 'He's out on the boat? After being bitten by a snake?'

Everand said wryly, 'You have a fine and most determined son.' His smile faded. 'The snake was in the Riverplain boat and I think was intended for Lamiya.'

Atage was quick to catch on. 'It was deliberate?'

'I believe so. We're facing someone who is cunning, and ruthless.' Rolling his shoulders to ease the tension, he refrained from adding 'and a coward'. 'It's imperative I understand the proposal for inter-province trade and who stands to benefit.' He tilted his head. 'More importantly, whether anyone stands to lose.'

Atage and Lyber both frowned. 'I don't see who could lose,' said Atage. 'We offer the same opportunities to each province, and the details are to be decided in discussions where everyone participates. What more could we do?'

Everand thought about this while Thulite placed a steaming mug and a platter of cakes before him. He tried to imagine how the unseen enemy's mind might work. 'It could be a perceived loss rather than an actual one, perhaps motivated by personal factors rather than consideration of what's best for the province.' The enemy was cunning, no doubt about that. 'This makes the danger no less. It just makes it harder to predict what'll happen. And when.'

'You still worry about the long race?' asked Atage.

'Yes, and the bridge and the dragon—if it appears. If disrupting the races doesn't result in the trade discussions being cancelled, or at least deferred, then the discussions or the negotiators could be at risk.' He looked at Atage. 'And you, as the instigator of the changes.' The colour drained from Atage's face.

Lyber frowned so deeply the creases on his face merged. 'Do you have a plan?'

Both Lyber and Atage watched his face carefully.

'There are a few parts to my plan. Some are not without risk. The first part we've discussed; we must have weapons made and people ready to use them to help protect the paddlers and boats.' Atage and Lyber fidgeted on their cushions and Everand raised his hands. 'I know this is uncomfortable for your good and kind people, but I can't be everywhere. Keep this strategy contained to those who will be trained and let's hope they're not needed. You have found enough men?'

Atage and Lyber nodded.

The silence stretched; it was time to tackle the more fraught component of his plan. 'Part of the ceremony is to give offerings to the river dragon?' When Atage confirmed, he asked, 'Where and when do you do this?'

Confusion spread across Atage's face. 'Near the town at sun-fade before the races.'

Everand sat back. 'Can I suggest you place the offerings near the northern gate? And put many more than usual and with much noise and celebration.' He thought more. 'Can you also take a cart-load of offerings to the bridge?'

Lyber's mouth dropped open. 'You really think the dragon might come?'

Everand stopped drumming his fingers on the table and spread his hands. 'I *hope* the dragon will come. Don't you need it to come so you can ask it to bring rain? Who better than a dragon to protect your bridge, river and town?' He hesitated. 'Assuming it will be on *your* side. *That* is the risk. The enemy could also be hoping the dragon will come.'

The air grew tense and still while they absorbed this. Thulite stood staring at him with her mouth open, a plate forgotten in her hands. He anticipated a multitude of concerns and questions.

A yellow and jade blur whizzed through the curtain and thumped into the side of his face. Everand extracted the wildly screeching Whirr from his hair. Cupping the bird in a hand, the way he'd seen Lamiya do, he said, 'Calm down. What?'

In his palm, the bird trembled with fear or exhaustion or both. Whirr screeched at him, his beak opening and closing rapidly and his black eyes darting everywhere. The bird snapped his beak shut and the golden feathers on his heaving chest fluffed up. Images bombarded Everand: the river, Flight, the team training, a view upriver with the bridge glimmering in the distance, a shadow before the bridge, the boat with the head of a fierce eagle, solid dark-haired men paddling grimly. What was Whirr trying to tell him?

The next image showed Lamiya standing proud at the back of Flight, mahogany hair blowing in the breeze, with the darker, larger boat right behind her. Whirr quivered.

'This is *now*?' Everand asked, not quite believing. Whirr peeped, offended. Meeting Atage's troubled eyes, he said, 'Riverwood arrives. By boat.'

'The arrogance!' spluttered Atage, thumping a hand on the table. Lyber knocked his mug over and didn't notice the liquid dripping into his lap.

Everand stood, cupping Whirr in his hands. 'I'll go to the boat ramp. You need to prepare a formal welcome?'

'Too right,' said Atage, compressing his lips. 'We refuse to be caught out like this. Thulite,' he said, 'scramble the women to prepare a welcome in the southern courtyard.' Looking back to him, he said, 'Ask Tengar and the others to do the team arch of welcome at the ramp when Riverwood lands.' Atage paused. 'Slow them down to give us time.'

After a curt nod, Everand stepped outside, still clutching Whirr. Making sure no-one was nearby, he made himself invisible and mouthed the translocation spell with the inside of the boat dome in his mind.

As he hoped, the boat dome was empty but the ramp was teeming with activity. The Riversea team and their boat were almost at the top of the ramp and the Riverfall boat was just landing. His heart skipped when he saw Flight turning mid-river to make her run into the ramp, with the larger boat from Riverwood not quite clipping her tail. His heart swelled with pride when Lamiya, balanced elegantly with her hair brushing her shoulders, gave a cool, imperious look at the Riverwood glide. 'My ramp,' he lip-read. After a beat, the Riverwood paddlers slowed their boat and Flight's tail slipped past the viciously curved beak of the eagle head on the Riverwood boat.

He was supposed to tell Tengar to form the arch of paddles. He opened his fingers and Whirr flew up to perch on his shoulder. Halfway to the ramp he remembered he was invisible, and relaxed the spell. Nodding in greeting to the Riversea paddlers, he paused when he reached Cowrie at the boat tail.

'Greetings, Cowrie. I hope your training went well?' Before the man could respond, he said, 'Atage asks the teams to form the paddler arch of welcome for Riverwood here, at the ramp.'

When the man opened his mouth, he added, 'I'll tell Tengar so he can organise everybody.' As he moved off, he heard Cowrie telling his team to move the boat to one side and line up in order.

When he took long strides down the ramp, the Riverfall team paused and looked at him expectantly. He quickly explained and Tengar took charge. Everand stood behind the Riverfall team, doing his best to blend in. He wanted a good look at the Riverwood boat and team. He particularly wanted a good look at their glide.

Flight stopped at the base of the ramp and Lamiya glanced around, working out what was happening. On his shoulder, Whirr flapped his wings and Lamiya looked relieved to see he was there.

By the time the Riverwood boat was aligned to approach the ramp, the other teams had raised their paddles in a V arch of welcome. Everand felt his lips twitch. The thirty-six paddlers waited, silent and immobile, as the eagle head drew nearer. Unfamiliar with birds, Everand deduced this eagle was one usually feared. Apparently of the same view, Whirr gave a shrill screech and dived down the front of his tunic. The feathers tickled and Everand thought, *Be still.*

He studied the boat. The eagle head had a curved and cruel ivory beak. Above this, grey cheek feathers surrounded vivid ochre eyes with large black pupils, the carved feathers feeding into a tuft of grey-brown crest. The neck was the same grey-brown, tapering to a solid boat, slightly higher and wider than the other boats, with grey and brown feathers painted along the sides. The boat tail was a spray of black, grey and brown feathers. Everand noticed the paddle blades had curved talons etched onto them.

The paddlers disembarking were all men, with deep-set, square faces and matching slab shoulders. Their dark hair looked wiry, and most had dark beards. Finally, the glide stepped forward from the rear, balancing perfectly on the benches with powerful steps and hopped out onto land. The shadow on his right shoulder unfolded to reveal a live eagle, the spitting image of the boat head. The eagle clacked its beak and cast intent looks.

Everand stared at the glide and his heart pounded against his breastbone. *This can't be.* The glide was a younger version of his former mentor! Same nose, same set of the chin, same hair and bristling beard, same eyes and even the same aloof expression. Everand felt light-headed. Everything about this mission was topsy-turvy and *nothing* made sense. He should never have agreed to come. He worked saliva into his mouth, his mind still floating.

Tengar stepped forward and bowed and the glide nodded curtly back. Behind them, the Riverwood team settled their boat on the grass and formed ranks.

'Yosh!' The Riverfall team snapped to attention when the Riverwood team walked forward.

'Yo!' the Riverplain team called as the dark men passed between them.

'Yee-ah!' sang the Riversea team as the men passed between them.

Once at the top of the line, the Riverwood team fanned to each side, joining the two rows, and raised their paddles. 'Ki!' they shouted.

The other teams lowered their paddles and hovered uncertainly. Tengar tilted his head at Beram, and they walked up the ramp to confer with the Riverwood glide. His mind still refusing to function properly, Everand saw Lamiya put a hand on Ejad's shoulder, probably asking if he was alright, and then direct her team to take Flight to the dome. Lazuli hovered protectively near her.

Lamiya's troubled gaze drifted to his face and he wished, so fiercely he gasped, to take her in his arms. His emotions eddied. Was it to reassure her, or did he need her to reassure him? Hopelessly adrift, his feet felt far, far away, and when he blinked the paddlers were carrying their boats up to the dome. He was by himself, except for the bird buried deep in his tunic.

He raised his eyes to the cluster of paddlers at the top of the ramp. Cowrie and Conch had joined Tengar and Beram to converse with the Riverwood team. The Riverwood glide stood on the uphill side. The man's eyes swept down the ramp and fixed on his face.

A jolt of recognition shot through the man. *What the?* Everand was assessed by piercing dark eyes. Did this glide recognise his powers? Sweat erupted on his temple. No, more than that. The man had recognised *him*. How was this possible? His mouth felt as dry as sand when the fleeting surprise on the glide's face was replaced by a look of satisfaction.

This mission was proving to be far, far worse than he had anticipated.

CHAPTER THIRTY-THREE

Everand took several breaths through his nostrils to draw courage before he set off up the ramp.

Tengar broke off from whatever he was explaining and beckoned. 'Traveller, come meet the Riverwood team.'

Forcing a neutral expression, Everand joined the group of men.

'This is Everd, a traveller from Axis. He's helping with the races as the position judge.' When Everand gave a half bow, Tengar said, 'This is Malach, the glide for Riverwood, and the pacers Torrap and Magle.'

Everand met Malach's intent gaze. Pushing down the thought about how uncannily like Mage Beetal's eyes this man's eyes were, he said, 'Your boat looks strong.'

Malach twitched an eyebrow, also uncannily just how Mage Beetal used to whenever Everand said something he considered to be stupid. 'You are from Axis?' The voice was deep, the words pronounced distinctly. 'It's unusual for anyone to travel from Axis.'

Everand winced and, eyes downcast, muttered as if reluctantly, 'If I'd been better at my duties I wouldn't have been allowed.'

A subtle probe touched Everand's forehead. The man was trying to see into his mind! He conjured images of the Guild kitchens, with Delma the cook standing with a beefy arm on her rounded hip stirring a large pot. He added the wooden racks and rows of hanging cooking utensils that he'd seen on his one visit. 'I put the wrong herbs into the stew and the mages all spat it out.'

He shrugged into the collective silence. 'I'm banned from the kitchen for twenty suns, so they didn't notice me leave.' He stopped there. Adding more make-believe details would raise more questions. Such as how he had passed through the granite wall and wardspell.

Beram clapped his shoulder with a laugh. 'You didn't mention this before. I'm glad we haven't let you near our food then!'

Tengar joined in. 'You stick to eating and drinking! Until after the races, anyway.'

Clommus and Cowrie took the exchange at face value and joined in the laughter. The pacers from Riverwood looked bored and Malach continued to stare at him.

Tengar rubbed his hands together. 'Speaking of eating and drinking, Atage has a welcome ready for your team in the courtyard.'

Everand hovered while the paddlers milled around, retrieving their paddles and over-tunics. The Riverwood paddlers carried their paddles and a small cloth bundle each. Was this all they'd brought with them?

'Is this everything you brought?' asked Tengar, speaking his thought. 'Will more people come from Riverwood?'

'No,' replied Malach firmly. To Everand's relief, the man stopped scrutinising him and followed Tengar and Beram when they walked towards the town.

Everand watched the receding backs of the Riverwood team. So, if only the team had come there was no possibility of any other visitors from Riverwood being caught up in any violence. This also meant he'd already seen who was to participate in the trade discussions. Was Malach a leader in Riverwood as well as being team captain and glide? Looking up at the clear azure sky, he decided to ask Beram to find out. He tailed the teams. The sun was nearly at its zenith and he only had from now to dark-fall and one more sun to unravel what was going on. What could he achieve in this time?

Walking slowly, he ran through his options. Given the involvement of magic, should he translocate back to the Guild to warn Mantiss and Agamid? But it had taken two of them to send him, and one had to dissolve the wardspell so he could pass through. Did he have enough power to send himself back *and* part the wardspell? Probably not. And what if Mantiss and Agamid refused to send him back again and told him to leave the matter for the provinces to solve for themselves? That would leave Lamiya and the people of Riverfall and Riverplain at risk with no help.

Fear ran a jagged course down his body. Why *had* Mantiss sent him by himself? Was it really because they'd thought it was a simple mission, or was something else going on? *I need your eyes on this.* Did his master anticipate a threat to the Guild but hadn't warned him? His legs felt weak. Never before had he doubted his fellow mages.

Next option: *if* he managed to get through the wardspell to warn the Guild and they believed him, they might send him back with another mage or two to help. What would they do? Coming back to the present, he saw the others were at the archway to the courtyard. A sour taste oozed into his mouth. The Guild's most likely path would be to move to obliterate Malach on the basis he was a half-mage. Strictly forbidden. Rule eight was unequivocal: mages must only breed with other mages.

His knees felt far away. While Malach looked like the traitor Mage Beetal, what if he was wrong? What if the likeness was sheer coincidence? He'd have effectively signed a death notice on Malach. His ribs felt as if they were trying to strangle his chest, and pinpoint white stars floated before his eyes. He heaved in a breath, and his ribs released their stranglehold.

Last option: keep going and do his best to protect everyone. So far, he'd not detected power in anyone other than Malach. *And an undefined ability in Lamiya, but she is on your side.* He flinched when the shadow of the archway flitted over him. Besides, he didn't know how much ability Malach had. As always, he needed more information. He would stay for the races.

Refocusing, he gazed at the clumps of people in the courtyard and the tables laden high with food and drinks. Warmth travelled through him: he liked these people, liked being here. What did that mean? Did he no longer want to be a mage at the Guild? He closed his eyes. *You're over-thinking. Find Lamiya. She'll make you feel better.*

His feet drifted towards the tables of food. Perhaps his hunger was due to all the physical activity as opposed to being cloistered in his study, the library or at meetings. Also, he was expending more nervous energy trying to remain undercover.

'Hey, Traveller,' said Acim, materialising by his elbow. 'Would you like to join us fishing?'

Everand focused on Acim's smiling face. 'What? When?'

'First light. We must catch the fish for the festival and the offerings to the dragon.' Acim waved his hands around. 'Zink and me, Lapsi and Larimar. Atage told us we have to catch more fish than usual.'

Zink joined them, clasping a mug. 'We thought you'd like to see more of the river.'

Everand almost smiled, then asked, 'Do you mean in a boat?'

Both gave him a startled look, and Acim answered, 'Yes, a small boat. How else will we follow the fish?'

'We'll go north, to the bridge,' added Zink. 'The river's deeper there.'

Now they had his interest; it was a good idea to check the bridge again. 'I would like to join you.' He paused. 'I'm not sure I'll catch anything, though.'

They both laughed. 'No need, Traveller,' said Zink. 'Atage asked us to leave offerings for the river dragon at the bridge. He said you might like to see the bridge again before the races.'

'We'll come for you at first light,' said Acim, touching his elbow briefly. 'The water is still then and the fish come out to feed.'

They moved away to mingle with others, leaving him to appreciate Atage's subtle move. Now that Riverwood had arrived and passed under the bridge, it was opportune to check that it hadn't been sabotaged before the long race. *If* Malach was indeed related to Mage Beetal, and *if* he was as devious, there'd be no further warning before the intended strike.

He thought of his previous mission. Without the warning that something was amiss through Elemar's arrival, the first the Guild would have known about any threat would have been Mage Beetal's army of dragons descending on the Great Hall. It would have been game over. Perhaps this Malach had erred by sending the tree-moths, the jumping fish and the viper. Assuming it was him.

Everand ran a hand over his jaw. If he was right about the glide's identity, then perhaps Malach had needed to test his powers. The situation was precarious and volatile but, even alone, as a fully trained mage he remained the best option the provinces had. It had been a bold move by the visionary and intelligent Atage to approach the Guild. Even so, how had he foreseen that they would need their own mage? His forehead throbbed with tension and a building headache.

For a while he observed who mingled with whom. Lamiya was with all the women paddlers, their faces animated as they chatted. The younger paddlers from Riversea and Riverfall sat together, bantering and joking. As before, Atage, Lyber and Tengar sat with the older paddlers. Malach and his pacers sat at the end of the same table, looking as if they'd rather be elsewhere. Everand felt an eyebrow lift. Malach turned his head and looked directly at him.

The air in the courtyard was heavy; his limbs and mind felt sluggish. How could he best use the remaining light? Information took time to gather and walking would keep him awake. Pushing up from the table, he saw Beram heading his way.

'What will you do now?' Beram asked.

'Walk a lap of the town. Can you show me where the men and weapons will be placed?'

Beram cracked his knuckles. 'Good idea.'

'Let's start south, at the boat dome,' said Everand.

Walking made him feel better and by the time they left the town, his mind was teeming with questions. They moved across the stretch of grass that led to the riverbank. 'Are more people coming?'

'Three more carts will arrive from Riverplain.' Beram led him to the boat dome and eased the doors open. 'We have tasked five men with guarding the boats after dark.'

Everand stepped in and stopped. The four boats were arranged in a neat line, occupying the width of the dome. In the front corner on each side were a jumble of cushions and a couple of folded blankets. Propped against the wall was a bundle of newly-hewn staves with sharp tips. He nodded. Hopefully, this would be sufficient to deter any saboteurs.

'When the races begin, these men will position themselves along the riverbank, behind the crowds. There'll be another ten men mingled there already.' Beram regarded him with anxious eyes.

Everand shrugged. 'Good, although I hope we won't need them. Do you have enough staves?'

Beram frowned. 'They are making more, hidden inside a dome. It's slow work trying to conceal the activity though.'

'Close your eyes,' said Everand. 'Go on,' he added when Beram raised an eyebrow. Everand murmured the spell of replication four times, so that the two piles of staves increased four-fold. 'There. That should help.'

Beram opened his eyes and following Everand's jerk of a head, gasped. 'Thanks!'

Everand looked at the boats. Should the paddlers have staves or these slingshots in their boats in case they were attacked directly? No, that would distract them too much and alert Malach that they were expecting an attack. They'd also be useless against the dragon. If it came to that, he'd need to protect the boats with his magic.

They left the dome and headed along the riverbank. Everand looked at the neat row of coloured tents along the bank. Beram walked behind every second tent and showed him a bundle of weapons concealed under grass-green cloth. Everand doubled these. Peering into the last tent, he saw neatly stacked wooden stools and piles of cushions. The tents would provide shade and a wonderful view of the races. He thought about the logistics of more carts arriving. 'What about the extra carts and hopeepa?'

'Riverplain will have a field and yards designated to their animals outside the northern gate.'

Everand thought about when he'd gone in the cart with Persaj to bury the bodies of the tree-moths. He remembered fields of yellow stalky crops but not fields of grass and yards. 'Are they behind the field of yellow stalks?'

'Yes, tucked away behind the wheat fields and nut tree groves.' Beram gave him a curious look. 'You seem unfamiliar with crops?'

Feeling inadequate, Everand shook his head. 'Mages don't concern themselves with growing and preparing food.' He winced; that sounded pompous.

Beram's eyes grew wider. 'They don't? Who does that then?'

Everand took several steps, trying to find a reasonable answer. 'There are farmers and cooks who do all this.'

'They're not mages?'

He shook his head, dreading Beram's next question.

'Who are they, then?'

Everand shrugged. 'Many people live in Axis too. They take care of the land and provide for us. In exchange we protect them and refine our magic.'

He'd taken another six strides before he realised Beram had stopped. With a sigh, he added, 'They help us willingly.' Beram's eyebrows rose and Everand felt his neck growing warm. 'When I return, I intend to ask many questions about things I had taken for granted.'

Beram's frown relaxed into a kind look. 'You are a good man. We're grateful you're here.'

Everand nodded stiffly. 'Please continue the explanations.'

The light was fading by the time they completed their tour. He now knew much about nut trees, hopeepa grazing, orchards and fruit harvest and, of course, cotton bushes. Beram explained about the irrigation, everything being grown within range of the river, trenches and wooden waterwheels. Everand was impressed by the economic and well-ordered layout.

As they headed back, he wondered how the farmers in Axis had set out their crops and, for the first time, wanted to see this. He understood how the silk moths were bred and the silk cultivated because this was managed by the mages, but he had little idea of how the 'people' conducted their duties, or how they felt about it. Did they enjoy their work? He shivered to dispel the sense of gloom drifting down in the fading purple light.

When they approached his dome, Beram said with a serious expression, 'The Riverwood glide told Atage that they don't require a trading table. What do you think this means?'

'Hmm,' said Everand, waiting until they reached the door. 'I think their glide, Malach, might have powers.'

Beram's step faltered. 'Like you?'

'Not as strong, but he is untrained, which makes him unpredictable. Also, he's not bound by the Guild Rules and constraints, as I am.'

They pushed through the curtain and Everand pulled out a cushion to sit at the table. His head throbbed. Why would Malach tell Atage they didn't need a table? That begged the question of why they were here.

After Beram had lit the candles, and soft light and a relaxing scent emanated, he sat opposite. 'What do you think this means? Do they all have power?'

Everand struggled to shepherd his mind back onto the task. 'I think just Malach.' Should he reveal his full theory? What would Mantiss and Agamid advise? A wave of nausea ripped through him: they'd counsel him to say nothing. Keep it secret that a mage had transgressed. Under the circumstances, was this fair?

'I'll make you a mug,' said Beram, rising and heading to the water jug.

Everand waited until Beram put steaming mugs on the table and sat down again. Then he told him everything. The air in the dome cooled as Beram listened, the creases in his face deepening.

Completely spent, Everand concluded, 'If something happens to me you must make sure the Guild is advised of all this.' His body aching all over, he wanted to slump over the table. 'Tell the same mages you met before, Mantiss in the green robes and Agamid in the purple robes.'

Beram looked distressed, but Everand had no energy left to provide him with reassurance.

Especially where none was warranted.

CHAPTER THIRTY-FOUR

Everand rolled out his mattress and fell onto it, pulling the blanket up snug around his ears. His entire body ached and sleep rushed at him.

He rested his hands on the mahogany table, head bowed. His master did not look pleased.

'I am disappointed,' said Mantiss sternly. 'You were supposed to be undercover and keep what we do secret.'

'It was a simple mission,' added Agamid. 'Go and find out who was sabotaging things and stop them. None of this complexity about raising water dragons and finding untrained mages.' He wagged a finger in annoyance.

Everand bowed, deeply uncomfortable. 'But masters, what could I do? The Riverwood glide looks just like Mage Beetal. Surely, he must be related? I thought you'd want to know!'

'Ridiculous!' snorted Agamid. 'How would Beetal possibly have fathered a son outside of Axis? He knew the rules.'

Everand floundered.

'How old is this boy supposed to be? Twenty or so? Are you saying Beetal deceived us for all that time?'

'You,' added Mantiss, pointing at him, 'you were always in Beetal's rooms, ever since you were a lad of twelve. You saw no sign of a transgression of this enormity? No evidence of Beetal popping out to rut with some peasant somewhere? Come now, some spy you have turned out to be!'

Words failed Everand and his mind whirred. How was he supposed to know what his mentor was doing when he was not in the study giving him his lessons? Mantiss expected too much!

'And,' Agamid was almost shouting, his purple sleeves flapping as he gesticulated, 'and you told them! We are supposed to be above the people. Untouchable.'

Everand bowed his head and let their tirade wash over him. He'd failed miserably, lost their trust and support. Would they remove him from the Inner Council? His scalp itched and he repressed the urge to scratch at his head.

'Nothing to say, boy?' probed Mantiss. 'How are you going to make this right?' Mantiss' chair squeaked as the mage sat back. 'You will bring us this half-mage, that's how. We will hold him to account.'

Agamid's face was a thundercloud as deep a purple as his robe. 'Indeed! This boy will wish he had never been sired!'

The prickling in Everand's scalp intensified, as if tiny scratchy feet were walking in the hair above his forehead. Something sharp pricked his forehead. Horror rising, he wanted to tell Mantiss and Agamid not to judge Malach too harshly for Mage Beetal's crimes, to at least let the young half-mage speak for himself, but something tickly and stringy was filling his mouth, sliding under his tongue, making his nose twitch. It was as if a web-like net was set to capture his words before he could utter them.

Everand flung open his eyes. It was pitch dark. He was lying on his side facing a wall and there was something tickling his nose and mouth. And something sharp *was* moving in his hair! Beram snored loudly on his mattress on the far side of the dome.

'Peep, peep.'

Alertness flooded into Everand. Whirr was walking on his head! He brought his hand up and felt in front of his face. Long hair. Lamiya was lying curled against him, her face against his chest and her hair tickling his chin and sliding into his mouth. He moved his hand lower and found her arms were folded up under her chin, her knees drawn up and resting in his groin. Closing his eyes, he hoped she didn't move her legs too quickly the way his body was responding to her presence.

'Lamiya,' he whispered. 'What are you doing here?'

She nuzzled further into his chest and whispered back, 'I couldn't sleep.'

His chest grew tight and, as in his dream, words failed him. Ever so gently, he brushed her hair away from his mouth and tucked it behind her ear. Using his thumb, he traced the outline of her eyebrow, her eyelashes fluttering against his palm, and then along the ridge of her cheekbone. His knuckles brushed the soft skin on her neck. That felt *so* nice. He trailed the back of his hand down her neck, enjoying the contours, noting where her neck fed into her collarbone. No wonder she always looked so elegant, her neck was long and her shoulders wide.

He slid his hand under the bulk of her hair and used his fingertips to tenderly massage the base of her neck, easing the tension he found there. His breath turned into a gasp as her hand crept over his waist in a hug. Scratchy prickles told him Whirr was marching down his rib cage, mercifully on top of the blanket.

'Can you ask your bird to sit down?' he murmured into the top of her head.

Her shoulders shook with suppressed giggles. In the dark, Beram gave a gurgle and blankets rustled as he rolled over, and Lamiya's shoulders shook some more. This was far from ideal! Surely his mission was not intended to include undercover romance as well? He could well imagine what Mantiss and Agamid would have to say on this aspect. *Not allowed. Not at all. Don't even think about it!*

293

Lamiya straightened her legs and he grunted at the bolt of pleasure that shot through his groin. She wriggled closer, until her whole body was snug against him. Burying his face into her neck, he tried to calm his racing heart. After a few torturous breaths, he realised she was content to lean into him, to just be with him. His heart slowed. Whirr marched back up his ribs and down over his shoulder, hopped onto the pillow, scratched around for a bit and then lay down.

With a deep sigh, Everand put his arms around Lamiya's lower back, rested his face against her neck and closed his eyes. He could get used to this; settling in with Lamiya every dark-fall and waking every sun-up to her beautiful, smiling face. Breathing in the grassy scents of her, the tension ebbed from his muscles. His mind filled with images of grassy plains and colourful birds like Whirr flitting among bright flowers.

In his dream the grassy plains began to shake, as if a hundred hopeepa were galloping towards him. Something pushed at his shoulder. He squeezed his eyes tightly shut.

'Wake up!' Beram's voice. Was he on the plain too? The ground shook harder. 'Wake up!'

With difficulty, Everand opened his eyes. Beram was crouched beside him, his face earnest.

'Quick, get up.' Beram sat back on his heels. 'Trust me, you don't want Acim and Zink to find you in bed. They'll wreak mischief.'

Acim? Zink? He bolted upright. The fishing expedition! What would Beram think about Lamiya being in his bed? Panicking, he looked around. He was alone. Confused, he licked his dry lips. Had he dreamed she came to him during the dark? Disappointment filled him; she'd felt so real.

He rolled onto his hands and knees and pushed up to his feet, groaning at the very real throbbing that travelled through every single one of his muscles. Carefully, he tilted his head from side to side to stretch his neck.

Beram was giving him a strange look.

'What?'

Beram twisted his fingers together. 'You have a feather in your hair,' he said politely.

'I do?' Everand found the offending fluffy feather and plucked it from his hair. Inspection revealed it to be one of Whirr's turquoise feathers. He couldn't suppress his smile fast enough.

Beram gave him another odd look and shrugged. 'You'd better get ready. I'll give you a cloth of food to take.'

Everand had barely struggled into his clothes and was lacing his sandals when Acim and Zink tumbled through the curtain.

'Yosh!' they said in unison.

'Yosh,' replied Beram, handing Everand a square cloth bundle, neatly tied at the top and smelling wonderfully of bread.

'Come, Traveller,' said Zink. 'Light breaks.'

After a quick thanks to Beram, he followed the pair from the dome, taking long strides to keep up as they trotted towards the northern gate. 'Isn't the boat ramp the other way?' he asked, confused.

Zink looked over his shoulder. 'Small boats don't need a ramp. Lapsi and Larimar are waiting with the boats.'

Everand strode faster, noting that people were stirring even though light was only just peering above the town wall. He saw Persaj heading into the hopeepa stable and gave him a wave. Persaj beamed and waved back.

The northern gates were already open and the beauty of the area greeted him as they marched through. A wispy mist curling from the river glistened silvers, pinks and primrose in the rays of early light. The cotton bushes glinted with dew, a subtle fragrance rising from the glossy leaves and white buds. Small brown birds darted to and fro, their peeping similar to Whirr's. Far away to his right, a green hue was edging into the purple haze of rounded hills silhouetted against the grey-gold sky. The air was crisp and fresh against his face and his steps lightened.

Acim and Zink turned off the path and headed towards the river. Everand clutched his cloth bundle tightly when he realised they were going to plough straight down the bank to the water. The shadows in the mist transformed into two small wooden boats, about two person-lengths long and wide enough for a person to sit.

'Yo!' came the soft greeting from one of the boats. Squinting, he saw Lapsi sitting on the bank holding the ropes to both boats. Larimar sat at the back of one, facing forward but with a paddle on each side. Two paddles? Lapsi stood and brushed grass from his trousers before he handed the rope of the empty boat to Acim.

'You can start out with us,' said Zink. 'If we catch as many fish as we hope, you might have to come back in Larimar's boat.'

Everand swallowed: the boats looked tiny. The dragon boat had been bad enough, and these looked far less stable. He took in the clean lines of the curved wooden slats they were built from, the three flat bench seats and a pair of oars nestled in a cradle on the rim.

Acim caught his eye. 'You can swim, can't you?'

When Everand looked at him in horror, all four of them burst out laughing. 'Don't worry,' said Zink, still grinning, 'we won't tip you in the river. You might have to take a turn at rowing, though.'

'And,' said Acim, 'the fresh fish may smell!' He paused. 'Would you like to try some raw?'

'Sounds wonderful,' said Everand, assuming this was another joke. When the response was a series of nods and smiles, he worried it might not be. Disliking the thought of cold, slimy, raw fish, he followed Zink to the nearest boat.

'Sit in the middle row,' said Acim, pulling the boat closer. 'We'll row and you can take a turn when you've had your food.'

Zink took his sandals off, stepped into the water and lightly climbed into the boat, balancing himself in the centre of the small wobbling craft.

Everand removed his sandals and followed, wincing as cold water closed over his feet and rose up to his knees. Good idea not to get the sandals sodden at the outset. Putting his sandals and cloth bundle on the middle seat, he did his best to step into the boat without tipping it. He dropped onto the wooden bench with a thump, his feet having snagged in a pile of netting on the floor. He nudged the net back with his feet and laced his sandals.

Acim pushed the boat away from the bank, adroitly jumped in and took up the pair of oars at the front. The boat surged backwards as the two rowed in time. Mist wafted around them in silver and primrose columns, hiding the riverbank and the town. The sounds of birds waking and calling reached Everand. He put his hands on the seat for extra balance while the rowers turned the boats to face north.

Acim looked over his shoulder. 'We'll row to the bridge first as this'll take a while. The rainbow fish gather under the bridge so we'll fish there and leave a pile for the river dragon, then fish for the supplies for the festival on the way back.' He picked up his oars and leaned into them.

Everand took a deep breath and heightened his senses while the boats glided along. Fingers of cool mist caressed his face and neck and he let his body sway with each surge of the oars pulling through the water. He'd have ample time to check the bridge thoroughly if the others were going to fish there.

Looking down, he observed the even and tight weave of the bundle of net and the small stones sewn in along an edge. Reaching down, he fingered the net, tough fibres rasping his fingertips. It was strong grass plaited and then woven into cross-lines resulting in neat squares.

'I made it.' Zink said, sounding proud. 'A new one for the occasion.'

'Hah! Let's see if it catches anything!' Lapsi's voice floated through the mist. 'Are your grasses tough enough?'

Everand smiled at the way Acim and Zink bristled and sat straighter.

'Compared to your stringy stuff?' replied Zink. 'You'll be amazed how many fish we'll catch!'

Soft laughter rode along the mists. Everand reached out through the shifting strands of grey to sense the bank on the Riverfall side. It was quiet, the only movement the rustle of grasses and leaves in a breeze. A shadow loomed, and when they passed close to it he saw it was one of the waterwheels Beram had mentioned. It rose large and round, with many struts lined with buckets. He peered through the grey eddies and saw that it reached higher than the bank. 'How does this work?'

Zink answered. 'There are ropes attached to turning spokes. We pull on these to rotate the wheel so the buckets dip into the water. When the buckets reach above the trench, there is a stand and a bar that tips the bottom of the bucket so the water drops into the trench.'

'And these trenches run down to the crops?'

'Yes,' said Zink, puffing as he rowed. 'Beram decides when we need to flood the trenches. When it rains, there's less work.'

Everand tried to visualise how the wheel worked, absorbing the implications of less rain than usual. Small wonder the town was hoping to please the dragon. The mist was dissipating and he could now see the other boat and Larimar and Lapsi rowing in perfect timing.

'We'll pass the second waterwheel soon,' said Zink. 'It's at the end of the cotton bushes, about three-fourths of the way to the bridge.'

'That's a good place for you to take Zink's oars so he can get the net ready,' said Acim.

Soon, sunlight trickled pleasantly onto Everand's face, neck and arms. The mist disappeared and he could see the cotton bushes on the left bank. He turned to eye the Riverwood bank. Tall strands of reeds and grasses grew densely along the water's edge, making it hard to perceive what lay beyond. It looked wild. A variety of birds swam near the shore or waded through the reeds. Did the eagles hunt these birds? Perhaps there were lizards and snakes worth hunting. The boat slowed, and he saw they were at the last waterwheel.

Everand swung around on the bench and put his weight on his feet. Zink grabbed his elbows to guide him to the rear bench and then sat backwards on the middle seat, facing him.

Zink gave an encouraging smile, small creases forming around his blue eyes. 'Now pick up both oars.'

Everand grasped the handles, marvelling at how smooth the wood was, and noting how the shafts fed through the guiding keepers.

Zink gave him instructions. 'That's it … keep in time with Acim.'

Everand hastened to copy Acim but his oars dropped into the water unevenly and he felt the tug across his shoulders and at the back of his neck as the weight of the water bit. Concentrating, he understood his hands needed to be in time with each other as well as Acim. This was hard work! How were the others going to race after all this rowing?

After a while he settled into a pattern. The water glittered in the sunlight and the rhythmic splashing of the oars was soothing, the tickling sweat running down his neck and back less so. On balance, he preferred the dragon boat where you faced forward and could see where you were going. If you had to be in a boat, that was.

'The bridge approaches,' called Larimar.

The two boats glided into the shadow of the bridge, where wisps of mist still writhed. He took the opportunity to catch his breath while Lapsi brought the boat closer and Zink cast the net to him. Looking up, he found Larimar watching him. The man didn't say much. Then he remembered Larimar was the other

Riverplain pacer and was no doubt close to Lazuli. Both men were probably wondering why Lamiya spent so much time with him. And what he was doing there.

He returned to observing Zink and the net. Soon he understood they were going to row under the bridge, with the net stretched between the two boats. The stone weights would drop it down into the water.

'On my call,' said Acim, getting his oars ready. 'Go.'

Everand pushed with his feet and leaned into his oars again.

'Slowly,' murmured Zink. 'We want to catch the fish, not frighten them.'

The boats slipped smoothly forward, a ripple showing where the net followed.

'Closer to the bank!' called Zink, leaning precariously over the side to peer into the water.

They passed under the bridge and the muscles on Zink's arms and shoulders bulged with the strain. Resistance built up in the net and it became harder to row, and soon Everand's muscles were burning with effort.

'Enough,' called Zink. 'Take us to the bank.'

Copying Larimar, Everand grabbed the mooring rope and jumped out, and they pulled the boats snug against the grassy edge. The others heaved the net onto the bank, where it flopped about, full of shiny, wriggling fish.

'Higher!' yelled Zink when the net nearly flopped back into the water.

Everand slid over the tufty grass to grab the middle of the net and helped them haul it to a flat patch, near the path leading onto the bridge. Chest heaving, he stared at the thrashing, dying fish. A pang throbbed in his heart as he thought of Mizu waiting for his return. He skimmed his gaze over the net, relieved none of the fish looked like Mizu. These were mainly covered in white scales, some tinged with rainbow colours, and he recognised the small, narrow fish as the flavoursome sliver fish.

Zink wiped sweat from his forehead. 'Will this be enough to please the dragon?'

Eyeing the massive mound, Everand said, 'I'd think so.' He wished he knew so. 'Nothing else will eat them?'

Zink shrugged. 'The birds might pick at a few.'

Everand stared at the wriggling catch. If the dragon remained deep in the lake by the waterfall it wouldn't know the fish were here. A flaw in his plan. 'Has the dragon taken fish from here before?'

With a shrug, Zink said, 'Usually we place the fish next to the town. And the dragon hasn't come.'

On impulse, Everand walked away and stepped up to the highest point in the centre of the bridge. To the north, the table-shaped mountain rose in the distance, with a silvery glint that could be the waterfall. Could the river dragon fly? Did it never come this way? Curse it, he should have considered this earlier. Was the rocky ledge a barrier to the dragon swimming downstream? Mage Beetal's dragons had wings and were adept flyers and lethal from the air.

Closing his eyes, he recalled the shimmery image he and Lamiya had glimpsed of this dragon. Did it have wings? They'd not seen enough of the beast to know. However, if no-one ever spoke about seeing the dragon flying then perhaps it couldn't. If one believed the dragon was actually connected to the rainfall, the people of Riverfall had erred gravely when they ceased taking their offerings to the lake. Curse it all! Could he go to the lake this dark-fall? No, too risky.

Hesitant footsteps disrupted his analysis. 'Traveller?' asked Acim.

Pushing down dark thoughts about the inconvenience of keeping his powers concealed, he swept a hand towards the downriver side. 'This is a good spot to judge the long race from. I'll be able to see the boats clearly. Can you give me a little longer?'

With a brief smile, Acim retreated.

Facing north again, Everand kept his hands hidden from the others' view and conjured a fist-sized, clear ball. Into this he fed an image of the bridge and the mound of fish next to it. On instinct, he added himself and Lamiya standing beside the mound with palms open in welcome. After a pause he added the boats, Mizuchi and Flight. Then a view of the path beside the rocky ledge, dropping down to where the river fanned out wider again. For good measure he added the sun rising.

Did dragons understand human language? Deflecting his doubts, he composed a message: *Come, Great Mizuchi. The people of Riverfall hold races in your honour. Come, they want to renew the friendship.*

Carefully, he sealed the ball. Tossing it lightly between his hands, he prepared to transport it to the lake. A quick glance told him the others were sitting on the bank, chatting. A shiver passed across the back of his neck. Glancing up, he frowned at the dark speck high above. One of Malach's eagles? Could he get the ball to the lake without an eagle intercepting it?

Grasping the ball firmly, he replicated three more with identical images and message. Lob them all together or separately? Separately, a better chance of getting through. Hopefully, the dragon would find at least one. Was there a way to mark the balls so he'd know? Cuddling the balls against his tunic, he drew a deep breath, searching for a suitable spell.

After what seemed to take so long he was amazed the others hadn't called him, he found a spell of marking, related to a spell of warding. With precision, he marked each ball so he'd know when it was touched. With intense concentration, he added the spell for an image of who or what touched it to be returned to him. Sweat beaded on his brow.

He threw the first one into the air, pictured the centre of Dragon Lake, and translocated it. The ball vanished. The next one he sent to the base of the waterfall, the third close to the pebbly beach where he and Lamiya had stood, and the fourth back towards the centre of the lake. Keeping his eyes closed, he visualised the balls plopping into the water and sinking, and not bobbing around on the surface.

The fourth one wasn't fast enough. Before it could sink, the screech of the eagle reverberated through him and a vision of flashing talons shot into his mind. Unthinking, he placed his hands over his ears to block the sound. He should have known the lake would be watched! Removing his hands and dropping them, he leaned on the bridge railing, drained. And he still had to row back! Would he know who the eagle took the ball to? He assumed it would be Malach.

'Traveller!'

'We must go!'

The others were standing and beckoning, so he pushed off the railing and walked down the bridge. If Malach could read the ball, the half-mage would know he had called the dragon.

His heart sank.

CHAPTER THIRTY-FIVE

Lamiya wriggled further under her blanket, wishing she could have spent longer snuggling against Everand, but she knew they'd collect him early. She rolled onto her back and stretched out her spine and neck. The team would rest this sun. A few more practice race starts would have been good, but not with paddlers absent fishing. Her pulse quickened.

Would the dragon come for the fish? What would happen if it did? Even underwater the beast had looked huge and fearsome. When Riverfall had issued their invitation to race, there'd been no mention of a dragon, because the notion had faded into stories the old told to entertain the young. *Race the boats and beat the drums to bring the dragon and make rain thrum* ... A wonderful idea, but not one she'd believed. Would what she and Everand had done make a difference? Sleep banished, she pushed back her blanket. She might as well do something useful.

Her movement roused others and soon a candle was lit and she and Lulite were heating water to make a brew. Lulite flashed her a wide smile. Of course! Her friend must be excited about displaying her clothes and jewellery. Smiling back, she asked, 'Would you like help to set out your wares?'

'I was hoping you'd ask,' murmured Lulite. 'Lapsi said he'd help but he won't be back until the sun is high.' The drummer slid her eyes sideways. 'It'll be more fun with your help, anyway.'

A twinge of guilt blossoming inside her, Lamiya decided to immerse herself with the team and help when the other carts arrived with the bulk of the Riverplain goods. She carefully filled three mugs with hot water, breathing in the aroma of the freshly cut herbs. Lulite picked up the platter of bread and fruit and put it on the low table.

Lamiya clasped her fingers around her mug; the air seemed cool. As she sipped, she assessed her paddlers. Lopa and Laza were excited, looking forward to showing off their products. Lattic sat quietly, watching Lopa. Suppressing a smile, she hoped he'd find the courage to approach her soon. Levog, Lepid and Lazuli sat together, discussing how best to parade their hopeepa. She gave a small frown; Lazuli looked subdued, his eyes cast down as if he were only half listening. On his far side, Luvu was looking at her over the rim of his mug.

'Alright, glide?' Luvu asked gruffly.

Appreciating the invitation to seek his advice, she put her mug down and asked the question she was pondering most. 'Which race do you think is our best chance?'

Luvu took a sip from his mug and said, 'The middle race. We are fast, lean and accurate. But ...' he held up a hand, 'the long race is the one we most want.'

'Can we achieve both?' As she spoke, she realised how much she wanted both.

'That's the spirit!' Luvu actually smiled, creases forming around his eyes and mouth. 'We can try. The other boats are strong. We'll lose the short race, just keep us close and not last. Remember, the overall points tally counts.'

Lamiya felt a huge sense of reprieve that this former glide and most experienced paddler didn't expect them to win everything.

'One other thing,' Luvu continued. 'Be careful of the wake from the other boats. Being close carries the risk of bumping, and the wake gives a choppier and slower ride.'

'Good advice, thank you,' said Lamiya. In the thrill of the race, she might not have anticipated this.

The meal finished, she led them through a thorough stretch session and fielded strategy questions. Ejad arrived halfway through and she admired his resilience in recovering so quickly from the viper bite. At the end, they formed a circle with raised right palms joined in the centre, and the strength of their 'Yo!' made her shiver with pride. She *must* bring her team glory.

The team had just lowered their arms when Beram stuck his head in the doorway. 'The carts from Riverplain are here.'

Lulite linked an arm around hers and the team tumbled out of the door. Lamiya leaned against her friend as they walked.

'Let's hope the trade discussions go well,' said Lulite when they entered the courtyard. 'Imagine being able to have races and trade like this more often!' She gave a small laugh. 'That'd be a powerful incentive for some new designs.'

Lamiya said around a smile, 'Just make sure you don't go home with more than you brought!'

Lulite turned with mock horror on her face. 'Who, me?'

Lamiya laughed freely; she knew her friend too well. Besides, the work from the Riversea artists was likely to be entirely desirable. Could she find a shell necklace to complement her new skirt? There'd be a feast and dancing after the races. A shiver chased down her arms at the thought of swaying in the moonlight wrapped in Everand's arms.

'What?' asked Lulite.

Lamiya shook her head.

Lulite faced her squarely. 'You are troubled. You need to tell me about this soon.'

Around a swallow, Lamiya said, 'After the races. Then I'd value your wisdom.'

Lulite gave her a searching look but didn't press her. Together, they turned to greet the carts that were rumbling through the archway.

Before Lamiya could register who was aboard the carts, people seemed to come from everywhere. She smiled when she saw two small boys daring each other to pat the nose of a hopeepa that looked down at them with fluttering eyelashes.

'Lamiya!' She looked around, trying to see who had called her. 'Lamiya!' The call came from above her. Amazed, she saw Latog, his broken leg stiffly bound with a rush and mud cast, standing on the cart supported by Luvu and Lopa.

'You came!' she cried in delight. Now all the team was present.

With much careful pushing and shoving, the others managed to get Latog to ground level. 'Wouldn't miss it unless I were dead,' Latog said gruffly as Lamiya grasped his hands. She let go when Luvu handed him a wooden T-frame to lean on.

Lulite tugged at her elbow. 'My things are on the third cart.'

Lamiya followed Lulite to the cart, drawn by two of Levog's hopeepa, their jade blotches striking in the early light. The sheen of sweat along the creature's necks and flanks told her the carts had set a good pace.

'We have two tables,' Lulite said. 'We've been asked to set out our wares before dark-fall so everything is ready. Trading will begin straight after the long race.'

Lamiya raised an eyebrow. 'How do you know all this?'

'Luvu asked Atage. He's been trying to find out as much as he can before the discussions.' She gave Lamiya a curious look. 'You haven't forgotten I'm a negotiator, have you?'

Lamiya gave a nervous smile. Actually, she had. She'd noticed Luvu made a point of sitting with the older men from Riverfall at each feast, which made sense. She'd not thought about Lepid and Lulite being the other negotiators. Thank the spirits she only had the races to worry about. The trade discussions would be just as complex. She gave a small swallow; assuming these went ahead and Everand's fears weren't realised. Her gaze moved around the courtyard and

307

the bustle of people. She noticed Beram and a couple of men putting a bundle behind one of the Riverfall trade tables. Were those spear points sticking out?

'Are you alright?' Lulite tapped her arm. 'You look worried.'

Lamiya blinked at her friend. 'Yes. Let's position your wares to advantage then.'

Time passed swiftly while she helped Lulite and the others unload basket after basket from the carts. The range was impressive: baskets of assorted weave, colour and size; feather ornaments; down pillows and cushions; dried flowers; jar upon jar of seeds, spices and herbs; pots of rice grain; jugs of rice-wine; and caskets overflowing with brightly coloured necklaces, headpieces and bracelets made from myriad arrangements of beads and feathers. Whirr hopped from basket to basket, puffing up his chest and preening. She sighed. It would have been good to bring some of her exotic birds to display, but the journey would have been too stressful for them. And she had enough to manage already ... Maybe next time.

'What do you think?' Lulite's question drew her attention and she gasped at the sky-arch-coloured scarf her friend held up, made of small feathers neatly stitched together.

'Incredible!' Lamiya fingered the edge, marvelling at the soft feathers. 'How long did this take to make?'

'Two seasons to collect the feathers, then five suns to lay it out in an order that worked and to stitch it.'

'I guess there's only one?' she said. 'It's exquisite how you made the colours blur into each other. How much will you ask for it?'

Lulite looked troubled. 'I have no idea.'

'At least eight fishes,' said Lamiya firmly. 'This is a prize piece.' She drummed her fingers against her thigh. 'We could go and see what prices the Riversea artists are putting on their work.'

Lulite lowered the scarf with a sly smile. 'That, my captain, is a most excellent idea.'

Lamiya waited while Lulite carefully wrapped and concealed the scarf and stood back to admire the layout of the table one last time. Then they looped arms and meandered to the tables designated for Riversea. Mookaite and Melanite were already there.

Mookaite greeted her with a kiss on the cheek. 'How's your head? All better?'

'Yes, thank you,' said Lamiya, smiling at Melanite too. 'Are your tables already set up?'

'Not yet,' said Melanite. 'We're observing the competition first!' With a wider grin, she said, 'You'll wear your new skirt to the feast?'

'Of course,' said Lamiya. 'I'm thinking it needs a new necklace to heighten its magnificence.'

They all laughed.

'We'll leave you to choose wisely,' said Mookaite, tugging Melanite's elbow. 'We'd better get started.'

Lamiya watched the two women nudge their way through the milling people. When the boats lined up she must forget their kind friendship and see them as rivals. Shaking her head, she stepped up to the Riversea table. Spirula, Charonia, Clama and Nawpra were busy laying out strings of shells and woven baskets. Of the Riversea men there was no sign.

'Hey, Lamiya,' called Charonia. 'How be you?'

'Good. Do you need any help?'

'No, we be fine,' said Charonia, laying out more strings of shell necklaces.

'Where's the rest of your team?'

'Hah!' said Spirula, putting down some small ornate boxes. 'The clumsy oafs be polishing the boat and keeping out of our way.'

While the women laughed, Lamiya eyed the small boxes. 'What are these?'

Spirula picked one up and handed it to her. 'To put your jewellery in.'

Lamiya rotated the box in her hands; it was made of a fine wood, with tiny shells and bits of coral stuck to it to form a pattern.

'Open it,' said Spirula. 'Use the wee catch at the front.'

Turning the box around, she found a tiny wooden peg catch. She slipped this and eased open the lid, which was lined with a smooth shell that hinted at pearly colours. The base was padded with a mat of tiny white feathers. Awed, she said, 'It's beautiful. Can you save me one?'

'I put your name on this one,' said Spirula kindly.

Lulite elbowed her in the ribs. 'Now who's acquiring more than she sells?'

'Very funny,' said Lamiya, calculating whether she had enough tokens to also buy a necklace. 'Have you seen prices to help you decide?'

'Not yet,' said Lulite. 'Come look at the necklaces.'

Lamiya let Lulite tug her to the next table where the range of styles was truly impressive: clusters of shells in a bauble on a string; individual shells of every shape and size imaginable; shells in a continuous thread, with an assortment of colours mixed or individually presented; and necklaces of intricate shells hung on fine strands in elegant web formats.

The sheer simplicity and elegance of one caught her eye. A fine white strand was designed to sit loosely across the neck at collarbone height. At the mid-point of each bone sat a small, silver-white, flat coiled shell, and from these fed two more fine strands so that in the centre, just above the curve of the breast, a pearly cowrie shell sat. The crinkly lips of the cowrie were blue-silver, like spun moonlight. Lamiya swallowed: it was perfect. The small wooden board underneath it on the table showed the symbol for three fish tokens. Lulite squeezed her arm and nodded.

'If we win the long race, I'll reward myself with this,' whispered Lamiya.

'As if you need any more motivation to win,' said Lulite. 'And I think six fish tokens for my scarf.'

Lamiya drew her eyes away from the necklace and crossed her fingers that it would still be there after the race. The next table was bare. 'Whose table is that?' she asked Nawpra.

The woman shrugged her solid shoulders. 'Riverwood? But we haven't seen them.'

'That's because they didn't bring any women.' Charonia laughed. 'So, no organisation of goods.'

'True. They're probably out training!' added Clama.

Reminded of the undercurrents attached to the races, Lamiya scanned the courtyard: there was not a Riverwood paddler in sight. What could they be doing? She thought back to their sudden arrival and the scant belongings the paddlers had carried from the boat. If they hadn't brought anything to trade, why come?

The back of her neck felt warm and she realised the sun was already arching towards its high point. The Riverplain carts had gone, presumably taken to the stables and fields. Lazuli's downcast face flitted into her mind. He hadn't spoken to her. At all. She should look for him. He needed to be full of his usual energy for the races.

Leaving Lulite chatting, she peeled away from the tables and set off for the stables. On the way she kept an eye out for any of the Riverwood paddlers, thinking Everand would want to know where they were. As she walked, she saw food being prepared and many more tables and benches being carried to the courtyards. She glimpsed Melanite and Ejad carrying armfuls of clothes. The Riverwood paddlers were nowhere in sight.

The hopeepa stable looked quiet. She slowed, thinking maybe she should check the yards outside the gate first. Then she heard voices. Drawing closer to the door that stood ajar, she listened.

'I don't know, brother. Can you ask her?' At Lepid's words she froze, one hand grasping the doorframe.

'How can I?' Lazuli sounded upset. His words grew alternately louder and softer, as if he were pacing. 'What could I say?'

'Honesty is usually best,' said Lepid. 'You've been friends since you were both knee-high. You're made for each other. Talk to her!'

Her breath caught in her throat. Were they discussing her? They must be. Lazuli hadn't shown interest in anyone else.

'What are you afraid of?' probed Lepid.

'Things are different!' snapped Lazuli. 'Since she spent time with the traveller something's different. She likes him better than me.'

'She's young,' said Lepid soothingly. 'Give her some time.'

'Time?' said Lazuli sharply. 'How much more time? Her mother and father were ill, then they died and she was grieving, then we were preparing for the races, and now we are at the race and festival and still she needs time? She has time for the traveller.'

He sounded bitter and Lamiya pushed her knuckles against her mouth. She had no idea he'd felt this deeply about her for so long.

'Yes, but he is a traveller,' said Lepid calmly, as if reasoning with a small child. 'He will leave, move on. Then what will she do?'

Lamiya felt ill. She had been trying so hard not to let her mind think along these lines.

'What if she goes with him?' Lazuli almost shouted.

Lepid sounded incredulous. 'No-one goes to Axis. How can she go with him?'

Her knees shaking, she leaned against the door. Lepid was right! *No-one goes to Axis.* And they didn't even know that

Everand was a mage! What had she been thinking? Angrily, she brushed at the hair tickling her cheek. How could she ever have thought it possible to be with Everand? A dull ache spread across her chest. She loved being with Everand. He was so brave, so selfless and kind in trying to help them all. Wait! Had Everand thought about this? He behaved as if he wanted to be with her. Was this why he drew back whenever their attraction seemed to be getting away from them? Did he *know* that she couldn't go with him?

She felt as if she were breaking in two. She wanted so much to be with Everand; she had trusted him, believed in their feelings for each other. Was Lepid right? She couldn't go with Everand and, worse, he *knew* this? She belonged in Riverplain. And now she'd hurt Lazuli. She leaned her forehead against the hard wooden frame. How could she make things right?

With a sniff, she straightened up. First things first: she had a team to command and glide to glory. Other things could wait. She took a deep breath and marched into the stable.

'Here you are!' Her lips felt numb around the forced smile. 'What are you doing?'

Lazuli and Lepid spun around and stared at her. Lazuli stood with his mouth open, a red flush creeping up his neck. Lepid winced and said, 'Hello, Lamiya. We're planning how to show off our hopeepa.'

'Well, when you finish that I was wondering if you'd help me polish Flight? I've heard the other teams have polished their boats.' She waited while Lepid looked at Lazuli, who remained at a loss for words.

'Of course,' said Lepid. 'We can come now.'

'Excellent,' said Lamiya. Her mind locked properly onto the task. 'Let's go by our dome to collect the feathers. We might as well put Flight's racing colours on.'

Lazuli gave her a nervous smile, normal colour returning to his face, and Lepid gave her a questioning look.

But they both followed her from the stable.

CHAPTER THIRTY-SIX

Everand eyed the glistening pile of fish at the base of the bridge, now surrounded by neat arrangements of fruits and breads and what looked like polished green stones. Where had they produced those from? He extended his senses. A grass plain stretched away from him, feeding to the base of grey-green hills in the distance. Behind him, the river bubbled and gurgled, the surface rippling gold and silver in the sunlight. He spread a subtle ward over the mound of offerings, one that would dissipate in the depths of dark-fall. Satisfied this would discourage any predators before the dragon arrived, he slid down the bank to where the others waited.

Acim and Zink had already pushed off from the bank. Larimar sat with his oars ready at the back of the second boat, and Lapsi held the mooring rope. Everand clambered into the tipsy boat and settled awkwardly on the middle bench. Lapsi jumped in and they rowed into the centre of the river.

'Could we go under the bridge and then turn around?' he asked, wanting to check beneath the bridge.

Without reply, Larimar and Lapsi rowed under the bridge. As its bulk passed above them, Everand twisted his neck and inspected the structure. The stones and woodwork looked solid; he could see no sign of interference. He roamed his heightened perception over the stones. Underneath the arch, in the very middle where it was highest, he paused. Something was amiss, a kind of lurking blot. A couple of shadows detached from the gloom and two bats flew at him. He ducked, then watched them curve around and scoot back into the shadows.

Larimar and Lapsi looked amused as they turned the boat around and passed back under the bridge to rejoin the others. Everand scanned the bank on the Riverwood side: tall reeds and grasses flapped erratically in a rising breeze and the sunlight glinted blindingly off the water. Nothing untoward. He tapped his fingers on the bench beside him, unease hovering. Larimar raised an eyebrow at him.

'All good,' he said without explanation. Both boats headed back downriver.

When they approached the largest waterwheel, the paddlers rowed slowly while Zink prepared the net. Lapsi asked Everand if he could row again.

Everand got ready to move to the forward oar bench. The two boats jostled and bobbed beside each other, the breeze whipping the water into choppy waves. On the far bank the tall grasses rustled sibilantly, sharing secrets. He saw a family of black birds with bright red beaks swim to the edge and scurry into the reeds, the younger birds calling as they followed.

The back of his neck tingled and a shiver passed down his arms. A warning? Suddenly, he realised how vulnerable they were on the river in a small boat and beyond the sight of the town. How many people knew they were out here? If Riverwood wanted to know where he was, they would only need to ask a Riverfall paddler.

Distracted, he eased past Lapsi and took up the oars, only half watching Lapsi and Zink cast the net between the boats. Rowing slowly, he tried to scan ahead, behind and to both sides all at once. The back of his neck tingled and prickled. Perhaps he should prepare a ward-shield to hover over the two boats.

Two calloused and strong hands flashed into his mind, followed by Malach's face. The man was standing just outside the northern gate. So, the eagle had indeed passed the message ball to Malach. Quickly, he closed down the marker and link, hoping Malach hadn't ascertained exactly where the two boats were.

He returned to preparing the spell of warding when the massive gold talons and then the face of the dragon completely filled his mind. He gasped, chest constricting. The wide nostrils flared a deep crimson and the dragon's gold whiskers bristled away from glinting, blue-scaled cheeks. The rage of the beast was overpowering and he struggled to sit upright, let alone row. Dimly, he heard the others shouting. Breathing hard, he wrestled to sever the link but the essence of the beast was too strong. The eyes of the dragon gleamed like molten gold with black slits in the centres as dark and deep as endless ravines and he was sinking, sinking into the depth of the gaze.

Gritting his teeth, Everand repeated the message in the ball and conjured the image of the pile of offerings by the bridge, he and Lamiya standing with palms open in welcome. Against the weight of the dragon's ire, he added images of the sun rising and boats waiting to race. Heavy, blue-scaled lids closed over the golden eyes in what could have been a blink of surprise. Then the dragon was gone.

'Traveller!' Acim shouted, waving his arms.

Struggling to bring his awareness back to his surroundings, Everand forced himself to sit upright, his mind sluggish. Time moving at half pace, he saw Zink and Lapsi scrabbling to bring the net in, fish leaping and writhing in its folds. Larimar sat staring upriver, oars dangling forgotten by his sides.

'We have no weapons!' yelled Acim. 'Get ready!'

His mind fuzzy, Everand watched Larimar take his oars out of their keepers, toss one at Acim and raise his up by his shoulder as if he intended to swing it.

'Tree-moths!' screamed Zink.

Everand looked upriver at the dark cloud zooming across the water straight at them. His bile rose. How could he have been so stupid and let these good paddlers be so vulnerable? Desperately, he tried to summon a warding spell, but his mind was wandering in a thick mist and was unable to latch onto the spell words, which slipped and slid beyond his grasp. Cursing, he tried to shake off the dragon's thrall.

Copying Acim, he flicked an oar out of its keeper and prepared to wield it like a weapon, his mouth dry and his grip clammy. Tackling the moths on firm ground with several other men had been one thing. Bobbing about in a small boat while the moths swooped was another thing altogether. The ominous brown cloud drew closer, and his mind grew clearer.

'Aim for the antennae,' he called out.

Larimar grunted and flexed his fingers on his oar haft.

The cloud of moths blotted out the light. Everand anchored his feet against the bottom of the boat and grasped the oar tightly. Larimar swung first and a moth screeched when the oar connected with its abdomen. The cloud of moths split and two eagles flew out of the centre, beaks open, talons outstretched — aiming directly for his face!

Everand gasped and swung his oar with all the strength he could muster. The eagles nimbly dodged. A quick glance told him he was on his own: the four paddlers were beset by moths, fully occupied swinging their oars. Out of the corner of his eye he saw an eagle diving in fast on his right. Resisting the urge to cringe, he swung the oar blade in an arc at the bird's head. With an ear-splitting screech, the bird veered away. A sharp clack of a beak erupted by his left ear. The second bird had attacked from the other side!

His head was engulfed in stifling feathers, clogging his nostrils and mouth, stinking of bird and cutting off his breath. Sharp talons raked over his head. Dropping the oar, he punched the bird and it shuddered when his fist connected with its rib cage. Excruciating pain roared across his head as a chunk of his hair was ripped away. The bird soared upwards, shrilling. Spitting out a feather, he breathed shallowly against the stabbing pain. A trickling sensation told him he was bleeding. Before he could investigate, the first bird swooped in again.

Sweat dripped into his eyes, his scalp stung like crazy and his arms felt like blocks of wood — but he kept swinging the oar or punching his fists to deflect the birds. The eagles flew in fast measured loops so that one was always swooping in from his right and the other from his left. He barely had time to breathe, let alone draw upon any spells. Angry, he observed that the eagles were the same as the one that rode on Malach's shoulder.

Eventually, an eagle crunched into his head and he yelled as another piece of hair was wrenched out. Keening wildly, the eagles flew in a triumphant circle, both with a tuft of blond hair dangling from its talons. Abruptly, they flapped away towards the Riverwood bank. By the time he'd blinked the sweat from his eyes, they had vanished. Simultaneously, the tree-moths broke off their attack and moved downstream, heading towards the town.

Drained, Everand sat with his head bowed and his hands resting on top of the upright oar haft to support his trembling arms. The boat bobbed adrift, the motion combined with the pain making his stomach churn. His mouth tasted of soggy feathers and blood.

'Traveller?' said Larimar tentatively. 'You're bleeding.'

He drew in a ragged breath. His thoughts circled like agitated butterflies refusing to land. What had just happened? An important idea flitted with his thoughts, amid flashbacks of the attack. Dazed, he looked at the other boat. Acim and Zink were staring at him, breathing hard and eyes wide. The net drifted on the water beside their boat, with fish wriggling free of the folds.

'Are you alright?' asked Acim.

'What happened to your head?' asked Zink at the same time.

'The eagles attacked me,' said Everand, wishing his heartbeats would slow down so he could think straight. He flapped a limp hand at the net. 'You're losing fish.'

Zink cursed and started to pull on the edges of the net to tighten it.

'Are there enough fish?' asked Acim, a frown etched between his brows.

'We should cast one more time.' Zink looked downstream, checking where the tree-moths had gone. Then he stared at Everand. 'What do you think? Is it safe now?'

Larimar and Lapsi sat wiping sweat from their necks and arms, waiting for a decision.

Acim asked, louder, 'Traveller? We need more fish. Is it safe for us to fish?' Then he said more softly, 'Can you hang on while we fish? How bad is your wound?'

Everand drew in a ragged breath, and the important idea emerged from his tangled thoughts. 'We can fish,' he said. 'I think they're gone now.' The attack had achieved its purpose: Malach had some of his hair, which he could use to craft spells of compunction or binding. Assuming he had sufficient skill.

Fatigue enveloped him. How could he make sensible decisions when what was happening kept shifting under his feet like this? Was he now a target? Malach had seemed to recognise him. What did this mean? Now he had to protect the boats and races, the trade discussions, the dragon and himself! How could one half-mage wreak so much confusion? He imagined his butterfly thoughts flopping down in exhaustion.

A piece of green cloth appeared under his nose. 'Here,' said Larimar kindly. 'Wipe away the blood. Dip it in the river.'

Gratefully, Everand took the cloth, dipped it in the river and dabbed at the back of his head. The cool water felt nice, although it made the cut sting. The cloth quickly became bright red. He rinsed it out and kept dabbing gingerly while Zink and Lapsi worked the fishnet. The cloth was fading to pink by the time they'd filled the net and hauled it into the boat. He rinsed the cloth out again and looked at the sodden, crumpled mess. Would Larimar be offended if he offered it back to him?

Reading his mind, Larimar said, 'Keep the cloth, Traveller.'

'Thanks,' said Everand. 'Sorry.'

'Why did they attack you?' Larimar asked, forehead drawn tight in a frown.

Everand shrugged and Larimar gave him a dubious look.

The row back to the town passed without further mishap, although he saw a brown cloud passing over the wilderness on the Riverwood side that looked suspiciously like the tree-moths heading back to their forest. The others didn't engage in their usual banter, and he guessed they were trying to work out why the eagles had focused on him.

'We need to tell Tengar,' said Zink when the town came into sight. 'What if this happens during the races?'

When Acim nodded, Lapsi gave him a sharp look and added, 'We'll tell Lamiya.'

Everand stared down at the water, wishing he could say something to reassure them. But maybe that was best left to the team captains.

At least the paddlers would now be more alert.

CHAPTER THIRTY-SEVEN

Everand looked at Acim when they passed the spot where they had boarded the boats.

'We're going to the ramp,' said Acim. 'Persaj is bringing a cart to take the fish to the courtyard.'

Everand sat quietly in the boat, watching the outer town wall and colourful tents slide past. He frowned at the lack of activity along the bank and near the tents. Had something happened here, too? They drew level with the southern courtyard and he heard many voices calling and shouting instructions. Something had happened. What would Lamiya be doing? He longed to lean on her shoulder, feel her arms around him and let her presence calm him. When the boats nudged onto the boat ramp, there was no sign of Persaj or any cart.

Acim jumped out and tugged the rope until the prow scraped the ramp, then put his hands on his hips and looked around. Everand stood, but his legs wobbled and he thumped back down onto the bench. White stars swam at the edges of his vision. He tried again and wobbled clumsily out over the front of the boat. The others watched without comment. His feet back on firm ground, he tottered up the ramp. After a few steps, he felt some strength returning and called down to Acim, 'I'll go and look for Persaj.'

Acim called back, 'We'll get the fish out ready.'

Walking slowly and drawing measured breaths, Everand headed for the courtyard. The sunlight hurt his eyes and his head throbbed with every step. He sent a dulling spell to the back of his head and the throbbing eased, but he still felt light-headed.

He passed under the archway and stopped dead at the frenetic activity. The courtyard was in shambles, with tables and benches overturned and products scattered everywhere. Paddlers and townspeople were righting tables and gathering up fallen goods. A familiar face caught his attention. 'Beram!'

'What happened?' Beram exclaimed as soon as he drew near. 'Your hair is matted with blood!'

'Eagles,' said Everand succinctly. 'What happened here? The tree-moths?'

Beram nodded. 'They swooped in out of nowhere and pushed over the tables, using their wings to scatter all the goods.' He shrugged. 'Much of it's covered in moth-dust that we'll have to remove. A few things got broken.'

Everand looked around the courtyard and raised his eyebrows when he noticed the Riverwood paddlers were helping.

Beram followed the line of his eyes and grimaced. 'As if it had nothing to do with them! What could we do?' He took Everand's elbow. 'Come. You must see Mookaite.'

Beram tugged him along until they found Mookaite helping the Riverplain women to set out their table again. Disappointingly, Lamiya was nowhere in sight. Neither was Lazuli. The throbbing returned to his head.

'By the river spirits!' Mookaite blanched when she saw him. 'To my dome. Now.'

He let Beram and Mookaite take an elbow each and march him to her dome. Halfway there, he remembered he was supposed to be looking for Persaj. When he said this, Beram peeled away, promising to fetch Persaj and make sure the pile of fish reached its destination.

Welcoming the cool, dimmer interior of the healer's dome, he inhaled the subtle fragrance of flowers and herbs and felt his mind calming. Mookaite directed him to a small bench by her low table and sat him down. He heard her humming while she warmed water and bustled about opening and closing jars.

'Here, sip this slowly.' She placed a steaming mug on the low table. 'It'll ease the pain.'

'What is it?' he asked, the pungent smell already clearing his head.

'Lavender, peppermint and a petal of rose,' she replied, coming to stand behind him. 'Take a few sips and let me look at your wounds.'

Everand blew on the scalding brew a few times before taking a cautious sip. Mookaite gently unbound his ponytail and parted and lifted segments of hair. Despite her efforts, pain lanced into his scalp.

'No moth did this,' she murmured.

'Eagles,' he said.

'Eagles!' Mookaite dropped the hair she was holding. 'You're lucky to be alive.'

'Mmm,' he said noncommittally. 'Can you clean it and redo my hair so others won't notice?'

Mookaite put her hands on his shoulders with a reassuring squeeze. 'I'll try.'

Focusing on sipping the entire mugful, he did his best not to fidget. Mookaite's fingers were sure and gentle as she sponged away the congealed blood.

She clicked her tongue. 'I'm going to wash your hair so you're presentable for the races.' A light hand rested on his shoulder. 'Your head will be too sore to touch for the next few suns so it's better to wash your hair now.'

He steeled himself for the discomfort while Mookaite prepared two large bowls of warm water and fetched a chunk of purple soap. Concentrating on breathing evenly, he revelled in her skill as she carefully wet his hair and applied the soap. A strong essence of lavender surrounded him. Avoiding the cuts, she massaged his scalp in rhythmic circles, the pressure just perfect. He released a long sigh. Soon, she was tipping warm water over his head and the length of his hair to cleanse it.

'Such a pretty colour,' she murmured. 'Like spun moonlight.'

His head became heavy on his neck and the desire to sleep oozed over him. What else had he intended to do before the races the very next sun-up? Was he supposed to meet with Atage and Lyber?

His mind drifted and he was back in Mage Beetal's study, his mentor pacing the silk rug and admonishing him for not paying attention. Was it possible Mage Beetal had cultivated *two* apprentices? Was it possible the mage had routinely snuck out of Axis to coach Malach? How else could the half-mage have so much power?

There were certainly times when his mentor had been late for his lessons, and occasions when the bristly mage had been in an unaccountably good humour. Who was Malach's mother to hold such attraction for him? But how could no-one have noticed? How could Beetal have got through the wardspell without drawing attention? Was there another way out of Axis? Everand yawned, his arms and legs pleasantly numb.

Light flickered as someone pushed aside the dome curtain and gasped, 'What happened?'

Lamiya. He wanted to smile but his lips were too heavy. As if inside a distant cave, he heard Mookaite mumbling something, more questions, more answers. Next came the pressure of Mookaite's hands on his shoulders and her voice close to his ear.

'All done. Rest for a while. Lamiya will sit with you while I go help the others.' The pressure of her lovely, warm hands eased. 'Don't rub or scratch at it.' Then she was gone.

He sat breathing slowly. Was Lamiya still there? Why didn't she say anything? When he tried to lift his head, his scalp gave a stab of pain. *Annoying*. He braced himself and looked up. Lamiya was sitting on a cushion on the other side of the table, her grey-blue eyes wide. She looked pale, upset and distant. A current of anxiety merged with his pain. Had he let her down somehow?

'What's wrong?' he croaked. When she didn't reply, he felt ill and out of his depth. With effort, he met her eyes. 'Lamiya, is something wrong?'

Her face softened and she came to sit at his knees. *Better*. Tears glistened in her eyes. *Not better*. She put a hand on his knee while she searched for words. Despair swamped him; she was going to choose Lazuli and didn't know how to tell him.

'This is so difficult.' She sniffed. 'I don't ... how can we be together?'

Such a big question! His head and heart pounding, he stiffly put his hand over hers. 'I don't know, Lamiya.' When she chewed at her lower lip he added, 'I'd like to try, though.'

She put both hands on his knee and rested her cheek on top of them. Her hair tickled his knee. He licked his cracked lips. 'We can only try and see what happens.' Assuming they survived whatever Malach had planned. Not to mention the dragon. A tremor passed through him and he frowned as the thought flitted into his mind that this dragon was far more powerful than Mage Beetal's dragons had been. Why was it so angry?

Lamiya gave him a wavering smile and, persuading the languid muscles in his arm to move, he stroked her hair. He adored her energy and boldness, but how much courage would it take for her to choose to love him? Their lives were so different. It'd be so much easier if he could fall in love with a fellow mage. But he couldn't. How could he commit to anyone, even as attractive as Tiliqua, unless his heart was in it?

His fingers caressing Lamiya's silky hair, he thought about her standing poised at the back of her boat, her eyes dancing with joy, her muscles rippling. His chest swelled and grew tight at the same time: he so wanted to be with her. How could he tell her this? Could he afford to lay bare his heart again? But if he didn't, he'd lose her. He slipped his fingers under her chin and tilted her face up so he could look into her eyes.

'I know we're different ...' he cleared his throat, '... but I'd like to be with you.'

Her eyes grew dark, pink infused her cheeks, and she gave him the mischievous smile he so loved. Eyes sparkling, cheeks dimpling, she squeezed his knee and said, 'Nice. *After* the races!'

He groaned and tipped forward to kiss her but stopped with a gasp at the pain piercing the back of his head.

'Oh, your head!' Her eyes filled with concern.

Sitting bolt upright, he murmured, 'You might have to kiss me. *Before* the races.'

Pushing up from the floor, Lamiya hesitantly wrapped her arms around the back of his neck and softly placed her lips on his.

Joy raced through him as he kissed her back. Gently.

Too soon, she pulled away. 'Mookaite will be back soon. And I must prepare my team.'

He held onto her arms. 'I can't say this in front of the other teams, but race well, Lamiya. Free the dragon in your boat and glide your team to glory.'

With a wide smile, she took his hands and squeezed them.

'Go,' he said reluctantly. 'I'll rest until Mookaite returns.'

After another squeeze of his hands, she backed out of the dome. The curtain dropped back into place and he swallowed. Something wasn't right; she was holding back. Something was bothering her. He closed his eyes. Lamiya's expression was similar to the way Elemar had looked at him when she was floundering with the realisation that she couldn't return to her own world: afraid and out of her depth but trying not to show it.

What had he done back then? He'd floundered then too, until Delma the cook, standing with her hands on her fulsome hips, had advised him that he needed to reassure Elemar — and that all women appreciated small gifts. Not really seeing the connection, he had presented Elemar with an ornate bottle of Bellflower perfume. Her eyes had danced with delight, she'd trusted him more and she'd rallied her courage.

Moving stiffly, he arranged Mookaite's cushions so he could lie down. His head throbbed relentlessly and he shuffled around until he eventually found he could lie on his left side. So, a present for Lamiya: there'd be ample choice from the trading tables. It must be elegant and exotic, to be given to her at the feast after the races as a reward for paddling well. Would the few tokens Beram had given him be enough? If not, he could magically copy them so he had enough. A minor digression from the Guild rules under the circumstances. *Guild rules*. A weight settled over him, pinning him to Mookaite's cushions. He shuffled, still unable to get comfortable.

After only two suns — one of races and one of trade discussions — his mission would be completed and he'd have to return to Axis. Suddenly, this felt far too soon. His head ached and his throat grew tight. Was *that* what was bothering Lamiya? She expected him to leave her? Of course she did. *Everyone* expected him to go back, because mages don't meddle and he would have to report to Mantiss and the council. Did Lamiya think he was just leading her on? He groaned. How could she think otherwise? But they were so drawn to each other …

He writhed on the cushions, every part of him aching. Was *not* going back an option? His breath caught. Why was he even thinking this? How could he not go back? Mantiss expected him to return and resume his duties, both overt and covert. He frowned. There was also Mizu, waiting for him to heal her.

The light behind the curtain grew and then faded while he considered what reasons he had to return to Axis.

CHAPTER THIRTY-EIGHT

There were only a few pages remaining to read. Mage Mantiss sat for a moment, staring at the threads of minerals trickling through the marble wall tiles. The soft light from the glow-orbs highlighted them like tiny golden rivulets. Thinking of rivers, how was Everand faring? The festival and trade discussions Beram had spoken of must be imminent. Had Everand found out who was trying to sabotage these events?

Mantiss rubbed his hands together to warm and loosen fingers that seemed eternally cold and numb. If anyone could unravel hidden plots, it was his spy. Everand's report would be interesting. Mantiss closed his eyes against an eddy of nausea. May Everand's report not identify any immediate risks. He didn't have enough energy to deal with another major crisis.

Enough of that gloom and doom! Mantiss tugged the notebook closer. Two reading sessions to go, then he was ready for whatever news Everand might bring back.

From the scrawlings of Mage Lapemis

Rules for the New Guild of Axis

By the end of the second cycle of the new Mages' Guild, six babies had arrived — three mage-born and three human children. To my profound relief, in the mage-born we had two males and Dtella blessed me with the yearned-for daughter. Although our daughter Oedura would have a choice of only two for a partner, our line would continue.

Humbly, I received regular power from the stone to share with the others. Already, we have completed the administration building, one residence dome and started the foundations for a library. We determined to call our new town Axis, because our lives and world revolved around it.

The key rules for the Guild were established and scribed as such:

Rule One —   The key purpose of the Guild is to enhance and refine the workings of magic, and to impart knowledge and training to younger mages as apprentices.

Rule Two —   The Guild will be led by an elected Head of the Guild.

Rule Three —   The Head of the Guild will be supported by an Inner Council and an Outer Council, member numbers to rise over time.

Rule Four —   The Guild will work 'to protect by sun and moon' the mages of Axis and the humans who work with us.

Rule Five —   The Head of the Guild has overall authority, and the code words to access the Staropal are to be known only by the incumbent Head of the Guild.

Rule Six —   The Staropal will be concealed and only accessed in times of dire need, as decreed by the Head of the Guild and with agreement from the councils. The stone must be used for honest purpose and for the greater good.

Rule Seven —   The humans who reside in Axis agree to work with and care for the physical needs of the mages, such as food, water, clothing and labour, in exchange for shelter and protection.

Rule Eight —   Mages must only breed with other mages to keep the lines of magic pure. Accordingly, the humans of Axis must only breed with other humans.

Rule Nine —   No mage or human shall pass outside the granite wall, unless ordered to do so by the Head of the Guild for special purpose.

Rule Ten —   Others from outside Axis shall not be allowed inside the wall of granite, unless authorised by the Head of the Guild for special purpose.

Rule Eleven —   Breaches of Guild Law will be judged by the Inner Council, with the final say by the Head of the Guild. Extreme digressions will be punished by obliteration or removal of power.

Rule Twelve —   Mage power must only be used for sound purposes with honest intent. Use for personal ambition or evil intent constitutes a breach of the direst magnitude and will be punished in accordance with Rule Eleven.

Not written in the rules was our sworn pact among the original eleven that knowledge of the acquisition of the Staropal and of the creatures called dragon would never be passed on. Our descendants must believe in the new Guild as an agent of integrity from its foundation. We have recorded in the annals that we found the stone in the eternal spring and realised it held magical properties. The presence of the granite wall is explained as a shield to protect us from invasion, such as the kind that forced us to flee our original homeland.

We will strive to remain a self-contained Guild and live harmonious lives.

Mantiss closed the notebook. Lapemis and the others had established outstanding foundations for a strong and peaceful Guild. They had chosen the land to live on well, even if the choice had been determined by distance from the red dragon. In his mind, he quickly ran through the reports each subsequent Head of the Guild had made on key events during their stewardship. Not one had referred to any red or blue dragon, or any similar creature.

The only reports with incidents of significance were the one that detailed the transgression of Mage Thrip and the Last Great Battle — and his own report describing the treachery of Mage Beetal. Mantiss swallowed. *His* report referred to dragons, the winged creatures from Terralis.

He rubbed at the base of his neck and a thrill of renewed terror ran through him. At the time, frozen with horror, he had expected the dragons to snatch the Staropal. But it was Mage Beetal who took the stone. He put a hand on his chest, feeling the ragged pace in his heartbeat, and took a breath. The winged dragons were not the same as the river dragons Lapemis had scribed about. Mage Beetal's dragons were savage and lethal. The ones Lapemis had encountered sounded more intelligent, and possessed some kind of innate power.

Mantiss sealed the notebook back in its nook, then sat flexing his fingers. Beram had referred to Dragonspine River but hadn't mentioned any *live* dragons, just petty sabotage of a pending event of boat races and trade discussions. Everand was tasked with solving a human squabble and finding out about the people in the provinces — and he'd been given strict orders to conceal his power and abilities.

Surely, Everand would not find any dragons. And he wouldn't be recognised as a mage. He was far too skilled for that!

It was a short and simple mission — it had to be.

CHAPTER THIRTY-NINE

Someone was rubbing her hand, the sensation warm and comforting. Lamiya wriggled. Someone squeezed her hand and whispered her name. Jerking awake, she found Lazuli peering at her.

'Great sleepy glide.' His words were slurred around the grin she could barely see in the dim light. 'Your team awaits your orders.'

Fluttering spirits! Had she overslept? She bolted upright, snatched her hand away and threw off her blanket. His laughter reached her ears just as she realised everyone else was still asleep. 'You beast!' She punched him on the arm.

'Careful,' Lazuli growled. 'I need this arm!'

Seeing that only faint light eked under the curtain, she said softly, 'Indeed, mighty pacer. And it's good to be awake.'

'Have you children finished?' came Lulite's voice from her other side.

Lazuli's pillow sailed past her nose and landed on Lulite. She only just managed to jerk her head back to avoid Lulite's pillow as it flew past and thumped into Lazuli. She laughed: her team was in high spirits. 'Enough,' she raised her palms. 'Save your energy!'

She neatly packed away her bedding, surrounded by the team all doing the same thing. The banter between the paddlers warmed her heart. So much training and preparation for *this* rising of the sun. Excitement shivered through her. And again, as she replayed Everand's earnest words, *I know we're different ... but I'd like to be with you.*

'Imagining our victory already?' Lulite nudged her and she realised she was standing there doing nothing. She flashed her friend a smile and went to retrieve her race tunic. A forest of limbs moved around her as the paddlers dressed in their green trousers and vibrant orange tunics. Lamiya wove an array of green and red feathers into her hair, Whirr obligingly tugging them out of her bag and flying them up to her. She puckered her lips and the bird hovered to give her a light peck.

'Stand still.' Lulite stood in front of her holding a small bowl.

Lamiya closed her eyes while Lulite painted red, orange and green stripes across her cheeks and then dabbed at her forehead, adding the image of an orange sun with red flashes around it. The brush tickled and the smell of the crushed flower dyes hovered in her nostrils.

'There. You look fierce enough,' said Lulite, stepping back to admire the effect. Whirr squawked loudly and Lulite waved her brush at him. 'Settle down or I'll decorate you too!'

Lamiya's stomach clenched when Laza nudged Lulite aside and thrust a platter of fruit and small pink cakes at her. 'Eat.' Whirr hovered over the plate chirruping, admonishing her. Taking the plate, she forced herself to start on the fruit, knowing she would need the energy. 'Have you packed the race food?' she asked. Laza nodded and smiled.

Next, Lopa handed her a small bag woven from rushes that smelled enticingly of Riverplain grasses. 'The sweet grass to bless the boat. I added red clover for luck. I found three four-leafed plants.'

Lamiya beamed. 'One for each race! Well done.'

She persuaded her stomach to accept the zesty pink cakes, washing these down with a mug of brew that had a zingy aftertaste. Lulite must have added ground ginger to give them all an extra boost. Using the bowls of water near the doorway, she rinsed out her mouth and felt refreshed.

On turning around, she found the whole team assembled with broad grins and paddles held proudly upright. With their faces painted, hair spiked with colourful feathers and vivid tunics, she almost took a step back they looked so fit and fierce. Movement slithered behind her and Ejad scurried past, clad in Riverplain colours. Lulite decorated his face while Lopa tied feathers into his hair. Now they were ready.

'Yo,' she said softly.

'Yo!' The team hoisted their paddles in one fluid salute.

Lamiya led them from the dome, choosing a medium pace to loosen them up but not brisk enough to raise a sweat. The first wan rays of the sun hovered above the town wall, spilling soft grey and primrose light across the courtyard and bestowing a yellow hue to the leaves on the bushes. Loving the heady mix of fragrance in the remnants of a dew, she drew in a deep breath until her ribs and chest expanded with crisp air. There was minimal activity, but she detected voices and movement in the domes. Hope blossomed briefly: they could be the first team to their boat. She lengthened her stride.

In the outer courtyard, a handful of Riverfall men were milling around the tables of products. Atage must have placed a watch over the tables. When the team passed by, the men nodded in approval. Her pulse fluttered as she imagined Flight and Mizuchi powering head-to-head towards the bridge. They swept out of the gate and swung towards the boat dome. The doors were already propped wide open, and she slowed for a few steps while her eyes adjusted to the dim interior.

'Yosh, Lamiya,' said Tengar's voice. Her eyes distinguished the shadows and shapes of the Riverfall team readying to lift their boat.

'Yo, Tengar. May the winds guide your boat.' She paused. 'In our wake.' Soft laughter came from behind her and from the Riverfall team.

Tengar wagged a finger at her. 'You'll eat those words later.'

She stepped aside as the curved tail of Mizuchi loomed blue and gold at her and the paddlers carried their boat out through the door.

'Wait,' said Luvu, snagging her elbow. 'Let me check our boat.'

Quelling a rush of nerves at the prospect of another viper, or something worse, she tried to look relaxed until Luvu and Lapsi gave her all-clear nods. Swiftly, the team lifted the boat.

On reaching the path, she saw the Riversea team on their way, white tunics and feathers standing out in the primrose light. Behind them, she could see the heads and necks of a pair of hopeepa, bringing the officials' cart with Atage and Lyber to oversee the lining up of the boats and formally bless the races. Her heart skipped a beat. *And Everand, as the judge.* Her heart skipped several more beats. In her concern for his injury, plus her misery about their doomed attraction, she hadn't asked him what she was supposed to do if the dragon came! Her palms prickled with sweat. Too late now, she'd have to work it out when it happened. *If* it happened.

'Lamiya, which side?' hissed Luvu from behind her.

Resisting the urge to wipe her palms on her tunic, she realised he wanted to know which side of Mizuchi they should place Flight. To her relief, Tengar waved his arm to the downriver side and his team shuffled Mizuchi over to make room for them. Her team reversed Flight down the ramp until the boats were snugly side by side and the two dragon heads were aligned. After they'd lowered the boat onto the wooden slats, Lamiya moved to stand by Flight's head. She was glad they were next to Riverplain and assumed the other boats would be placed higher up the ramp. She rolled her shoulders and stretched her neck.

'Slow the boat!' called Cowrie, and the tail of Seasprite rushed at her. While he directed his team until the boat was perfectly aligned in front of Flight, Lamiya admired their uniform of startling turquoise trousers below pearly-white tunics. The bare brown arms of the paddlers rippled with muscles and inked images of racing fish and sea serpents. Around their ankles, strings of shells and pearls gleamed and clinked. Long white feathers waved from their hair, and around their necks hung strings of shells. Hanging in the centre of each string was a dried star-shaped sea-creature. A symbol of good luck? The overall impression was of white waves riding on crystal-clear water.

Clama and Nawpra gave her excited smiles over their shoulders, their teeth flashing white in tanned faces. Lamiya grinned back, hoping Spirula would remember to put that jewellery box aside for her, and that Charonia's beautiful necklace would still be there. Closing her eyes, she muttered a prayer to the water spirits that she would glide her team well enough to earn the necklace.

The Riverwood boat was reversed down the ramp. From below it, the fanned wooden-feather tail of the eagle was imposing, the brown and grey colours blotting out the rising light. Malach strode beside it, his dark eyes fixed upon her. Black stripes stood out along his cheeks, and enormous grey and dark-brown feathers snaked from the back of his head. His jet-black, bristly hair was bound in a topknot in an austere warrior look.

Her chest constricted at the knowing look he gave her. She nodded stiffly and his eyes glittered with amusement. Dismay swirled through her. What was his plan? Her palms prickled with sweat again. Curse it! She'd have trouble gripping her oar if this kept up. Malach spun away, dismissing her, and strode to the front of his boat. The Riverwood paddlers, dressed in dark-brown trousers and storm-grey tunics with feathers and stones tied around their necks and ankles, rigidly faced the front. Did all their faces look as stern and cold as Malach's?

Lazuli poked her in the back. 'Don't worry. If they're behind us we won't see them.' He put a reassuring hand on her shoulder, and she brushed his fingers in thanks.

'Paddlers, attention!' called Tengar from the top of the ramp.

Lamiya squinted up at Tengar, silhouetted against the sun. Atage, clad in a formal blue jacket and beige trousers, stepped beside Tengar.

'Welcome to Riverfall!' Atage's voice rang down the ramp. 'And to what we hope is the first of many races and festivals to come. We thank you for your journey and look forward to seeing your prowess.' His voice gained in clarity and timbre when a taller person came to stand at his side. Her lips twitched when she suspected Everand was enhancing Atage's speech.

'In honour of your racing, we have small gifts for you.' Four children, each carrying a small basket, rushed past Atage and approached the head of each boat.

A girl with blonde hair bounced up to Lamiya with a shy smile. From her basket she fished out a handful of bright ribbons tied to a small thong. 'For your hair to wish you luck. May the wind chase your boat's tail,' whispered the girl, handing the ribbons to her.

Lamiya clasped her palms together around the ribbons, as if in prayer, and bowed to the girl. 'May the sun brighten your face and bring you joy.' The girl beamed and moved past her to approach Lazuli. Lamiya held up the ribbons, spun from the finest cotton and dyed in the primal colours representing life: blue for water; yellow for the sun; green for crops; red for fire; brown for the earth; and silver-white for the moon.

After a moment's thought, she tied the set of ribbons behind her left ear, where they wouldn't blow into her face but she'd catch sight of the coloured ends as they raced.

Soon the children were skipping back up the ramp and four Riverplain women walked down the ramp, each clasping a woven basket.

'To help you race with passion and energy, we give you each a fire cake,' called Atage.

A woman, who could have been the girl's mother, approached Lamiya. With a warm smile she reached into her basket and took out one of the small, perfectly round pink cakes that glittered with spun flower nectar. 'May fire and energy drive your limbs,' said the woman, plopping the cake into Lamiya's outstretched palm.

Lamiya repeated the response she had given the girl and respectfully placed the cake onto her tongue. Zesty flavours burst over her tongue and made her eyes water. Behind her, Larimar stifled a cough. A hubbub reached her ears with the crowd gathering along the riverbank. Soon the tents would throng with people cheering and waving streamers. She hoped they'd found a good spot for Latog to watch, where he wouldn't get bumped and his mending leg would be safe. Anticipation flushed through her veins. She couldn't wait to get Flight onto the water.

'Now for the blessing of the boats,' called Atage. 'Glide Tengar, please awaken your boat.'

Lamiya held her breath as Tengar hurried down the ramp and took a small pouch from Mookaite. The poor man had so many duties! The Riverfall paddlers stood solemnly to attention facing their boat when Tengar reached Mizuchi's head and withdrew a handful of rushes and a sprig of cotton bush from the pouch. A young Riverfall man came down the ramp and waved a short, lit torch under the bundle. Smoke that smelled like river and cotton wafted into the air. Tengar waved the smouldering bunch under the dragon's nose, and in a circle around the head.

'Great Mizuchi!' Tengar shouted. 'Awaken and rise! Bring us your power, fire and speed for we race in your honour!'

'Yosh!' The paddlers arched their paddles across the boat's width, the blades with the sketched blue dragon facing upwards.

The rushes crumbled to ash and Melanite passed Tengar a small bowl and a brush. Entranced, Lamiya watched Tengar reach up to place a dot of lurid red dye in the centre of each eye. 'See us, Great Mizuchi! Race with us!'

For half a breath, Lamiya thought the boat rippled. She blinked while the paddlers repeated their chant. It was now her turn and she stood as tall as she could.

'Glide Lamiya,' called Atage, 'please awaken your boat!'

Conscious of everyone's eyes upon her, she faced Flight's head. The large yellow eyes seemed to be watching her from amid the vibrant orange and green scales. The green whiskers bristled, and the tips of the gold horns gleamed despite the early light.

Whirr pushed up out of her tunic, holding in his beak the string to the pouch of herbs. Lamiya tugged out the pouch, breathing in the aromatic grasses. The young man with the torch hovered while she withdrew the large handful of sweet grass and extracted the carefully pressed heads of four-leaf clover, each on a conveniently long stem. *One for each race.* She licked her lips, held the sprig above the flame of the torch and, her eyes watering in the smoke, waved the burning sprig beneath Flight's wide crimson nostrils.

'Majestic Flight, come fly the waves with us!' she cried, mustering all her energy. 'Skim us over the waves, leaving white clouds in our wake! We race in your honour!' As the last four-leaf clover started to burn, she visualised Flight's nose speeding under the far bridge first, white water flying behind them.

'Nice,' murmured Lulite, passing her the small bowl and brush.

Feeling as if she were floating above herself, Lamiya stood on tiptoe and carefully dotted Flight's right eye in the centre. Her breath caught, for the eye shimmered like a textured gold iris and glanced at her, then returned to being yellow paint. She stumbled to the other side and reached up to dot the left eye.

'Majestic Flight, see us! Come race with us!' Again, the eye shimmered like a golden iris, and she fancied that the painted scales briefly took form. Everand's voice reverberated inside her head. *Yes, Lamiya. Call your dragon. We will need her because Mizuchi will come.*

She resisted the urge to spin around, sure that Everand wasn't right behind her but was still standing with Atage at the top of the ramp. Her paddlers called 'Yo!' and arched their paddles above the boat. They all looked focused and ready to race, so if Flight's eyes had glimmered, she was the only one to see it. *Mizuchi will come.* How could he be so sure?

Impatiently, she waited while Cowrie and Malach awakened their boats and dotted their dragon's eyes. The Riversea burning sprig conjured images of a briny shore laden with seaweed. The sprig Malach burned had a heady, pine scent mingled with what she thought was fungus. The result was not pleasant and she wrinkled her nose. Although she was watching closely, she didn't discern any flicker of life in their boats, which both remained solidly wooden. A tangle of nerves formed in her stomach. Was she the only one who could speak to the spirit within her boat?

Atage, Lyber and Everand were walking down to stand between the four boats. Although Tengar had already told her what the racing rules were, she pinched the back of her wrist to make herself pay attention. The four glides moved to the front, close together, and the paddlers turned to face the officials.

Atage gave a broad smile and waved his hands. 'Good paddlers, I won't keep you. I'm sure you're keen to get racing in what no doubt will be fierce and close contests.'

Lamiya's gaze drifted to Everand's face. He was holding his head stiffly and she guessed his wounds hurt. He avoided eye contact, keeping his gaze firmly on Atage. Risking a fleeting skim over Malach's face, she saw that he was observing Everand through half-slitted eyes. Her palms prickled. How did Everand always look so composed when all this intrigue was bubbling below the surface?

Lyber held up a wooden frame with rows of coloured tokens strung along it. 'Good paddlers, we'll vary the line-up order of the boats for each race. You must race straight and true and not block or impede another boat in any way.' He waited until all four glides nodded. 'If you cross the path of another boat you'll be eliminated from that race.' He looked up at Everand. 'Our traveller will call the positions as the boats pass the finish flags, and I'll keep tally on this board. At the festival feast we'll award prizes for the winner of each race, and the overall best boat.'

'Yosh!' yelled the Riverfall paddlers.

Lamiya flapped a hand at her team, warning them not to respond. Larimar and Lazuli scowled at her, and she glimpsed a sardonic look on Malach's face.

'Yes, quite,' said Lyber, flustered.

Atage took over. 'We'll allow time for you to warm up. When the horn sounds twice, come up level with the flag marking the edge of the boat ramp.'

Lamiya noticed a Riverfall man waiting to the side, holding a pole with a bright-blue flag on it. Around his neck hung a long, wooden horn.

Atage gestured towards the man. 'Jibo will watch the noses of the boats line up and you must follow his instructions. When you're all level he'll call you to attention and sound the horn for go.'

Tengar's growl quelled the rising 'Yosh!'

With a smile, Atage concluded his instructions. 'The order for the first race, from the ramp to the southern gate, is as you are lined up now: Riverfall on the far side, Riverplain next, then Riversea and Riverwood closest to this bank. Don't stop paddling until your boat tail is past the yellow finish flag. May the wind follow your boat's tail! Enjoy your race and we'll see you at the finish line!'

The glides bowed and the paddlers inclined their heads, acknowledging the rules. Lamiya straightened up, and Everand flicked her a hint of a smile. Then the three men walked away, leaving the paddlers to launch their boats.

She watched the Riverfall paddlers file smoothly into Mizuchi, then her team nosed Flight down the ramp. Before she boarded, she put a hand on Flight's forehead, murmuring, 'Come to us, Flight. Skim us above the waves, for we want you to bask in glory.'

For an instant the wood warmed under her palm, and a huff of breath flew over her elbow from the nearest nostril. Buoyed, she skipped along the benches to her position. Flight surged away from the ramp, and the Riversea team carried Seasprite into position.

Lamiya turned Flight downriver for their warm-up, away from the gathering crowds. She heard cheering as Tengar chose to parade Mizuchi past the tents, inciting the audience. Ignoring the other boats, she took her team through warm-up drills. Their timing was good, their strokes strong and relaxed. Hope beat through her. They could do this!

'Feels good,' Luvu said gruffly. 'Current is pulling to the far bank.'

'Noted,' said Lamiya, for she'd felt that too. Lulite drummed a steady rate and after a while Lamiya turned the boat. Just as Flight's head faced north, Jibo sounded the horn twice, calling them to the start.

She rolled her shoulders and said, 'Everyone looks good. We can do this! Remember, eyes in *this* boat, ears on *our* drum. Deep, fast start of ten followed by twenty brisk, powerful strokes. Then power, power, power it home in this short race. One team, one breath, one heart. Yo!'

'Yo!' called the team softly.

CHAPTER FORTY

Concentrating on keeping Flight straight, Lamiya gauged the water. Sunlight coruscated across the surface, giving the small waves pretty yellow-pink caps. Luvu was right; the water had a slight pull to the far bank and a soft breeze was blowing upriver from behind them. She'd have to make sure Flight's nose stayed straight; it would be easy to veer towards the bank if the wind caught her. The current was moving slowly downriver. Not too bad, but they'd be paddling against it. Ahead of her, Tengar had stopped Mizuchi and the Riverfall paddlers had their paddles submerged deep, holding the boat in place.

Flight slid smoothly alongside and Tengar gave her a nod. As far as she could see, their two boat noses were just behind the blue flag and Jibo was watching the Riversea and Riverwood boats approach. The head of Seasprite glided by and Cowrie called his team to hold position. She was glad Riverwood was further over when their chunky boat slammed into place. Showing off, or lack of technique?

From the ramp, Jibo yelled, 'Riversea, back two strokes … all boats hold position!'

Seasprite moved back and she had a brief moment to admire the boat's artwork, but was conscious not to make eye contact with any of the paddlers. She flexed her fingers on the oar haft. *Only this boat matters. Only this boat.*

'Paddlers, get ready!' Jibo shouted.

Lamiya gripped the haft and her team bent forward and dug their paddles in deep. 'Paddlers, attention!' At Jibo's call, her team's backs heaved as they drew in breath. She shifted her weight onto her toes and bent her knees ready for the sudden movement. Behind the drum, Lulite leaned forward.

The horn sounded! Beneath her feet, Flight jerked forward so fast she almost lost her balance. Pride shot through her: what a start! Ten strokes sped by. Without her call, and in one beat of the team's heart, they stretched into fast and powerful strokes, their blades biting the water and the front of the boat lifting superbly. Lulite drummed *Doom! Doom!* Blocking her ears to the other drums, Lamiya counted to twenty.

'Long and strong!' Flight surged forward again. She couldn't believe how far forward Larimar and Lazuli were reaching, the entire team stretching to match them. Huge bubbles of white water sped along Flight's flanks. She felt the dragon breathe.

'Power for home!' she yelled and Lulite drummed faster while the paddlers' arms and backs flexed and arched in perfect time. The boat was almost flying.

'Lift! Lift!' A glance told her they were almost at the southern gate. The town wall loomed on her right, with the yellow flag flapping on the bank and the cart with the tall frame of Everand intently watching the flagpole. Splashing surrounded her as Mizuchi and Seasprite surged alongside.

Tengar screeched, 'Yosh! Lift! Yosh! Lift!'

'Yee-ah!' yelled Cowrie.

'Yo! Yo!' she screamed, her throat hurting. Lulite drummed even faster and the team gamely strove for more speed, their arms swinging in a blur. Tengar was slightly ahead, the blue-clad team pulling hard, and white water rushing past Mizuchi's blue and gold scales. On her other side Cowrie was almost level, the Riversea paddlers' grunts sounding above the drums. A horn blasted, then again, again, again, and they were past the flag.

'Let it run!' Lamiya called and her team slumped over their knees, sides heaving. She met Lulite's eyes. The drummer sat with the drumstick resting on her knee. She shook her head and jerked it towards the Riverfall boat. As she thought: Mizuchi had edged past the flag just in front.

Disappointment rose, but they hadn't expected to win the short race and second by a nose was an impressive outcome. Luvu had said to keep them close. The two key races were still to come. She became aware of the tumult from people along the riverbank. In front of the tents, people clad in tunics of every imaginable colour were running to and fro waving streamers. She ran her tongue over her lips and tried to slow her galloping heart.

'*Great* work. The start was amazing. I nearly fell off!' When the team sat up and started to laugh, she added, 'Seriously, it was impressive.'

Lazuli twisted around, his face flushed and sweat pouring down his neck. 'Where did we finish?'

Lamiya shrugged. 'It was close. I think second. Let's cool down while we wait for the judge's decision.' As they paddled slowly, Lamiya nodded at Tengar then at Cowrie. 'Good race,' she said to both. On the second pass by the finish flag, she observed Atage, Lyber and Everand deep in conference. The race must have been incredibly close.

Surreptitiously, she peeked at the Riverwood boat. The ten men paddled in silence, not looking around. Malach, however, was taking note of everything. After watching the boat for a few strokes, she saw that it sat lower in the water than the others. Due to the bulky paddlers? And maybe the chunky structure of the boat itself. Her heart lifted: this would offset the strength of the men in the longer race, especially as the current was against them.

Her pulse hammered when Atage, Lyber and Everand stood up on the back of the cart. The four boats lined up in front of

345

the cart and the fluttering yellow flag. Her team straightened their backs. The crowd on the banks quietened, and she heard parents shushing noisy children.

'Paddlers, we salute you.' Atage's voice carried with eerie clarity across the water. 'You tested our judges sorely.'

Lamiya stopped her lips from etching into a smile when Larimar nudged Lazuli, telling him not to be so impatient.

'The winner of the short race is … my pride is so great I can hardly form the words … our very own team from Riverfall!'

The noise from the bank was deafening, matched by the war cries from the Riverfall team: 'Yosh! Yosh! Mizuchi rises!'

Lamiya waited until there was a lull and then shouted, 'Three cheers for the winner!' She gave Tengar a respectful nod while the teams cheered, then ran her tongue around the inside of her dry mouth. Who was second?

Looking at the cart, she giggled. Atage stood ready with Lyber, who was holding up the tally board, but Everand was busy batting at the nose of the tallest hopeepa, which was trying to lick his face. Giggles passed through her team. Everand swatted at Crystal and the hopeepa hurled her head away as if something had stung her. Her tail swished violently. Still smiling, Lamiya watched Everand wipe his face and run his hands down his tunic. When he realised most of the paddlers were laughing, he looked horrified and stood ramrod straight.

'Second, by a mere dragon nose, was … Riverplain!'

'Yo! Yo!' Her team loosed their cries and rattled their paddles. Beneath her feet she felt the boat take a breath, and hastily firmed up her balance. The boat wobbled when her team turned to one another and smacked hands.

'Good work, glide,' said Luvu. 'Now let's get serious.'

Leaning forward, Lamiya asked, 'Where's Latog? I can't see him.'

'At the next finish flag,' said Luvu. 'Fewer people, and he can see the finish of race two and the start of race three.'

Atage held up his hand. 'We declare a tie for third between Riversea and Riverwood! It was impossible to separate the noses of these two boats.'

The crowd on the bank cheered until they sounded hoarse, and Riversea and Riverwood tried to outdo each other with their paddling cries. Lamiya lifted an eyebrow, surprised the Riverwood paddlers were entering into the spirit of the competition.

Jibo came to stand by the yellow flag and Atage called, 'The line-up for the middle race is: Riverplain on the far side, Riverwood, Riverfall then Riversea on the near side.'

Lamiya's heart fell. They would be on the far side with Riverwood right next to them. *Not relevant,* she tried to tell herself. Just keep out of the wake of the heavier boat. While her team paddled a loop and took turns to have a drink, she reconsidered her strategy. Could they head out fast again and fight to keep in front? Or would they pay for that later? The last start had felt so good; perhaps it would work. Out of the corner of her eye she saw the Riverwood boat behind her drawing closer. Bending over, she tapped Luvu's shoulder.

'We must stay ahead of Riverwood. Pass this along: *fifteen* fast start strokes, followed by twenty faster ones to get the boat nose up, then settle into long and strong. Listen for lifts as I try to keep us ahead.'

Luvu grunted and bent forward to tell Lepid and Lapsi. When the orders reached the front of the boat, Lazuli gave her an excited nod. Jibo sounded the horn twice and she directed Flight towards the far bank. The river was wider where it flowed past the town and it would be more difficult to judge their alignment with the start flag. They paused by the far bank, grasses waving above them, and waited.

Malach turned his boat too close behind her and the head of the eagle slid by in silent menace. A shiver passed down her at the cruel ivory beak, the flat black eyes and the aggressive crown of storm-dark feathers. *It is only wood.* Taking an even breath, she forced herself not to look at Malach when he stopped so close that his shadow fell across her feet. She thought she heard Luvu murmur, 'Good girl.' She frowned. *Curse Malach.*

Peering subtly sideways, she saw the Riverwood paddlers hunched ready, but they were staring stone-faced at her team trying to intimidate them. A spark of anger lit in her chest and, inside her tunic, Whirr peeped.

The current tugged at Flight's nose. It would run stronger closer to the bank; another reason to get out front fast. Resigned, she stared resolutely ahead, waiting for the horn. Lulite gave her a sharp nod: get ready.

She only just heard Jibo's shout. 'Paddlers ... attention!' The horn blared.

Flight surged forward, the rushes on the bank flying past. Fourteen ... fifteen ... 'Fast twenty!' Flight's nose edged ahead of the beak of the eagle. Twenty strokes passed.

'Long and strong!' she yelled and Lulite started to drum. The current kept snatching at Flight's nose and Lamiya had to concentrate on keeping the boat straight. There was no margin for error with the bank rushing by so close and Raptor crowding her on the other side.

Raptor nudged subtly closer, almost pushing her into the bank. Panic rose: Malach was intentionally crowding her! Her heart hammered. Just before the northern gate the river meandered to the right, and the bank would get even closer! The ominous eagle head was level with Lopa and Laza in the second row, throwing a shadow over them. The girls paddled valiantly, their shoulders tense. Lamiya felt this was the moment: all or nothing.

'Give me a lift!' The team plunged their paddles deeper. The eagle head edged backwards, closer to Levog and Lattic in row three. The Riverwood men dug their blades in, white bubbles curling underwater, and the eagle head crept back closer to Lopa and Laza.

'Lift! Lift!' Lamiya cried. Tears prickled the back of her eyes when her team lifted, breaths rasping. Ejad's tunic was sodden against his back and Luvu was grunting with each stroke. She extended her senses and called, *Flight, come save us.* Despite the effort, her team paddled with one heart, one breath, one soul. The Riverwood paddlers started to look ragged: their timing was slipping. *Finish them off.* 'Lift again!'

Lulite pounded the drum and exhorted the team, 'We can do this! Go! Go! Go!'

The beak of the eagle slipped back to level with Lamiya. Setting her mouth into a grim smile, she edged Flight's nose away from the bank. She mustn't cross in front of Raptor, but she could move Flight away from the bank ready for the meander. The tug on Flight's nose relaxed as they hit smoother water. The northern gate approached, the curve of the bank stretching inward on her left, and the red finish flag snapping on the right bank. A hundred strokes to go and the head of the eagle was still annoyingly level with her. *All or nothing.* More effort now might cost them the longer race, but it had to be done.

'Power for home!' she called, ignoring Lulite's look of disbelief and the skip in her drumbeat. The team threw their backs into it, reaching deeper and faster. Lamiya shifted her weight forward as the boat nose lifted and white water gurgled by at astonishing speed.

'Yo! Yo!' she sang. The boat sighed, the wood tremored under her feet and for a blink, the dragon head looked real. The beak of the eagle receded and she sensed clear water opening behind her. She allowed herself a smile; Malach would have to deal with *her* wake. Dimly, she heard Malach shouting, 'Ki! Ki! Pull!' She also heard Tengar and Cowrie yelling at their teams to bring it home. With a start, she grasped they were *all* behind her. A loud horn blasted.

Lulite shouted, 'We can stop! We finished!'

Lamiya leaned her weight back and yelled, 'Let it run.' Sweat ran down her arms and neck and her legs were shaking. Lazuli and Larimar both twisted over the boat side and threw up. Lulite screwed up her face and the paddlers behind them hastily jerked their paddles up out of the water. The entire team doubled over, heads on knees, paddles dropped to the floor. Luvu was grunting alarmingly.

Whirr climbed out of her tunic and shook sweat-laden wings at her with shrill peeps. Leaning on the oar, she felt laughter rising. Malach's plan had well and truly failed. Wiping her eyes, she let her laughter bubble out. In a heartbeat, the team was laughing with her.

Mizuchi glided past and Tengar called out, 'Nice work, Lamiya.'

Seasprite was next past and the Riversea paddlers gave her bows of respect.

Jibo sounded a few hoots on the horn to call the boats to the officials' cart. Joy filled her at the excited chatter among her team as the boats slid into a line in front of the red flag. Riverwood chose the position furthest away from them, which brought another smile. She wished she could jump up and down with happiness in front of Everand and babble at him about the race.

There was no conferring of the officials. Atage stood straight up on the cart with a broad grin. 'I'm sure we just witnessed a performance that will be hard to best in future races. The winner is Riverplain — with clear water behind them!'

The crowds on the bank shrieked, clapped and stamped their feet and the paddlers in the other boats put down their paddles and clapped. Heat rose up Lamiya's neck and flamed across her cheeks. Whirr hopped up and down on her shoulder, fanning her with his wings. Pride threatened to drown her at her paddlers' shining eyes, happy smiles and jubilant postures.

Lazuli and Larimar raised their paddles. 'Yo! Flight rides the waves!'

The rest of the team took up the chant while the crowd applauded. After a moment, Lamiya called, 'Steady. Let's hear who was second.' A stillness grew along the bank, and Everand's voice reverberated inside her head. *'Well done. You and your boat looked superb.'* She sensed a smile around his words before his presence withdrew. She glanced at the officials' cart, but he seemed to be looking at Atage.

'Although the winner was clear, the contest for the other positions was again close. Riverwood held on for second, with Riverfall just pipping Riversea for third place.' The crowd hooted and burst into applause.

'Ki! Ki!' The Riverwood paddlers chanted and their drummer gave a roll on his drums that sounded like the rumble of thunder.

'Acknowledge Riverwood,' instructed Lamiya, feeling they should be humble in their victory. Obligingly, her paddlers looked over at Raptor and nodded.

Lamiya's heart jumped into her throat when Malach twisted to look directly at her. However, he dipped his head, accepting her skill. Relieved when he immediately turned away, she wiped her palms on her tunic, wishing she could shake off the sense of threat. Whirr nestled against her jaw as if he agreed.

Atage called, 'Prepare for the long race. The line-up order will be Riverwood on the far side, Riversea, Riverfall and Riverplain on this near side.'

Yes! They'd only have one boat wake to contend with, and Riverfall was the strongest opponent. Being beside each other, they'd be able to race more intently. Was this by design? No matter, it suited.

'Jibo will give you time to have a drink and a snack,' Atage said. 'It'll take a while for us officials to reach the bridge.' He raised both arms open wide. 'Paddle well. See you at the bridge!'

Excited chatter rose along her boat and Lazuli endowed her with a wide smile.

Chapter Forty-one

Tuning out the bustle of the crowds as the officials' cart reversed and headed north, Lamiya decided they should warm up away from Mizuchi to discuss strategy. As she turned Flight, she noticed a second cart fall into place behind the officials' one, a familiar figure propped up on the back platform. She gave a cheery wave, heartened when Latog waved back. The team lifted their paddles in salute to their former glide.

'Let's make him even prouder, eh glide,' muttered Luvu.

With Flight's nose facing downriver, the team relaxed and took a drink. *Finally*, the long race. Closing her eyes briefly, she thought of the magnificent necklace. Would she be wearing it at the feast? She must win this coveted race.

Opening her eyes, she observed the other boats. All four boats had separated, presumably to review strategy. The Riverwood boat had stopped over by the far bank and Malach was bent over retrieving something from under the last bench. Recalling her premonition of the Riverwood paddlers carrying weapons, unease edged into her. An eagle rose from the grasses on the far bank and hovered just above Malach. Surely, he was up to no good! She turned Flight into a loop to pass closer, her tongue stuck to the roof of her mouth. Everand was certain the danger was to the long race, and maybe she could find out something useful.

'Don't forget to eat, glide,' Luvu said gruffly before turning to Ejad. 'You too, young paddler.'

Lamiya forced herself to take some star-fruit from her bag, the sweet flavour refreshing her mouth and spirit. They were halfway across the river when the eagle flapped its wings ponderously, lifted up and flew away upriver. Flight rode smoothly over the deepest part of the river, the team bantering. For a heartbeat, there was a disturbance in the water, and a shadow passed underneath. On her shoulder Whirr gave a chirp. Beneath her feet the wood warmed and rose imperceptibly to put pressure under the soles of her feet.

Blinking, she gazed into the river but saw only dark water sliding past. The team paddled unaware, and the impression faded. She observed tension setting into Lazuli and Larimar's shoulders as they drew closer to Raptor.

Abruptly, she directed Flight away. She must not distract her team. When her boat turned side-on to Raptor, Malach glared at her. Forcing a polite nod, she called for her team to lift the rate. Then they were past Raptor, and on the other bank the horn sounded twice. Turning Flight towards the red flag, she frowned. She should have been bolder. But what could she do? *Trust Everand*, said her heart. *You just race.*

'Best team in Riverplain,' she began, knowing that would make them smile, 'let's be the best team of every province.' She paused. 'Riversea could surprise us, but we know Riverfall is the team to beat.' Ejad beamed. 'Begin with fifteen fast strokes and stretch into our long-effort powerful rate. We can't afford to lead all the way, but we mustn't let Riverfall get ahead. Match them, *whatever* they do, and aim to power away over the last hundred strokes. Lazuli?'

Lazuli ceased conferring with Larimar and looked over his shoulder. 'We should power home from a hundred and fifty strokes. Tengar's team is too strong and at a hundred strokes they'll aim to come with us.'

Luvu grunted. 'Could be so.'

Lamiya took two breaths. 'Agreed. We lift, and keep lifting, from a hundred and fifty strokes out. Are you ready?'

As one, the team saluted.

Lamiya made a straight line for the red flag. Whirr climbed inside her tunic and she took a moment to roll her shoulders and flick her hair back. Her fingers brushed the ends of the vibrantly coloured ribbons of life. Stroking the ribbons, she drew in a breath until her ribs could expand no further. Next, she flexed her fingers and her toes, adjusting her balance until she felt impeccably poised.

Flight's nose was in line with the fluttering red flag, and Jibo gave her a nod. Mizuchi slid into place on her left. She licked her lips: this was it. A first and a second positioned them well: if they achieved first or second in the long race they could win the races overall. Riverfall's third in the middle race gave her team the edge. Her heart beat against her breastbone while Seasprite and Raptor moved into position. Keenly, she watched Jibo crouch behind the flag and squint, checking the alignment of the boats. He stood up and lifted the horn halfway to his lips, calling, 'Paddlers, get ready.'

Her team dug in their paddles and flexed forward. She stood balanced with her right knee fixed out in front. The horn sounded and amid tumult from the crowds and a great swishing of water, Flight jolted forward. The bank and tents flew by in a dizzying blur of faces and colours and chaotic movement and noise.

Fifteen … the team swapped to fast and strong strokes. Tengar was perched dead level on her left, his stance mirroring hers. Curse it! He'd copied their start. She blinked: the two teams were not only paddling in perfect time but were also in time with each other! The beats of their drums were indistinguishable.

'Long and strong!' Lazuli and Larimar speared their blades into the river, the muscles on their shoulders and arms bulging. Enormous clouds of white bubbles raced along the boat's sides.

'Eyes in this boat!' she called when Larimar turned his head slightly. From the corner of her eye, she knew why he'd peeked. Curse Tengar! The Riverfall paddlers had matched their stroke and the two boats powered through the river in dead alignment. *Relax. There's a long way to go, and this will keep the team focused.* Mizuchi and Flight had already gained a good half boat-length on both Seasprite and Raptor.

The first waterwheel loomed on the bank and zoomed by. Still, they raced side by side. Random clusters of people gathered along the riverbank cheered and waved. 'Mizuchi!' 'Mizuchi!' 'Yosh!' Tengar's boat lifted, encouraged by the support, but before she could call for a lift, Lazuli and Larimar had matched them, her entire team sliding into a perfect new rate. Surely, she had the most glorious team in all the provinces!

Crisp grassy banks and neat rows of cotton crops sped by. Sweat ran in runnels down her face and arms, the sun beating down. The team paddled as if joined by invisible threads, their orange tunics dark with sweat clinging to their backs, the feathers in their hair drooping. Behind the drum Lulite flashed her a tight smile. The Riverfall team was a mirror image, blue tunics dark and dank, but paddling in perfect time. The two boats skimmed the water.

Risking a peek over her shoulder, she gauged Seasprite was two boat-lengths back. Possibly still close enough to come home strongly. Raptor was another boat-length behind them. The Riverwood team paddled in time, but the boat looked heavy and flat in the water.

Time stood still with the feel of Flight beneath her feet, the glinting water rushing by, the splosh of paddles and gurgling of water. The larger waterwheel loomed, and receded. The crops changed to waving golden wheat. The sun's rays bit into her head and arms and sweat poured down her back, arms and legs. She held the oar straight; the boat was running true on course.

Soon, she moved Flight's nose slightly to account for the approaching modest curve in the bank. Her heart beat more quickly; once around this bend they'd be able to see the bridge. 'Great work!' she called.

They skimmed around the bend and the bridge rose as a firm shadow, stretching across the river some five hundred strokes away. Squinting, she discerned Everand and Lyber standing in the centre, azure sky behind them.

'Great work! Hold the rate!' Adjusting her balance, she eyed the river ahead, fixing in her mind the spot she thought would be a hundred and fifty strokes out: where the land became untended grass and bushes. Sneaking a sideways glance, she saw Tengar adjusting position, getting ready for the sprint finish. Whirr shuffled to the centre of her breastbone with his beak poking out.

Lamiya visualised life flowing into the boat. She brought to the front of her mind the boat's yellow-painted eyes becoming textured golden irises. Thinking of the four-leaf clover, she murmured, 'Come, Dragon Flight. Take this race. Ride the waves with us.' The boat pulsed beneath her feet and the prow imperceptibly lifted. Lazuli and Larimar straightened their backs, filled with new resolve. Three hundred strokes to go.

The bridge loomed brown and grey against the sky. Now she could make out the stonework and the wooden rails. Everand stood at the crest of the bridge, leaning over the railing ready to judge positions, sunlight sparkling off his hair. Suddenly, he straightened up and looked the other way, upriver. Her breath caught. What was he doing? No time to look.

'Power!' she called. With a grunt, the team plunged their paddles in. The Riverfall team matched them. The boats were racing so close she imagined the two dragon heads snapping at each other.

Everand's voice snipped into her mind. *'Find your dragon!'*

Her gaze lifted to the bridge. *What the?* A wall of head-height water rushed under the bridge, coming straight at them. 'Tengar!' she shouted in warning. Her team missed a beat. 'Hold course!' she shrieked, facing Flight's nose straight into the massive bubble of river. 'Keep paddling! The river dragon comes!'

Behind her, the Riversea team began chanting, 'Ee-yah! Ee-yah!'

She ground her back teeth together, remembering Clommus' story of how they paddled the waves in the sea. Riversea could gain ground if they rode this wave better than they did.

The wall of water raced at them, a rising menace of blue-grey. Her heart faltered when the dragon's massive blue and gold face jutted out through the curtain of water. 'Lulite! Hang on!' If they capsized, would the dragon eat them? She bit her lip. 'Flight! Come! Come, my dragon.'

The front of the boat started to rise. As the back of the boat tilted upwards, the wood softened and warmed beneath her feet, giving her better purchase. She withdrew deep inside, to her inner well of summoning power. Calm washed into her and she cupped handfuls of summoning light from a pool of silver: *Flight! Breathe. Swim and race with me.*

Eyes wide, she saw the back of a live dragon head riding up the wave, arching its neck to keep its balance. A long purple tongue flickered out to one side, a vivid red mane rippled and the sun gleamed off a long neck of orange and green scales. The body mercifully remained in the form of a wooden boat and her team paddled amazingly, powering up the wave to poise on the crest.

The beat of a larger, greater heart rolled beneath her feet as the boat perched between water and sky. *Dragon Flight! Take us to the bridge!* She sensed the textured golden irises looking back at her. *I hear you, Lamiya of Riverplain*, rumbled words seeped through the soles of her feet. The dragon eyes blinked and the front part of the boat stretched as the live dragon's neck arched and the head moved downwards.

Lamiya tensed her knees and leaned hard on the oar. The team flipped their paddles out to the sides, ready to stabilise the boat. In the water between her boat and Tengar's, a massive, blue-scaled tail flicked out and a wall of water roared past.

Her boat plunged alarmingly and she clung to the oar, heart in her mouth, knees flexed against the inevitable slap that was coming. Her heart pounded a beat, a parallel stronger beat resonating beneath her feet as the half-boat and half-dragon splashed onto level water. The live orange-green dragon took the brunt on her chest, powerful forearms clawing out at the front, reaching out with her head and neck for balance.

Joy filled Lamiya at the sight of the elegant, vivid dragon with the flowing red mane. The boat-dragon lurched upwards and ploughed forward before any river water could spill over the sides.

Tears of exhilaration streamed down her cheeks. 'Bring it home!' she screamed. 'Go! Go!' Better not to give the paddlers any time to think. The dragon Flight extended her neck and the team responded.

'Yosh!' came from next to her. She dared not look. Riverfall must be right there.

Lulite pounded a rapid beat and yelled, 'Mizuchi and Seasprite challenge!' Then she shrieked at Lazuli and Larimar, 'Go! Go! Go!'

The prow lifted and the boat flew. The bridge lurked high above, and just as they entered the shadow of the bridge a whole, real, orange and green dragon with a red mane peeled away from the front of the boat.

Lamiya's heart ached.

CHAPTER FORTY-TWO

Everand held his breath when the blue-and-gold river dragon rushed under the bridge, creating a massive bubble of water. When he, Atage and Lyber had arrived at the bridge he'd noted the clawed gouges up the riverbank and thought the pile of offerings looked smaller, but there was no sign of the dragon. He drummed his fingers on the bridge railing, rapidly concluding there was no plan better than the one he and Lamiya already had. Befriend the river dragon and try to release the dragon spirit in her boat. Lamiya stood at the rear of her boat looking elegant, poised and alarmingly desirable as she exhorted her team to challenge the Riverfall boat.

Suddenly, she stood taller and stopped yelling, as if she were concentrating. He threw his power to her and joined in her call: *'Flight! Come, sweet dragon.'* He perceived Lamiya reaching inside herself, drawing on her uncanny calling ability. A golden iris filled his mind and blinked. Satisfied Lamiya's summons had been heard, he withdrew and focused on the race.

Heart in mouth, he watched the blue-and-gold river dragon speed through the water between the Riverfall and Riverplain boats. The way the dragon flicked its tail to one side boded well. Perhaps it did not intend harm.

Lyber gripped his arm, face pinched in terror. 'The boats!'

Everand extracted his arm. 'Stay calm. Wait,' he said, wishing his heart would follow his own advice instead of hammering so wildly he could barely think. He ducked when Malach's eagle swooped right above his head, following the path of the river dragon below. Then he stood taller, his pulse racing impossibly fast as he fought to look everywhere at once.

Down and to his left, the Riverplain and Riverfall boats were plunging downwards as the bubble of water passed. Lamiya's boat seemed to be half-dragon and half-boat. In the middle of the river, Seasprite was rising up the bubble of water, the paddlers *laughing* and yelling their team cry.

A couple of boat-lengths behind, Raptor paddled solidly on, the eagle now circling above Malach. The man had lowered his steering oar and was lifting something else. Everand enhanced his sight: a crossbow with a thick, stone-tipped bolt fitted into a mighty powerful looking string. The stone tip dripped a dark liquid. The dragon! Malach *was* after the dragon. Why harm the dragon? *Not harm, you buffoon.* The thought was oddly tinged with Mage Beetal's voice. *Influence.* Control the dragon and control the river. Control the river and control all the provinces. So neat.

He glanced at Lamiya's boat and his mouth dropped open. Neither boat had tipped over and the two teams were battling it out for the bridge, with Seasprite close on their tails. 'Yosh!' 'Yo!' 'Ee-yah!' 'Lift!' 'Lift!' filled his ears. Awe filled him at the indomitable spirit of these paddlers. The eagle circled behind the boats, presumably marking the river dragon's path. At the back of Raptor, Malach stood ready.

The boats were almost beneath the bridge, the paddles splashing fast and furious, the drummers pounding an incredibly fast tempo and the paddlers gasping and grunting. Beside him, Lyber leaned on the rails, watching intently. Reluctantly taking his attention away from the dragon, Everand leaned over and focused on the edge of the bridge: the teams were so evenly matched. Keeping his sight enhanced, he fixed his gaze on the line created by the outer edge of the bridge.

The instant before the two boat noses zipped below him, the form of a lithe orange and green dragon with a red mane slipped away from the front of Lamiya's boat and dived under the water. The boat's dragon head turned solid again, the stretched neck shortened to its wooden form — and Mizuchi's blue nose flew past the line as the Riverfall team took one great powerful stroke.

Everand grimaced; Lamiya would be so disappointed. Then he smiled. On balance, it was the best outcome between these two superb teams. Riverfall would have the glory of the long race but Riverplain would possibly take the overall race glory. By the time he'd stood up straight, Seasprite had also paddled under the bridge. Raptor was closing on the bridge, but Malach was looking over his shoulder at the water behind him.

Frowning, Everand spun around and found Lyber had been joined by Atage. Both men stood looking at him expectantly.

'Who won?' asked Atage, his eyes shining.

Everand stared: a live dragon, possibly two dragons, were romping in their river and they wanted to know who had won the race? A laugh simmered in his chest. 'Riverfall, by a breath.'

Atage and Lyber clapped hands and let out whoops. Lyber started moving the tokens around on his tally board. 'I know the other positions,' he said.

Leaving them to it, Everand peered down just as the river dragon swam back under the bridge, heading upriver after the boats with its tail flashing through the water and leaving massive trails of cascading silver bubbles. He ran to the other side of the bridge and grasped the railing. Mizuchi, Flight and Seasprite hovered in the centre of the river with the teams slumped over regaining their breath. Lamiya was scanning the water around her, braced for any unexpected movement.

The eagle was turning in a broad circle about ten boat-lengths upriver. Everand guessed the river dragon had overshot, not expecting the boats to stop, and was coming back. Raptor was nudging upriver towards the dragon and Malach stood with his legs planted wide and the crossbow hefted in his hands.

Watching the ripples on the water below where the eagle skimmed, Everand threw his presence at the dragon, visualising the dragon face he'd seen in the message ball. A weight buffeted him and his knees wobbled as the essence of the dragon hit him, but the dragon's mind was bouncing around like a pebble in a wave. A whirl of emotions assaulted him: curiosity, excitement, a tinge of caution, an urge to play. The excited dragon was circling the boats but with no idea of what to do. And no idea of the danger it was in.

Everand severed the link and frowned. The ancestor's tales hadn't specified whether the river dragon was a male or a female, but this dragon felt decidedly male. His chest tightened. The annals of Axis made no reference whatsoever to *any* dragon, male or female. Did the mages not know of the river dragons? He took a painful breath. No-one, not even Mantiss, had said anything, not even when Mage Beetal's dragons arrived. But then, the mages did not live near a river or lake. They mustn't know.

Everand looked around. Atage and Lyber were still conferring over the tally board. Aware of the dragon, the paddlers were sitting up with their paddles held flat to stabilise their boats against the wash from the dragon's frolicking. The crowds gathered next to the bridge were huddled together, pointing at the water. A band of ripples raced past Raptor and Malach shot a bolt into the water, then reached down to get another bolt. A second ripple moved past Raptor and the paddlers exclaimed and beat the water with their paddles as if deflecting a large fish. Everand smiled: the other dragon from Lamiya's boat Flight.

His smile faded; he *must* get the river dragon's attention. There was still potential for disaster if Malach succeeded in hitting the dragon with his crossbow bolt dipped in potion. It was likely the potion was one that would compel the dragon to obey him. His former mentor had created such a potion and had used it on his army of dragons.

A cold sweat broke out on his neck. Was it possible Malach had some of *that* potion? He swallowed painfully. That raised many, many questions. For now, the dragon was curious and excited and intended no harm — but if the potion hit the dragon, it would turn, in a heartbeat, into a massive beast of war — under Malach's direction. And the boats were all still on the water, with Lamiya, Beram, Mookaite, Acim, Zink and all his new friends. His heart ached and his pulse raced.

Shielding his eyes with a hand, he scanned the skies for any other threats. There was no sign of any tree-moths, or any eagles other than the one tracking the dragon, just clear blue sky. He scanned the river. No sign of anything else odd in the water. So, Malach was focused on the dragon.

The eagle screeched, braked with a great flapping of wings, and changed direction to follow the river dragon as it raced a circle around the boats, going the other way. The surface of the river grew choppy and the boats bobbed about. Lamiya's paddlers cheered and he had a brief glimpse of the head of the smaller, orange, green and red dragon as it peered above the water near the boat. Then the dragon from Flight dived and a bubble of water chased after the river dragon. Malach loosed the second bolt when the smaller dragon zipped past his boat, but she was too fast.

Everand felt tension growing in his neck and jaw. When the dragon Mizuchi grew tired of circling, he would approach a boat. Ironically, the dragon seemed unaware of the second dragon tailing him. How could he get the dragon's attention and make it listen?

Everand climbed over the bridge railing, perched on the narrow ledge with his toes dangling in space and scanned the flowing water below. *More getting wet.* As if to make a point, the wounds on the back of his head started to throb. Atage and Lyber shouted at him, asking what he was doing. Dragon Mizuchi sped towards the bridge. Everand sent power into his feet and legs, took a great gulp of air — and jumped.

His feet sliced into the water and he barely had time to bend his knees and lean forward before he landed with a great *ooph* on Mizuchi's neck. The mane spikes were sharp and he just stopped his chest from hitting one, sitting up and grabbing the base of the nearest spike with both hands. He sent a spell of adherence to make sure his grip stuck.

Mizuchi breached the surface with an ear-splitting roar. *Don't drown me! I'm a friend*, Everand thought at the dragon. In response, the dragon dived and humped through the water, trying to dislodge him. Everand squeezed his eyes shut against the water rushing past his face and held his breath. A silver thread slashed through the water a finger-width from his shoulder. One of Malach's bolts! Stupid, he should have considered that! Getting hit himself would be even worse. *Great Mizuchi! Go greet the blue and gold boat.*

Who are you to ride me? The dragon's voice, definitely male, exploded into his mind.

I've come to warn you! Everand flung back, difficult while concentrating on not slicing his hands open and not taking a breath.

No! You have power. You can't be trusted! The dragon humped and writhed with more effort.

Everand felt himself slipping. He gripped so tight the mane barb cut into his hands. Ignoring the stinging cuts, he tried again. *I am your friend. I want you to meet the local people who honour you.*

Tricksy two-legs with power must be avoided! Snarled the dragon. *Get off me!*

Perplexed, Everand clung on. If the mages didn't know of the dragons, why did the dragon think they couldn't be trusted? Was it something Malach, or perhaps Mage Beetal, had done?

How could he convince the dragon? *Go to the blue boat, made in your honour. Riverfall want to be your friend and race their boat with you.* He projected the image of the boats racing. *They gave you the fish.* He projected the pile of offerings.

A rumbling shivered through the dragon's body, but he was still annoyingly underwater and veered away from where Everand thought the other boats were. Peering through the dragon's ears, which were pricked intently forward, he saw a shadow moving on the surface ahead, the paddles dipping in and out of the water. Raptor! *Not this boat!*

This boat moves. I will race it. Everand groaned. Malach must *not* gain control of this impetuous and over-excited dragon. They would be an entirely dangerous combination. Mizuchi powered along the side of the boat and the paddles dipped faster, trying to keep up. Another rumble passed through the dragon and he edged closer to Raptor.

A silver line buzzed through the water right by Mizuchi's shoulder. Quelling his fright, Everand seized the opportunity. *See that? Danger! Stay away. As your friend, I'm trying to warn you.* To his horror, Mizuchi swam in a wide curve, lining up for another pass.

Mizuchi surged towards Raptor again.

Blinking furiously, Everand scanned ahead. The Riverwood team was paddling faster, Malach realising the dragon wanted to race. Arms aching, he clung on while the dragon's body moved in sinuous wide curves at indescribable speed. Water rushed by him so fast he worried he'd lose his clothes. The dragon zipped past the boat, and a bolt sliced the water right next to Mizuchi's head.

A trail of black ink hovered in the water behind: strands of the potion. *Don't touch that! It's a spell!*

The dragon hesitated mid-writhe. At last, he might have got Mizuchi's attention. *That boat wants to control you. You must trust me.*

Mizuchi swam a slower, wider loop. *Are they from the western shore?*

It took Everand a moment to work out what the dragon was asking. He visualised Dragon Lake with the waterfall cascading in the centre, Riverwood on the far shore with the forest, and Riverfall on the near side, closer to the sea. *Yes. The western shore. Near the trees.*

The eagle goes with them? A growl reverberated through the dragon.

Everand swallowed. He didn't want an angry dragon that was even less predictable. However, lying to Mizuchi wouldn't bode well. *Yes.*

They tried to trick me, growled the dragon, turning his head towards Raptor. *Slippery fish and bird with not spice.*

Everand had no idea what Mizuchi was referring to. Alarmed, he felt the dragon's powerful muscles bunching. Mizuchi stretched out his head and neck, his tail swishing faster and faster. Hunching over against the force of the water pushing at him, Everand tucked in his head. There was nothing he could do to deter the dragon. He secured his grip just before Mizuchi slammed into the side of Raptor, put his head under the boat and tossed it as if it were a feather.

After a brief pause, the feet and legs of the Riverwood paddlers plunged into the water around them. The boat landed with an almighty thud and splash, mercifully not on top of them. Everand clung on, watching Malach's crossbow sink in a slow spiral until it disappeared into darker, deeper water. The dragon hovered, snorting bubbles, then snaked his great head from side to side, eyeing the kicking legs and feet in the water. He opened his mouth to reveal long, gleaming, ivory fangs.

No! Everand hurled the command.

Why not? Mizuchi snapped, swimming casually towards a pair of thrashing legs.

You'll scare the other boats and they won't be your friend!
He took a desperate gamble that friendship was what the dragon
wanted. His chest ached and pinpoint stars were swirling at the
edges of his vision. His bubble of air was running out. Beneath
him, the dragon's forearms ceased clawing the water and the
tail swished more slowly.

Please take me to the blue boat. I need air. The dragon
hovered, possibly thinking. *Let me introduce you to the team
who race in your honour.* Mizuchi curved away and Everand
hoped he was going to the other boats.

The dragon came to a stop and raised his head and neck out
of the water. The sunlight hurting his eyes, Everand sat blinking
the water from his face. His sodden clothes were moulded to
him, but started to warm in the hot sun. He blinked harder and
his vision returned. Everyone in the boats from Riverfall and
Riverplain was gaping at him and Mizuchi in stunned silence.
Where was Seasprite? Glancing around, he saw the Riversea
team paddling over to help the Riverwood team, who clung
like limpets to their overturned boat on the far side of the river.

'Yosh!' called Tengar. The Riverfall paddlers raised their
paddles in homage to the dragon and bowed so low their noses
brushed their knees.

'Yo!' Lamiya said quickly, and the Riverplain paddlers
saluted the dragon.

See? Everand thought at the dragon. *I am your friend. All
these people want to be your friend.*

The dragon pricked up his ears. 'Great Mizuchi!' called
Everand, extending his voice so everyone could hear. 'This
team from Riverfall race in your honour. Their boat is named
after you.' He paused while the team bowed low again.

The dragon tilted his head. *My mother was Mizuchi. They
honour her, not me.*

Everand gasped. Of course! That explained the time lapse,
and why this dragon hadn't come down the river. Ignoring the

expectant gazes on the paddlers' faces, he communicated back: *Great River Dragon, we didn't know. May I respectfully ask your name?*

The dragon rumbled, *Mizukaze, meaning water-wind.* The dragon preened its whiskers and added immodestly, *Because I am so fast.*

You are impressively fast, agreed Everand. *They will build another boat in your name, Great Mizukaze.*

Will they race with me? The dragon turned his head and fixed massive golden eyes on him.

Everand averted his look so as not to be hypnotised. Did Mizukaze mean now? Movement slithered into the side of his vision and the orange and green-scaled dragon from Lamiya's boat poked her head out of the water. That dragon looked decidedly female, although he couldn't reason exactly why. Perhaps it was her more graceful, lithe form and the way she fluttered her golden eyes.

'Dragon Flight!' cried Lamiya. 'Welcome! We from Riverplain race in your honour!' Her team saluted with their paddles and bowed.

Everand's heart lifted to see Lamiya so radiant. *See?* he directed at Mizukaze. *These are friends.* The next words were difficult to form around the breadth of his smile. 'Tengar! Mizukaze wants to know if you will race him. You'll need a newer, faster boat!'

Tengar's smile slipped. '*What* did you say?'

Still smiling, he said, 'This is Mizukaze, *son* of Mizuchi. You need a new boat.'

Tengar bowed low, the team hastening to copy. 'Great Mizukaze, welcome. We will build a new boat in your name.'

And race? Mizukaze rumbled.

'Great Mizukaze,' said Everand loudly. 'The boats would like to parade past the town with you.'

Is parade a form of race? asked the dragon, his golden whiskers bristling and nostrils flaring wide to show crimson pockets.

'More of an honour. They want to show you their town and let you meet all the people. You can swim downriver with them while they paddle the boats there.'

In a race? persisted Mizukaze.

Everand sat straighter and looked at Tengar as he said, 'When you reach the town walls you can race the last part in front of everybody. The crowds will love that.' He sensed the dragon pondering this and added by mind-link, *Besides, you have your new friend to show around. In our language her name is Flight.*

Very well, rumbled the dragon, twisting his head on an angle to look at him again, the golden irises intent. *I would like to hear the drums.*

His vision beginning to swim in the depths of Mizukaze's gaze, Everand lowered his eyes. *I'll ask them. Can you put me on the boat?* Mizukaze nudged forward beside the Riverfall boat, nosing gently at the wooden head.

Everand hesitated, wondering how he was supposed to get in the boat when it was full of paddlers, until Tengar took a step backwards to make room for him on the glide platform. The paddlers stared at Mizukaze in awe, mouths open, and Persaj kept raising and lowering a hand as if he wanted to pat him. Beram leaned inwards while Everand clambered off Mizukaze's neck and tried to step into the boat. His foot slipped and he fell, face-first, across Beram's lap.

'Traveller, you are priceless!' Beram laughed, grabbing the back of his tunic and tugging to help lift him up.

Heat flaming in his face, Everand pushed up and stiffly climbed back to sit cross-legged at Tengar's feet. The paddlers in both boats were laughing and Lamiya was wiping tears from her eyes. He grinned at her, loving the way her eyes sparkled when she looked at him. His heart skipped, like that first moment when he had seen her poised at the back of the boat while he floundered in the river. He swallowed. Now the races were finished, surely they could spend time together, alone? His heart skipped several beats. What about at the feast? Would she wear the new tunic and skirt that so accentuated her beauty and grace? A gift! Would he have time to choose something elegant and lovely?

'Traveller?' said Tengar sharply.

'Sorry. What?'

'Will you come back to the town in the boat or in the cart with Atage?'

Everand eyed the dragon heads peering out of the water. 'In the boat, please.' Hopefully, he wouldn't need to curb the dragon's exuberance on the way.

'Good plan,' said Tengar. To the other boat, he called, 'Lamiya, are you ready? Paddlers, swap sides for the paddle home.'

'One more thing,' said Everand. 'Mizukaze asks that you beat the drums.'

Beram twisted around with a grin. 'You must tell us how you can *talk* to the dragon!'

'Only when he's listening,' admitted Everand, holding up his hands to stop the team's flood of questions.

'Let me tell you at the feast.'

CHAPTER FORTY-THREE

The two boats moved back downriver and Everand sat quietly at Tengar's feet, letting the rhythmic sounds of the paddles and the murmured chatter ebb over him. His clothes steamed and the back of his head throbbed. He must see Mookaite for fresh salve. Looking over his shoulder, he saw the Riversea boat Seasprite making ready to head downriver. Miraculously, the Riverwood boat, Raptor, seemed intact, with the paddlers back on board and tipping water out of the base of it. Malach was standing at the back, retrieving his oar. Would Riverwood slink home or return to the town?

Facing forward, Everand listened to the chatter, but nobody was discussing Malach's attempts to shoot the dragon. Was it possible that in the chaos the other boats hadn't realised what was happening? Or had they thought Malach was trying to protect his boat? If this were the case, then Malach's intentions remained undetected. A knot formed in his stomach; he'd be unwise to underestimate Malach.

He closed his eyes, swaying in time with the boat. The Guild had underestimated Mage Beetal and that had nearly cost them everything. Untrained he might be, but Malach could have inherited all of Mage Beetal's cunning. Assuming they were related: that was yet to be proved.

He snapped his eyes open: the races were over but the mission was not. What would Malach do next? Would he disrupt the feast, or the trade discussions? Perhaps the Riverfall men with weapons would still be needed. He must talk to Beram and Tengar.

He looked at the dragons swimming alongside the boats, their backs rising out of the water at intervals, scales gleaming as they moved with power and grace. What about them? His forehead ached. His mission had not included anything about any possible river dragon. The Guild expected him to return as soon as the trade discussions were concluded.

He'd missed something. Again, he thought of Mantiss' earnest look before he was translocated and the ambiguous words, *I need your eyes on this.* Aside from protecting the festival and finding out about the people who lived in the provinces, was he supposed to do something else? Did his master know, or suspect, something that he hadn't shared? Was he *supposed* to have found out about Malach? But how would Mage Mantiss possibly know?

Well, now that he *had* found Malach, what would Mantiss expect him to do? Should he openly accuse Malach of his attempts at sabotage and tell Atage to send him and the Riverwood team home? Not really his decision, and such a move would leave a resentful half-mage on the loose. That wouldn't help future province relations. Could he reason with the half-mage to leave the other provinces alone?

The knot in his stomach clenched: this would also be viewed as meddling. He would be expected to report that Malach existed and to let the councils decide. Could he persuade the Guild to take Malach in for training, as unprecedented as it would be to accept a non-pure mage? He put his head on one side to ease the tension throbbing in his neck. That assumed he could convince Malach to accompany him to the Guild.

What if the Guild voted to obliterate the half-mage in accordance with Guild Rule Eight? He swallowed with difficulty. He couldn't even suggest Malach go to the Guild without knowing what the Guild would do ... but leaving him loose in the provinces … he felt a muscle in his jaw clench and twitch.

No meddling. Find out about the provinces and report any emerging risks. He imagined Mage Mantiss' stern voice as clearly as if his master were sitting in the boat beside him. He sat straighter. Fine, he'd leave it to Atage to decide whether to send Malach home or let his team stay. His forehead pounded. What should he tell the Guild, though?

The second waterwheel loomed and the town walls rose ahead. Everand shuffled to look up at Tengar. 'Could you and Lamiya summon the teams' energy to race to the ramp?'

'I expect so,' said Tengar with a grin. 'Hey, Lamiya! Race you to the ramp!'

Both boats surged forward and the drummers began to beat their drums. Mizukaze lifted his head out of the water and released a pleased roar. Behind him, Flight's head poked out of the water, her golden eyes blinking in curiosity. Everand lifted and then flung his arm forward, thinking *'Go!'* at the dragon. Mizukaze dived with an elaborate swish of his tail.

Soon, water rushed by the boat's flanks and he wished he had something more secure to hang onto. The two dragons easily matched the boats and spent a lot of time lifting their heads and flicking their tails. When they passed the tents along the riverbank, tumultuous cheering and clapping accompanied the dragons' antics. The drummers beat louder and faster while the teams tried to outdo each other, chanting 'Yosh!' and 'Yo!'

They sped past the boat ramp and both teams lifted their paddles and started to laugh. Everand laughed with them. Part one of his mission had turned out well, for the races were undoubtedly a success. Relief and pleasure coursed through him.

The dragons sped past, heading upriver, and he saw they had gone to race Seasprite. 'Ee-yah!' came the Riversea call as they took up the challenge and power-paddled towards the ramp. Tengar nudged his boat out of the way when the dragons gambolled back by them, and Seasprite skimmed past the ramp.

Everand looked upriver again: where was Raptor? The Riverwood boat was approaching with more caution. So, Malach intended to stay.

Mizukaze! He concentrated on the bubbling water where the dragon was. *Let this boat land. Leave it … for now.* Mizukaze didn't respond, although the dragons frolicked a circle around Raptor to make the water choppy and did nothing more. Everand's lips quirked while Malach wobbled at the back of the boat and the paddlers gave grim glances at the water. Raptor approached the ramp in silence and hovered a distance away from the other boats.

Everand frowned, then turned back to the dragons. Would they get bored and head back to their lake when the boats were put away? Did Atage need a more formal agreement with Mizukaze?

Movement on the path caught his eye. The cart with Atage and Lyber arrived in a cloud of dust at the top of the ramp, and then the driver coaxed the hopeepa down the ramp. The two hopeepa lifted their necks in alarm at the sight of the massive dragons. Everand sent a calming nudge to Crystal, and she swished her tail. Atage wouldn't be pleased if the hopeepa bolted and he got unceremoniously tipped onto the ramp.

Great Mizukaze! Come meet the leader of these people. The bubble of water glided towards the bottom of the ramp. The dragon stopped level with the boat and stood up, towering above them, water cascading off his back and the blue scales gleaming in the sun, as vivid as the sky above. Crystal bellowed and stamped her hooves. Atage gripped the front rail of the cart and looked extremely nervous. Mizukaze arched his neck and the gold spikes stood out and glinted in the light. Atage seemed frozen to the spot.

Everand scrambled to his feet and bowed to the dragon, relieved when Atage took the hint and he and Lyber bowed too. When no-one said anything, he sighed. 'Esteemed river dragon, this is Atage, the leader of Riverfall. Beside him is Lyber, the second leader. They welcome you to their town and are delighted their offerings and the races pleased you.' To Atage, he called, 'Atage, this is Mizukaze, *son* of Mizuchi. This dragon is unfamiliar with the ancient customs.'

Perhaps he should have consulted with Atage about the protocols, but he guessed that not even Atage had actually expected the dragon to come. 'Great Mizukaze, the people will hold more races in your honour and race against your speed and might.' Everand made a pounding motion with his fists and the drummers beat their drums.

Mizukaze arched his neck higher and puffs of smoke came out of his nostrils. Everand sensed approval radiating from the dragon. He wished Atage would recover his wits because he was well and truly meddling now. Mantiss and Agamid would be appalled.

Facing the cart, he said respectfully, 'Atage, leader of Riverfall, the dragon asks why you have summoned him. Is there something you need?'

After an awkward pause, Atage stood straighter. 'Great Mizukaze, welcome! The people would be glad if you could make it rain to foster our crops. For this we will ply you with offerings and race with you in our boats.'

Everand added, 'And beat their drums.'

I accept, appeared in his mind. Mizukaze dipped his head and gave such a thunderous roar all the paddlers flinched. The two hopeepa bellowed and fidgeted, restrained expertly by their driver.

Everand looked at Atage, who was clinging to the railing with a pale face. 'Mizukaze agrees. He will be your friend.'

'Wonderful!' cried Atage, lifting his arms high. 'Three cheers for Mizuchi er ... Mizukaze!'

Everand winced at the whooping and hollering. The water behind Mizukaze's tail burbled as dragon Flight emerged. Holding his breath, he watched the elegant dragon wade to the Riverplain boat and extend her nose to touch Lamiya's hand. Lamiya gently stroked the top of the dragon's nose and her lips moved as she murmured something. Then she looked directly at him and beamed such a smile that his heart did a somersault.

In the cart, Atage and Lyber bowed again and everyone in the boats and on the bank clapped. Mizukaze's mouth dropped ajar, reminiscent of a grin, and more smoke puffed from his nostrils. Everand's legs began to shake and the back of his head felt as if someone was sticking knifepoints into it. *Thank you,* he thought at Mizukaze. *We people must rest now.*

The dragon dipped his head and conveyed, *Rain soon.* Mizukaze shuffled his massive body around, nudged the other dragon, and then they both ploughed away from the ramp.

Entranced, Everand watched the dragons give a tandem wave with their tails and swim upriver side by side.

CHAPTER FORTY-FOUR

Everand flopped down at Tengar's feet. Wishing he could just relax, he tapped Beram's shoulder. 'We need to meet with Atage to talk about Riverwood.'

Beram nodded. 'Why don't you go to my dome and get changed? I'll arrange the meeting then come to collect you.'

They disembarked and Everand wound his way through the paddlers, who were all hanging around the boat ramp going over the races with much banter and exaggeration. He tried to wave at Lamiya but she was surrounded by people. Fatigue weighing down his arms and legs, he hurried to Beram's dome.

After a quick wash and change into crisp, clean clothes he was considering a rest on the cushions when Beram marched in.

'We're to go to Atage's dome now,' said Beram while he stripped off his team uniform and grabbed clean clothes. 'Lyber is fetching Malach and his pacer.' He swigged down some water and dragged the back of his hand across his mouth. 'Atage thinks we should meet with Malach immediately and resolve this sooner rather than later.'

Putting the cushion back under the table, Everand sighed and followed Beram. They navigated a path through throngs of people milling in the courtyards, the noise making conversation impossible. He'd like to have asked what strategy Atage had in mind. Hopefully, the man would be bold and make decisions and not try to pass the responsibility to him. It seemed wise to call Malach to a private meeting. Who knew how the half-mage would react when confronted? So far, Malach had been cunning and ruthless. Could he be trusted to honour any agreement they reached?

When they reached Atage's dome, Everand flexed his fingers and summoned his power ready. The inter-province trade was Atage's vision and although he didn't think Malach would overtly attack the man, it was better to be ready. Thulite showed them through to the meeting room where Atage and Lyber were waiting. Everand sat without comment; he must let Atage drive the meeting and not be tempted to intervene.

Atage nodded. 'Thank you for coming. Beram told me how you saved the river dragon. We are immensely grateful.'

'You're welcome.' Everand smiled. 'I'm glad we've worked out this is a different, younger dragon. It explains a lot.'

'Indeed,' said Atage with a smile of relief. 'We'll make sure we keep the full tradition of races and offerings going from now on!'

Voices sounded at the entrance, then Thulite ushered Malach and one of his pacers in. Atage immediately became a shade paler, and Beram fidgeted uncomfortably.

Malach remained standing and looked down at Atage. 'You asked to see me?'

Atage waved a hand. 'Please, sit.'

Malach and his man sat, their backs stiff.

'First, thank you for coming and competing in the boat races.' Atage rested his hands on the low table.

Everand raised an eyebrow. Would this soft approach work? Malach looked amused. Perhaps he should read the man's mind so they would know fully what he was thinking. He subtly extended a mind probe.

Malach turned to him and growled, 'I wouldn't do that.'

Keeping his face calm, Everand withdrew his probe. Curses. Malach had sufficient ability to detect even that lightest of touches. They'd be forced to take whatever Malach said at face value.

Atage frowned, not understanding the interaction. 'This matter is somewhat delicate ... but I need to ask whether you intend to join in the trade negotiations. You don't seem to have brought any goods to trade.'

Malach shrugged. 'We have no need of your goods. Now that I've seen what each province has to offer, this confirms that we don't need to trade with any of you.'

Everand waited through the heavy silence that followed. He looked at Atage, willing the man to find his courage.

'I see,' said Atage, clasping his hands. 'In that case, do we assume that you won't be attending the discussions?' He swallowed. 'Will you be leaving?'

Malach leaned forward and jutted his jaw out. 'Are you asking me to leave? Is my team not welcome?'

Everand frowned. Was Malach looking to cause a confrontation, or banking on Atage backing down? The pasty colour to Atage's face suggested this was entirely possible, and Beram was casting pleading looks his way. He clamped his tongue to the base of his mouth to curb the temptation to accuse Malach of trying to sabotage things. He itched to know whether he'd sent the tree-moths. The back of his head gave a sharp pang, suggesting he should also ask why the eagles had attacked him. He clamped his tongue down harder. Wait and see what Atage did next. Malach gave him a brief but smug glance.

'Well,' Atage floundered, 'you were welcome, but why stay if you don't want to trade?'

Malach looked at each of them, his gaze lingering on Everand. Beside him, his man sat rigidly, one hand by his hip as if reaching for a weapon. Malach shrugged. 'We can leave. But we need time to repair our boat. The river dragon cracked it.'

Atage sat straighter. 'Yes, that's fair. So, can we assume you won't be joining us for the negotiations and will depart after light when your boat is fixed?'

Malach stood up. 'You may assume.'

Everand stood, and the others hurried to follow suit.

Atage gave Malach a tight smile. 'Of course, your team is welcome at the feast this dark-fall. It is right that all teams celebrate the races.'

Malach nodded brusquely. Hanging behind him, his pacer frowned, looking displeased.

Everand gave Malach a measured look. The man retained an annoying subtle air of amusement. Did he think they were cowards because no-one had openly confronted him? If he said nothing now the opportunity would be lost.

'Wait.' He stepped between Malach and the door. Holding eye contact with Malach, he pushed down his thoughts about how like Mage Beetal the man's face and sardonic expression were. 'The tree-moths ... did you send them to undermine the festival?'

Keeping a straight face, Malach said, 'Why would you think that?'

Forcing himself to sustain the eye contact, Everand said evenly, 'The moths are not from the other provinces, and Riverwood is the only province not welcoming the trade.'

The air in the room grew thick with tension. Everand dare not look at Beram or Atage, keeping his full attention on Malach and the crackling static passing between them.

Malach snorted, his nostrils flaring. 'Do you have any evidence these moths came from Riverwood? Perhaps they are wild. There is a lot of untamed land to our south.'

Everand slowed his swallow down so it wouldn't be visible to the others. This probable half-mage was as devious as his former mentor had been. Was it worth pushing the point about the eagles, which clearly *were* from Riverwood? Or about his endeavours to shoot the dragon? Malach was watching him with a smug air, waiting for his next effort. The burly pacer's frown deepened into a scowl, but the man also looked confused. Interesting. Was it possible the team did not know about or understand what their leader planned?

'Well,' said Atage loudly, rubbing his hands together. 'Thanks for that. So, we are agreed that you will leave as soon as your boat is repaired, and you are welcome to join us at the feast.'

Grinding his back teeth together, Everand took a step back. If Atage wanted to leave matters without an open confrontation, he should respect this. If Malach and his team left without further incident maybe this course would turn out to be wise. After all, the provinces would have to fend for themselves once he returned to the Guild. He kept his face neutral when Atage waved a hand at the door, indicating the meeting was finished.

Raising a bushy black eyebrow, Malach pushed past Everand, leaning in so their shoulders brushed. 'I know exactly who *you* are. You and I are not done yet.'

Everand stared at the man's back, a shiver crossing his nape. How could Malach know *exactly* who he was? Did Malach mean he knew he was a mage, or that he knew precisely which mage he was? *You and I are not done yet.* Everand swallowed.

'Well,' said Atage, rubbing his hands even more briskly. 'I think that went about as well as could be expected.'

'Maybe,' said Beram, his brows furrowed and looking at Everand. 'Do you think we should have pushed him harder and asked him why he tried to shoot the dragon?'

With a tired shrug, Everand said, 'Hard to say. I think he would've continued to deny everything. It would have been my word against his. This way, you've given him no further cause for resentment, which could be a good thing. Let's hope he leaves sooner rather than later.'

He pushed down unease that he had managed to redirect Malach's focus to him, and the eagles had collected some of his hair that could be used in a spell or potion, depending how much ability Malach possessed. Again, if he returned to the Guild would that matter? His unease surged back up: it would matter if the Guild found out about Malach and decided to take action. A great weight pressed down on his shoulders.

'You look tired, said Beram. 'Let's go see Mookaite for fresh salve for your head.' He beamed. 'Then we have a feast to prepare for!'

Everand started towards the door and then remembered his plan to buy a gift for Lamiya. 'Can we stop by the trade tables after seeing Mookaite?'

'If you insist.' Beram rolled his eyes before following him to the door.

Disappointingly, Mookaite was not in her dome. The back of Everand's head was throbbing, and it would have been good to settle that down before the feast.

'Maybe she's at the trade tables,' said Beram, next heading to the trading courtyard.

Everand followed, finding it harder to keep lifting his feet against an encroaching bone-deep fatigue. How would he manage a feast and more revelry? When Beram nearly disappeared into the press of people, he reached out and put a hand on his friend's shoulder to keep track of him. The level of noise was not helping his headache.

Mercifully, they found Mookaite at the Riverplain trading table. Everand looked over the heads of the crowd to confirm the Riversea table was the next one along. Mookaite saw him looking that way, arched a fine eyebrow at him and tugged Beram away to look at something.

Hiding a smile, Everand slipped sideways through people until he could see the Riversea jewellery. Taken aback by the extent of the array, he skimmed his glance over the table — and stopped at the centre. His throat grew tight with emotion. Yes. That piece was perfect. It was so … Lamiya. He counted out the fish tokens — he had just enough — and passed them to the Riversea woman serving. She wrapped the piece in a fine cloth and gave it to him with a look of curiosity. He hurriedly dipped his head and stepped back.

'That was quick!' said Beram when Everand reappeared by his elbow.

A warm stain began to creep up his neck.

Mookaite snagged Everand's elbow and smiled at Beram. 'See you at the feast.' Then she pulled on Everand's sleeve. 'Come, Traveller, let's put fresh salve on your head and make you presentable.'

Everand slipped the soft pouch into his pocket before she could ask what it was.

CHAPTER FORTY-FIVE

Mage Mantiss hurried along the path to his dome. The sun's yellow warmth was waning, but dusk was not yet nigh. He had ample time to read the final entry in the notebook before Tiliqua arrived for the dusk meal. Elytra was looking forward to seeing Tiliqua and had asked the cook to prepare spiced sunflower seeds with mashed petals to start with, one of their daughter's preferred dishes.

Once inside, he went straight to the reading desk and summoned the notebook. Solemnly, he opened it and turned to the final entry.

From the scrawlings of Mage Lapemis

Handing over to Carlias

I feel the strength fading from my limbs and the light dimming in my eyes. My magic lurks, reluctant to obey my summons. The Council met last sun, and elected Carlias as the new Head of the Guild. An excellent choice. Although sixty season-cycles in age, he should be able to lead for the next twenty cycles or so. By then, the Guild will be established enough for a second-generation mage to lead. Carlias will arrive soon and I must reveal the code words to him and hand over the Staropal.

When I look out the window, I feel most proud. After forty-five cycles, we have made good progress. The library gleams in the sunlight, and we have added to the sparse collection we saved from the boat, recording new spells as we devised them. The administration building stands solid, with an ornate polished wood floor for the Great Hall on the ground level, and a table and chairs of the finest and richest mahogany. The Guild Rules have served us well so far.

The attractive ponds and gardens are colourful and peaceful. The humans have sown a wide array of crops, and we have used our power to augment some to great use. The forest of sunflowers yields abundant oil and the stalks make for strong baskets and woven products. The beetle breeding program has surpassed our expectations, with three species now tamed and available.

Carlias extended his ability to produce giant silk moths, and he and Aclys manage the moths and worms. Aclys is having more domes constructed devoted to breeding and spinning, and the luxurious silk is a delight to wear. Best of all, we now number twenty-three mages, with five more to be birthed imminently. The humans surpass us, with a population of sixty already. Our aim to replenish our Guild to a hundred mages may be achievable.

Sometimes, when the wind blows strongly from the east, my ears tell me they can hear the red dragon calling. The stone whirls with red hues, suggesting this is not my imagination. Of the dragons, however, we have seen no sign. And we have not gone looking. The granite wall provides an effective circle of protection, and Guild Rule Nine, that no mage shall step outside the confines of the wall, has not been broken. We are self-sufficient and safe within its solid grey arms. Our lives are harmonious.

Ah, a tap at the door and Carlias has arrived. It is time. Heavy of heart, I retrieve the Staropal, shrouded in its silk cover, from the hidden alcove under my desk. Once it has accepted Carlias, he will return it to beneath the marble emblem set into the floor of the Great Hall. The stone murmurs and warms beneath my hands. Will it miss me, I wonder? Lifting my gaze, I rest my eyes on Carlias' lined but dear face.

'You will take care of it, won't you?' I say, more lucid words eluding me.

Carlias' eyes crease with his gentle smile. 'Of course, my friend. I am honoured to carry on in your footsteps. You have led us well and coaxed this stone so expertly.'

I slip the silk shroud off and hold the stone out to Carlias. To my relief, the sapphires, turquoises and emeralds dominate, reflecting the stone is content. 'Lake-cave-star-opal,' I say distinctly. 'You must use these words to converse with it.'

Awe on his face, Carlias reaches out his hands and, with profound regret, I place the stone upon his palms. 'Lake-cave-star-opal,' he murmurs and the stone flares the brightest, incandescent blue.

'It has accepted you,' I say. 'Copy my path and take only small amounts of power at a time, and keep it concealed otherwise. Do not let anyone else know the access words, and do not let anyone else touch it.'

Carlias raises his eyes. 'Why so?'

'You must know,' say I, 'this stone was formed by tears from the red dragon. It contains ancient and unknown power. We have tapped into the merest fraction of its capability. The stone is pure, as is the magic.' I lift my shoulders. 'Those who seek power ... those with ambition ... must *never* be let near it. If wielded unwisely, this stone would grant untold power and could be deployed to wreak great damage.'

Carlias draws air in a gasp. 'I see. You have concealed this well, old friend.'

'Another thing.' I lift a finger in warning. 'The stone does not forget the red dragon. We have no idea how long the creatures live for, but most likely far longer than any of us. Perhaps even generations of us.' My throat grows tight.

'Never ever take the stone outside of our Guild, or be tempted to wield its power to see beyond our wall.' I hold his troubled gaze. 'Keep it safe, my friend. Bury it and keep the wards in place. Promise me this.'

'I promise,' says Carlias, and the stone glows with an unusual array of jades and emeralds.

'Cover it,' I say, my heart yearning to snatch it back. I clasp my hands behind my back to suppress the desire. Weariness steals over me.

'You look tired,' says Carlias. 'Do you need anything?'

I shake my head. Now the stone has been safely passed over, I sense my breath will leave my body before the moon rises. 'Good luck, my friend. Be a wise and astute Head of the Guild.'

Carlias bows and leaves, the stone murmuring farewell from beneath its shroud as he closes the door.

With shaking hands, I complete this final scrawling in my notebook and ward it so that only Carlias can open and read it. I place my final instructions, reinforcing that this information must only be passed from Head of the Guild to next Head of the Guild. The history of how we came by the stone has been recast for future apprentices so none are tempted to search for the red dragon. Let the creature's existence pass into mythology, for we have no river.

Choosing my favourite chair, I crumple into it and watch the sunlight fading outside.

The pull of the stone and the acute sense of loss dissipate.

Peace ebbing into my body, I close this notebook.

Releasing a deep sigh, Mantiss softly closed the notebook and murmured the code words. The book slid from his fingers, nudged into the hidden alcove and the wall tile reformed. He rested against the chair back for support. To whom would he pass the Staropal and the notebook? Ideally, Agamid or Everand. However, Guild Rule Two declared that the Guild would be led by an elected Head. The other mages might possibly accept Agamid. He sighed again. Agamid was a loyal friend and skilled mage, but he did not have the political nous to lead. Pelamis and his colleagues would run rings around him.

He tapped his fingers on the desk. After the battle, once Mage Beetal was dead and the invaders defeated, for a short time the Staropal had hung in the space between them, undirected and unclaimed. It had then bobbed towards *Everand*. The stone must have sensed his purity of intention, his complete lack of ambition. Everand had grasped the stone, but had then brought it straight to him, placing it in his shaking fingers and closing his hands over it.

Grateful, he'd rallied the surviving council members to raise the marble emblem in the floor and had concealed the stone deep underground again. Removed from temptation. Was there a way he could get the Staropal to indicate a preference for Everand? Would this persuade the others to elect him?

A door closed somewhere.

'Father? Oh, here you are.' Tiliqua came into the room and walked over to give him a brief kiss on his head. 'What are you doing? Nothing?'

'Contemplating matters, my dear.' Mantiss pulled up out of the chair and turned to take his daughter's arm. 'I'm looking forward to hearing how your research is progressing.'

Once seated at the dining table, he looked across at his tall, elegant and clever daughter. 'Thank you for suggesting where Everand was at the last meeting–' he held up a hand when she went to speak. 'Can you interview the apprentices and ascertain their strengths and preferences?'

Tiliqua's eyes narrowed. 'Everand is still mysteriously detained?'

Resolve firming, Mantiss nodded. 'After we have eaten, I will explain.' He smiled wryly at the way Tiliqua's blue eyes sparkled.

'At last,' she murmured. 'You take me into your confidence, too.'

Mantiss felt his chest tighten. He hadn't thought that his daughter might resent his trust in Everand. If he encouraged them to work together ... yes, that could work out well. Very well.

CHAPTER FORTY-SIX

Dusk light eked into the dome. 'Are you ready?' asked Beram.

Everand patted his tunic pocket for the tenth time to check he had the gift for Lamiya, wrapped in a soft cloth. 'I believe so.' He was as ready as he would ever be for yet another activity at the end of what had been a frenetic sun-up to dusk. An eddy of nerves collected in the base of his stomach: he hadn't seen Lamiya since the races.

'Don't worry,' said Beram, touching his elbow. 'The tunic suits you. Besides, the team asks that you sit with us.' He grinned. 'You promised to tell us about speaking with the dragon.'

The man's grin was infectious, and Everand's shoulders relaxed.

They passed under the arch into the southern courtyard, weaving through the long, plaited streamers in the six colours of life that hung down from the arch to brush them at waist-height. How familiar the sounds and whirling colours of these festivals had become. The river provinces revelled in their lives. With a pang of sorrow, he thought about how much the mages could learn from these people.

The bonfire's massive yellow and orange flames danced hypnotically against the darkening sky, sending up crackling sparks like a swarm of a thousand fireflies. The courtyard walls receded into the shadows, forming a dark protective cocoon around the milling clusters of people.

Beram nudged him towards a table close to the knee-height wooden dais that seemed to have magically appeared on the far side of the bonfire. The carpenters must have been busy.

'Traveller!' 'Dragon rider!' 'Everd!' The team greeted him enthusiastically, clapping him on the back, multiple hands offering him mugs of feeja wine and plates piled with small loaves and sweet cakes. Tengar gave him a more restrained nod, but the man's eyes crinkled with a smile.

Persaj shuffled along the bench, shooing Ejad the other way. 'Sit here, Traveller!'

Everand obligingly squeezed between Persaj and Ejad. Mookaite sat opposite, and Beram folded down next to her. Noticing the way that the healer smiled at Beram, he realised it was Mookaite's attention his friend was aiming to attract. It looked as if he'd succeeded.

Persaj leaned closer and Everand smelled feeja wine on his breath. 'You've such a way with creatures. You must tell me how you do it.' Persaj's tongue was running away with him for a shy person. 'Crystal adores you. That hopeepa would follow you anywhere.'

Tongue-tied, Everand shrugged, uncertain whether he did have a 'way' or whether it was his subtle use of power. Before he could answer, Acim and Zink bounded up to the table, carrying enormous platters mounded high with steaming, spiced fish.

'Eat up,' said Acim. 'Atage will start the presentation soon.'

Each dish outclassed the previous one. The fish was as tasty as it smelled, followed by bowls of spiced vegetables which crunched in his mouth to release unidentifiable juices dribbling over his tongue that he wanted more of. His mug of feeja wine remained full no matter how many times he sipped at it, and he worried about the possible effects, given that he didn't usually drink wine. He'd embarrassed himself enough on this mission as it was. The team clamoured to hear about his ride on the river dragon. His tale went over well until he paused for breath and Beram said loudly, 'It's the dismount that needs some practice!'

The whole team thumped their mugs on the table and laughed so hard they had to wipe their eyes. Everand bristled, and then laughed with them, supposing that his face-plant into Beram's lap must have indeed looked hilarious.

The sound of a stave hitting wood interrupted their laughter, then Jibo climbed onto the dais and sounded the race horn three times. A hush spread over the courtyard, as if a giant hand had draped a blanket of silence over the crowd. Atage stepped onto the dais, clearly visible in the light of the fire. Everand admired the way the dais and tables had been arranged in neat curves so that everyone would be able to see and hear. The flickering firelight glinted off the tokens of office hanging from Atage's neck. Lyber stepped up too, the tally board in his hand.

Atage began his speech, and Everand gazed to the next table over. Lamiya sat between Lulite and Lazuli, wearing the turquoise tunic, and he presumed the moon-coloured skirt was flowing around her legs. His throat constricted. Lazuli was playing with her hair, which shone and glimmered in the light, although Lamiya was focused on what Atage was saying. Slowly, she turned to look right into his eyes and his heart sped up. Was their attraction so strong she always knew when his attention was on her? With a smile, she waggled her fingers at him.

Tearing his gaze away, he discovered the Riversea team was seated at the first table on the other side of the dais. The paddlers wore their team colours, the pearly white tunics gleaming with orange hues in the firelight, and they were adorned with numerous bracelets, necklaces and feathers in their hair. His curiosity was piqued when he saw the drum from their boat on the ground at the end of the table next to Clommus, with a jumble of other odd-looking instruments.

A shiver crossed the back of his neck when he detected the Riverwood team, sitting half in shadow, on the far side of the

Riversea table. So, they were bold enough to attend the feast. Malach sat the furthest away, obscured in the gloom, but he sensed the man's glittering dark eyes were fixed upon him.

A colder shiver chased across his nape. *You and I are not done yet.* His stomach roiled. *Focus, you need to set Malach's parting words aside. Soon, they will retreat to their elusive province. And you will return to Axis, where you belong.*

With a shaking hand, Everand took a sip of his feeja wine and rolled the liquid around his tongue. What could Malach possibly be planning now? It felt as if he were back right at the beginning of his mission, with no comprehension of the real threat. Or, he almost choked on his mouthful of wine, what if he *had* been right all along, but his presence had changed things? Gulping down the wine, he focused on Atage.

'I'll present the tokens of honour to the winning team for each race, and then the overall winner of the races.' Atage waited for the bedlam to subside. 'First, I thank our esteemed judge, the traveller.'

Everand sat up, surprised. Persaj and the others clapped him on the shoulder and he winced at the bruises forming.

'Raise your mugs to the traveller. Our evenly matched teams gave him great challenge and we're most fortunate to have had his keen eyes. Three cheers for the traveller!'

Heat flowed through Everand while the entire courtyard cheered and stamped their feet under the tables. Opposite him, Beram and Mookaite wore knowing smiles. He didn't know where to look and was relieved when Atage held up his hand, the crowds hushed and everyone's attention shifted away.

More relief filled him that, as requested, Atage hadn't mentioned his role in calling and then saving the river dragon. He'd told Atage that he wanted the province people to believe that the inter-province races and the revival of the old traditions had summoned the dragon. Atage and Beram had seen the wisdom in this.

Atage turned to face where the Riverfall team were sitting and smiled broadly. 'The first race was won by our very own Riverfall! I call glide Tengar to the dais!'

Tengar eased off the bench and strode to the dais, enhancing his swagger so that everyone laughed. Stepping up, Tengar shook hands with Atage, who presented him with a handful of gold-sprayed circular tokens hung on vivid blue strings. Everand assumed there was one for each paddler.

When the noise ebbed, Atage added, 'Second in this race, by the smallest of margins, was Riverplain, followed by a dead heat between Riversea and Riverwood.'

Clapping and cheering with everyone else, Everand concluded his hands would also be sore by the end of the presentations.

'The middle race,' said Atage, 'was filled with surprises from the astonishingly fast start. The winner, with clear water behind their aptly named boat, was Riverplain. I call glide Lamiya to the dais.'

Everand thought his chest would explode as Lamiya rose and with poise and grace, the moonlight skirt swishing around her ankles, stepped to the dais. She bunched the skirt with one hand and jumped up onto the platform, the rosy glow to her cheeks not entirely from the firelight. She put out a hand, but Atage grabbed it and tugged her close so he could give her a kiss on each cheek. The Riverplain table erupted into delighted laughter while the Riverfall and Riversea tables let out wild hoots.

He felt dizzy at the emotions tumble-turning through him. Lamiya received the team's tokens and he couldn't take his eyes off her as she walked back to her table, where she was swamped by hugs from her team. He only distantly heard the rest of the announcement with Atage proclaiming that Riverwood was second, followed by Riverfall and Riversea.

Mayhem accompanied the presentation of the tokens to Tengar for the long race. Everand was buffeted by the team as they thumped each other on the back and hugged, including him. He began to wish he hadn't eaten so much, or imbibed so much wine. Persaj excitedly showed him his tokens, and he admired the neat work. Each clay token was a perfect circle, with an intricate outline of a dragon rising above some waves etched into the centre of the disc. The string was of the finest, softest cotton, dyed a vibrant blue.

Finally, the team sat down to hear who had won the races overall. An expectant hush settled over the courtyard, filled by the crackling of the fire and the popping of sparks sashaying up into the cooling air.

Atage stepped forward into the light. 'Good people, in this first festival we were fortunate to witness four great teams and races that were nothing short of spectacular. After the three races, the teams of Riverfall and Riverplain were tied with ten points each.'

Everand's attention sharpened and a loud 'Oooh' came from the crowd. Of course! He should have done his calculations better: two firsts and a third was equal points to two seconds and a first. What would they do?

'After much deliberation, requiring many mugs of brew from Thulite and many sweet cakes,' the crowd chuckled, 'we decided the honour should go to the only boat that won a race with clear water behind them. I call Lamiya and her entire team to the dais!'

Everand flicked his eyes to Tengar but the man didn't look surprised. Instead, he gave a nod, as if to say, only fair. All around, the paddlers clapped and cheered, good-humoured despite the closeness of an overall victory. Lamiya hopped up onto the dais, and he felt as if his heart was thudding its way up his chest ready to jump out of his throat. His eyes burned with emotion and he lowered his gaze.

Sensing scrutiny, he peered from under his eyelashes to find Mookaite watching him. While the rest of the table applauded, she leaned over and beckoned him closer.

When he tipped towards her, she murmured, 'Her heart is yours, Traveller. You need to tell her yours is hers.'

He sat back quickly. Was he that obvious? For a moment, he watched Lamiya being enveloped by her team and squeezed and hugged while the courtyard packed with hundreds of people celebrated her team's prowess. How could he possibly claim her? She was special to these people.

It was as if a bucket of cold water had been tipped over his head. *This* was what she saw; *this* was why she was holding back. He was supposed to return to Axis, where she could not go. And he did not belong here. Sitting stiffly, he coaxed air into his chest.

Forcing a swallow, he looked at Mookaite and muttered, 'How can I?'

CHAPTER FORTY-SEVEN

Memories poured in and Everand drew the protective walls into place around his heart, until he was alone despite being surrounded by people. Self-sufficiency he could do, had done since he was small. His presence had repulsed his mother. His father had been kinder, but aloof and busy.

When he was twelve and his father died — by his mother's hand, and she'd then vanished — Mage Mantiss had assigned him to study under Mage Beetal as an apprentice. A bitter taste flooded his mouth. *That* had gone well, hadn't it? His mentor had turned out to be a rogue and a traitor. Icy coldness splashed over him and the bands around his chest grew excruciatingly tight.

Then Elemar had arrived. For a brief time, he'd had a friend, had dared hope she cared enough to stay. But she'd left, the allure of the handsome warrior who loved her and her home world too strong. His tongue burned with acidity.

Despite vowing never again, he'd dared hope Lamiya might love him. How stupid. How could she? He must return to his Guild duties. Mage Mantiss was relying on him, and Lamiya must stay with her people who adored her. In Axis she would wither like a flower without light. His neck succumbed to the weight of his head and his chin sank to rest on his chest.

'Traveller?' Mookaite leaned further forward and Beram sat staring, concern in his expression.

He put his hands on the table and forced himself to say, 'Yes?'

397

Mookaite's warm hand closed over his, forcing his fingers to be still. 'Beram, tell him!' When Beram shuffled on his seat but didn't speak, she blew impatiently at a wisp of hair across her mouth and said, 'He needs to know *now*.'

To his astonishment, Beram put his hand over Mookaite's so that both their hands covered his. With sheer force of will, he repressed the urge to snatch his hands away, to shriek at them to leave him be.

'Traveller ... Everand ...' Beram fished for the right words. 'Atage was going to tell you after the trade discussions. We don't want to offend you, being a mage and all, we mean it as an honour, but you are welcome to stay in Riverfall. As long as you like.'

Everand blinked. What exactly was the man saying? Did they need his power and ability for longer?

Mookaite threw Beram an exasperated look. 'Men never say the whole thing! What he means is, the people of Riverfall like you. If you want to stay here with us, we'd be happy. Not because of your power, but because you are a good and true man. Atage wants to tell you this after the negotiations. He intends to make you a formal offer to stay and live here. If you wish it.'

Beram gave her a fond smile. '*We* would like you to stay. My dome is yours, for as long as you need.' He gave Mookaite a sly look. 'And after I don't need it, it is yours.'

Everand gazed at their faces until his eyes hurt. He could stay? They *wanted* him to stay? His eyes drifted to the Riverplain table, to take in the sight of Lamiya chatting with her team. If he stayed ... a butterfly of hope flittered unsteadily in his chest.

Mookaite grasped his hands and tugged until he looked into her large brown eyes filled with kindness. 'Go be with her,' she said softly. 'You both need to allow your hearts what they so want.'

Still, he faltered. What about Lazuli? What about the people of Riverplain; would *they* have him? His lips compressed: the

Guild would not let him go so easily. No mages and no magic, none whatsoever, outside of the Guild.

And Mantiss ... who was like the father he'd never had ... even he couldn't sanction a breaking of Guild Law like this. He would be betraying Mantiss and all the teaching and support he'd received from him over the past fourteen season-cycles. Most of his life. Words failed him. These people wouldn't understand this.

'If you can ride a dragon, you can do this.' Beram's grin widened. 'You can dance, can't you? Clommus and his band are about to start playing.'

Dance? Everand felt the world tipping beneath him. Before he could say, 'Mages do not dance,' Mookaite was pulling him to his feet and Beram too was standing. Persaj moved aside to let him out, and his feet floated him behind Beram and Mookaite to the Riverplain table.

'Congratulations!' called Beram, clapping Lazuli and then Larimar on the back. 'Great racing.'

'Yo!' shouted most of the Riverplain team.

Everand hovered while the women hugged Mookaite and the men nudged and clapped one another on the back. The press of bodies around him gained density as the two teams merged.

A roll of a drum sounded, followed by an array of musical notes. He peered over the heads of the paddlers and saw Clommus standing in the centre of the dais with four of his team fanned behind him. Conch was beating the drum and Pippel was playing a long, narrow horn that emitted sweet, high notes. Clama was shaking and patting a circular disk with bells on it, and Limpel was blowing a different, deeper horn. Clommus tapped a foot and began to sing loudly.

They rode the sea and mighty high waves
A'fearing they be sent to watery graves
Until lo and behold rising darkly ahead
Land they see and a new life instead ...

The Riversea team whirled out in front of the dais and began to jiggle about, their shell necklaces and bracelets jingling. The women swayed their hips, and their grass skirts shimmied and shook. Everand shook his head. Was this dancing? Townspeople converged between the bonfire and the dais until the space was filled with bouncing, smiling bodies. Clommus sang enthusiastically, starting a new ballad as soon as he finished the first one. The tempo quickened and people shrieked and whirled around one another.

Uncertain what to do, Everand shifted his weight from one foot to the other until he felt a soft touch on the back of his hand. He looked down. Lamiya stood before him smiling coyly, her mahogany hair cascading over a shoulder. Whirr's head popped out from underneath her hair and the bird peeped. Well, he assumed that was what the opening and shutting of the beak meant; he couldn't hear anything above the pandemonium. The paddlers flowed around them, heading to the dance area.

Slowly, he reached out and caressed her cheek, warmth flowing into him when she leaned her face into his touch and smiled. 'Congratulations, Lamiya. You raced so well.' That sounded awkward, but he meant it. 'And you called your dragon.'

Her smile widened, her teeth gleaming and dimples forming in her cheeks. 'Flight came,' she said as if still in wonder.

There was a brief flurry of movement behind her, and Everand saw Beram guiding Lazuli away. He swallowed: he needed to find his courage very soon. 'I have something for you.' He fumbled in his pocket to draw out the cloth pouch and gently placed it in her hands. 'To celebrate ... everything.'

Her throat moved in a large swallow as she picked at the string with her fingers. Carefully, she lifted out the necklace and stared up at him with glinting eyes. 'Put it on for me?'

Time stood still as he lifted the necklace and stepped closer. With shaking fingers, he nudged her hair up and slid his hands around the back of her neck, fumbling with the clasp. Whirr hopped onto his hand and ran up his arm to perch on his shoulder. The bird's wings tickled his cheek. Lamiya waited. His heart thudded and he wished his fingers would cooperate. Her skin was so soft he wanted to caress it forever. With a miniscule click, the tiny wooden peg snicked into its keeper and the necklace was attached.

Resting his hands on her shoulders, he looked down. The pearly cowrie shell with the crinkled blue-silver lips that perfectly matched the moonlight skirt rested neatly in the cleft just above her breasts. The two flat, silver, coiled shells on their fine strings sat perfectly at the midpoint of her collarbones. The piece looked as if it had been made for her.

Lamiya's eyes glinted. 'How did you know?'

Confused, he peered into her face. 'Know what?'

'I vowed to have this beautiful necklace if we won the longer race.' Her smile wobbled. 'I was heartbroken when Charonia said she'd sold it.' Wiping a hand across her eyes, she added, 'I thought this was because we didn't win the long race.' She smiled warmly. 'So, how did you know?'

He shrugged helplessly. 'It reminded me of you. Balanced, beautiful, elegant.'

Her smile grew mischievous and she reached up to lace her hands behind his neck. Whirr ran down her arm onto her shoulder. 'Say that again …'

Heart thudding impossibly hard, Everand put his arms around her lower back and pulled her close. 'It's also to thank you,' he murmured into her silky, fragrant hair.

'Me?' The word was muffled against his chest.

'For helping me.' He kissed her hair. 'And believing in me.'

'How could I not?' she said, snuggling closer.

The hubbub of sounds and activity faded into a background blur, as if just he and Lamiya stood in the dark by the bonfire. Clommus' voice and the music filled the surrounding space, and he became conscious of pinpoint stars far, far above, and the sparks from the fire flying up to greet them. Her breasts pressed against his chest and he burned to sweep her up into his arms and carry her away to a quiet place by the river.

'Your legs are shaking,' she whispered. 'So are mine.' Her shoulders shook. 'Do you have to go?'

He thought he'd misheard, but she raised a solemn face and asked again, 'Do you have to go?'

The roaring in his ears drowned out even Clommus and his band. His future hung in the balance on her question: two paths opened before him and he must choose which one to tread. His heart wanted to jump and skip down one path, but his mind wryly cautioned that if he did, there'd be no going back — and there would be consequences. His throat aching, he swallowed.

Lamiya waited, hurt and doubt creeping into her eyes at his hesitation. Her grip behind his neck loosened. She was preparing to withdraw.

'I ... I ...' *Go on, say it!* He unclasped his hands from behind her back, and touched her cheek tenderly. Her eyes were wide and dark, her breath warm on his wrists. 'I want to stay with you. If you'll have me.' His mouth went dry and her eyes sparkled with hope.

'We only just met, but I'm drawn to you as a humming bird to nectar.' She tightened her grip around his neck and pressed closer. 'Please stay. With me.'

Everand crushed her against him: how could this beautiful, strong, brave woman possibly want him? She was right that they barely knew each other, but the pull was beyond reason and ... irrefutable. He kissed the top of her head, laughing when Whirr pecked at his hand. 'Do we need your bird's permission?'

Lamiya leaned back, eyes shining. 'Whirr is an *excellent* judge of character.' Her face became serious and she chewed at her lower lip. 'Can you really stay?'

This was the crux of it, and he must be truthful. 'There will be complications, but Beram told me Atage will invite me to live in Riverfall.' She regarded him with anxiety in her intent grey eyes. *Well, you've taken a step on this path, take another.* He slid a hand around to cup the back of her beautiful, long neck. 'I like Riverfall, but I'd love to see Riverplain, if your people will let me come.'

Light shone in her eyes and deep dimples formed in her cheeks. 'I'll ask them.' A shiver of energy and excitement ran through her. 'There's so much to show and tell you! Wait until you see *our* lake. It is clear turquoise, even more vivid than the tunics of Riversea! And soft, green hills tumble down to it.' Whirr flapped his wings.

He gave the bird a dry look. 'And I suppose there are a thousand of these?'

Lamiya burst out laughing and Whirr scolded her with high-pitched peeps. 'Traveller,' her eyebrows pinched together in a frown. 'Traveller no more, Everand ...' she rolled her tongue around his name, savouring it. 'Everand, you do make me laugh.' Mischief sparked, highlighting the blue flecks in her eyes. 'I look forward to teaching you how to paddle properly. And swim.'

Everand groaned and pressed his lips together. Lamiya giggled and tipped her face up expectantly. He melded his lips over hers, revelling at the sweetness of her mouth. His heart raced and leaped, but then he realised it was both of their hearts, racing together. Lamiya moulded her body along his and the tremor started in his knees again. Deflecting the idea of being alone with her, worrying that he wouldn't be able to control his body, he concentrated on kissing her deeply for as long as he could.

You've done it now. Tread this path while you can, because you know the Guild will never let you go. And Mantiss ... what would his master do? If he stayed there was also still Malach to deal with.

The light dimmed and he broke off the kiss to look up. A cloud had wafted across the moon, and he could see others trailing in after it. For a moment, darkness closed in around him and his heart thudded with fear instead of joy.

'Finally, it might rain,' murmured Lamiya, taking his chin between her fingers and making him look at her. 'We called the river dragon, you and me. That was amazing! And as a bonus you will stay. Tell me I'm not dreaming...' She stood on tiptoe and brushed her lips tenderly over his.

Breathing in the essence of her, he allowed his fears to slip away. If she could be this bold, so must he. Planting his lips over hers, he pulled her close and resumed the kiss.

He had chosen his path.

About the Author

Kaaren has always loved stories, and as a child was often sprung reading by torchlight long after 'lights out'. When she was twelve, she tried to write the eighth Chronicle of Narnia. Hand illustrating along the way, the story was going well until her father took back his typewriter and her mother reclaimed the family dining table. Pushed by her mother  to enter, Kaaren won the Year 12 section of the inaugural Canberra Times Short Story Competition.

As an adult, Kaaren returned to writing with a two-part fantasy series *The Saga of the Ambitious Mage*, released by IrrePRESSible Press in 1998–2000 and a trilogy *The Prophecy of the Sharid*, released by Loranda Publishing and Australian Speculative Fiction in 2004–2006. She then changed tack to become a freelance editor, achieving accreditation with the Institute of Professional Editors in 2012. Over the past decade she has worked with many first-time authors to help bring their stories closer to their vision and to submittable standard.

Always fascinated by the history and mythology of oriental culture, Kaaren graduated from the Australian National University with a B.A in Asian Studies, specialising in East Asian Civilizations and with Honours in Japanese language. One of her awesome life experiences was running a half marathon on the Great Wall of China in 2010.

Despite being a life-long fan of dragons, it wasn't until she moved to the South Coast of NSW in 2017 that Kaaren took up dragon boat paddling. Which somehow, combined with plenty of time created by the Covid lockdowns, led to a new fantasy trilogy containing romantic elements, dragons and several teams of dragon boat paddlers…

Dragons Abreast Australia

Many tears are shed over a breast cancer diagnosis – the disease robs us of many things, our energy, our appearance, our confidence. Once a survivor has had surgery and other treatments, we need hope and to connect with those who understand and others who have this lived experience. We need to be physically active; to tread a new life by learning something new; to attain peace through mindfulness — and we can give advice and support to help other survivors. Then the tears will be of happiness, while we power down many rivers and waterways of the world.

Founded in 1998 on the principles of participation, awareness and inclusiveness, Dragons Abreast Australia is a national charity with groups spread across the country. We are a network of paddling groups comprised of breast cancer survivors of various ages from a great variety of backgrounds, athletic abilities and interests. High on our list of priorities are having fun and travelling across the rivers, lakes and harbours of the world to help us restore ourselves.

Being able to paddle and socialise in the company of others who have travelled the same path helps to restore the confidence, spark and sense of adventure we need to permit a full and active life after treatment. We invite you to join us in the boat at *www.dragonsabreast.com.au*

Many regattas hold designated 'pink' races, where paddlers combine to form 'pink' teams and meet new people. There are numerous Dragons Abreast Clubs around Australia. To find a club near you go to https://dragonsabreast.com.au/location/

The author participated in 'pink' races at the Masters Games in Adelaide in 2019, and had an absolute ball! Kaaren is thrilled to be able to donate some of the proceeds from book sales to support DAA.

About the McGrath Foundation

The McGrath Foundation's mission is to ensure that no one goes through breast cancer without the care of a breast care nurse.

We raise funds to support people with breast cancer by providing specialist McGrath Breast Care Nurses where they are most needed across Australia.

The McGrath Foundation currently funds 185 nurses who provide essential physical and emotional support *for free* to anyone experiencing breast cancer and their families from diagnosis and throughout their treatment.

Breast cancer is the most commonly diagnosed cancer in Australia, the risk of diagnosis for women in Australia in their lifetime is 1 in 7. As the rate of diagnoses increases, so too does the need for more McGrath Breast Care Nurses.

Funding is needed to meet our goal of 250 McGrath Breast Care Nurses by 2025.

To find out more and ensure that no one misses out on care go to:
www.mcgrathfoundation.com.au

As a survivor who has benefitted from the advice and compassion of a breast care nurse, the author is also pleased to be able to offer the McGrath Foundation some of the proceeds from book sales.

How to find out more about dragon boat paddling in Australia

Dragon boating originated in China thousands of years ago, but the sport has spread to be taken up in many countries around the world.

Dragon boat races are held in Australia from Broome to Brisbane, from Perth to Sydney and from Adelaide to Darwin. The first Australian involvement occurred in 1980 when the Penang Tourist Development Corporation invited the WA Surf Life Saving Association to send a team to the Penang Festival. The next year WA and NSW sent teams to what was then considered the unofficial world championships on Hong Kong Harbour.

In 1984 Sydney held the inaugural Sydney Dragon Boat Festival at Farm Cove. The Western Australia Dragon Boat Association was formed in 1985, and was soon joined by associations in all the other states. Australian Clubs tour regularly overseas and have been sighted at least once at all the major international festivals.

The overarching governing body in Australia is The Australian Dragon Boat Federation. More information can be found at https://www.ausdbf.com.au/about-us/

Alternatively, visit the website for your state Dragon Boat Federation, which will have details about the clubs in your states and the calendar of regattas and other events.

Paddles up! Give it a go.

The Mage and the Bird Caller Trilogy

If you enjoyed *Undercover Mage*, the good news is there are two more books.

Fugitive Mage — coming late 2022

Just when Mage Everand thought his mission was drawing to a successful close, the unthinkable happens. Lamiya is kidnapped. Aware of the trap, Everand allows himself to be taken too. He must save Lamiya — and use the opportunity to find out whether the rogue half-mage Malach is who he thinks he is. Forced to continue Malach's training in magic, Everand is faced with yet more dilemmas.

Matters turn bleak when the Council of Mages forcibly translocate him back to the Guild, where he must report on his mission and reveal the existence, and identity of, the half-mage. Now, Everand finds he must conceal his true thoughts from his master, Mage Mantiss, as well as persuade the Guild of his continued loyalty. Can he bide his time and escape to be reunited with Lamiya? How can he foil the Guild's plan to entrap and obliterate the half-mage?

In the meantime, Lamiya's powers evolve and she calls her own dragon. Or wait, did the dragon Akachi call her? Nothing is as it seems. The events unfolding hint at deeper secrets and betrayals ... and undetected forces and connections. In a twist of irony, both Everand and the rogue half-mage become fugitives. Everand and Lamiya come to realise the stakes are far higher than imagined.

Eminent Mage — coming mid-2023

Fugitives in Riverplain, Everand and the rogue Malach prepare to face the ire of the Mages' Guild. Lamiya and her people stand ready to protect them. Much depends on the politics of the Guild and whether Everand's master, Mage Mantiss, retains his position as Head of the Guild or is overthrown by the ambitious and ruthless Mage Pelamis. Conflicted, Everand fears he has betrayed Mantiss, but he must stand firm to protect the river provinces and the people he has come to respect and love.

On top of this threat, the dragon Akachi sets Everand a nigh impossible task — one that would right past wrongs, but would unravel the very foundations of the Guild. Everand struggles to chart a course through conflicting, turbulent waters. There is also the rogue Malach ... can he be trusted?

Lamiya, rapidly increasing in power and authority, devises her own plans to protect the mage she loves. The way forward becomes increasingly fraught and unpredictable. The future of the dragons, the Mages' Guild, the river provinces — the entire population of Ossilis —is at stake, with only the mage and the bird caller to save them.